Danny Mo

A Novel

John Haines

"The greatest thing in family life is to take a hint when a hint is intended – and not take a hint when a hint isn't intended."--Robert Frost

Cover illustration by R. Christopher Cain

First Printing, 2011

ISBN 978-0-9833249-7-3

Library of Congress Control Number: 2011905863

Chambers Street Press
www.chambersstreetpress.com

For Chico and Mo
My folks, the finest of their kind.

Special thanks to my value-added editor, Holly Pendleton, to Gary D'Amato for belief in D Mo from the get-go, to Gary Van Sickle for the walk-off winner, and to Mike Nichols and Drew Olson, whose contributions lend dignity to the cutting room floor. (Cold NY call.)

To my beta readers: Diane, DLesz, Kaz, "J," T.Halla, G-Swiss, JK, Willie Jo, Jesse, Joe P, Intermezzo, JCE, PMP, EE3, Aimee, Swanee and the Snake – your input is treasured. And to my family, friends and everyone else who asked how ol' DANNY was doing, your faith is energizing.

To the pros at PS Finishing Inc., for embracing a challenge and delivering priceless 'know-how.' Specifically, Paul Slotty for his generous outreach, Justen "Doc" Preiss for his cool command of files and fonts, and the uber-talented R. Christopher Cain for an amazing and prescient cover design and illustration.

To the hard working collective at Chambers Street Press for their conviction, to the creative crew at Hollygrafix for always stepping up, to D. S. Robertson and Leah D for those triangular egg salad sandwichettes in the clutch, and to Robert G. D4EO for taking a shot.

To Rachel and RJ for getting it. And finally, a huge thank you to my wife, Mary, for all that patience over all those weekends for all those months when you had to be wondering what the hell. (More than usual.)

Prologue

The kid tried to look casual.

But typical of most efforts at effortlessness, the boy's hop-steps as he half-ran toward the far end of the practice tee were contradiction in action.

The small green and black golf bag strapped over his shoulder wasn't heavy, but its length was enough to disrupt the natural bounce of a nimble boy of nine.

The kid was on a mission -- determined to follow his dad's first rule for a busy range: "Get your spot, then get your balls; but you need some balls to get your spot."

There was one open spot left, at the far end of the slightly-elevated hitting area that butted up to some bushes and a stand of trees. He couldn't help imagining that someone might materialize from the trees and take *his* spot.

Grownups waited behind other grownups on down the line, yet the vacancy at the far station was calling out only to him. Most everyone avoided that spot. Not only did the older folks think it was too long a walk from the range's cart-park area, but there was a scrub oak that crowded in from the right like a construction crane blocking the driving lane. But, damn…it was open. And that tree was actually why his dad preferred that spot.

His dad's final reminder from the night before echoed inside his head: people busy yakking often missed the next open spot. "Stay ready, Mo Mo," he had said, "and then pounce — like a jungle cat with say-so."

It was the boy's first time to the range at The Old Barn without his dad; a rite of passage for the serious junior golfer. As it was every weekend, The Barn was packed with regulars, most of them well aware of the unaccompanied kid because of his well-known dad. His mom had dropped him off after he finished his Saturday chore, which, this week, was digging out the lines of weeds between their driveway's concrete slabs with a screw driver. His dad who was probably close to finishing out on the course, would be by soon after to watch the boy hit for a bit before they headed over to The Aftermath for Steamin' E burgers and giant diet colas that came with free refills.

The boy galloped...up, down, and ahead on a one-kid cavalry charge, his bag banging against his leg with every anxious stride. Old-timers tossed friendly chirps his way, which he returned occasionally with some nods and brief glances just to be polite. With his heart thumping loud inside the confines of his bony little chest and his fixation turning to obsession on that last open spot, he abruptly chucked the tatters of his vanity and hopped the last train to Geeksville.

Disengaging from the shoulder strap, he thrust his bag under his arm and ran full-out, stooped like a soldier saddled with the not-so-portable rocket launcher. His legs were shaky from fear and he began to worry that some scheming golfer might just parachute onto *his* land and take *his* spot. He checked the sky... empty but for the blue on a bone-dry day in June at The Old Barn.

Senses alive, he leaned forward and pushed harder. Forty feet to go. No planes, no chutes. Good. And no one emerging from the trees. Cool.

And then, after all the weight of so much worry, it was his. He plopped his bag down and took command. *This land is my land.* Finally, a place to call his own, a home on the range, at least for as long as one big-ass bucket of balls covered his rent. His dad would be proud; he indeed had the balls to take some turf and make it his. Now, he needed balls to hit.

He dug out two tokens from his pocket and clutched them tight, feeling their captive value. With his back to the range, he looked to his right, all the way back down the line of golfers. No one was coming. A few golfers were still waiting for their turn but weren't nearly as focused as he had been. One more check for shadowy figures lurking in the willows and bushes, then back at the ball dispensing machine. He was pretty sure his imagination wasn't messing with him. The scrub oak, 50 or so yards out and at about the twelve-thirty hour-hand angle, had too many leaves to see if anyone was hiding in the branches. Go time.

He darted to the army-green ball dispensing machine, which stood just back and center to the range's hitting area. He glanced at the area from where he came. His bag still staked claim to his territory. Many of the adults at The Old Barn accused the clunky ball machine of "playing favorites" and not "putting out," but it was a snap for the boy. He'd been working this machine for a third of his life with his dad, who somehow had acquired a cigar box full of tokens. His touch was practically to the manner born.

Insert token, shove the lever in like you mean it, hold for one Wauwatosa, and yank it back out like you want it back. With a rumble of holy thunder the machine doled out a half bucket of gold. He positioned the second token in his right hand; one more push-pull from having his big-ass bucket topped off with yellow and black range balls. But somewhere, either in the distance or in his mind, he heard a sickening sound. An engine. *No.* Growing louder. *Aw...come on.* The boy's instincts went on red-alert without knowing exactly why, until the man with a long mane of salt-and-pepper hair came roaring around the corner bushes in a gas-powered cart and right up to the ball machine. The boy fumbled his 2nd token off the asphalt and it vanished in the untrimmed grass around the side of the ball machine. His ears got hot and his scalp had the bad tingle.

"Hey kid, shit or get off the pot," said the man as he snapped his fingers four or five times, loud and fast. "I'm on the tee in 10 minutes." What he said every time the range was crowded.

The boy's dad did not like the big long-haired man... and the boy hated him.

He decided to take the balls he already had and get back to his turf, because this man, whom the boy called "Hair Dude" (among other things with the root word, "Hair") would be the type to bully his way onto property that was not his. He was known for it.

The boy refused to even look at the Hair Dude. He turned with his half bucket of balls in hand and started to run back toward his spot. But within four steps, the wire handle on his now half-ass bucket slipped its hinge and shiny yellow balls scattered in every direction. Instinct took over. Born of a kid-centric understanding of free enterprise, the boy rounded up his balls with the kind of Darwinian street-guile one learns from years of parade candy free-for-alls (his dad tried to calm his mother every 4th of July by putting a twist on the claims made by professional athletes: "It's not about the candy, it's about respect."). Two kindly old men tried to help the boy, but they would have had better luck reaching for river minnows from a foamy shoreline.

He heard disembodied voices above him, "Look at those hands fly," and, "Just like his old man collecting bets."

Everything else was the white noise of a packed cafeteria. He saw colors and hands reaching down and moving shadows and feet turning all different ways; a dog's eye view of humans in mid-flounder. Then he heard a sound that cut to his core. The beeping sound a cart makes when backing up. The Hair Dude. There was no doubt in the boy's mind that the Hairball had saddled back up in his cart like Lucifer rearing up on his evil steed, and would soon launch an invasion on the boy's land.

He nearly forgot to keep breathing, but managed to get to his feet and broke towards his property. The Hair Dude had jumped in front of him after first swerving around the "NO CARTS BEYOND THIS POINT!" sign and began to cruise along the tee line in his cart, waving and smiling like a Third World dictator parading past the oppressed. When the cart slowed so the Hair Dude could watch Mrs. Pearson's mid-waggle ass-wiggle, the boy surged ahead and up the incline to his hitting station. The adrenalin and the nerves and the fight-for-all-worth-fighting-for gave fuel to one last burst -- and he pounced like a jungle cat with say-so. The sudden acceleration caused the boy to stumble and spill his range balls all over again. But this time they fell around the small stand bag that staked out his territory.

Hair Dudezilla smiled and dismounted the cart. He grabbed a few clubs and walked up to the boy's spot with his own half-bucket of balls and casually placed his clubs against the wire bag port. The boy may as well have been invisible.

But the kid held his ground, pointing to his bag and his scattered balls. He was intent on showing some balls, alright. "This is my spot," he said, but his voice squeaked on "spot."

"I was here first," came out a little too ballsy for a nine-year-old boy addressing the six-foot four-inch Hair Dudeasaurus. People were looking at them now.

"Boy," said the follicle god with a chuckle, "you and your old man think you own this spot, don't you? Well here's a news flash, kid -- you don't. You might wanna break it to him." The Hair Dude was nodding now. His hair held its position.

The kid stood statue-still as he faced the large man; he focused only on the Hair Dude's hefty man-breasts, some big ol' boobs aimed straight down at him. Gross. Somehow, staring at the Hair Dude's tits kept him repulsed enough to fight off a sneak-attack from his own tears; one of those defense mechanisms triggered by a survival instinct in tough kids who get dumped into awkward scenarios, like man/boy showdowns. Like this. A kick to the nuts was what was really in his heart but he had to keep it together. His first day alone on the range could not end in combat with his dad's archrival at The Old Barn.

"I'm off in 10 minutes kid," said the Hair Dude, "now step aside. You wanna hit now, you can hit from there." He pointed at the miserable side-slope falling off the elevated hitting area. Hardpan bare spots littered with clumpy, Chia-like islands of longer grass... it was no choice at all. "Or you can watch and learn." The Hair Dude tossed an unlit cigar aside, signaling that the raid was now over.

The boy decided to slowly pick up his balls and then, eventually, stand at the side and stare at the "Fat ol' Doobie Brother," as his dad sometimes referred to the man with the classic rock look. But the Silvery baboon knew what the boy was doing. It was making him angrier by the second and began kicking some of the balls to the side with enough soccer-style gusto to make an extra point. After gathering the balls as if unbothered, the boy noticed that for all the hard-guy bravado of the big shaggy jackass, he was mumbling. Not cool. Again, the boy's instincts flexed; the Hair Dude was not comfortable. Messing with the son of the guy who…well, it just wasn't smart.

Hairy Cleavage loosened up with a few short-iron shots. Most were okay but the bad ones were alarmingly bad for a good player; a couple thin come-offs that sounded as bad as they looked and a big succulent fatty. The boy enjoyed those. When he slowly put his hand over his mouth after such shots, the mane man got even angrier.

It was then that Hairosmith/Dude-looks-like-a-lady decided he was through messing around and grabbed his driver from the metal bag stand. The boy knew the guy was proud of his big sweeper off the tee; he'd seen him show off before; blasting bombs like he was the King Kong of golf, sometimes in all directions. "High wide and everywhere" as the boy's dad liked to say.

The boy watched the man tee up a yellow range ball, then walk slowly behind it, waiting for others to notice that the Mighty Babe with the Gorman Thomas locks was about to start blasting with the big stick. He waggled as his swagger returned, took the club back, hair still motionless, and put his considerable T & A into a big intimidating swing.

For all the Hair Dude's disgusting traits, the man did have a beautiful golf swing and an annoyingly large amount of talent. Talent that was missing this time, though, as he snap-hooked a tee shot into the woods along the 18th hole. A near-impossible feat of powerful pull-hook physics. The boy had his hand halfway to his mouth before the Hair Dude turned and glared directly at him. The Hair Dude enunciated clearly, neither loud nor soft, one word. "Fuck." His eyes drilled into the boy a few seconds longer after he said it. It gave the kid the creeps, but he forced himself to stare back until the Hair Dude turned away. Both had made their points.

The Disciple of Hair swung even harder on the next one. Better… but not great. Hardly worth the build-up.

"Goddamn tree," hissed the Hair Dude. "Gonna chop its ass down someday."

An organized division of hair broke formation from the frontline unit and scaled down the Hair Dude's forehead. He slammed the club down, flipped at the clump of misbehaving hair with his fingers — and the clump came right back as if to flip *him* off. The boy could not wait to tell the whole story to his dad — and the Hair Dude had to know it.

As if on cue with the boy's thoughts, his dad appeared over the crest of the bunkering by the 18th green and was heading down to the range. The dad carried his bag with an athletic grace that had been passed on to his son. Grace that was evident in every activity either of them performed, unless, of course, the boy was bustin' hump hauling his golf bag trying beat skydivers and traffic violators to a spot on the range.

The boy waved to his dad, who was approaching quickly from less than 50 yards away. The Hair Dude looked over to see the boy's dad, everybody's hero, heading their way and said something under his breath. After Big Shaggy returned his attention to his teed-up ball, the boy's dad gave a single nod to his son; the dad always used one, big, slow, nod from a distance to acknowledge those worthy of acknowledgment.

The boy shuffled his feet. He had his range balls gathered around the bucket after he had secured his spot, just as he was taught. But the fat ass Hair Dude had blown it all up. The boy had imagined his dad coming down to the range, where he would be all set up, in his dad's favorite spot no less — the one where the oak tree made you cut the ball to hit the range targets. He would have been showing off to the grownups his amazing ball striking skills, and making sure to be good and humble about it. It *should* have been that way.

A resounding crack cut through the range. The sound was unmistakable. The man had crushed a shot with his driver. The boy was unable to resist turning to look even though his plan was to look away if the Hair Dude caught one good. He saw the ball smash into the scrub oak, a common occurrence for many when hitting from the far spot on the range at The Old Barn Golf Course.

The unforgiving sound of the ball hitting the oak was startling. It happened quickly, but for an even briefer instant, it registered with the boy that everyone was tuned in to what was happening at the eastern most end of the range.

Some called it a raptor; others would claim it was some sort of vulture. Most would agree, however, that it was a red-tailed hawk. In any case, a large bird of prey in the tree was even more startled than the folks on the range.

The Hair Dude's shot caromed off the scrub oak and straight back in their direction. The yellow ball unleashed what turned out to be the hawk's nest protecting instincts, and it honed in on the intruding orb in an instant. The ball slammed into the Hair Dude's golf cart — parked defiantly at an angle well beyond the NO CARTS sign — and ricocheted into the boy's chest. He barely felt the ball, but powerful talons tore into the right side of the boy's jaw as the boy was momentarily overtaken by an obscenely large wingspan and paralyzing fear.

"Jesus Christ!" the Hair Dude screamed, backing away just as the boy's father arrived at the scene in a full sprint, coming right through the hitting line like a jungle cat with say-so and God help anyone who got in his way. The hawk figured things out quickly and disappeared almost as fast as it attacked.

The Hair Dude kept repeating "Oh Jesus Christ," in a raspy voice. The boy lay perfectly flat. His hand went to his face and his small fingers pulled parallel streaks of blood across his cheek. Depending on one's point of view, the look suggested either Native American warrior or...Adidas. The boy's eyes stayed dry, but his pants did not.

The story -- of how Danny Moran's boy had to be rushed to the hospital for stitches due to a shot hit by his chief rival Andy Salamone -- grew more fantastic over time. Danny Mo didn't say anything at first. He had raced straight to his boy. And when Salamone looked at him and said, "I'm sorry," he thought he might just let it go until after taking his son for medical help. But when Salamone didn't add a period after "I'm sorry," Andy doomed his fate by adding "...but I'm on the tee." Danny Moran calmly stood up and turned, and unleashed a short, piston-like straight right hand directly below the man's unsuspecting rack. The blow knocked every bit of air from the lungs of the now doubled-over Andy Salamone.

"I don't ever want to see you bring a cart down this range line again. You got that, Sally?" Then Danny messed up Salamone's hair with an upside-down range bucket making nicely do as a dunce cap, and pushed him over. It took less than five seconds.

Maurice "Mo Mo" Moran felt his dad's presence. He was safe now, as always, when with his dad. The boy was wet, sheet-white and shaking. Still, he was on his feet before Salamone. He didn't cry until the car ride to the hospital – when he told his dad he had gotten his spot, the way he was taught. As Danny Mo drove, Mo Mo's unrelenting sobs and occasional words merged and little was intelligible beyond "stupid Hair Dude" and "my spot." Danny's love for his son bordered on debilitating. He felt owned at times by irrational fears… that he wouldn't be able to keep his boy from the bad things, and crappy luck, the inevitable jags of sadness that are the litter of life and the byproduct of growth. Things he himself had suffered, bouts that could have turned worse had he not learned to beat them back with the sheer force of his daydreams or the rescue efforts of his memory's greatest hits. Would he even want his son having to lean on such abstractions? Didn't matter, it would be out his control, would have to let go. His parents had made it look easier.

At the moment, however, they indulged in the kind of love that had led to the loathing of another human being. Going back to his own childhood and his dad, he had felt an inexplicable bond when a father and son could share their contempt for a mutual enemy. Like Andy Salamone. But then Danny Mo heard his boy rush to the finish with a string of words that drilled their way into the tender parts of him. Words handed down from his grandfather decades ago, and now a "saying" between just them.

"'Cuz… I was bein' like a jungle cat with say-so, Dad, really I was….you shoulda seen me. I pounced! I…" Then, through muffled heaves, everything fought its way out from inside the little boy – words no longer possible. The jungle cat in the passenger seat was a hyperventilating storm of mucus and tears and pee and streaks of blood.

"I know Mo Mo, I really do." It was Danny Moran's turn to have his voice catch. He pulled down the sun visor, just to do something. His right arm a screen from the passenger seat. He didn't want his son to see the squall brewing in his own eyes.

∞

BOOK I

Chapter 1

Butterflies. Their very nature. Competing feelings. Season after season a summertime dichotomy.

Those damned butterflies.

Creature of beauty and grace, fragile yet strong, divine art displayed upon the canvas of their wings, flitting along with carefree ease on nature's playful course, forever in the moment. Throughout the world and for many centuries, butterflies have remained sprightly reminders of celebration, of transformation, of rejuvenation. Antic dancers knifing the air in fixed space, seemingly indecisive and perfectly certain at once, performing the miracle that turns silent motion into melody and daytime cheer.

In one's stomach, though, butterflies can mean anxiety, vomiting, and spirited rectal discharge. Danny Moran had played tournament golf for over three decades, and butterflies were nothing new. The fluttering in his midsection had become a part of his life; to the point where it was a bit disconcerting if the butterflies missed their cue. Untimely discharges were not an issue for him – the odd experimental salsa or kitchen-sink chili dare aside — though he had known plenty of golfers less fortunate when it came to "the butterflies." Guys who knew it was just part of the game, guys who were forced to factor in their required restroom time as part of a pre-tournament regimen.

But anxiety is a recalcitrant son of a bitch — and when the needle on his flutter meter went crazy, it was usually for golf-related reasons unrelated to actual golf performance. Usually the symptoms hit him in the car, working like caffeine, keeping him awake and a bit jittery if not necessarily alert at the wheel. It would likely intensify as he neared his destination, where the source of his stress awaited.

It wouldn't matter so much if he didn't care, but care he did. And caring, he believed, was anything but the popular notion of tapping some regenerating reservoir of desire. "Golf, marriage, certain cuts of meat, whatever — make a choice, put in the effort, apply some heat and everything should take care of itself," was his take on the subject. Still, his recent bouts with the butterflies came from the possibility that his best may no longer be enough.

This made things difficult. Doing his best meant trying hard. And for him, trying hard was as natural as trusting the organization of his own biology. How could it ever be wrong? The thought of backing off always seemed pointless; like getting a good night's sleep by skipping most of it the night before (something he did all too often when he was younger). Ironic, then, how the same program that had always gotten him through had now come back to haunt him. These days, nighttime thoughts poked at him like pointed fingers. Sleep came only when the jabs missed sensitive areas, which was not often. Now he was being advised to *not* try so hard? Well, that *would* be hard, but he sure as hell would try. *"Strike a wet match, Danny, and all you get is friction leading to a mess — but let the matches dry, and the heat and light is again yours."* Legitimizing the act of doing nothing was just too... Zenny Zen Zen for Danny Moran.

He turned onto a neat suburban street banked with lavish colonials stuffed into pristine lots that begged to be recognized with high world rankings in miniature lawn and garden excellence. It was apparent to Moran that it took crews of earnest Mexicans to stay competitive. He cruised slowly by the various parked equipment trailers while catching bits and pieces on the local sports talk radio station. Host Steve "The Homer" True, the self-proclaimed "host of the world's greatest talk show," apparently had decided it was a day for callers to spar over which brand name free agents the Packers' GM was ignoring despite a bunch of cap-room flexibility. It was already early May and many were fretting that the Pack hadn't signed a proven cold weather long-snapper yet.

Danny turned off the radio and put on his new CD, an Irish band called The Saw Doctors, led by a distant cousin named Leo Moran, and eased his way through the swanky neighborhood. He crossed the railroad tracks and County Highway P, which led to a lower tax bracket and a subdivision of older and smaller houses on spacious and more natural settings. The lots were wooded and rolling and mostly maintained by their owners. Danny, amused by the contrast between each side of the road and tracks, once said it was "look *where* I live versus look *how* I live," and it had become a silly family debate as to which applied to whom. He didn't remember exactly what he meant at the time he uttered the load of crap, so now he argued it in different ways for fun. It beat the hell out of real arguments.

A few more minutes and he'd be there. He stuck an arm out the car window to feel the warm rush of air against his damp and cold fingertips. He continued to slalom through the countryside and neighborhoods that comprised his shortcut routine. There were variations to this shortcut, but the neighborhoods were virtually indiscernible. A unique thing about his so-called shortcuts: they were verifiably shorter in distance, but generally took more time.

He came to an intersection at another county crossroad, this one Highway PP, where a sign pointing right directed golfers to an upscale, privately owned public golf course called The Hill Farm. It was three miles away over twisting roads, and was the site of much success for Danny, in both state championships and national amateur qualifiers.

A local mortgage insurance magnate had bought the property for the course over a decade ago after making three different offers to Norby Hill, a farmer whose family had owned the land for over a century. The property was once home to different factions of Hill family members who alternated between feuding and having sex with one another. At times it appeared to be more of a settlement camp, with people living off the land, inside the barn, and in a rickety three-story house, reportedly in some kind of family arrangement draped in folkway grays and the kind of taboos that give "close family" a bad name. The local authorities had left the Hills alone for years beyond the enforcement of the various required permit regulations, but a few of them claimed to know some mind-numbing stuff about the family.

Before a final land deal could be struck, Norby died of a heart attack while on his beloved John Deere tractor, crashing into the kitchen and straight through a large liquor cabinet containing stacked cases of Early Times Whiskey. According to the gossip, Ol' Norby, probably already dead, fell from the tractor and came to rest face down in an 80 proof river of whiskey and broken bottle shards. The tractor continued driverless through the porch skeleton and outside, plodding on for about a half mile before conking out 20 yards from the county highway, where it remained to this day a many-times repainted tribute to Norby Hill. His illiterate but long-winded wife, Crazy Norma — maiden name, reportedly, also Hill — accepted the first (and lower) offer for the land in exchange for naming the course, "The Hill Farm" — and for leaving the John Deere in place. She had claimed, according to reports, that Norby had been coming to take her with him when his "heart blowed up," but it remained a mystery as to whether she thought it an act of love or something more ominous.

Before the contractors had moved any earth, Crazy Norma's severed head was found on the property, a broken bottle of Early Times shoved so far into her mouth that much of her face was torn apart, her lips but grisly flaps, as if somebody had finally "shut that bitch up for good" according to a cop Danny knew. The incident added fuel to what Danny considered an outlandish legend of a semi-wild sub-Sasquatch-type character that the locals referred to as "Nimrod." Some believed the man-beast was some kind of secret Hill family progeny who still lived in the remote wooded areas on what was the Hill land.

Over a six or seven year period, grounds crew workers occasionally found surgically eviscerated deer carcasses and other creatures that were most likely dragged onto the course, later, post-op, presumably by other wildlife. There was no easy explanation for any of it.

A three-hole stretch along the back nine was an area where some golfers made a show of avoiding even the shade from the adjoining woods, much less step foot in them, for fear that the mighty Nimrod would drag them into the forest and behead them before eating their meaty parts. In the State match play five years ago, Danny told the press he always "played away from Nimrod" by working the ball to the far side of the fairway on the forest holes. It was the play anyway, Nimrod or no Nimrod, but such was the nature of match play.

It became a story of local intrigue when a series of graves were discovered during construction of the course. It was rumored that several belonged to infants, possibly stillborn, along with other supposedly in-bred Hill children and offspring misfits. According to local folklore and a blatantly gullible golf community, the ghosts of the various Hill children would wreak havoc inside the heads of the golfers who played The Hill Farm. Just about every brain-dead decision and any hint of poor course management were frequently blamed on the "Hilldren." Danny maintained that rampant stupidity could be found on every course, every day…but not every course had an incestuous farm family and an ill-mannered ape-man to blame.

Still, when Danny Mo had captured the second of his two State match play championships at the Hill Farm, he managed to win his semi-final match because Tripp Wagner somehow lost track of how many shots Danny had played on the 16th hole — which they both had butchered — and charged a putt nearly off the green as a result. The 16th is the last hole along the woods, and many wanted to believe that when Tripp (who had control of the match for most of the way) leaked a tee shot near the woods, he became unnerved by the lingering myth of Señor Nimrod, and was probably finished off by some Hillbilly spell cast by the spirits of the dead slow children.

Danny smiled, recalling the memory. He had his Chevy Impala on autopilot and motored by rote through the familiar suburban order as he continued to prep himself on the "art of not trying so hard." *Let the matches dry, babe. Heat and light.* A few minutes later, he pulled into the driveway and eased his car to a halt next to a spotless white Camry. He exhaled with enthusiasm, giving the butterflies another chance to flee. Again, they did not. He exited the car and slammed the door with a behind-the-back dribble action.

And entered his home.

∞

Chapter 2

Danny entered through the garage. The walk down the back hall toward the kitchen was yet another trigger for the butterflies to ratchet up their activity level. He paused for a moment before entering the kitchen, for it was there where more times than not his wife would be preparing, organizing, or cleaning something. She never made it look easy, which made it all the easier for her to show indifference about her husband's return from the golf course. It was just the way it was, most every day, May through September.

Full throttle passive-aggressive married love. Butterflies and cold fingers. Life in the rowboat of love. Hard work, slow progress. He entered the kitchen. No one was there. Danny considered the possibility his wife had gone for a walk, but it didn't feel right. She had to be nearby; the butterflies wouldn't be flipping out otherwise.

He slalomed through the well-appointed spaces of their long ranch-style house. Nothing. He listened. Still nothing. He furrowed some brow and reconsidered the walk possibility. It was still almost 80 degrees out; and the butterflies have been confused on the odd occasion before. A walk would give her a break from creating proper domestic order. Good. Though she might be ornery about having to take a walk alone. Bad. But if she wanted to take a walk with her husband, she could have called him to check on his arrival. Something she did not hesitate to do when she needed him to stop to pick up something up, frequently it was a "bottle" of Reduced-fat Wheat Thins. Their code for wine going back to when the kids were little.

The bedroom? Possibly, but she pretty much avoided the place in daylight hours these days. She used to utilize their room for both standard and major Laundry Ops, their king size bed being an optimal surface for break bulk, fold and stack maneuvers. He had taken over most of the post-dryer sort and fold duties as a way to "help out around here." It took some of the heat off, but there were still things to condemn — like timing and technique.

∞

He had insisted that folding laundry was primarily an "evening sport," and just like any other sport he believed that skillful folding came from being in the moment, and that this was only possible if he didn't rush the process by wanting to be elsewhere. His wife, however, felt that he didn't despise the process enough. With a prime-time ballgame or some political snark and bark between ideologues on the bedroom TV, Danny would fold, separate and stack with the hand-jive rhythm of the gifted athlete he was. She hated that he didn't hate doing it, especially after Molly had yelped about the wretchedness of folding laundry for years. The truth was — it simply didn't count as "helping out around here" if the chore didn't go a long way toward sucking the life out of him.

Danny — whose part-time job in fine retail clothing as a college student had outfitted him with some fabric management fundamentals — could not win. The lone domestic activity where he was more fastidious than his wife became, unsurprisingly, a point of contention. Several years earlier, a calm demonstration using a sweater Molly had given him for his birthday was quickly dismissed even though they both knew he had won on points.

"There's nothing wrong with shoulder-to-shoulder folding. It takes up less space," she had said, hissing in a way that sullied one hell of a pretty face. "See?" She went on to demonstrate the shoulder-to-shoulder fold. A 'Danny don't' if ever there was one.

"That, Molly, is so…C-flight. The fold line down the center is the giveaway, like a ball-retriever in a carry bag. Now, in the right environment, with a good ballgame on TV, I can deliver Tour level folding. Would I be ranked top-five worldwide in certain statistical categories? I wouldn't bet against it."

"Right back to golf, huh Danny? Always."

"Not true, but I'll say this. I've won how many state championships," Danny said, palms up, shoulders hunched, "yet my fabric management fundamentals are greater than my golf skills. Easily. And sock sorting? Top-five hands down, that's a gift I got in the cradle. I mean...I was born to sort things out."

"Your top-five nonsense, it just gets... old." Molly Moran's head shakes were meant either to make her exhaustion obvious or Meryl Streep envious. "What was it the other day...spreading cold butter on your toast? Always a joke."

"Spreading cold butter evenly is no joke, Molly. But getting back to socks; you know I take on the toughest baskets, the toughest mixes, I'm not afraid to stand in the crucible and attack piles of those all white but subtly different inside-out footies, not to mention those abused and confused static-charged stretchy socks you wear. And mine, I mean...are they navy are they black are they graphite, deep charcoal, dark chocolate? And you know I never back down no matter how it hurts my eyes. I stay positive and take it one basket at a time, just get after it, go right at 'em, dig down deep, give 110%, leave it all on the on the bedspread. I know my family looks to me, and I want those socks in my hands at crunch time...though I must first and foremost give all glory to God."

Molly shook her head. "It's your stamina that amazes me." Her voice was flat this time.

"Really...longest string of sports clichés in a domestic dramedy or reality series?" Danny beamed. "Or do you mean in the sack?"

"No. Hauling around such a colossal ego everywhere you go like its nothing."

"The Id is just mind over gray matter, Mol." One cryptic credo followed by another. "My common sense tells me to rise above a sense of common."

Danny and Molly Moran's then 19-year-old son, Mo Moran, had just entered the house and heard his folks' exchange as he walked down the hall, though he'd heard it all before. Mo Mo Moran was pitching for the Chicago Cubs' Class A team in Peoria at that time. He had a day and a half off and had come by to see the 'rents spar and eat as much of their food as possible.

"Same ol' same ol'," said the son as he entered the room. "Dad, everybody knows you shave the top of a cold stick of butter. You can't be top-five based on just that."

"Hey, come on in, Mo Mo. Good to see you. But, please, don't think shaving the top is any kind of toast-app answer when you're sourcing from a chilled stick, kiddo; don't be bringing checkers to a chess match. We're talking about warming the knife under hot water, working the corners. Bevel 'em good and you make more corners." Danny chuckled. "Some suggest using a cheese grater, but that's a crutch, and messy, and microwaving… that just takes the sport out of it, like internet porn has done. Anyway, I was just proud of how well it went the other day. But I've moved on. How you doin', man?"

Mo had already turned to his mother for a quick warm embrace, and like that the spirited laundry folding, sock sorting and butter spreading debate was diffused. Molly left the room shaking her head. "I'll whip up some BLTs," she said from the hallway.

∞

Danny and his butterflies proceeded down the hall towards the bedroom where he was certain no folding of laundry would be going on. If Molly wasn't there, she had to be out walking and his caged butterflies could be cited for a false alarm.

There was no one in the bedroom, and the two baskets of laundry were not warm from the dryer. Hmmm…

Danny went from room-to-room, giving each a quick look. The butterflies were now providing energy more than discomfort as he moved swiftly through the house. He kept his technique efficient, more effortless glide than showy juke. What veterans do.

Mo Moran's room remained mostly unchanged since the day he left for pro ball. A mother thing. Their 18-year-old daughter, Rinny, was out of town for the weekend and her room was an orderly tomb. Guest room, same. His wife's glowing white tennis shoes were at the front door. Basement rec room? Nah, she hated the basement. Danny's sanctuary for big games on the big screen left her cold, literally and not literally. He checked anyway — nope, not there. Danny would not be surprised if he achieved a top-five, worldwide time in the over 40 division for descending 12 or more steps in a non-emergency situation. Two at a time on the way up. Solid, but not elite. Unforced railing-grab. Mandatory deduction.

Car in the garage, Molly's walking shoes at the door, butterflies suggesting she was close. Weird. There were other possibilities, but other than the fallibility of the butterflies, none were coming to mind.

What to do next. He could fold and/or sort the two baskets of laundry so that if she walked in the door he'd be "helping out around here." But it was only 6:50 p.m. and there was nothing on TV worth watching yet. Some good games would be on later — he would fold the laundry then and undoubtedly perform to his full potential.

What Danny most wanted to do was sit on the deck with a beer and catch up on some golf magazines before capping off a peaceful easy evening with a Palermo's Hand Tossed Frozen Cheese Pizza. Not an option, but just knowing all the required materials were on hand brought its own kind of peace. Truth was, if Molly were to come home and see the unfolded laundry while he sipped a beer and read a magazine her reaction might, without making a sound, result in a sudden climate change along Milwaukee's suburban north shore. Maybe even parts inland.

He mulled it over. Yesterday Molly had asked him to trim some overgrown branches belonging to their yard's five major trees, "whenever you get some time." He could do that, but to do it so quickly could conceivably raise expectations for any future "when you get some time" chores. This might be considered trying hard, but it was the "acceptable" kind of trying hard. The "trying hard" he was to avoid, according to some expensive advice, was his tendency to provide his own brand of insight to his loving wife, Molly Margaret Moran. His own little 'cause and effect' breakdown, maybe a pearl here and gem there to expedite the discovery process; something, anything, to open her up to what she may need to feel happier, more fulfilled, something that might not adversely affect the tri-county climate. But "even the right answers are not a good idea when they come from a spouse," he was told by the expensive advisor, "especially if it's a bunch of good answers in a row." Whatever, dude (though the counselor was a woman), and you keep raking it in with your wet matches and shit.

Danny went to the garage to get the deluxe extendable stepladder and was a little surprised to find it wasn't there. For a moment he considered whether that was a sign that he was supposed to have a beer and read some magazines. He went around to the side of the house and checked a bushy area beneath the widest and lowest part of the soffit, an area where he liked to stash the deluxe extendable ladder for easy roof access. No one on earth could see the ladder in the bushes, but Molly could sense it was there and it affected her well-being. But it wasn't in the bushes either. Danny Moran had now lost his wife and the deluxe extendable aluminum stepladder she couldn't resist buying through an infomercial.

He walked around to the back yard, just beyond the deck, and there it was. The aluminum stepladder was lying flat on the grass and fully extended beneath the huge maple tree with the billion leaves that littered the deck and clogged the gutters every fall. Next to the ladder was an orange and silver bow saw.

He heard the sound of flesh smacking flesh. He continued toward the tree and looked up, full detective mode now. Voila. There she be. Molly, stranded in the tree. Perched on a sturdy branch that reached away from the house, but still too high to risk a hang and release landing. The ladder must've fallen away from the tree, likely on the push-off to mount the aforementioned branch.

She was slapping at mosquitoes, teary-eyed and angry, looking as if it were both a good thing and a bad thing that her husband had found her.

∞

Chapter 3

Something in his gut. Certainly not butterflies, he couldn't recall what the so-called butterflies even felt like anymore. This was something of a more troubling density, closer to some unfortunate marsupial, like a 'possum, that you find in the middle of the road still kicking and heaving in those messy moments before the end. But it wasn't pretending — it was making him sick to his stomach.

Mo Mo Moran was in the middle of the diamond, in the middle of a ballgame, in the middle of a mess. He kicked lightly at the dirt on the mound like nothing was wrong. A tough thing to do with what felt like the better part of a letter-opener half buried in his shoulder. The pain was bad, the fear worse. Enough to put a thrashing 'possum in his gut. Or so it felt.

One out, nobody on, no hits, no runs, not even a loud foul through five and a third. Didn't even have the real good stuff; shoulder a little stiff from the start; and now — after trying a new pitch, a less than genial circle change — his shoulder flat erupted, spreading a dread that turned his heart to lead. Dark and heavy, it just sank.

Mo Moran stepped onto the rubber, then off, then waved his catcher to the mound with his gloved hand. Not that he had to; his catcher, Billy Rick Trueblood, was already on his way.

"The hell, Mo? It's bad isn't it? Tell me it ain't bad…"

"Is," said Mo. "Like it blew up. Shouldn't have done it. Son of a bitch is hurtin' just from talkin'."

"Aw hell, Mo Mo, you got a no no going."

"Nothin' gets by you does it Billy Dick?"

"Yesterday's deal?"

"Yep. Somethin' happened… I knew it. I'm such a stupid ass."

∞

Mo Mo and Billy Rick had just finished 18 holes at Silver Meadows, a tony country club in western West Des Moines. They were guests of Henry Lankhammer, a local business owner who had done quite well in the institutional salsa industry and was big into the local Triple A team, the Iowa Cubs.

Sitting in the men's grill room, Lankhammer was into his post-round ritual: Ketel One, on the rocks, in a tub, with a twist -- repeat. After two and a half "Big Boys," as he called them, he became even more animated over how far Mo Moran had hit some of his tee shots.

"I'm not sure even Randy ever got to where Mo Mo hit it on number ten today" he announced, just loud enough to reach the ears of Merle Keenen, of the Keenen Upholstery empire, who was slamming dice two tables down from Henry and the two ball players. Keenen was the foremost champion, among many, of his 25-year-old "step-nephew," Randy Ride, an assistant golf professional at Silver Meadows.

Ride, a sinewy 6 feet 3 inches, was considered the longest hitter in Iowa. And for good reason. "Rocket Ride" had won the Iowa State Long Drive Competition both times he entered the event, which in turn qualified him for the Midwest Regionals of the National Long Drive Competition. Last year, Ride finished 7th in the Nationals and got a little airtime on ESPN. In a very specialized golf competition featuring raw power and extra-long custom drivers, it was an amazing feat for a young assistant club pro to place that high using his 46-inch everyday driver.

Mo Mo was fresh off a 75, and felt pretty good about his score considering he had flaunted a little of his Unfrozen Caveman touch around the greens. He'd felt a little twinge in his right shoulder, pretty painless, but a twinge nonetheless. Besides, little twinges were nothin' about nothin'. Everyone gets 'em. Ignore 'em and they go away. And probably a few more clichés if he would give it just a little thought. The niggling pang had actually kept Mo's swing all the smoother, and he imagined that his fluid swing during the round was possibly, like, helping, maybe stretching something, working it out. Whatever — he had bombed it all day

Mo Moran's tee shots, when he stayed smooth, often went so far that people mostly just laughed. He had played a few tournaments as a junior and with his many times state champion father and his friends enough to determine that "no one go where Mo Mo go." The regulars at The Old Barn Golf Course and The Aftermath Pub and Grill had elevated Mo Mo Moran and his historic tee ball bombs to the same god-like status given axemen ranging from Joe Satriani to Paul Bunyan depending who was doing the mythologicalizing. Mo had to admit he dug the rep.

"You think so, Henry, seriously?" said Keenen the upholsterer. "You think your boy even wants you talking such nonsense?"

"Be a sight to behold, those two going at it," said Henry.

"That's you talking, Henry...you and those big boys..." The guys at Keenen's table smiled, nodding. "...and I've always found that talking don't prove a hell of a lot."

Henry Lankhammer sold too many truckloads of salsa every week to care much what anyone thought. "You're getting yourself worked up, Merle. Hey, I think the world of Randy, love the kid. But I'm tellin' ya, Mo Moran can hit it right with him...unless, as you say, my boys are making me loco."

"Jaysus Henry, I like Mo Mo too, we all do...he's a Cub, but come on... you don't cover couches and I don't make sauces or dips or whatever, and Randy Ride? He don't throw 95 either, he simply has the power to drive a golf ball beyond comprehension. You just embarrass yourself talking crap like that."

Lankhammer looked around the grill room. The topic and volume of the debate had perked up ears in the room, spawning independent discussions and various tales about the prodigious distances of Randy Ride's tee shots.

"Well, Merle," said Henry, "how about I quote you, huh? Here's what I heard you say... 'I've always found that talking don't prove shit.' Or something like that."

Mo, deep into his fourth diet cola, grabbed still another handful of peanuts from a wicker basket despite serious doubts over having enough cola remaining in the ice-cube crevices of his glass to properly quench his dry-roasted thirst. The bomber talk was always flattering, a bit embarrassing even, but this time it was intriguing. Indeed it was; most the Thursday afternoon crowd inside the Silver Meadows men's grill quit talking when Merle the upholstery baron stood up.

"All right Henry, $500 bucks. Mo Mo Moran versus Randy Ride, providing Randy's available, first tee, five drives, longest one in the fairway, winner feeds his horse $250 minimum. That is, if Mo wants to." Merle raised his eyebrows, anticipating some kind of 'thanks but no thanks.'

Henry looked at Mo, not wanting to push it, but clearly giddy with the possibility.

"Hey, ho," said Mo, "let's go." He stood up. "After I take a leak."

Two people in the Grill believed Mo Moran could stay with "Rocket" Ride in a bomb off — Henry Lankhammer and Billy Rick Trueblood a/k/a "Billy Dick" — and they were jacked about the showdown. So was Mo. How he'd fare, he had no idea, but this was right in his wheelhouse.

On those occasions when he had a chance to play some golf with his dad, when Mo would unleash one — talking tee shot of historical significance – Danny Mo, who'd seen it all, would launch into one of his pet sayings, "On under and until...No one!" There was always the pause...followed by the karate chop before the defiant "...No one!" The saying was an abbreviation for "On this hole, under these conditions, until the end of time — no one will ever hit one there again." Eventually it was shortened to a karate chop and, simply, "...No one!"

Of course, Danny said the same thing when Mo Mo pumped one of his interplanetary tee shots so far into the wild frontier some undiscovered species would try to hatch it before any earthling stumbled upon it. "...No one!" was not always a compliment, but it became a ritual between father and son. Mo Mo once mentioned to his mother that he would consider using the, 'On under and until...No one!' version for his wedding vows some day. When she said, "Please, don't," without a smile, Mo Mo no go-go there again.

Through the use of handheld radios, communication between the grill room bartender and pro shop personnel was simple and setting up the bet took very little time. Randy Ride was given clearance; in fact, the head pro even had an assistant put a quiet $50 on the Rocket. A couple dozen men were transformed into kids at Christmas — but instead of cookies, toys, and eggnog, there were cigars, side bets, and cocktails in plastic to-go cups as trimmings to the cheer. Henry and Billy Rick had to write everything down on a scorecard as the action came too fast for the collective memories of a minor league catcher and the Midwestern king of food service and private label salsa.

The men filed out the door into the late afternoon warmth and made the short walk to the elevated first tee amphitheater. At the moment, there was no place that these particular members of Silver Meadows would rather be. Ali/Frazer, Pacquiao/Mayweather, Olbermann/O'Reilly, you name it…nothing could have brought more electricity per capita than Rocket Ride versus Mo Mo Moran facing off in a thunder-bomb throw-down smack-off in West Des Moines.

With four post-round pints of diet cola under his belt, Mo was geeked on caffeine and ready to go. When Rocket Ride almost cruised right by the first tee in a cart on his way to the range, Mo Mo shook his head and gestured in the universal 'ref waving-off-the-hoop' signal.

"We go now or we don't go at all. We gotta be getting back, unless you wanna do this some other time," he said, tweaking the crowd, taking command, just like he did in every sport he ever played.

Rocket Ride smiled and hit the brake. "I'm ready." He bounced off his cart like a Marine dismounting his jeep. He had the contempo-pro look down cold. Crisp black slacks with black studded belt, shiny black golf shoes, French blue golf shirt with short Euro-sleeves, black glove, blond hair and the casual manner of a lion that had been prodded into tearing apart another of Nero's discards for the entertainment purposes. Mo could tell Ride was astounded by the fact that someone would willfully enter the belly of the beast and take him on -- in front of people no less. He had known that Mo Mo was the Cubs number one pitching prospect, but how that mattered he did not know. Before returning home to Iowa, Ride had name-dropped plenty of pro athletes he'd played with when he worked at a club near Chicago. He liked to say "hitting .300 makes you an all-star in baseball; in long-drive competitions 300 makes you a threat…in the women's division."

Mo Moran, a solid 5'11", 185, wore tan shorts, tennis shoe style golf shoes, no socks, no glove, and an XL white shirt with "Taylor and Dunn's Public House" on the breast. There were a couple guys from the pro shop with radios waiting some 320 yards away on either side of the first fairway to do the measuring and reporting. They would be alternating tee shots.

Two sleeves of golf balls were handed to each guy. By mutual agreement it was decided they would hit six balls instead of five, since neither would be getting loose on the range. In fact, the members who had been toiling on the range had been informed of the countdown to blast-off and were also now on hand to catch some of The Rocket's red glare.

Both players quickly executed the stretches they'd learned in their respective sports while they waited for Henry to come back from the men's room. He ambled back smiling, re-tucking some fugitive shirt fabric while muttering something about a "catch and release program for his Big Boys." But no one was interested in anyone's talk anymore. Like a healthy dusting of milled lightning, an electric atmosphere had descended upon the first tee at Silver Meadows Country Club. A slight breeze would be helping the players.

Mo, suddenly looking a bit uncomfortable, went first and slapped one down the middle that went nowhere. Caught it on the bottom of the club. Thin. His dad would say "Catcher in the Rye, did ya?" Or, "She was quite skinny, was she?" Mo never understood what the hell he was yammering about until he finally asked him and was sorry he did. His dad said it was from J.D. Salinger's "short, thin novel" and "she was quite skinny," was supposedly a line from the book. To Mo it was just another of his dad's comments for which "whatever" was the only reply. Something he'd learned from his mother.

The guys with the radios failed at muffling their laughter when they reported back a distance of "just over 250 yards." Randy Ride smoothed one "just about 320 yards." Someone said, "Same time zone anyway" before adding "I think." A few smiled, others looked curious.

Mo Mo's turn. Impassive mask in place. No jungle cat in him at all. Strange. He stepped away from the ball. Twice. Finally, he locked in on his target, a maple tree just off the right side of the fairway that served as the 150-yard marker. The hole was 460 yards from the black tees, putting the tree at 310 yards. Mo Mo would count on his normal draw — some would call it a hook — to bring the ball back to the fairway. A last look at the maple tree and go. He smothered it. Horribly. A nose-diving piece of shit. The ball went, maybe, well, it didn't matter. Left of left, it was hard to even guess. Raspy chuckles and a few whistles from the crowd, but still mostly polite.

Rocket Ride then easily carried one close to 300 yards, the ball ending up more than 330 yards away. Ride appeared to be plenty loose; and quite comfortable in doing what he could to make Mo less so. Smiling, winking and pointing at different members, the occasional ho hum head cock. All effectively understated — confident the members at Silver Meadows Country Club were enjoying another chance to glimpse the jaw-dropping firepower emanating from their lanky home pro bomber. And, of course, make them some money.

But there was no escaping the truth; the spontaneous blast-off had sprung a big ol' buzz leak, and it was all on Mo. He believed he could match any drive Randy Ride had hit so far, but so too did Mo have an awkward issue he'd need to overcome first. At the moment, he had no idea if that would be possible without significant embarrassment.

Again, he shuffled up to the tee markers; he knew he looked tentative. That, in fashionable terms, his body language sucked. He took extra time teeing up his ball as if contemplating something he would likely dismiss. Eventually he stood behind the markers and looked down the fairway. He stood up to the ball and did a half waggle before suddenly shaking his head, spinning around and walking off the tee box. Whispers and murmurs came streaming from the members now. Mo heard some comments on the pressure getting to him. They had no idea just how right they were.

Mo signaled for Billy Rick to meet him as he walked toward the practice putting green some 40 yards left of the tee box. The cocktail-fortified onlookers babbled on in hushed tones. He knew Billy Rick would be stunned, and he was, but his buddy bounced up from his spot on the grass behind the tee like the catcher he was and hustled over to his battery-mate.

"You okay Mo? You ain't lookin' yourself." Henry had started toward the two teammates but Mo waved him off. The two friends huddled on the fringe of the practice green. Just like on the mound.

"You remember, Billy, when I told you I played in a charity golf outing a few years ago and I got paired with Brett Favre?"

"Yeah, said he was funny, hit it good. Chipped like a guy diggin' ditches, the hell..."

"What else?" Mo looked around, paranoid. "Something he's also good at, unofficially recognized as being maybe the best ever?"

"Hell if I...ah, Christ Mo, the farting thing. You said he could fart on command. He'd hit a good shot and then fart a long one, kinda proud of 'em, you said."

"You got it...ripped 'em at will. The guy's known for it. He even claimed Favre was French for fart." Mo looked into the middle distance as if lost in reverie, but he was focusing internally on something else.

"Mo, babe, you know I love a good fart story, but..." Billy Rick Trueblood stopped cold, eyes narrowing, listening. Then he burst out in laughter. "Damn you." Billy Rick tried to gather himself, "I thought there was a Harley in the parking lot or somethin', man, but it's you, you skunk... I mean, dude — that fart was longer than a 'Crazy Game of Poker' live."

The gallery behind the tee was too far away for anyone else to hear, but everyone there was looking in the direction of Mo Mo and Billy Rick, watching them laugh. They laughed at them laughing, and the speculation intensified the laughter even more.

Mo looked at Billy Rick, "All the soda...and peanuts. It was so quiet on that tee box and everybody's so close, watchin'. I didn't think I could swing hard and hold it in…I mean, I tried twice. On the mound I just let 'em fly."

"Well, go let one fly now, everybody's waiting."

Mo Moran's body language changed completely. He hustled up to the tee and apologized for the delay. No explanation. He teed up his ball, practically dancing through his pre-shot routine, not that he really had one.

He located his target, the maple tree, and swung, smooth, powerful, rejuvenated and free. The ball and clubface contact was flush, sweet. Pure as pure gets. The gallery, now reinvested, made 'that's more like it' noises. When Mo looked for the ball in the sky, he was a little surprised that it was a ten or twelve yards right of the maple and wasn't moving left as much as he expected. He walked a few steps to the right to make the ball appear to move left. Then, slowly, it worked toward the maple tree and for the briefest moment he wondered if a bird of prey lurked within. Two things were for sure: one; it was as good as he could hit a golf ball, and two; something a little funky happened inside his shoulder on the follow through. A twinge, but…twinges, hell, they're as much a part of life as compounding flatulence.

The Titleist Pro V1X, carrying lightly on the helping breeze looked like it would hit the maple tree. But the arc of the descending ball came under the overhanging branches and hit just past the base of the tree about ten yards from the fairway. The ball was given new life and shot forward and a little left. Hard. The gallery was startled and laughing less than happy laughs as the ball rolled out on the right center part of the fairway. The radioed voice announced the distance at 366 yards. Both the applause and commentary was respectful.

Mo told Randy Ride to finish out, that he was through. The guy with the radio reported that the ball fairly close to the base of the tree, and, no, he couldn't find any visible roots though it was quite firm in the shade there.

Rocket Ride's smile was reduced to the paste-on variety, and his ho-hum head cocks and shy-boy shrugs were reworked to play the role of a 'what-you-gonna-do' casualty. Ride made four more wonderful swings, two balls ended up in the fairway maxing out at a little over 350 yards, not really close enough to measure.

∞

The ride home was a triumph in storytelling among friends. Mo Mo Moran and Billy Rick Trueblood each cleared $800 from what turned into a $2,400 pot. Billy Rick, having reduced a bunch Bud Lights to nothing over the course of the proceedings had put his southern accent in overdrive.

"Can't decide what buttered my corn more there Mr. Mo Mo…the length of that hardly-human tee shot or the length of that hardly-human BP-like gas-leak of yours. Dude, that fart was like…like a gymnasium buzzer got frozen stuck or somethin'."

Mo took it all in. He had competed since he could walk. Whatever the sport, always the star; countless championships and awards and trophies and interviews and attention were part of the program. Conquests never got old. Mo still cherished memories of triumphant playground races and countless driveway basketball wars and even a few tape-measure walk-off Whiffle Ball moments of come-from-behind neighborhood glory. The long drive face-off with the Rocket Man had materialized from the sort of spontaneous locker-room combustion that egos and alcohol create, and yet listening to Billy Rick's recap on the drive home felt just about as rewarding as when he got the call that he had been drafted by The Cubs, probably because the rush from being picked in the third round was more about relief, having blown off a bunch of college scholarship offers to play for the Cubs.

He looked forward now to calling his dad with the story. Mo Mo would get him all frothed up leading him to the 366. The whole thing; The Upholsterer and The Salsa Man, Billy Rick, the bets, even the emancipating cutting of the cheese. It was the kind of story his father loved. He knew he'd be able to hear the karate chops in his dad's voice coming through the phone when he'd finally get to "No one, Mo Mo… No one!"

As Mo drove, he hardly even bothered to worry about the shoulder tugs he felt with every turn of the wheel. Some Advil and it'll be gone in the morning. It better be gone, he was pitching.

∞

But that was then. When he had the chance to talk to his dad the following evening, he rattled off what he had to tell; the long drive duel and the no hitter for 5 and 1/3. Then he told him his shoulder had blown up. That his season was probably over – and, who knows…

The wave of 'possum rot returned. And festered.

∞

Chapter 4

With an order of Farm Bites in one's immediate future, even unworthy lives and unlucky souls had a right to feel blessed by the gods of gusto and good-living.

Garlic-smashed Black Angus tenderloin medallions atop pickled cucumber doubloons both riding high on golden saddles of buttery Texas Toast, they were called Farm Bites; *the* appetizer at The Farmstead Restaurant. Danny Moran believed these cell-phone-sized delights to be top-five worldwide in the hot, cool, and crunchy category. "Might be the finest beef-based appetizer of the modern era," he would tell friends, though always quick to acknowledge that he had no way of knowing what the Aussies were up to, nor did he have firsthand knowledge as to the marbling qualities attributed to Argentine cattle pampered on pampas grass, and that he'd only heard and read stories about Kobe beef, reportedly a tender mercy possessing a mouthfeel many consider too pure to risk mixing with other textures. Maybe some day, but for now it was Farm Bites, twelve dollars for a serving of five, he always had four, Molly one; it was their deal.

∞

Standing at the bar in chilled silence, Danny had a Black and Tan in play while Molly nursed a Merlot from the Greg Norman Estates. The frost, of course, was Danny's fault. Pissed his wife off with another shorter-but-longer shortcut. Train-crossing delay. Who knew? Molly, a junior high English teacher at Holy Apostles Middle School, had taken to countering Danny's "stupid ranking fixation" by grading everything. She was a hard grader.

"A D-plus…and the plus is a gift, only because we're still alive and they're still serving," she had said as they entered the restaurant. She was starting to have some fun with the grading thing. Danny saw this as progress.

They eventually wriggled into some small talk about a few of the antique tools and farm implements affixed to the rustic walls throughout The Farmstead; Danny wondering how some of the tools worked, Molly expressing a pronounced lack of shock that her husband found tools confusing. After a brief relapse into the trademark malaise of couples who've run out of things to say, they were summoned and seated by The Farmstead's affable owner, Dallas Birk.

A large man, "Big D," the story goes, was raised by a single mom who became pregnant by a well-known former Green Bay Packer during the Lombardi era. The player had apparently failed to mention he had a wife back in Chevy Chase – Redskin Country — so Marcy Birk named her boy Dallas.

At Danny's second favorite table at the far end of the restaurant, and with their second round of drinks rounding the sharper edges of their daily bothers, Danny and Molly melted into some momentary peace. At least, peace in the way the Morans knew it, where they let bygones mostly be gone — unless called upon later. But for now, there was peace. Maybe it was the Merlot. Maybe because, moody as she often was, Danny never tired of his wife's face.

"May I take a moment to be shallow, Molly? Take a crack at it anyway — and I do mean shallow in the best sense of the word, but anyway, let me just say...you, Mol, are, to my eyes...still a babe."

"Sure. Thanks. I think." Molly shrugged, not particularly touched.

"You know what I mean."

"Let's just say I'm wary," said Molly. "I mean, I just slapped you with a D on your driving."

"Plus. It was a D-plus. Better than an F," said Danny. "The F you tagged me with yesterday for the toast crumb violation was over the top. You flunked me...even after I drove the bastards into the sink?"

Molly smiled and shook her head in disbelief. "How can you go to the trouble of wiping the crumbs off the counter and into the sink – and then, not...rinse them down the drain? You did the hard part, and then just left them there to wreak havoc. Why? It boggles the mind."

"The crumbs are simply awaiting disposition, Molly. They're in our custody. Once they're rounded up and captive in the sink, they can't hurt anyone anymore. For crumbs, honey, the sink is death row."

"So just wash 'em down the drain, for God's sake." Molly's voice grew more intense. "Use the spray hose, like your dad always said, "go right at 'em, show 'em you own their crumby little asses!"

"Oh, I do, Molly Mo. But I do it when I return to the sink to rinse my plate. The water I use to do that also runs the crumbs to their final resting place. Water is a dwindling resource, can't just take it for granted."

"You were using a paper plate, Danny."

"Well...yes, yesterday I was, but my point remains the same. The next person to use the sink, to rinse a coffee mug for example, it's that multi-purpose run-off water then that completes the mission. Bottom line...its arrivederci crumbs. And -- we don't waste water."

"Right on, Mr. Tree-hugger, ignoring the paper plate issue for a moment, why don't we look at the root cause? Put it this way... you once told me how you deserved one of your high world rankings for toast-buttering. Right? Well, I'm not so sure. It's not all about managing a stick of butter or clean-up...shouldn't it also include controlling your overall crumb count right from the start?"

Danny loved it when Molly went with the program. It was the silence he hated. Silence he encountered on too many summer evenings upon his return home after practicing at the Ol' Barn – what he called his "preparation sessions." It was the possibility of another dose of cold, wordless discontent that brought on his butterflies. And what Danny feared most of all: that he would, again, insist his wife explain her chilliness — and that, again, she wouldn't.

And so Danny would inevitably contemplate an array of possibilities before unloading truckloads of logic in artful but useless soliloquies that did nothing but address his own guesswork. If he pushed it, his wife might offer a weary counterpoint. It might be snippy, irrelevant or a startling counter-punch, but hey, it was something.

"Something" usually went a little like this: Molly would seethe or sigh over something like, for example, a kitchen sponge blunder (color-coded by application). Danny wouldn't get it, she would resent it, he'd get sarcastic, and she'd nitpick in retaliation. Then, he would resent it, she wouldn't get it, he'd get sarcastic, and she would nitpick again until her words were like the poking fingers of another Mo, the Alpha of The Three Stooges. (Actually Moe.)

It was during those stretches that Danny felt more tension dealing with his wife — even if it was simply talking on the phone or driving somewhere – than he ever did competing in some golf tournament.

Danny sipped through the Tan and headed into the Black of his beer and smiled. "Well, you've got a point Molly; my crumb management hasn't been what it used to be. The healthier, multi-grain breads that are out now, like that Fiber One stuff we buy… they're veritable crumb factories. So you're right. I probably haven't adjusted to the newer whole-grains as well as someone with my skills should. Seriously."

Molly knew her husband's partial put-on act too well, but she had a little momentum now. She sipped her Merlot, and then quickly returned her glass to the table. A sign she had more to say.

"Let's put it this way…everybody talks about how great your short game is. 'Oh man, that Danny Mo, he can pitch and chip it as good anyone on the PGA Tour.' And you do that 'aw shucks' thing. You go 'Yeah, short game's gotta be good, bad as I'm hitting it.' Or you say, 'Wouldn't have to count on it so much if I'd hit some greens.' I've heard you say those things enough times. Well Danny, even I understand you don't have to chip if you hit the green to begin with. Right? It's the same thing here. Why don't you just back off with the butter knife, and slow down a bit. Same damn thing, you'd have easier cleanups and waste less water if there were fewer crumbs to begin with."

"Wow, yes, a tempo thing" said Danny, nodding. "That's not bad, Molly. In fact, it's incredibly astute." He inspected his butter knife intently. "Maybe I should think about an equipment change too, maybe we find some butter knives with finer ridges, or better yet, none at all. But yeah, I very well may have gotten quick. Could also be my grip pressure. A guy gets into bad habits. You know as well as I do, Mol...at one time, even with cold butter...man, I could really spread it."

"Top-five worldwide, no doubt." said Molly, drolly. Then, with mock enthusiasm, "You can get it back, you always do. You, sir, are Danny Mo."

"Your support is everything, Molly Moran."

"Right," said Molly dismissively. She looked around the restaurant and turned serious. "Let me ask you something, Danny."

"Yeah?"

Molly hesitated. She had never been all that comfortable with compliments. Giving or receiving. "What did you mean... a compliment in the shallowest sense, or shallow in the best way or whatever you said? I mean, you 'babe' me all the time, I get that, but..."

"Well," Danny brought his elbows to the table and leaned in, "you know how sometimes, the more you're with someone, and the more you see both their best and less than best qualities, they become, I don't know... you've seen them look good, bad, rough, tired, occasionally stunning or suddenly strange, or maybe it doesn't matter as much or maybe it's a comfort you have with the devil you know... Ah hell, I don't know..."

Danny's explanation felt like he was walking on wet cement. "I guess I just wanted to tell you that — even if I hadn't known you for so long, or even if you weren't quite so bright... you know, someone who couldn't liken a crumb reduction initiative to a part of my golf game — well...on a purely visceral, somewhat shallow level, you'd still be 'a babe,' even to a handsome, head-turning man like me. Sure, I wish you weren't as crabby as you get sometimes. But, really, that's only when you're awake."

He wished he could have resisted the quip. Sort of. "That was, uh, poor on my part."

Molly's big eyes narrowed. "The stinger's always hiding in the honey with you, isn't it Danny? But, really, that's only when you're talking."

Touché.

"You grade, I rank. Women are from Venus, Men are from Serena." *Where the hell am I going here?* "I mean, hiding my stinger in your honey will always be my activity of choice, Molly, Babe." Danny was backpedaling like a politician caught telling the truth to the wrong crowd.

"Sure. But you never tire of throwing your little jabs. Why? Do you feel vulnerable…and sarcasm's your escape hatch? Or is it a need to feel smart and wisecracks are your little brain snacks?"

Danny shrugged. "Maybe I need more than a sigh or a blank look sometimes. So… I make a crack, see if anything spills out. Something is better than nothing. Maybe I should email Dr. Phil and see if my sarcasm is actually related to your silence.

Molly took the daintiest taste of her wine, turning the last sip into two. "Well, please get back to me."

Danny picked up his butter knife again. No ridges. Good heft. "Wonder where he stands on toast crumbs?"

Molly raised her glass and swirled the little that remained. "The kitchen floor, I suppose, if at all."

∞

The Farm Bites arrived. Good timing. Danny was able to stay calm, but barely. Hungry puppy noises at a frequency range he hoped only he could hear arose from a place deep within him. Delaying such forms of gratification took all the mannered pragmatism and stifled enthusiasm Danny could muster. Affectations that were also equally prudent when it came to competitive golf, games of poker, and even, more times than not, fistfights.

Danny watched Molly's eyes follow every action the server made in arranging the appetizer plates and the linen and the water glasses. It was a tactic, actually; a conspicuous preoccupation with something that was really nothing to keep from having to say anything further about something else. In this case, Danny figured it was him bringing up the whole "babe" thing — his fixing-a-watch-with-a-hammer way of telling his wife he still found her attractive, still a babe. It was a reference to their first date, when Danny Moran had stretched the truth beyond recognition by claiming he hadn't dated all that much before her, and said their relationship was his "Babe-tism," a groaner between them back then and for years after, if not at all recently. Nevertheless, for the moment, Molly seemed content.

Like a whole lot of The Farmstead's famed honey butter, peace was on a roll.

∞

The remainder of their dinner did not disappoint. More importantly, Danny and Molly had fun. They sparred like they did in the days when their chemistry never slept. The conversation was balanced; they didn't just click over to their default option – the lives of their kids, Rinny and Mo — though they did touch upon their goings-on. After the toast crumb resolution, they had stayed pretty much in the moment, finding meaning in meaningful and meaningless things, and laughing like they hadn't for too long.

Danny was signing the check when Molly asked a question at a slightly higher, probably wine-related volume. "I heard that some people think you may try to qualify for the Senior Tour when the time comes. Wouldn't that be something you'd maybe discuss with me first?"

"It's called the Champions Tour now, but that's neither here nor there, but… Danny had to laugh. "Where'd that come from?"

"Joanie said Paul heard it from Iggy or Randy or someone. So…are you thinking about it?"

"Not. At. All." Danny put down the pen and looked over the labyrinth of table coves and booths throughout the restaurant. Monopolizing a booth maybe ten or so feet away was a guy with a face he knew but couldn't place. The man looked remarkably like a puffier John McEnroe. "In fact, it's ridiculous. Think about it. That would be what, five years away, right about the time Mo is coming into his own. We'll be practically living at Wrigley. I plan on embarrassing you, me,

Mo, us. We can just paper the place with 'Mo 'em down!' signs." Not
Danny's style, but he enjoyed threatening the proud dad shtick.

"I know — and you know I've come to accept you regularly making
a fool of yourself a long time ago. But all that aside, you've taught your
boy well." Molly's eyes brought light. "It's going to be fun."

"Sure will. And, well...been thinking a lot lately, Mol. Thinking I
might even cut back on competitive golf...period. Maybe sooner rather
than later. Hell, I don't know. I do enjoy the friendships and the
competition, I just don't need it like I used to."

"You'd miss it," said Molly, "and you know it."

"Maybe. But if I could somehow win the State Open this year, I'd
probably just pull the plug. I may anyway, win or lose."

"You think you can still win a State Open? Didn't you say the kids
are winning it every year now...the mini-tour guys and the college
stars?"

"Pretty much. But this would be the year to pull it off."

"I'm sure I'm supposed to know, but...why this year?" Molly had
been through so many seasons of tournament golf she more rolled with
it than kept up.

"It's at The Hill Farm. Won the Match Play there, qualified for The
US Am there...just play well there. Plus, it's close. I can sleep, or attempt
to, in my own bed. Just a feeling." The Farmstead was nearly empty
now, and he realized that the puffy Johnny Mac appeared to be listening
in, and that the guy was drunk, his head rocking in slow ovals. Danny
stared at him, waiting for the dude to retreat. He didn't.

"Remember the year it just poured. Early nineties? What a mess."
Molly, actually engaging her hubby with some golf memories. Rare.
Sweet.

"Yeah, what a shame. The leaders all stumble in like drunks; Sally
posts a low one over an hour earlier, before the storm. Only round he
broke par."

In the booth over, Puffy Mac was laughing now, one of those raspy,
coughing, laughter-supersedes-breathing kind of cackles, wobbling in
his booth and glancing back and forth at Danny and whoever he was

with. "That's right, Dan Moran," the man half-shouted. "Andy always says he got his when he was young enough to do it." He was slurring his words between cough-laughs. "He knows you'll never, I mean... he says he feels bad you never got one." Blotto.

Then it hit him. The guy was Andy Salamone's brother-in-law. Puffy Mac hadn't always been quite that puffy. As much as Danny could tell from looking at a guy in a booth, his body didn't appear proportionately all that different, but the guy's face was all jowly chins and misappropriated flesh now. The man had followed behind, or caddied for, Salamone at different tournaments over the years, though not so much lately. He worshiped Andy, and worked for him at Salamone Fabric and Rollers. Danny couldn't come up with a name but recalled Andy treating the guy like a pet he was tired of feeding.

Molly and Danny Moran got up to leave. It was almost closing time for the dining room. As they came upon the booth where Puffy Mac sat, Danny noticed the guy across from him wearing an eye patch and about to do a face-plant in his drink. Judging by the trajectory of his drool, he would not have missed. Puffy kept talking to eye-patch man who was about as alert as a totem pole. P Mac turned and reached for Danny's elbow.

"You really gonna quit, Dan Moran?"

"Well, Mac, I will when I do." *Mac?*

"Hey, Mac, who you callin' Mac?" slurred the puffy faced man. "Tha's what I heard you just said."

The bloated man's breath smelled like some sort of janitorial strength crap-removing acid, the kind of breath that bites into the eyes. His hand slipped off Danny's arm and he almost toppled out of the booth.

Molly moved Danny along and said, "You gentlemen drive carefully, now."

Danny went to the bar and talked to the bar manager. Danny gave him some cash and told him to call a cab for Puffy and the pirate — and to be sure to call the cops if they refused.

Walking through the parking lot on the way to the Impala, Molly broke the summer evening silence. The wine had her using an amazing amount of words to say two things. One, the cab gesture deserved an A, and two; the eye-patch man appeared to be in a coma or dead.

"Nah," said Danny, addressing her points in reverse order. "If you looked close, he was winking at you, Mol. And why not, you're…"

"I know," she interrupted, "…a babe."

"So, Babe, how about you grade me again when we get home? Maybe on one of your curves?"

"No."

"No?"

"No… a curve would mean I'd have to grade others."

"That might be okay…" Danny tried to look lecherous.

"Really? Hmm…"

"…as long as I can wear your panties and hide in the closet, keep the door open just a crack?"

"You're a fiend…" Molly smiled and grabbed Danny's arm "…but you're my fiend."

∞

Danny passed on taking one of his shorter-but-longer shortcuts on the ride home. No butterflies, no sniping, no tension. The phone was ringing when they entered their home.

It was Mo Mo. Bad news. His shoulder…

∞

Chapter 5

Danny Moran was the youngest competitive golfer ever inducted into the Wisconsin Golf Hall of Fame. Included in his over fifty titles were four state match play championships, three of them before he was thirty.

The State Match Play Championship is played over four mid-June weekdays. After a Monday qualifying round, there were two matches a day until you lost, if you lost. If the event was out of town, you had to check out of your hotel every morning and then check back in if you won both matches that day. In Danny's case, by the time he checked his work-related emails, called home and ate dinner, there was barely enough time to crash, usually with his face in a book or magazine before having to get up and do it again. Play well and you could easily kill the better part of a workweek, blow a quick $500 on food and lodging, and feel your wife's exasperation swell with every day you're away — just to bring home a wooden plaque, maybe some new balls and bunch of dirty laundry. And sometimes it was just the dirty laundry and a sour attitude.

He loved it.

So when Danny came into the office on a perfect Tuesday morning, he was predictably prickly. Any time he had to forgo a meaningful golf competition, it was difficult; even reading about it in the paper could bring about involuntary shudders or a twitch to the face. Still, he couldn't resist checking the results. There were always buddies to check on and pull for — and a few tank-jobs to celebrate.

At his desk, he held the newspaper so that it concealed any involuntary activity on his face as he scanned the qualifying scores. Five of the seven golfers from The Old Barn had qualified for one of the 64 spots that would make up the matches. Good. Andy Salamone qualified third with a 70. Too bad.

Despite Danny's past success in an important event, business had to take priority over golf now if he were to compete in even bigger tournaments later in the summer. He rarely missed the State Amateur, also held Monday through Thursday and an event he had also won four times. Nor was he likely to skip the qualifiers for the three US Amateurs — the US Amateur Public Links (for public course players only), the US Amateur, and the US Mid-Amateur (presumably for amateurs who have jobs... that is to say, non-college players, or, technically, qualified participants over the age of 25).

In 1990, the year Phil Mickelson won his US Am at Cherry Hills near Denver, Danny had survived several mountain lightning delays during the stroke play qualifying, and then went on to win enough matches to make it to the final eight. But playing in any national amateur meant another week off of work, another week away from the family, and with the extra travel, at least a thousand dollars just to do it.

Years ago he would play the occasional Western Amateur or Sunnahanna Invitational. But when Rinny in soccer and Mo in golf and baseball started competing at higher levels in their respective sports, time and money had to be spread around. And so the state's major match play event with its mid-week format and uncertain elimination was one event he reluctantly passed on. Like so many responsible decisions, it felt like he was ordering cauliflower from a custard stand.

Danny Moran's list of golf achievements was spectacular – but even with his four State Amateur titles, four match play championships, and four State Best Ball championships, even with seven State Public Links trophies and some three dozen other victories in prestigious but mostly weekend events, his resume still had one glaring omission: The Wisconsin State Open, featuring the state's elite pros and amateurs both. He had four top fives, twice the runner up. Three times it looked like he was a lock to win coming down the final nine and let it get away. And so for a good decade and a half, Danny had no higher priority in competitive golf than to win the Open. Maybe then he could relax a little, back off on the nightly practice grind, the endless preparation he felt it took to win. He had hoped it would have happened by now. But hope never beat anyone.

Danny Moran employed two others at MO Solutions (along with contracting out for tech and web support), and they did not directly bring in revenue. It was about five or six years ago that he hired Evan Orsman, an old friend from his college days who handled all the finances and, when required, reviewed the more complicated accounting aspects of the different businesses that hired MOS. Carla Wicheczmowski, (pronounced pretty much "which is my house key?") handled absolutely everything else. Those close to her called her "Witchy," which she preferred. Danny trusted Evan and Witchy like family. Sometimes they scrapped like family.

When Danny started a business consulting business 11 years ago, he named the company Modus Operandi Solutions; MO Solutions for short and MOS for shorter. He liked to claim that the whole MOS/Mo's, connection never occurred to him. Without missing a beat, Witchy had said, "Modus Operandi Business Solutions would have been more accurate, we'd be MO BS...and completely accurate."

Witchy was a sandy-haired, athletic woman in her mid-forties. She had violet eyes, a year-round tan, and one of those boxer's broken-nose bumps as part of her slightly larger than average beak. Not classically beautiful, but attractive, fit and smart. She helped coach a high school girl's tennis team on Milwaukee's North Shore, and competed in some tennis tournaments herself. She once had a suit brought against her for fracturing the skull and severely damaging the genitalia of a serial mugger who tried to roll her outside a downtown club. In court, a point of contention became "How many kicks and blows does an unsuspecting mugger have to endure once his clock has been completely cleaned and his ass properly kicked?" It was comical really, and the incident became a two day hot button on local talk radio when damages were sought from Witchy by the mugger for reportedly reducing the quality of her attacker's current and future erections. The morning team at WKLH, Milwaukee's classic rock radio station, dedicated *Witchy Woman* by The Eagles to her over that span.

∞

Orsman, Witchy and Danny met in a small conference room inside their small suite in Stonebridge II's office park. Orsman reported on some capital allocation irregularities after a wide-ranging process review for a snack food company that had hired MOS. Danny was a whiz at sniffing out process hiccups and other flows that weren't quite right as well as what was actually working, and he was good at creating promotional waves with sometimes novel marketing strategies, but when it came to breaking down the hard numbers, he needed Orsman to summarize everything without interruption, then again with questions from Danny, before finally giving a critical listen to a work-in-progress version in strategic Danny-speak.

Evan Orsman was short, thin, veiny-armed and 45 — the same age as Danny. He liked going on about his family ad nauseum. "Is there something so wrong about spoiling my chubby wife and my two chubby kids" was a common refrain. He had never played a single round of golf in his life. In fact, he never really played sports at all. That, however, didn't keep him from pouring over the standings and statistics like nothing else. A sports factoid buff, he knew the latest line on everything. Danny would often say "No one… I mean, no one…" *(Karate chop included)* "…knows sports trivia or MLB statistical minutia like my man, Orsman."

Witchy went over Danny's schedule for the rest of the week and assorted company reminders. "So, we'll be expecting you to be slightly irritable this week, Danny?"

"What burns inside me shall be buried, as usual – but by all appearances I'll remain my statesman-like self."

Orsman nodded. "Can we expect this approach to fizzle early and fall off from there?"

"You two are predisposed to know my pain. Please don't make it worse."

We won't, Danny" said Orsman, "at least not like if Salamone has a good week."

"Didn't even know he was entered," said Danny as he pretended to scan an Excel spreadsheet printout. "I'll be in my office."

Before leaving the conference room, Danny saw Witchy give Orsman a hard look. As far as she was concerned, all talk about Salamone was to be off limits in the office. The guy had hired MOS over a decade ago, and when Danny mentioned some irregularities he had discovered about the company's purchasing practices, Salamone went on a rampage that resulted in him firing an entire department. Salamone then opted out of a contract with MOS that he had supposedly signed yet failed to return. Finally, the Hair Dude, as Mo Mo called him, offered something paltry to end an agreement Danny believed was already a verbal contract. A lesson learned the hard way. What's worse, the married Salamone began futilely calling Witchy for delusional reasons, which she ended in no uncertain terms with the verbal equivalent of what she did to the hapless, would-be mugger whose balls she punted deep into his own territory.

It was less than a month later that Danny Mo dropped Salamone on the range with a single right hand, when the hawk tracked Sally's ricocheted shot directly into Mo Mo's body, leaving little question mark scars from the razor-sharp talons that tore into his face.

∞

Chapter 6

Cut - you craptacular punk-ass yank-job sow. No effing way. No Sir. Not you. Go. Stay. Yeah. Go stay left and live there. Yes. All...freaking...day. Welcome to the Jungle...damnit, not Jim Rome -- again. Go again. Don't suck. Great. Okay. Back in the stance a little bit. Alright. Waggle... fluid... clear the left side...

Whhhompht! Solid...

Great. Push draw. Hit the oak while you're at it... everybody does... freakin joke. Incredible. Where I wanna go and yes you can go to hell and hide for all I care. See cut, hit draw. Errrr! Yeah. Reliable. That's why we're here. To putrefy this range with noxious methane from my golf game. STOP talking like Rome every time you stink. Yeah. Got more where that came from. Just watch. Yeah. Open the shoulders a bit. Alright. Have a take now. Nice little D Mo baby fade. Waggle... fluid, clear...

Whhhompht! Flush...

Left...hmmph. Shocking. Shocking development. Shocked? Not! Cut. You freak-dog spawn of Lucifer piece of... Nope. Sorry. Can't. Not today. Not me. Not even borderline worthy. Just another over-the-top piece o' slop. Smack-off? Seriously? Get real. Pull it again why don't you. Right down my shoulder line. Unbelievable. Straight. Perfectly straight. Great. Block-ass push-draws and stay way left and don't you come back no more. No more. No more. No-freaking-more. Put-a-bullet-in-my-brain. Straight-balls. Great. The cut-shot king. Danny-freaking-Mo. The hell? Rome is burning. State Am around the corner and you go get lost in the Lefturn hemisphere. How great is that. The Lefturn hemisphere. You clueless line-crossing jack...wagon. I'll give you waggle, fluid, clear, ah...flush that crap...

Whhompht! Pure. Pure left...rack that, you reek, I'm out. ...aww...come on, not Marty, not now... Damn, Reeky don't lose that number.

"Getting ready for the Am, are ya?" Dragging his butt up the incline to the hitting area of the practice tee was Marty Archibald.

Ol' Marty was one of the lords of Wisconsin golf, and one of his trademarks was the "one tough hombre" limp. In his middle 60s now, he'd had a heart bypass a year ago. Prior to that he had two new knees and a hip put in. Still, if Marty was capable of standing on his own, he competed. For trophies or money, it didn't matter. He played out of The Old Barn golf course and encouraged Danny to make The Barn his home course when he moved to the area from Door County a couple decades earlier. Marty was the only person ever to play in the US Amateur Public Links Championship in five different decades. Now, while in a perpetual state of recovery, he was the only regular who dared to bother Danny when he was at his work station on the range. Not even Crusty Sindorf went there without an invitation.

"Oh, hey there, Marty," said Danny, stepping away from his spot at the far end of The Old Barn's range. "Didn't see you sneaking up on me."

"Just wanted to say hello. Been getting in some chipping and putting, letting the body heal, you know."

"Well you know what they say, you're always stronger where the scars remain, and you're probably nothing but scar tissue these days."

"You may have point there, Danny. So...you hittin' it okay?" Marty had a hint of a champion's arrogance, but what amused Danny most was Marty's tactical humility, the type of guy who turns humble when he senses he might get some credit for it. Or...when an opponent might just drop his guard.

"Pretty good. Feel good about it." A lie, of course, and Danny knew Marty saw through it too.

"Just wondering... Am's Monday, ain't it, or is it the next?"

"This. Churchy Hills CC."

"Ah...The Church. Nice track. Too long for me now. Put in some new tees I hear — can really make it ridiculous if they want – except maybe for someone like Mo Mo. And you too...you're still taking it pretty deep." Marty shook his head. "But that's why I came to over to bother you. Checking on Little Mo. They cut on him yet?"

"Yeah, surgery supposedly went well. We'll see. The real work starts now. Bad tear though. He's a little down, but I'm probably the only one who can tell."

"Say hello, would ya? He's a helluva kid."

"Sure will, Mart, though Mo Mo's no kid anymore."

Marty nodded and started to limp back towards the putting green as if it were excruciating. With Marty, a man with even more total victories than Danny, everything always hurt like hell. The guy verbalized and emphasized his every ache since anyone could remember. Then, most times, on the course he'd crush you like a spent cigarette.

Danny watched him walk away. He knew Marty well enough to know the old warhorse would turn back to pass on one more comment. He always did — it's what great men do. Danny put his head down. Out of respect.

"Oh, and Danny?"

Danny snapped his head up, as if surprised.

"You'll figure it out. You usually do." Marty didn't wait for an answer. He turned, slowly, and the 'one tough hombre' hobbled away. His work was done.

Danny's was not.

Love ya Marty. But it'd sure be nice to be left the hell alone... Ah... Get back to work would ya, Danny boy. Waggle... fluid... clear... screw it. That ain't workin'...what was it that worked for a while last year, some kind of travel-sized Zen thing... ah yes, I remember... Port... o... let... Yeah.

Whhhompht! Hmm...much better.

Port...o...let.

Yes. Better.

∞

Chapter 7

The small apartment was not the classic pigsty one might expect of a couple of 21-year-old minor league ballplayers with limited household skills, but neither had the place been the recipient of many hissing fits from the likes of *Lysol, Pledge* or *Windex.*

Mo's casual approach to order was as many miles south of his mother's devotion to it as it was north of his roomate's indifference, though it was Mo who pronounced that "the best weapon against a dirty apartment is a dimmer switch." The dimmer switch, however, could not make the empty bag of *Cheetos* disappear from the middle of the floor. Still, tidiness and Billy Rick notwithstanding, Mo Moran had been comfortable enough sharing an apartment that was – give or take a shade or two of muted ecru – just like a couple dozen million others.

The televised coverage of the British Open had just wrapped up and Mo Mo was not all that comfortable on the couch. And he sure as hell wasn't in the mood to lean forward a full five feet to grab the ringing cordless phone from the coffee table in front of him. Mo regarded the thing as an intruder. It was an old – practically Seinfeld era - stand-up that belonged to his roommate Billy Rick Trueblood. It was during the previous presidential election that he decided the phone's geometry resembled the shape of one candidate's head. And like that particular Senator back then, it, too, was now begging for attention without changing expression.

But it kept ringing, and warrior that he was, Maurice Moran took the challenge. He made his move. He grunted aloud, but only because he was alone, before making a clumsy lunge for the phone.

And knocked it over.

The slender gray stand-up phone tumbled end-over-end like a gymnast toward the middle of the small living room floor where, remarkably, the receiver stuck the landing, but only after cartwheeling into the empty *Cheetos* bag that Billy Rick had polished off during a late-night loop of Sports Center.

"Damn you," said Mo, uncertain if "you" referred to the phone, the bag, Billy Dick or himself. Regardless, capturing his phone was now a full-blown mission. And so Mo carefully rolled onto the floor and crawled on his three functional limbs, stalking a former presidential candidate, who was still droning intermittently as he looked out from inside the empty Cheetos bag. Problem was, it wasn't entirely empty. Mo Mo picked up the bag and dumped out the phone; and with it came a healthy stream of Cheetos dust that left a fresh, orange, Nike-like swoosh on the cream Berber carpet.

"Aaachh…dammit, uh, hello?" said Mo after hitting the 'talk' button. For the first time in his life he hadn't checked caller ID, sure he was close to losing the call to voice mail. He wasn't in the mood for losing.

"Mo Mo, Honey, am I interrupting something?"

"Hey, Mom. I…well, I just dumped powdered Cheetos on the carpet trying to answer the phone… shook me up a little," said Mo, laughing, a bit relieved that it was his mother. "One of those things, all of a sudden, something you think'll never happen to you and then…what is it — denial, anger, bargaining — the whole deal. So, how are you Mom?"

"My God, you've become your father." Molly sounded like she was half-pleased. "We're good here, Mo… but maybe we should call back when you come to, uh, 'accept' your *Cheetos* incident? What are you eating *Cheetos* for anyway?"

"Billy Rick loves 'em then leaves 'em," said Mo. "All over the place."

Molly laughed. "Don't mean to nag, Honey; but I'm your mom, and as your father likes to say about being a father as well as his day-to-day nonsense, 'There's no off-switch for that.' Anyway, we were just checking on you. Figured you'd be watching the British Open. How are you feeling?"

"I'm fine. Shoulder hurts a little…but it's supposed to. The PT makes it worse. Otherwise, it's all good. Gets boring."

"Well, don't try to do too much, honey. Is Billy Rick helping you I hope?'

"Sure, but he's gone most of the time, playing. I only go to the home games now. They don't want my shoulder bouncin' around too much. What's new with you guys?"

"Not too much. Rinny's getting ready for her first semester away. Your dad says she's pre-planning contingencies for her back-up plans."

"Of course," said Mo. "Two of a kind, aren't we?"

"Two amazing kids — raised in the same house and as different as chalk and cheese. A blessing." It was a favorite observation of Molly's. "I wouldn't have it any other way…and I'm sure you haven't a clue what you're doing after this call."

Mo Moran could attest to that.

Molly went on for a while, ending with how everyone at the Daugherty wedding asked about how her son was doing, how her husband drank a little too much and danced embarrassingly like Michael Flatley channeling Prince.

"Well if his behavior becomes an issue… Let me know, I can always come home for an intervention."

"You *are* your father's son." Molly laughed. "And you know what?"

"No, tell me, Mom." Mo knew what was coming.

"I love you anyway." Mo's mother signed off and handed the phone to his dad.

"Mo!"

"Thought you gave up the goofy dancing, D Mo," said Mo Mo.

"I dance, therefore I am. So let it go." Danny shifted gears. "How are you Mo Mo?"

"Never better," said Mo, "stuck on worse." Mo, reflexively becoming his father's son. "Mom will break the news to you on the Cheetos mishap I'm dealing with."

"Good, I'll take notes," said Danny. "How's the wing?"

"Growling. Certain actions. You know — the ones you need for basic survival, moves that ensure proper hygiene and limit itching…they're tougher than you think with your off hand. How 'bout you, other than embarrassing Mom... State Am starts tomorrow?"

"Yep. Churchy Hills...afternoon tee time to start."

"You ready?"

"Nope. Didn't get in my usual prep, and what work I did do, stunk. Stunk bad. Sulphur Dioxide bad. No time for a practice round either, but I know that track pretty well. Pulling my irons. Just not cuttin' back. Have to figure it out as I go."

"You can lean on Lazarus 'til you get it worked out?" Mo was referring to Danny's sand wedge. An old, refinished, groove-sharpened, 56 degree Cleveland bent to 57.5 with the flange ground to have very little bounce. According to his dad's friend Crusty Sindorf, with Lazarus in his hands, Danny Mo could "get up and down from anywhere inside the nine circles of Hell."

"Well, I'd prefer to hit a few more greens, Mo. Seems the more greens I hit, the better I butter my toast. Makes your Ma happy. Or is it the other way around?" Mo Mo could hear his mother in the background practically sing the words, "That's right."

"Yeah?" said Mo, "I don't think I wanna know."

"S'posed to rain tonight, and that place is long enough. Ran into Marty the other day, said they built some new tees, moved 'em way back."

"Must be so if Marty said so. He'd know all about moving things." Mo Mo belonged to a growing fraternity of people who believed Marty Archibald was a rule-bender, a cheater, especially in big money games. Word was spreading fast, and as far as Mo was concerned, too fast not to be true. He actually had good reason to believe the old man would fudge the golfing process, be it a little bit of gamesmanship or bumping a ball in the rough. Anything to gain an advantage.

"Mo -- it's a little more complicated. And I believe you saw what you saw saw..."

"I did see, and I know what I saw," said Mo, his voice went up a quick half-octave and returned to normal. "Davy saw it too. That is, if you don't believe me. And what do you mean 'complicated?' What happened to 'play the course as you find it, play the ball as it lies and count 'em all?"

Silence from Danny.

"Not to belabor this dad, but…we were looking straight down on him. You think everyone else is making stuff up too?" Mo's shoulder pain made it easy to vent.

"I'm just saying it's not worth letting it consume you. As for Salamone, Larson and Rabin, if those guys saw it too… gotta be Gospel."

"Earth to Danny Mo, me, your son, I saw it. The dude was playing for big dough that day"

"I've known the guy a long time, Mo…" Molly interrupted again; in the background Mo Mo could hear something from her along the lines of "…for God's sake you two let that damn Marty thing go!"

Mo Moran had drawn a line in the sand on this issue. His dad was his hero, but if he saw what he saw, why couldn't his dad give him this one. Mo Moran believed he had earned the benefit of the doubt.

It was nearly five years ago. Mo and Davy White, 17th hole at The Old Barn. Mo Mo had bomb-bombed one into the woods to the right of the fairway. There, the wooded area dropped about 30 feet down and 60 yards total to the fairway of the 15th hole. While looking for Mo's ball, Davy quietly called Mo over to look below and ahead, just off the 15th fairway, a little ways into the woods that put the teeth in both holes. The two boys stood like 16-year-old Peeping Toms, watching the legendary Marty Archibald, relocate his golf ball with a couple furtive foot nudges. So subtle, so cliché, but perfectly clear. Two bumps, same foot. They were sure Marty didn't see them, but the two boys sure saw him and what he did.

And since that day, it seemed every time he ran into Marty, the guy would be so over-the-top friendly to "Little Mo" that it felt like some kind of cover. Marty had always been friendly and gracious before, but after the boys had their sneak peek on 15, bumping into Marty usually blossomed into so much back-slapping affection that Mo feared Marty might just start scratching behind his ears if he'd let him.

Once, when Mo Mo brought it all up to his dad — that Marty's friendliness may have raised a modicum of doubt as to whether the old man had actually caught a glimpse of the boys in the woods — his dad had stunned him with one sentence. "But, you were so certain that he didn't, Mo Mo," his dad had said, "you know — so positive about what you saw."

∞

At the other end of the line, his dad changed the subject. They covered the British Open, Mo's rehab regiment, the state of the Brewers and the Cubs, and finally his dad began one of his protracted wrap-ups, "Witchy and Orsman say hello, as do the guys at The Barn, and that includes Marty, if that's okay. They all miss you Mo Mo, everyone is wishing you a fast recovery."

"That's great, tell everyone hello for me too. I'll be following the Am on that Blue Golf Internet thing. That real-time scoring they do is awesome."

After a little more chitchat designed for nothing more than making the moment last, Danny signed off.

Mo said "You go right at 'em tomorrow."

Mo Mo heard his dad laugh in appreciation before hanging up. "You go right at 'em" was a Grandpa Curlyism. He tossed the phone, lefty, underhanded, onto the couch and tracked down the Dustbuster, but it wasn't charged enough to handle the Cheeto dust, so he turned off the lights and plopped back onto the couch, and paid the price for plopping in shoulder pain.

∞

Chapter 8

A hard rain came at 4 a.m.

Danny, fully awake now, figured it was a good bet that the first round of the State Amateur would be postponed a day at best, or delayed until late in the day at worst.

If faced with an afternoon tee time for a tournament ravaged by early morning downpours, Danny Moran preferred to have the round washed out completely. Way better than waiting around all day just to plow through Bentgrass goop for a few holes until an air-horn ended the day's play on account of darkness. The wet course wouldn't have had time to properly recover before the morning groups were sent back out to trample it even worse in the process of finishing their rounds. Only then would the afternoon pairings begin to squeeze in however many holes they could.

The setting sun would cast the rest of its light at the putting surfaces from an oblique angle that lengthened the shadows of the trees, shrubs and bunkers around them. The individual blades of grass on the greens took on a grainier texture, and worse, the side-winding sun had a way of making the freshly-stamped heel prints, ball marks, and other wetness dents more conspicuous. The resulting morass of contrasting shadows and light could mess with a player's perception more than an upside-down M.C. Escher print. So, with the conditions toying with the senses, and his ability to focus under siege, a good start was rare for Danny Mo. On top of that, the mosquitoes and their kind invariably descended at dusk to prey upon the weakened wills of moribund golfers already slipping toward the purgatorial wretchedness that festers between anger and apathy.

For a guy who otherwise preferred tough set-ups and difficult conditions, the uncertainty of the rain delay was the one thing that Danny let get to him. He'd take a make-up day of 36 holes later in the tournament over a mishmash of baffling shadows, hungry bugs, and purgatory on earth.

Now, sitting at his desk in front of his laptop and in his blue robe, Danny analyzed every scrap of meteorological data he could glean from the radio and The Weather Channel's website before running the timeline in his mind. He concluded the inevitable, shut down his laptop, and went to sink into the couch in his darkened living room. Looking out the window, he saw the dark silhouettes of fallen branches and leaves as well as lolling plastic garbage cans and tipped-over lawn furniture strewn about in his and other yards throughout the neighborhood. Throughout a restless night, he could tell just by sound, the different house-slamming angles that the summer storm delivered to his home. All of it pointing toward the worst case scenario; that of playing who knows how many holes until the bookmark of darkness was placed into an abbreviated round of mucked-up tournament golf.

The morning paper wouldn't arrive for another hour. Danny decided to go back and lie down in bed next to Molly. She immediately flipped away from him like a boated muskie's last lunge toward the lake, and then repositioned her slender form under the covers into the "I'm comfy, don't touch me" position.

Lying on his back with his eyes closed and a mind at anything but rest, Danny Mo pulled some of the comforter his way, just to show some say-so.

∞

Chapter 9

It was a self-fulfilling prophecy.

One as inevitable as the studio audience finding Leno's or Letterman's opening monologue hilarious every night whether it was or not.

The contagious momentum born of mutual expectation - it was a phenomenon Danny Mo had benefited from many times over the years in becoming a champion. It was as simple as this: He expected to win, and others expected him to win. Even some of the state's hardscrabble veterans were sometimes betrayed by smiles of false bravado and other stabs at masking concessions to the inevitable. Turning an opponent's trepidation into one's own momentum wasn't anything new, of course, just the way it's been ever since the serpent sandbagged Adam and Eve in the Garden of Eden. Harder to watch but just as welcome were those who collapsed quickly, like easily spooked kids who see people-eating monsters in random shadows. Ironically, it was the best of the younger players who feared absolutely no one these days. Not even Danny Mo.

In the consulting world, MOS's clients hung on its principal's stream of consciousness observations. Most were predisposed to embrace the substance between the laughs. It spoke to the power of reputation. Danny fed off the mojo and surprised even himself sometimes with the 'what do ya know' wisdom he dropped into his free-wheeling presentations and stand-up improv. His insights came mostly in generalities and teed-up hypotheticals, the sizzle before the substance. The data supporting his observations, organized by Orsman, was then handed over to management teams that could integrate the metrics into measurable process improvement strategies and in some cases, culture change. Despite his indulgence in creating a brandable persona, Danny's true gift was leading his clients to a larger perspective where they could incorporate their own industry-specific solutions as if they had been independently discovered. (A useful approach to parenting as well, Danny had often thought) Bottom line: everybody won, but none as much as Danny and MOS, Inc.

It was how he rolled. Be it busting previously unimagined moves on the dance floor at weddings, or cold stick toast-buttering, or hand jive sock-sorting or jitterbugging down basement steps at unthinkable speeds – all of them top-five worldwide and hypothetical as hell – he took pride in dealing with the mundane. Though silly to some, the bit-by-bit accumulation of little victories and his ability to stack even wafer-thin moments of self-belief undoubtedly played at least some role in Danny's larger successes. "Never underestimate the value of overestimating yourself," was just one of his self-affirming credos and, to him, a pearl of wisdom worth polishing up not only for certain business applications and golf competitions, but also for how such thinking had a way of lightening various household chores and injecting a little rock anthem magic into his downtime daydreams.

But self-fulfilling prophesies could become double-edged swords. Danny's disdain for late starts in rain-delayed events usually delivered the downside that he, too, deserved for being weak. After hanging around the men's grill room telling lies and refurbished truths for several hours, word came down that play would resume right about the time Danny had anticipated while pouting in the early morning darkness almost half a day ago. And though Danny was uncanny at projecting weather-related starts and restarts, he was generally clueless as to when the tournament committee would play God and proclaim that "proper daylight" had expired.

And so the first round of the Wisconsin State Amateur went exactly as Danny had feared. He went off at 6:15 pm and slogged his way further and further into the front nine at Churchy Hills. After an opening par, he made two bogeys on his second and third holes that were as sloppy as the turf. Two more pars followed on holes four and five; the latter benefiting from Danny putting a bad stroke on a misread putt that, had he done either thing right, never would have given his group the chance to see his ball to dive into the cup like it did.

Having a bad putt go in only raised Danny's self-contempt. He hated the not knowing, hated having someone else decide when his middle-aged eyesight would fail in the fading light. It reminded Danny of his high school hoops days and the difference between having to run a prescribed amount of sprints, no matter how many, versus running them until his big, fat, made-for-the-early-grave-he-earned coach decided to blow his damned whistle and end another arbitrary power trip. As if on cue with his thoughts, Danny unleashed a big fat nine iron, laying a bible-sized hunk of sod over a casual puddle just ahead of him on his way to doubling the sixth hole.

Finally, in the gloaming, he chopped at his ball in the rough until placing a three-putt cherry on top of an ugly day of work. It was then Danny Mo had the honor of putting down a triple bogey seven on his card for the seventh hole to finish seven over for seven holes just as the air horn sounded suspending play. Danny and the two others in his group could not have been further away from the clubhouse and still be on golf course property. Just freaking beautiful.

The clubhouse could be seen in the distance, only because it was now lit up like the state capitol, which also could be seen in the distance. To Danny, each building looked to be about half a day away on foot.

He did the card signing stuff in a daze at the scorer's table and headed immediately to his car. He had zero interest in checking the scoreboard or talking to anyone. His scorecard would talk his trash for him. The scoreboard area was always littered with players who had played well. Doped up on their good play, they sought to extend the buzz by lingering where other wandering souls might ask how things went. Danny bought into what Steve Stricker's father-in-law and fellow hall-of-famer, Dennis Tiziani, had to say on the subject: "Half the people don't care what you shot and the other half wish you'd shot worse."

His irritation intensified at the hotel until he could dilute it with the passing time. He ordered a pizza, took a shower, and called home.

Molly said "I'm sorry," as she always did when Danny reported a failing of any sort. Part of Danny felt that part of Molly felt a little humility was good for Danny Mo.

"Winning too much makes people delusional," she liked to say, "especially you."

Danny, of course, told her that he was top-five worldwide in handling bad days and tough defeats. Any irritability, he claimed, was just him making a point to not handle it too well. "Losing in stride? That would be the beginning of the end," he'd say. Molly's eyes glazed over whenever he tossed that one out.

"The end," however, was a subject Danny had been contemplating more of late. While neither a young gun nor a senior, he still loved to compete and enjoyed the camaraderie. But after the better part of three decades spent competing, the idea of cutting back was picking up momentum. Maybe redefine the fun of golf; focus more on those good walks, big laughs, and beautiful days amid the natural splendor of so many well-designed golf courses in Wisconsin, the stuff that too often gets taken for granted when one becomes obsessed with how recent ball flight trends might bode well or spell trouble for the next tournament. Every event brought another set of expectations, his and everyone else's, and setting aside the fact that this worked to his advantage, if the success was the fun, did the commitment to success eventually squeeze out the various rewards so ballyhooed by those who've been baptized into the holistic glory of golf? Maintaining his place on the pedestal - be it pride, vanity, whatever, Danny enjoyed the esteem in which he was held. Still, the commitment to prepare was never-ending, and that part was getting old. For Molly, his relentless practicing had evolved into something approaching guttural snoring. His penance paid through protracted stretches of his wife's ambiguous silence.

Nevertheless, Danny's primary objective, perhaps obsession, was all about winning a State Open. The allure of the one that got away, the one to cap his competitive golf career, the one he should have already won, and the one that was further evidence that golf was the ficklest of all sports. If he could just get one, maybe it'd be easier to kick back a little, chip away at the bucket list, his *and* Molly's, finally take that trip to Ireland that the Moran's had long promised themselves once the kids were gone.

Now, on the phone, Molly seemed sincerely sorry about Danny's rough start. Especially since Rinny had indeed been able to get off of work for the final two rounds. This was supposed to be their chance to hang together for a few days, just them, before she was to leave for Boston College the following month. It was very important to her - and everything to him.

But if he insisted on continuing to hack it up in this State Am, he wouldn't be around for the final two rounds. He'd be reading about it in the paper - if he even bothered. And so he would fight like hell, mostly to share a couple days with his daughter – but also because of the responsibility that went with being Danny Mo.

∞

Chapter 10

6:30 a.m.

Danny stepped up to the tee on the eighth hole to start the second day of the State Am at Churchy Hills and crushed a tee shot straight into the glare of the rising sun. He never found his ball - at least not within the allotted five minutes before it had to be declared a "lost ball." And so it was a long, wet walk back to play three from the tee with the stroke and distance penalty.

It didn't help that some happy-go-lucky guy in the threesome behind Danny's found a Titleist imprinted with what he pronounced as "*ow p*" – and a sprinkler-head scuffmark - a few feet into the rough on the opposite side of the doglegging fairway from where Danny and everyone else believed his first ball would be.

Stress has a way of revealing qualities in people that range from a kitten-like anxiety to a counter-puncher's composure. Danny took the morning shot to his mid-section on the 8th hole and calmly played the last 10 holes in one under par to complete his first round. He made nothing with his putter, but did two-putt for birdie on the 17th and posted a sumptuous 80.

He started to see a few positive signs in the second round, which began immediately after the first. Then again, a positive sign is also a plus sign, as in +4. He was still pulling too many shots that wouldn't cut back in the way that was his way, and almost every putt longer than a sub sandwich remained above ground. His sand wedge, the death-defying Lazarus, did however come alive. Had Lazarus not risen up, Danny would have been above the cutline and down the road.

Danny's 76 allowed him to make the cut right on the number - 156. Of the 180 players to begin the tournament, the cut pared the field to the low 70 and ties. Thus, after the cut, he was tied for last place. That was okay. Danny Moran was not going to win his fifth State Am this year anyway, but for the remainder of the tournament he could work on his game, and more importantly, simply enjoy every step with his daughter in the forecasted better weather ahead.

The State Open was a month away. The final two rounds of his State Am would commence an intensified preparation for that. Andy Salamone had gone 73-73 playing 18 each day; a full ten shots ahead of Danny. He knew this after hearing "Hey there, Dan Moran," in the parking lot. It was none other than the jowly John McEnroe look-alike guy, "Puffy Mac," who had caddied for Salamone. He looked a sweaty mess, baggy-eyed and rumpled, as if he had just emerged from a two day nap in the trunk of a car.

To shoot 146 in the heat and humidity with no carts allowed due to the wet conditions, big ol' Salamone would've needed someone to tote his bag. It looked like Sally's brother-in-law had barely survived doing so. Dude had to be thigh-chafed and beat from walking two rounds in the muck. Maybe a bit of diaper rash and some nipple sensitivity...

Ten shots in back of Salamone. Two rounds to go. Something to gun for.

∞

Corrine Louise Moran possessed a fresh and simple face that was usually free of makeup. Her features had a fortunate symmetry and an appearance that certain fashionistas might see as the exact opposite of exotic. From a distance, many thought she looked younger than her 18 years. Up close she looked even younger, yet her "PMS in reverse" as Danny called it - her good humored concoction of savvy, moxie and poise - ripened her in ways unrelated to appearance.

Danny once told his buddies at The Aftermath that if he could start his life over, he'd try to be more like his daughter. To which Carter Slane, Danny's Best-ball partner and long-time friend replied, "Sweet thought Danny Mo, but you're always gonna be dumber, uglier and odder than Rinny."

∞

The presence of his daughter got Danny focused fast. Much like her brother, Rinny could hit a golf ball with power and purpose; but having excelled in other sports, the talented Moran kids never developed into the golfers they might have been. Danny never believed that his kids were at all wary of comparisons to him; their decisions to pursue other, more athletic sports had more to do with the fact that they happened to dig other, more athletic sports. Danny was the same way as a kid.

Hard to question that - one was a top pitching prospect in the Cubs chain, albeit an injured one, and the other was on the brink of trading on her soccer skills for a free education at Boston College. Both subscribed to the "I've got my whole life to play golf" refrain. Mo had entered a few junior events, and despite some wildness off the tee, his "power to all fields" as his dad put it, he did pretty well for the time he didn't put into it. For his kids, golf was as much a social activity as it was sport. The fun was in the fertility of the chatter and the sensory pleasures in the smack of a ball; short-term challenges individually defined and thus became its own reward. A perspective Danny sometimes envied. He cared only that they were happy people and enjoyed whatever they pursued. Danny had long thought soccer was a game invented before the world discovered something called…imagination. Seemed like an endless game of tag to him. When Rinny took to it so passionately, he soon found soccer to be as riveting as any contest ever waged - at least as long the game involved Rinny and her team.

He felt it coming in the windy third round. His ball striking was still annoying the hell out of him, but his putting stroke somehow went through some born-again kind of thing and his outlook brightened. Showing off for Rinny didn't hurt. Danny shot an ugly looking feel-good 70, two under par, and moved up to 29th place. A couple collegiate standouts shared the lead at four under and Salamone hung tough with a 74, keeping him in 8th place, six strokes clear of Danny.

∞

Rinny, across the booth from her dad, shook her head; Danny saw traces of Molly's practiced pooh-poohing action. Rinny was observing her dad's attempts at applying half tabs of firm butter to his breadsticks. It seemed he was committed to breaking through the browned surface of the bread for some reason. Not an easy thing to do - slippery butter chunk into rounded breadstick - but there was no back-off in Danny Moran.

"You know Daddy, a little delicacy with your hand action…"

Danny was curious. The bread buttering thing again. "Okay, Rinny."

Rinny smiled, "I'm no expert, but…"

"Yes?"

"The veins in your forearms…they bulge…just watching you do battle with the breadsticks…looks exactly like when you held the club today."

Danny shook his head. "Interesting that you mention that, too."

"Crusty?" Rinny smiled and nodded as if proud to be in such company.

"It was your mother. We talked about a bread buttering thing a while ago. You know, just breaking down different approaches to reducing my toast crumb output versus trying to manage a higher volume disposal program. Thought maybe it was a grip tension thing."

"Funny," said Rinny. "Mom won't even let me make my own toast lately. I mean, if she's around. She used to insist I do everything for myself. I suppose now that… " Rinny's words trailed off as she looked away.

"Yes, your mother's working through the idea of your leaving. It's tough. The empty nest looms." Danny felt the emotion welling inside him. "Some things are easy to hold near, Rinny…" Danny stalled a bit, losing himself in his golf grip on the butter knife, so he could look down. Cover. "…and harder to let go of."

"You had to be doing something right, Daddy. Only two scores better today." Rinny, bailing out her choking dad by jumping back into golf.

"Yeah, amazing, bad as I hit it. Probably because my daughter was with me. Kept me grinding, kept me in the moment." Danny looked around the restaurant, at nothing. "These are the days I'll always remember, you know, you and Mo, it's just really cool having your kids caddie for ya…." Right back to the well.

"I love it too. Especially now, of course, being at the precipice of a whole new deal. New city, new friends, new everything…it's a little bit sad, little bit exciting." Rinny's eyes balanced watery sentiment with a readiness for come what may.

At that moment, what came were two servings of steamy, creamy, Chicken Alfredo Linguine.

∞

The wind had turned around completely for the final round of the Wisconsin State Amateur. Light southwesterly breezes became a steady, two-club Nor'easter. Scores would soar more than normal for the fourth round of the Am, when the hole-locations were at their most devious. Danny Moran let the wind fill his sails. This was his kind of day.

On the range he was able to determine the nervous types by sound alone; their breathing, the little laughs and the tone of their voices as they made small talk. The more dramatically inclined usually rehearsed their roles as victims as early as possible, perhaps so it would sound more natural later.

Rinny stood back a short distance from the line of fire, half turned away from the earthen buckshot the wind fired back. She cleaned each of her father's clubs as he worked through the bag. She never once looked to see where Danny's shots were going. Instead she watched his reaction, and the attention he was paying to his grip. Danny looked at her and winked; he was on to something.

∞

Chapter 11

He found the key to his ball striking also unlocked his touch on the putting green. Weird how that happens.

After rolling a final ball nearly the length of the green, he took some practice strokes. Stance opened, eyes shut, shoulders going up and down, his spirits rose even as an elasticized bit of spit slowly escaped his lower lip and landed on his shoe. Then, Danny Mo's mind went for a joyride.

This time, perhaps because he was feeling it, he thought about joy, and whether true joy could really be true joy without at least one accompanying sound or gesture. Some form of corroborating sensory evidence like a smile or a chortle or beer shooting out the nose. Even the overly stony look of someone attempting to smother such humanness could be telling. And willful restraint was something he had become quite familiar with over the past two-plus decades of marriage.

But reactions, especially joyful ones, fascinated Danny Moran. At the office, even the endless phone calls Evan Orsman made to his chubby wife or one of his chubby little kids – "commotion management," he claimed - would have him nodding, wide-eyed with the phone to his ear and an ambiguous smile on his lips.

At home, Molly did not nod. Ever. There were times, however, when those largely illegible, frequently laughable and highly illogical miseries of everyday life somehow got sorted and put away properly in her rather particular world, when even Molly Margaret Moran gave herself over to life's warmer waves, letting them wash over their marriage as if to remind Danny that it was all under her control all along.

Even with a stomach riddled with butterflies, he would roll with it (*Let the matches dry, Danny*), working to make her momentary joy seem routine instead of some kind of half-court swish, that maybe Molly's hyena-like jaw-hold on her day-to-day stress might be loosened by Danny's loyal dog example.(*That's right; don't try so hard*). And in those moments, when Molly could neither divert her life's blessings nor hide from the happiness that was hers for the taking, Danny was freed, in turn, to embrace the promise of peace in his world (Pax Morana) for however long the angels chose to sing.

But now, in the middle of the putting green in front of Churchy Hills' clubhouse, a pinwheel of giddiness within him was beginning to spin. Powered by an internal awareness of everything momentarily relevant and a blossoming optimism about his immediate future, he felt time slow to the pace God designed for savoring sunsets and outdoor music festivals. If his expression had changed throughout all this, he wasn't aware of it.

Just before making his way to the first tee for the final round of the Wisconsin State Amateur, Danny Mo stood up straight in the middle of the putting green and looked into the distance. The cool, freshly northern breeze was easily redirected by his face. Others, Danny knew, would let it inside their heads.

Rinny broke her dad's reverie when she walked back the three balls Danny had lagged to the far cup some 60 feet away. "Feeling good with the flat-stick too, aren't you Daddy Mo."

"I am, Rinny. Got the lighter grip going, landed on a nice jingle-jangle tap-tap putting rhythm." Danny wasn't keen on talking about it before the round but wanted to involve his daughter in every possible moment. "I just feel…"

"…like butter. I know. You got it going on. Let's go prove it." Rinny cocked her head towards the first tee and went for Danny's clubs.

Danny could only chuckle. "Alright then," he said to no one, and trailed his daughter to the first tee.

∞

Danny felt relaxed and excited at the same time as he waggled his driver above the ball on the first tee. A sense of mirth came over him now, but he stifled the budding smile out of respect for those less fortunate. He then exaggerated his new lighter grip key over the first two holes, blasting tee shots far and wide, the kind any golfer would be happy to simply find. But two pars were saved and a whole lot of faith restored through the selfless short-game dirty work of Lazarus.

After that, Danny locked into everything he believed would happen when he was warming up on both the practice tee and the putting green - all fades and tap-tap bang-it-in putting. He turned in 32, four under par. Experienced and instinctual, he knew the wind was simply a calculation divided by feel. Combine the given data, i.e., yardage and estimates of the wind's mph translated into club differentials, account for the variables of trajectory and spin, and finally, the measured application of angles and energy more easily explained as "feel," or in the case of shorter shots, "touch." In sum, it was called execution. For others in the field, the wind was a reason to snivel aloud, to feel persecuted rather than to do four and a half hours of messy work in tough conditions. Danny anticipated exactly that, and found a reason to fight; this round would be the start of his State Open quest, still a month away. August. The Hill Farm.

Danny and Rinny both fell into a rhythm. The objectives became all-consuming and they knew not to over-analyze a good thing happening naturally. The one concession to serendipity in the convergence of these father-daughter discoveries was the mutual decision to refer to most every shot as a "butter cut." Before, in flight, or after, "butter cut" became a mantra that said more than two words. It said, more or less that less is more. It said that everything would fall right for a ball falling right. It said that letting go brings more control. And, it was a move toward "no crumbs."

On the 10th and 11th holes, beautiful putts of 12 and 15 feet burned the high side of the cup. A fraction less confidence and they would have disappeared. A birdie on 12 brought him to five under, and a poised shot from an old divot in the fairway on the 13th kept him there.

Amped, he airmailed the 449 yard 14th with a downwind eight-iron. He exploded his ball from behind the green, the nastiest rough on the course, and made par from nine feet. Danny doubted Lazarus ever made contact with the ball during the explosion of chlorophyll on his recovery shot.

On 15, a 189-yard par three into a crosswind wind and over water, Danny cut in a little three-quarter, choke-down, slam-trap, punch-cut, hang-on four-iron - to three feet. Then he just shoved his d mo-marked ball right down the throat of the cup. Six under. The gallery for Danny's group had grown from a half-dozen to a couple dozen. And it was, without question, Danny's group. Neither of his partners, nice players both, would have to grind hard to break 80 in the prevailing conditions of the day.

Most of the field were getting bullied by the breeze and victimized by some traditionally torturous final round hole-locations. A couple flags looked as though they could be wayward foul poles on little ball fields. A guy whose name Danny could never keep straight, either Frank or Fred, from the Madison area and a director for the state golf association, told Danny as he walked to the 16th tee that the competitive course record was a seven under par 65. Danny thanked Frank or Fred.

Butter cut, butter fade, tap-tap bang it in - bird. Danny said to himself "Nowhere to hide baby," referring to the hole presumably. Seven under, with the reachable-in-two par five 17th ahead. Danny could feel that he had reached a level of excitement that was his cue to throttle back a bit. He found himself yawning, and while the yawn turned into a real one, it started out as an affectation to trigger his own calmness. Danny rhythm-rocked a tee shot down the left rough line and let the crosswind melt his butter into the 17th fairway. From there, 222 yards away, Danny played the same kind of shot with his 19 degree hybrid, what a friend of his referred to as a "Shaq-toe," but he overcooked it and his ball ended up in the right greenside bunker. With Lazarus and the wind throwing the eruption of sand back into his face, Danny Moran snapped his head around and down with the overblown reaction of golfers who know they left a bunker shot way short of the hole. (Tiger's eyes are especially susceptible.) But the hole took in the ensuing 15-footer like a vacuum-tube sucking in a ping-pong ball. Eight under par and one hole to go. The state golf association official, Frank or Fred, was following along now and marshalling the growing numbers who'd come out to see Danny stalk the course record.

The 18th hole was, at the moment, brutal. Though only 414 yards, it had out of bounds on the left and water right. The wind was mixing it up now, quasi-quartering one moment, and then coming straight at the players like repeating sneezes of varying force the next. Danny teed the ball low and corked a knuckler that knifed the symptoms of the Nor'easter and found the right side of the fairway. His second shot, however, caught a gust and came up five yards short of the green in the neatly mown but narrow throat between two bunkers. It was either lucky, or good and lucky, but ending up in either bunker would have made his sand shot on the previous hole seem elementary.

Danny circled the scene, sizing up his shot to the back left pin. He took his time to let the multiplying onlookers settle in. They fully encircled the green now, the cheers of "Danny Mo" at standard "you da man" volume were becoming louder and more frequent as beery enthusiasm flowed from some of the early finishers who were apparently looking to salvage something from a tough day at Churchy Hills Country Club.

It was not a difficult chip at all; plenty of green to work with and no real pressure - the championship wasn't on the line, nor was this some match-play firefight. Danny wasn't sure where he stood in the tournament other than the fact that he wasn't going to win. The places after first didn't matter much to him, playing well did. A course record, however, warmed the cockles of his heart more than any single malt ever could.

He'd been resigned to sharing the course record of 64 at The Old Barn with a certain Andy Salamone. Danny had fired his round in a U.S. Mid-Am qualifier. Salamone's 64 occurred in a club championship match where there was one witness, Salamone's opponent, Jack Schmackl, who at the time swore Salamone putted out on every hole. Later, Schmackl, (or "Captain Jack" as he preferred to be called) after a day of drinking and playing gin, had the misfortune of driving his car directly into a beloved local family standing near the entrance of The Old Barn Golf Course. They were farmers in straw hats, five of them plus their dog and a rooster and a goose; all made of some plaster- or cement-like substance. Little painted statues. All of them crushed by the

Captain. (There are those who claim Captain Jack blackmailed Salamone into paying his legal fees for the accident, which had resulted in Schmackl's third drunk driving conviction.) Somehow the Captain made it home, and when the cops came knocking he denied everything…but a busted piece of goose bill wedged in his grill did him in.

The Captain, when lit up on drink, sometimes became quite lucid about his match with Salamone and the 64 that tied Danny's course record set two weeks prior to Salamone's. People still talk about Captain Jack, sitting at The Old Barn's tiny bar, completely plowed after a miserable round where he had contracted the shanks and couldn't stop. Salamone had carried on too long, making joke after joke while the Captain just sat there taking it, seemingly out of it. Suddenly, he stood up, all wobbly, and through some violent hiccups declared that, "Not only did Andy Salamone not putt out on every hole when he posted 64…he never even played the 18th!" Obfuscation from Salamone somehow carried an ounce more weight than the Captain's slobbering declaration, and the course record continued to be "officially" shared.

Rinny had Lazarus in hand, ready to pass to her father. Danny took the wedge like it was made of blown glass and said, "No crumbs." But not like he had earlier, when his "no crumbs" had the feel of chops being licked. Danny furrowed his brow and filled his cheeks with air.

"Daddy? Uh…" Rinny stepped into Danny's personal space and looked at him. "Everything okay?" Rumblings around the green were mostly about how Danny Moran could get this up and down in his sleep.

Danny came to; Rinny's words were as if a hypnotist had just snapped her fingers. He took Lazarus, his 57.5 degree sand wedge and personal savior, and waggled it until peace came over him like a smoker taking in a Marlboro Red too long denied. The crowd hushed. Danny shook his head, almost in resignation. Fred or Frank stood well away from the flagstick but far enough onto the green to let people know he was running this show. The wind brought its energy directly into Danny, a factor that actually made the shot easier to get close.

Hands forward, no veins, buttery touch, no crumbs but very crisp. He nipped the ball cleanly and it rocketed forward with alarming speed. The ball hit, skipped and then screeched to a halt as if by magnetic force. It ended up 18 inches from the cup. Laughter, applause, delight. An eight under 64 in the final round of the Wisconsin State Amateur under tough conditions; the new course record at Churchy Hills now belonged to Danny Moran.

On under and until someone beats it...No One.

∞

No one could have known Danny's one reservation as he walked off the course to back-slaps and cheers. Sure, he felt wonderful about the course record, and was jacked that he had a final round that could catapult him into the second half of the year with some momentum. He was appropriately humble in his brief dealings with the media; talking up the joy of having Rinny on his bag and at his side ("No Rinny, no record - simple as that."), and the satisfaction he gets competing in golf ("Every round's a new chance for something never done.") but a tiny reservation remained.

Near the scoreboard, he pried Rinny away from some of the younger golfers she knew and/or those who wanted to know her. They left the property before the leaders had even finished.

∞

Chapter 12

"That, Papa Mo, was so, like, postmodern cool," said Rinny. "Showing the kids how it's done."

She repositioned herself in the car's front seat next to her father, certain she was too casual for Danny to notice her furtive appraisal of the young, strapping and clearly pissed-off Peter Allis as he stormed toward his car, his shouldered golf clubs clacking with every angry stride.

Father and daughter fell silent, awash in the post-round glow of partners taking stock. "What was going on with you before the chip on 18? You got a little funky."

"You think so, huh?"

"Yep…and a little after too."

"Hmmm…"

"In fact, you seem funky still."

"Maybe I'm just a funky guy."

"But it was perfect. Skid, skip, stop. Everybody went whoa…like it was a magic trick, or like when Mo Mo smashes one. Or used to, anyway."

"And I'm sure he will again. A healthy Mo can hit it with Bubba and the boys. And past Tiger. Why I'm always sayin' 'No one!' so often." Danny smiled. "Talk to your brother lately?"

"Last week," said Rinny. "Seems okay. Not great. I think the rehab routine has got him a little down."

"He's tough."

"He is." Rinny went to a deeper place. She looked out the window as Danny merged onto the interstate. She looked back at her father without saying anything.

"Yes?"

"Mo Mo. We were talking, like we do. He started going on again about Mr. Archibald. Almost like he has some sort of fixation…"

"I know, Rinny."

"He thinks…"

"That Marty's a cheater." Danny was nodding. "Right? And I give him a pass because he's a buddy…?"

"Yeah…same ol'. I know he doesn't really believe it, but he…acts like you're choosing Marty over him. Not exactly, but… Now he's heard some other stuff. Let's just say I don't think we've heard the last of it."

Danny smiled.

"Yeah," said Rinny, trying to help. "I guess some old buddies were downtown to see some band, and they got turned around, you know, like, lost, in a bad area downtown looking for the club. One of the guys supposedly recognized Marty - he had a young Black or Hispanic girl in his car. Supposedly looked, you know, young, the wild clothes, tons of makeup…you know…"

"Really," said Danny, "and what do *you* think it means?"

"I don't know," Rinny sighed. "Mo Mo thought it was like, vindication. Proof Marty isn't the guy he tries to pass himself off as."

"I see. So you don't think Marty's long dead wife would approve, not that…"

Rinny smiled, almost to herself. "Don't go bringing me into this, but Mo Mo said that you'd say something like that." Rinny shook her head like she couldn't believe they were talking about this. "I've probably said too much."

Danny chuckled in one syllable - something Rinny called a "chuck." "Thanks Rinny, but, again…who knows what anything means until you really know what it means. You can quote me."

"Very… 'it ain't over til it's over' of you, Yogi Mo," agreed Rinny.

"Maybe - except Yogi's line is a 'yes or no' thing. Now - the meaning of things? Those are essay questions." Danny paused as if considering leaving it at that. "But Mo Mo has been 'Little Mo' for a long time. He's become, as I've heard him say, 'his own damn Mo.'"

"So…" Rinny shrugged, regrouped, and smiled wide again. "…what was up wit da funkiness on that last chip shot?"

Danny did his one big nod thing. "I was torn, Rinny. I could play the safe shot - the one that would set the course record. And I did. I wanted a little place in history for however long. Square up the wedge, couple hops and, with the wind coming at me strong and it's, 'check please.' Knew I'd get it close."

"And that's bad, why?"

"Not bad, per se, it's just that…that shot doesn't have much chance of going in. It's actually sort of…showy. But for me, it's the easiest type of shot to get close, if that makes any sense. I wasn't protecting a lead, and I wasn't going to win - so why not bump and run an eight or nine iron and try to make it. Or even hood Lazarus. Hook and roll it - maybe right into the hole. 63 feels a shot and half better than 64. Maybe pass a few more players."

Rinny got it. "So you thought trying to make it brought bogey into play. Maybe you roll it past the cup, end up just sharing the course record."

"Yep, said Danny. "It's nothing I'm ashamed of, but I know inside…"

"Uh…I think you're being a little hard on yourself. I mean, I don't think many people would admit as much. In fact, 'no one,' I'd bet." Rinny was beaming. She karate-chopped the air and again said, "No one."

Danny felt his heart become big and light. He dug it when his kids went with his cheesy sayings. "I wanted the record more than I wanted to do what it took to shoot the lowest score I could today. Goes against everything I believe in." Danny caught the reflection of his eyes in the rearview mirror. "Think about it. I was protecting a consolation prize."

"It was the course record, Daddy. You said it yourself - you weren't going to win the tournament anyway. Everyone thought it was a great shot."

"It was a very good shot," said Danny, "but maybe not the right one. And I don't want to sound like some 'God I'm good' whiner, but I didn't go for it."

I-94 east of Madison and west of Milwaukee droned on with leafy green sameness, interrupted only by the colors of intermittent strip mall sprawl and some new clusters of living quarters developed for the maintenance-averse semi-wealthy. Rinny drifted off, seemingly in the act of looking at her father. Danny Moran's thoughts of his State Amateur slowly shifted to what awaited at home and at work.

As they approached the Marquette interchange, where I-94 elbows into I-43 North, Danny felt a vibration near his genitals. It startled him momentarily, as it always did. Danny had a history of missing key phone calls due to the fact that he never outgrew cranking up his favorite tunes on the open road. To counteract this, he developed the habit of keeping his cell phone on vibrate and between his legs when he drove. When his balls would tingle, he knew someone was giving him a jingle. Molly thought the practice about as sophisticated as burping the melody of the Ave Maria.

Danny checked the caller ID. Without his reading glasses, cheap cheaters form Walgreen's, he couldn't always be sure who was calling, but he pretty much always answered cell phone calls. This time he could make out the number.

"Hello Lady Mo," said Danny. Rinny stirred in the passenger seat but her eyes remained closed.

Molly voice was even. "Well, I must admit; I checked your score online. I'd say Himself must be feeling pretty good."

"I would consider knighthood from the Queen a lesser honor than faint praise from Molly Moran."

"I would hope so."

"Need some Reduced-fat Wheat Thins or anything?" The 'Wheat Thin' reference had become code for 'wine' going back to when Rinny and Mo Mo were very young."

"No thank you, I'm set. Is Rinny with you?"

"No, I left her with the Allis boy. They wanted to catch the last six days of the Heartland Hemp Festival. Guess some good jam bands are gonna be playing. A few days in Iowa, over to Indiana up to Mi..."

"Knock it off, Danny," Molly cut him off. "I have to talk to you about something." Rinny was awake now, gazing at nothing.

"What is it?" Danny half-laughed. "Some dark spots in the shower tile grout?"

"What..." Molly sighed loudly for effect. "Just because at least one of us is concerned with the basic upkeep of our home."

"What is it Molly? Just tell me."

"I'll tell you later, when Rinny isn't around," said Molly, withholding, in control.

"And yet where else would she be? And yet you still called; therefore I must conclude that the main reason for calling must have been to give me faint praise."

"If you say so."

"Thank you."

"I'll talk to you when you get here...say hello to Rinny."

"Sure will."

Rinny shook off her grog and raised an eyebrow. Danny pushed the off button on his cell phone and then stopped cold, eyes wide, and his body motionless. "What?" said Rinny.

"I just felt something powerful, like your mother and I hit the off buttons on our phones at the exact same moment. I'm sure we are somehow connected by the timing of our disconnection. And this is not the first time it's happened."

"You know Mom..." Rinny said, laughing. "And she knows you. So there..."

"Oh I know, Rin. We almost take for granted that we can't take each other for granted. Along with sex, God and money, tension is a key part of any relationship."

"Yeah, well, I..." Rinny hesitated. "...ah, I might as well...a couple of months ago I pressed Mom until she confirmed what a Rattler was. I was pretty sure, knew it was code. Like you do with the Wheat Thins thing." Rinny was blushing.

"Reduced-Fat...Wheat Thins" said Danny, who felt his world momentarily go to rewind and fast-forward at once. First with the thoughts of Mo Mo, and his son's own opinions and perspective and how he was becoming "his own damn Mo." Now Rinny, suddenly all matter of fact with her unabashed willingness to broach the subject of "Rattlers." That, Danny thought, was pushing it.

∞

It was nearly a quarter century ago. At a "dreaded couples baby shower" for Molly's older sister Virginia. She was expecting her third child, Madison - Maddy, as she's now known. Ginny went into labor an hour before the dreaded shower commenced, but since so many had come so far, the dreaded couples shower went on as scheduled. One Daniel James Moran stepped up and decided to help open gifts - after Molly volunteered him to help.

When one of the gifts turned out to be a collection of infant rattles with suction cups designed to stick like hell to the tray of a baby's highchair, Danny, well into his 4th Guinness, licked a suction cup and aggressively planted it on his perfectly rectangular forehead. It was a reasonably funny moment. But it turned hysterical later when the best efforts of nearly 20 women - whose collective domestic know-how easily equaled that of the Martha Stewart Corporation's entire R & D department - were unable to remove the baby rattle from Danny's dome.

That night they stayed at a Ramada Inn no more than a mile from the site of the shower. The rattle remained attached to Danny's forehead, of course, and the woman at the front desk looked at Danny for a full five seconds without saying a word. Danny returned her stare, and then they both smiled weakly and went about doing the paperwork for the room. When Danny signed his name, the effect was light Latin jazz.

Molly seemed to get more agitated with his every rumba-rhythm movement as her husband unpacked his overnight bag in the hotel room until she shut down completely; a fast-attack version of the silent treatment.

Like a television analyst, Danny did his best to break the incident down for his wife, step by step; how he did his best to "keep things loose in a situation where everything was changing so quickly," and how "people will reminisce about the time that Danny Moran, yeah, Danny freaking Mo, with a reckless lack of concern for his own safety, slammed a suction-cupped baby rattle on his forehead and couldn't get it off. How it wasn't much different than entertainment for the troops, something to take people's minds off a dreaded couples baby shower, a family story to be passed on by everyone who was there, and some people who weren't but who would one day claim they were ala The Ice Bowl in '67. And why? Because one man refused to let a party die when the whole idea was to celebrate a life. That's why. And by the grace of God, Molly, you get to sleep with this story's leading man and rub your sexy parts on him for as long as we both shall live." Danny finished with his inviting arms opened wide.

Molly caved. Danny's monologue, which included rattling at key moments, eventually got Molly to giggle, which then gave way to a laughing jag so intense just the thought of it, to this day, could make Danny's heart swell with gladness.

And so that evening, after midnight, with a baby rattle stuck to his forehead, Danny made love to his wife in such an ear-shattering rumba rhythmic manner that the session indeed went down in history as "The Rattler." The noises filling and spilling from their hotel room sounded like a train gaining speed, slowing down at times, and when circumstances led to the baby rattle working side to side, Danny felt he was reproducing the transitional grooves of certain live Santana songs. Extended jams, of course.

On some occasions, after a couple glasses of "Reduced-Fat Wheat Thins," Molly would sometimes bring up how the conditions might be right for a Rattler. And Molly requesting a Rattler was the type of thing that got Danny through the detours, fender benders and road ruts of home life, those times when Molly's sighs were audible to half a zip code and little fits were pitched over laundry violations or color coded kitchen sponge crimes. The baby rattle eventually came free during a most peaceful sleep that night, a sign that again pointed to the folly in trying too hard, nearly two decades before Danny began working to make the concept a creed.

"How on earth did you hear about…that, uh, you know…?"

"Rattlers, sure." Rinny was prepared. "I've overheard you guys for years, when you thought I was clueless and young. But I was only young, not clueless. I had badgered Mom long enough, just wanted confirmation. I already knew what it was code for, I just wondered why you called it what you called it." Rinny made a point of showing how wonderful she thought the whole story was, maybe because it helped balance out the exasperation her mother showed a little too often - and her father's smoldering frustration in all that. "It's a story that makes me think even more of both of you."

"Well, Rinny. What can I say? That rattle… thing was kelly green, had a little seal-bark squeeze-horn thingy along with the rattling stuff…let me tell you, we're talking studio quality." Danny, deflecting via minutia. "They don't make 'em like that anymore. Unsafe for children. I have to agree…had a purple hickey on my forehead for ten days."

Danny pulled into his driveway. Having Rinny with him had kept the butterflies at bay. Still, as he recalled Virginia and baby Maddy, he became aware that his fingers were cold.

∞

Chapter 13

Danny Mo did not have a dog (Molly claimed to be "allergic to them all"), but he did have recurring dreams about a beloved yellow lab named Hank who went missing on a regular basis.

In these dreams, Danny would usually, eventually, find Hank being Hank in strange places; racing through the aisles of a bead show in New Mexico, or sniffing around a beach along Galway Bay, or hamming it up in the back of a dilapidated pick-up truck for a bunch of dirty-faced kids at an unfamiliar Dairy Queen. Since these were merely dreams, Hank alternated between being a rambunctious pup and stately ol' Hank. Yet, always, there was the despair of losing him and the death-defying efforts to find him, over and over. On those occasions when he couldn't locate Hank, Danny would turn increasingly stupid. He'd feel his tongue swell and his legs grow heavy as they took him to a cliff he wouldn't mind going over. Sometimes he woke up teary-eyed whether he had found Hank or not.

Now, Danny bounced out of his car and entered The Aftermath Bar and Grill feeling like a man who had just discovered that Hank the Wandering Dream Dog was alive and well and waiting at the bar to toast him with something in a frosted mug. His fondness for a mythical dog and cold beer notwithstanding, it was actually Danny's fan-boy fervor for The Aftermath's Steamin' E Burger that had him giddy about his immediate future.

Danny claimed The Steamin' E was "the only burger in the world with intuition," claimed the burger had an almost evangelical sense for dispensing whatever level of redemption or inspiration that the faithful required from their Steamin' E. And the final bite, as Danny liked to say, was like "Hay Wrap" by The Saw Doctors, his favorite band's traditional final encore, delivering one last satisfying burst that leaves everyone wanting more. The owner of The Aftermath, a guy named "Kai" with no known last name, maintained that the keys to his Steamin' E were preparation and execution, "exactly like the keys to great golf, only different."

"Preparation of the fresh ground beef is what we call a pre-hot routine, and the grilling execution is simply patience under fire. Basic fundamentals. Still, debate centered on the sirloin-to-chuck ratio in Kai's recipe, and rumors related to the judicious use of rendered duck fat simply would not go away.

The Aftermath was less than a mile down the road from The Old Barn Golf Course and had become its de facto 19th hole. After Captain Jack Schmackl wiped out the little plaster farm family and their pets, county executives reduced The Old Barn's food service to canned beverages and small bags of peanuts, pretzel twists, and standard chips with slider-sized Sloppy Joes available for a buck each on weekends. Though The Barn's pro shop remained moderately stocked with golf equipment and accessories, the clubhouse became pretty much a blandly carpeted room of windows and underutilized tables but for one Monday night a month when a local chapter of the American Association of Amateur Arborists met there.

Kai had since purchased what was once a beat up old biker bar called The Get Suckered Inn, and remodeled it with a lot of good wood and turned it into The Aftermath, a bona fide destination known for dense sandwiches, stinging drinks and a versatile ambiance. The inside boasted a whole lot of good wood and electricity - flat screen televisions, a state of the art sound system, and the amber washes of indirect lighting that highlighted the good wood. While possibly a contradiction in terms, The Aftermath could be rightly called a high-tech roadhouse.

"Yo, Danny! Help us settle something." It was a thick and familiar voice from a circular table surrounded by five regulars from The Old Barn.

Thad Booher was waving. Ubiquitous, decent, and friendly, "Boo" was a permanent middle-handicap golfer, a willing marshal or spotter at local tournaments, and one of those golf guys who openly admired good golfers, especially Danny Mo. And yet Danny struggled to like him as much as the guy probably deserved to be liked. Boo was loud. And the truth was, Danny had a hard time getting past Thad's tongue - the thing was a beast; it looked and sounded much too big for his mouth. When he talked, Danny feared the slithery mass just might spring from the darkness like an anaconda from a river cave. His laugh was worse, when he gave an irresponsible amount of freedom to the thing. And Thad, wanting to be Danny's buddy, laughed at most of whatever Danny said. It was just the way it was.

"Hey there, Boo," said Danny, nodding to everyone as he attempted to slalom by the table of Boo and the boys. They were all good sorts and avid "Barnstormers," as many of the Old Barn regulars called themselves. He stopped at their table and everyone smiled and nodded.

Boo beamed for having been personally "Boo-ed" by Danny Mo. "We're coming up with golf-related oxymorons, Danny. Started when I popped up my drive on 18 today and K-Dawg claimed I 'flat-skied' it, so we were arguing about whether that was an oxymoron, then 'metal-wood' came up, of course. So far we've come up with 'pure shank' and 'nice lip-out' and 'toe-skull.' You have any, Danny?"

Danny had to admit, Boo and the boys were taking their 19th hole banter to a new level by tackling something as esoteric as the golf-related oxymoron. He looked into the middle distance trying to shake the image of the acrobatic eely thing in Boo's mouth after having watched him enunciate "golf-related oxymorons."

Danny gave a pained expression, his mind sailing through a wordy wonderland of his own creation. "Well, how about 'clutch-flop?'" Danny was pleased with himself. Boo and the boys laughed freely. Their reaction was inspiring. "Then there's 'easy-putt,' at least that's what I think of every time Johnny Miller, who quit the game because of the yips, says 'easy-putt, right Rog?'" The group nodded, knowing, welcoming the custom-made stuff coming from Danny Mo. Danny ran with it. "And...don't quote me, but it's my understanding that Golf House in Far Hills has gotten together with The R & A in Scotland to, among other things, rule on whether 'too much jizz' can be officially classified as a golf oxymoron... or a medical condition."

The Barnstormers erupted. Boo's glistening organ worked back and forth as if the air were ice cream. Danny smiled, waved a brief *adios*, and moved on to the bar. His work was done.

Kai smiled from behind the bar as he toweled off his hands. He looked at Danny approaching and said, "E, cheddar?"

"E me…cheddar, but Kai, uh…last time my cheddar was translucent in spots and Crusty's Colby was a melted heap of opaque glory. He'll be here shortly, he'll want the usual."

"Cheese densities differ, Danny…I assure you the net weight was very close."

Danny had argued for more cheese since anyone could remember. Kai, however, refused to turn his creation into "a mere vehicle for cheese."

Danny settled onto a wooden high-back bar stool, pleased with the spacing at the bar and the promise of his immediate future. No Hank, but damn, the E was imminent.

Crusty Sindorf entered The Aftermath with an animated and talkative Andy Salamone alongside him. Crusty looked around, no expression, spotted Danny and headed towards him. But not before Salamone mostly whiffed on a back slap. Danny could hear Andy say, "Right, Crusty…don't ya think? I sure as hell do." Crusty rolled his eyes as he walked away.

Salamone waited near the door for three of his minions, including the guy with the eye patch who Molly and Danny had seen bobbing for whiskey at The Farmstead. Danny figured they must be the ones allowed to walk two steps behind their Big Andy, as Salamone preferred to be called, though he insisted it rhyme with Gandhi.

Crusty made his way through the tables tossing out friendly hellos to some folks, and cool ones to some others who got cool ones for reasons known only to Parnell "Crusty" Sindorf. He didn't care what anyone thought of him and played no games. He had spent the first two decades of his adult life in the military, then a brief stint caddying on the PGA tour, and currently had a one-man business fixing and flushing the water hydrants that even the best city and municipality workers across the country struggled to repair. Communities either had some guy like him, or paid Crusty's price, because they would spend a whole lot more replacing the hydrants and the water mains linked to them if they didn't. Crusty never negotiated and was fine with any decision. With his military pension, he made a nice living with eight to ten trouble-shooting jobs a year, mostly in winter, mostly in the south.

"Dannymo," said Crusty, one word, always, "ya get me on the board?" To Crusty, life was about getting on the board. Whether he, or anyone else for that matter, finally made a birdie, won a poker hand, got laid, completed the day's first bowel movement, or made what he deemed a worthy contribution to a group discussion, or, like now, got an order in for a Steamin' E Burger - it was always 'getting on the board.'

"You're on the board. Colby, probably get a little less cheese than me."

"Of course."

"Good playing today. Even par weren't you, Crust?"

"One over. Best I can hope for." Crusty shook his head as if to acknowledge Father Time. In his mid-50s now, he wasn't going to find any more length, having already tapped out all that technology had to offer. He clasped the gnarled fingers of his weathered hands together with an elegance that belied their appearance and placed them on the bar. "But who gives a shit."

"You and Salamone come together on something?" Danny looked straight ahead.

"He was going on about your Am round, what he calls your 'sixty fucking four.' Says you and a few of the mini-tour pros gotta be the guys to beat at The Hill Farm. Usual bullshit."

"Bein' the big man. Still frosts me that he chipped in on 18 for 70. Heard he ran around half the green like a fat, foofy Hale Irwin at Medina."

"Coupla old goats you two…only guys to break par in all that wind. Had to crap his pants when he found out you caught him." Crusty's expression confirmed he knew Danny didn't exactly live to tie Andy

Salamone. "You know, a tie coming up the dirt road is better than some other ties, Dannymo. Last after 36 and 6th at the end - not bad."

Danny felt the funk from not trying to make his chip on 18 all over again. "I guess. But you'd have to say, technically, he caught me after I passed him."

Sindorf turned toward Danny and looked at him. "Salamone wants you to feel the pressure going into the Open. Says he heard you were pulling the plug."

"What?" Danny's eyes went wide. "Crust? How the…? I told you, Carter, and my family. That's it."

"He can't be guessing, Dannymo."

"Carter's a vault, it ain't him." Danny taxed his memory, searching. "Not that it matters a whole lot…but, how the hell?"

"Who gives a shit is right," said Crusty, "But maybe I do…" Crusty looked at his lap, straightened an imaginary kink in a perfect crease on his pant leg, and then, eyes narrowing, looked back at Danny. "Just so ya know, Dannymo, I'd be happy to caddy for you at The Hill Farm."

Danny had already turned toward the TV screen showing something on ESPN Classic from the days when NBA players wore short and shiny freedom-fighter shorts.

"Seriously, Crust?" Danny glanced back at Crusty.

"Absolutely."

"Be beautiful, man. I mean…poetic even. I can play that course a bit."

"Any course, but you can take 'em all at The Hill."

"Alright then," said Danny, just a trace of a smile, "we ride…" He turned back to the bar, partly for dramatic effect, mostly looking for his Steamin' E Burger, "…once again."

"I know Rinny's your go-to looper these days… read what you said about your princess warrior in the paper, but she'll be out east by then, right? Mo Mo's surrounded by corn and grinding out his rehab. You and me, we got it done before."

"And dig this, Molly's gonna be out of town that week too," said Danny, his voice rising. "The house to myself, The Hill Farm, Crusty on my bag...damn if Jesus don't love me some."

"And...an E on the board," said Crusty. "What a life. Where's Molly going?"

"Gonna spend some time with her sister and niece. The niece, Maddy, guess she's having a tough pregnancy. Bed rest, doctor's orders. Molly's gonna hang around and help out for a week or two until Maddy delivers."

Salamone came up behind Danny, having circled back from the men's room, no doubt to take him by surprise. "Well Dan Moran, sixty fucking four is pretty fucking fantastic, I must say. Maybe you can carry it over to The Hillbilly Farm for your swan song...maybe get yourself that Open, huh."

No doubt, Salamone relished illuminating the fact that he had an Open title and Danny did not. Danny looked at Salamone without saying a word.

Crusty turned away, only too happy to receive The Steamin' E Burgers from Kai. It was one way to keep from getting into it himself with Andy Salamone. Ex-military man Crusty and his 5'"9" and 160 pounds of sinew feared Salamone not at all.

"So, Sally..." Danny paused. "Who gave you the idea I was pulling the plug?"

Salamone laughed, a quick snort really, not a bona fide chuck, but clearly enamored with having knowledge others didn't have.

"Why it was your buddy, Moran, the Hall of Fame cheater on the loose." Salamone waited a beat, then cocked his head and raised his eyebrows in mock shock. "Marty Archibald."

∞

Chapter 14

Danny was sitting up in bed in darkness, legs compressing the feathery comforter under him like heavy pliers on a pile of frosting, his mind momentarily summoned by the past. It was 3:15 a.m. according to the clock radio; sometimes Danny would note that that was the time of the demon visits in Amityville. Now, Danny was thinking about coasters.

Some years ago, Molly had purchased a set of decorative perimeter-etched glass coasters that protected the wood finish of their respective nightstands. They were, as coasters go, fine looking coasters, some would even say elegant. That Molly had spotted them on a clearance table at a chic mall boutique damn near turned them into trophies.

But as elegant as those coasters looked to the discerning eye, they weren't all that functional. The small glass knobs that kept the square coasters slightly elevated from the nightstand's surface had a way of amplifying the sound when a glass of water was placed upon it. When the ever-restless Danny Mo would do so, that very sound would often startle his light sleeping wife. She'd instantly sit up, convinced she'd heard something like a butcher knife clanging on the tile floor in their bathroom or some such. Even worse was when the condensation from the drinking glass on the coaster created a tentative bond, with the coaster hitching a ride with the lifted glass before falling, or back-flipping, onto the hard maple with the night-shattering clatter of a forced-entry raid. More than once Molly had jumped from the bed, gasping, ready to call 911.

Not good. When Danny went retro with his solution to the problem, Molly, of course, balked. Eventually Danny approached Molly and laid it all out on the table. Simply stated, he wasn't at all pleased with Molly's ruling, handed down early in their marriage, that outlawed him from keeping the latest golf magazine on his nightstand. "It looks so tacky," she would say. "All you need to do is put it in the wicker magazine basket next to the couch in the morning…that's all."

It was then that Danny Mo made his stand. "No. It's a ritual. I read my golf magazines in bed, before going to sleep. No need to move it back and forth just so if I forget you can whistle me for a periodical foul." Danny had said this like the folly of it would have to be obvious. "So, Molly, Hon, unless we are having people over, the magazine will stay put. Plus…they're quiet."

Molly had stayed calm. "Danny, I know you started setting your water glass on the golf magazine so the coaster noise wouldn't wake me up. That's sweet, it really is. But by the time you're through reading a magazine, however many nights it takes, there are so many water rings on the cover…it literally makes me shake. It looks so tacky." Molly started to cave in. "When it's new and neat, and there aren't so many rings…I don't mind so much."

Danny thought about it. Half in, half out, he lingered in that metaphorical doorway of bedroom compromises among spouses. Then he rushed in, boldly opening himself up by suggesting he would simply turn the magazine over when he placed it on the nightstand for the evening, and then flip it right side up in the morning. He summarized quickly: one, the cover stays neat and clean, two, it was his bedroom too, and three, it was win/win.

∞

Now it was 3:16, which was always a bit calming after 3:15… at least he knew he wouldn't perish – John 3:16 was pretty clear on that. He drifted back to that key marital moment in their great magazine-as-nightstand-prophylactic debate. He recalled how Molly had taken a deep, slow, breath, how her shoulders rose then dropped, how she looked off into infinity, taking in some world he could not know, pensive, fighting off doubt, and how she then turned and stared hard into his eyes. "God help us," she had said, "but let's give it a try."

It didn't lead to an immediate Rattler, but after proving himself over time to his wife that the same laser-like focus that made him a hall-of-famer would prevail with the flipping of the magazine, regardless of the alternating influences of fatigue, alcohol, or Molly's migratory moods, and that it wasn't the kind of gateway shortcut that might sully the pursuit of proper order and explode into unmitigated household anarchy, the Rattler did finally come. Danny consistently flipped that dadgum magazine every night without fail and he damn-well earned that rattler. *They* had earned it. Sweet and salty, it was a creative, athletic and celebratory Rattler by which all Rattlers would one day be compared.

∞

And so as Danny lay awake he wrapped up the memory with a sip of water, and by rote, replaced his water glass silently on the backside of his golf magazine. He looked over at Molly. She was on her side and buried in comfort, at peace, her quest for order momentarily set aside for slumber, her mouth a long latitudinal line with a slight curl, like a friendly porpoise or dolphin… whatever the hell Flipper was.

Then he attempted to let his mind run from the historic magazine resolution of over a decade ago and began to imagine what was to come, for him and for his family. It would be just another night of getting poked by thoughts that came in flurries and melted away when they felt like it. As usual, Danny's thoughts on the future rarely "went quietly into that good night." No matter the silence.

∞

Chapter 15

Danny switched the phone to his fresher ear. He was in his office at MOS and had heard it all before. Marty Archibald's directions were painstakingly specific and filled with warnings of imminent danger. Always the case when it came to dealing with "his girls."

"Alright…keep your window open a few inches so she can hear you start to play the Jay Z guy on your stereo. No Jay Z, no go. Her name is Cindy Young…been around off and on for a while now. A cut above, bright, really good and really pretty - still young, but not as young as she looks.

"Got it," said Danny.

"Remember - tell her you are Jonah's friend."

"I know the game, Marty."

"Good, now…understand, Cindy's got one hardcore bad ass stalking her, got a thing for her, keeps resurfacing…asshole's got nothing to lose, Danny. And he's a shooter…" Marty Archibald's voice went softer. "She says she can lose him if he shows up tonight - but be careful Danny. Remember…no music until and unless you think it's safe, and she'll be digging in her purse if she thinks he's watching."

"Got it."

"I'm telling you Danny, safe passage is our thing and this guy's a nasty son of a bitch."

"Whatever happened to the friendly neighborhood pimp, you know, havin' a drink with the alderman?"

"Only in the movies, my friend," said Marty, before switching gears. "So…get back yesterday did ya? Everybody okay?"

"Got back late…and I'll tell you, I thought I had prepared myself, but it was gut wrenching leaving a daughter to her big new world.

Molly was sobbing, but, man, I was absolutely dying inside. Rinny, gone. College, so far away. But you know her, she was nothing but excited, taking over her dorm room like a jungle cat. Good thing she didn't have to meet her roommate with Molly still around." Danny chucked, and then manufactured some extra chuckles, for cover, masking an ongoing recovery from a heart tipped over. Seeing Mo Mo off to pro ball was one thing; a daughter leaving was quite another.

Danny's tone changed. "On the other hand, I was not unhappy to leave Molly with her sister in Chicago. What a nightmare - Molly and me traveling together. We used one of Carter's company vans and Rinny's crap filled every cubic foot — and what do ya know, in an upset, Molly gave me consistently bad grades in Driver's Ed. Every lane change…too fast, too slow, whatever, she fired off the bad grades."

"Yeah, well hell, ya made it didn't ya…what else is there?" Marty knew the Morans well enough to know the devil was in the details. "Traveling well is pretty much about being on time and living to tell about it."

"Exactly. I just smile and tell Molly I'd never let anything happen to her." Danny closed his eyes and regretted saying it the moment he did. He quickly added, "Didn't get any tickets either," trying to move on.

"No tickets. Good for you, Danny," said Marty, a touch patronizing, like patting a kid on the top of his head for having a cavity-free check-up. "Well, anyway, I got nothin' but time and I'm two days behind. I'll catch up with you later at The Barn. I take it you'll be getting ready for the Open. I'll bring that Jay Z guy's CD then too."

"Sure Mart, good… something else I'd like to ask you about then, too, so yeah, come to the old green later. All short game work tonight."

"Okay then, Motown it is," said Marty. "See you there."

Danny quietly placed the receiver in its cradle, but the silence didn't erase anything. He sat back in his chair…couldn't help but think of Joy, Marty's one in a million wife, how she died, Marty reaching to her in the passenger seat so she could die in his arms, and how Marty, however wrongly, blamed himself.

∞

The Old Barn had two practice greens, the old one and the new one. The new one, big and undulating, was now nine years old and located directly in front of the clubhouse and just to the left of the first tee, but it was still called the "new green" to most of the old timers. To everyone else, it was, simply, "the putting green." The other practice green was the "old green," and it was just barely on the far side of the new maintenance shed, the old shed having been removed to make room for the new tee for the fourth hole, which used to be the old first hole when the course had only nine holes. It was maybe 150 yards from the clubhouse and butted up just short of the old barn, the one for which the course was named. The old green, then, could not be seen from the clubhouse and pro shop because of the new shed, and golfers headed to or on the fourth tee could only be heard and not seen from the old green because of the old barn.

Because of the new shed's size and a recent addition to the barn, the old green didn't get the sun and air circulation it used to. The surface was usually a blend of light green and olive brown, often showing a random constellation of khaki-colored turf circles of various sizes. The green was perpetually sparse and looked horrible, but it was firm, smoother than it looked and about two feet faster than the new green, which was about a foot slower than the greens on the course. Danny found it to be a perfect place to prepare for major state and USGA events, where hard and fast greens were the norm. He loved the old green, a secret courtyard hidden at the feet of an old yellow barn and a new aluminum shed, a place he called Motown. Motown almost always guaranteed Danny some privacy for his short game practice since very few wanted to walk 150 yards for something so ugly; especially when the huge, smooth (but slower) new green was so convenient.

The grounds crew and cart-barn kids hated the old green, but hey, they came and went over the years, and Danny could not care less if they were forced to use only one of the two big doors to go in or out of the Old Barn, at least when someone was using the green. A couple of longtime members of the grounds crew respected Danny and his habit of passing out tickets to Summerfest and Brewers games, but to everyone else, he was the embodiment of self-centeredness, the guy who never took a day off from practice and it was his Motown bullshit that made their jobs a little tougher. Danny knew it wasn't very practical but his view was 'Hey, serious golfers can be selfish bastards and just be glad that I'm the best of the worst of 'em.' Nevertheless it was a generally negative attitude that the crew had toward Danny, and it started at the top, with the superintendent.

Red Haskins, The Old Barn's "Super" for the last 10 years very much wanted to let the old green die and go to hell, or heaven, he didn't care which, he just wanted it dead. But Danny was big on defending his turf. A half-dozen years ago Danny showed up just before sunset to hit a few putts, only to catch some cries coming from inside the old barn. Seems Big Red and a big, ol' beverage cart girl named Phyllis were into something that was clearly consensual. Big ol' Phyllis was loud, and moaned with a modicum of creativity when she expressed her hunger for "Red meat," and that she wanted it "well done"; but a sudden cheerless chuckle suggested that everything came grossly under-cooked. So when Red Haskins proposed removing the old green at a greens committee meeting, Danny walked up to Red at the head of the table and whispered, "Red meat, not very well done," the greens keeper turned even redder and immediately tabled the proposal until the next meeting. A meeting at which Red suddenly had an idea for keeping the old green viable.

Occasionally some wandering chop or nostalgic old timer would saunter into Motown to use Danny's little piece of land, and if Danny was present, he'd go into cocoon mode, hoping it would discourage a long stay.

From the near end of the old green, one could see the last sliver of the old parking lot which was still used for overflow parking for some of the bigger outings held at The Old Barn. Danny noticed Marty's "merlot, not maroon," Crown Victoria ease to the very end of the lot.

Danny could almost hear Marty's customary groan as he performed the pain-defying act of getting out of his car. As if his mission was to create widespread awe about how this great man somehow continued to carry on, every single day, for people of all colors, of every age, from all walks, especially women. It was his calling, he felt, to be something others could believe in.

Marty would describe in detail his injuries, operations and replacement parts as if he were the only one to ever have or require them. Then he'd rip a tee shot right down the pipe using his God-given eye-hand coordination and a couple forearms that were about as big around as Danny's carry bag. It amazed Danny almost as much as it amused him how very few truly knew Marty Archibald.

These days Marty was still the grandfatherly legend of Wisconsin golf, though more and more people had heard the stories of his trash talking and gamesmanship and, reportedly, out-and-out cheating when competing in certain circles. And in golf, stories about cheating got passed around faster than tales of neighborhood bestiality. Marty had taken to hanging with a few of the area's bigger golf gamblers, high times guys who enjoyed playing thousand dollar Nassaus, a hundred if that was all the action they could get – or if they were playing against, and therefore usually donating to, Marty Archibald.

Andy Salamone mixed with this crowd and probably wailed the loudest about Marty's ways. There was a time when it was worth the head games, playing for smaller stakes, just to be seen with the legend and have some stories to tell about him. Nevertheless, Salamone probably played Marty for cash more than anyone else. Over the years their battles had grown increasingly contentious.

The whispers had grown louder and more frequent until Marty had to take a break, maybe for good, to have by-pass surgery last year. Danny generally believed that where there was smoke, there was probably fire. And Danny had no doubt that Mo Mo saw what he claimed to see. As with most folks who have secrets to keep and are hard to understand, Danny usually went with Marty simply being "a piece of work." And that, Danny believed, said it all. Or at least enough, because Danny also knew there were some secrets he would just have to keep.

"There he is…" said Marty as he approached the stifling air of Motown. Marty said it early enough so that Danny, who was acting oblivious, would have the chance notice his gimp-a-long gait before shutting it down. "…soon to be maybe, hopefully, the oldest State Open champion since, well, I guess that would be…me. Would it not be, Danny?"

"Oh…hey there Marty, what're you doing sneakin' up on me like that?" Danny smiled, he gave him the good one, still feeling bad about what he'd said on the phone earlier, but not enough to indulge Marty's wounded warrior act. He went back to his putting.

"How you playing, still good?" Marty nodded like he already knew the answer.

"Feeling okay, Marty." Danny did not want to talk about how good he felt about his game. He changed the subject. "You bring me some Jay Z, yo?"

"I've got the young fella's music recording with me." Marty clumsily pulled the CD from, of all places, his back pocket and handed it to Danny. "Guess he's pretty popular…this Jay Z."

"Cindy likes him, I take it."

"Don't know, just so she can hear the man's singing voice I guess, Cindy says she would 'know the Jay Z anywhere.'"

"Marty, I gotta talk to you about something." Danny looked at the yellowness of the old barn as if something in its wood was captivating. "Old Yeller," some called it. "First off, Marty, I'm sorry for my…"

"Dammit, Danny…" Marty had grabbed Danny's sand wedge and was waggling it, checking how it set up. "…I do miss the action."

Danny saw the sparkle in Marty's eyes and decided to put off the apology about his passenger safety comment. It would only dredge up some unpleasantness and Marty wouldn't care unless there was an audience for him to impress anyway. "So, Marty, how the hell did you know - and why did you tell Salamone, that I had pretty much decided to…possibly, retire from competitive golf after the open?"

Marty's eyes turned serious, but a smile remained. "I didn't, Danny. I don't talk much to him since the quadruple-bypass with complications - other than 'hello' and 'how ya playin'?" Marty then squinted, thinking. "But now that you mention it, the subject did come up. Where were we? Sally's got some buddies, actually think one of them is a cousin or something...and some other guy, a guy with an eye patch. Bump into them once in a while, wasn't too long ago at George Webb's it was, they started asking me stuff about you maybe wanting to step back from the game, you know, to watch Mo Mo and Rinny is what they said. No surprise there, so I just say, 'well...that sounds like Danny.'"

"Ah," said Danny, "I get it now. Sally's brother-in-law and the plastered pirate."

"That's right...the skinny guy with the eye patch, kind of sickly lookin', said he saw you somewhere."

"Yeah, Molly and me. Farmstead. They were highly intoxicated, but not too gone to eavesdrop I guess."

"Danny, I don't know nothin' for sure anymore, but I know you and me, and we keep our secrets don't we?" Marty delivered his 'sad man' look. He brushed back a unicorn horn of silver hair. "You can always talk to me, you know."

"I know Marty, I just didn't want it getting out...and now it is. Sally and his posse squeal like schoolgirls. Not sure I need the game like I used to...the preparation, the grinding...the guilt if I'm not. And I can't compete for fun if I'm not competing to win."

"You know what, Kid, you've done it all...all except win the damn Open and that's just bad luck...happened to Snead too. Way it goes. You might change your mind about quitting...or decide as you get into your fifties that you want to be the best senior in the history of this state. Strong as you are? Matter of decidin' more than tryin'." Marty was visibly impressed with his last sentence. "But, as Crusty says, "who gives a shit - you do what you want."

"Ol' Crust is gonna caddy for me at The Hill Farm."

"That can't hurt," said Marty. "Man was a pro."

"Yeah, the man's got some stories from those days. Hard way to live, though." Sometimes Danny felt a little too insulated from the more ragged edges of life. Crusty the military man who'd played minor league ball, (despite not being a homerun hitter, he once hit two homeruns off of Hall-of-Famer Dennis Eckersley in a minor league game in Bumphuck, Montana or Wyoming or wherever) he'd go on to fight for his country, win a bunch of military golf tournaments on 4 continents; and for a short time was a nomad living in cheap hotels as a caddie on the lower fringe of the PGA TOUR before it was all-exempt. Now he worked when he wanted to. "You know, Marty, I look at what Crusty's been through and you too, with all your surgeries, the big action games, and…" Danny chucked, "all your girls. I'm just…I dunno."

"Well, Danny" said Marty, "your life has been successful and blessed…just a little more, I don't know, conventional. Nothing wrong with conventional, not that *you're* conventional, hell no, you're actually a little weird, and you sure don't talk conventional. You ask me, I think you talk kind of strange." Marty laughed, maybe a little too long. "But you do know how hard it is to run a business - and drive anywhere with your wife."

Danny shrugged and chucked.

"You're a helluva guy, Danny Mo, living a helluva normal life." Marty nodded a couple times. "Probably why you make up that top five in the world stuff, like when you replace divots, or bounce a ball on your wedge for an annoying amount of time." Marty looked at his watch. "Ah, I best be going."

"Alright." Danny moved closer to Marty. "Two things: I don't make up my top-five, worldwide rankings, I earn them. And, two - don't worry about me and Cindy tonight. We'll be fine."

"Sure Danny, whatever. Take note, though, she's really something special. Call me tomorrow." He turned and started to walk away.

Danny Moran watched the old man with more championships than anyone in Wisconsin state history and seven surgeries and four bypasses, a new hip and two fairly new knees and a whole bunch of troubled women who lovingly called him Jonah. Danny lost himself in the rhythm of some practice putting strokes. He waited for what he knew was coming.

Marty limped several steps toward the old parking lot. Finally, the great man turned. "Oh, and Danny…"

Danny snapped his head toward Marty, their routine.

"Cindy suggested you play the song 'Feelin' it,' and not to freak out on the lyrics."

"Feelin' it'…I like that." Danny smiled. He had nowhere to be until much later tonight, at the corner of 13th and State. Cindy.

He stroked an eight-footer into the cup.

Feelin' it.

∞

Chapter 16

Mo Mo Moran opened the refrigerator door with his good arm just to confirm some bad news.

Again.

Wasn't news at all then, really, and Mo thought for a moment he might be creeping toward what his dad had often cited as the definition of crazy; "doing the same thing over and over expecting either different results or the girl in the magazine to materialize in your bed." The elder Moran was referring to the habits of many a delusional soul, but Mo suddenly saw it relating to the baseless hopes of obsessive refrigerator door openers.

He had just done the same thing a little while ago, and a little while before that, but how long ago those whiles were was tough to say. Frankly, he wasn't clear on much of anything at the moment. He knew that Billy Rick Trueblood and all his healthy teammates were playing a four-game series in Albuquerque. He knew his mom was in Chicago with his aunt and uncle and cousin Maddy, and he knew his dad was no doubt happy at home because Mom was indeed with his aunt and cousin Maddy, and he knew his sister was getting settled in Boston, or some city near there on some hill named after some kind of nut, Walnut Hill or Chestnut or Coconut…he couldn't remember what Rinny had said, but it was whatever city Boston College was actually located in.

The one other thing he knew for sure was that no matter how many times he opened the refrigerator door, a tray of sliced cheese and salami was not going to suddenly materialize on the middle shelf the way it often did when he lived at home, and worst of all, he was still completely out of beer. Other than that, he felt like he knew nothing else for sure. Sure, some folks might have suggested that he was, at the moment, perhaps…a bit drunk, but Mo Moran would have slurred that he degged to biffer.

After an accelerated climb through the Cubs' farm system, Mo Mo Moran had become the top pitching prospect in only three years before crashing onto the rocks known as the "out for the year" injury list. He had gone from prospect to suspect in less than three months, and now, Mo felt he'd found still another way to spiral even further south, from a place that wasn't very high to begin with no less. How do you come down from the pits? He had never had a serious injury before this shoulder mess, and he had never spent so much time alone before. And until now, he had never felt any real significance in finishing the last can of beer.

Now it was a revelation. Finishing the last cold one after 9 p.m. meant there would be no more unless he were to drive, left-handed, at night, while fairly shnockered, to a place like Mondo's, just to sit at the bar and look pathetic. Since he left home Mo Moran had always been more into drinking copious amounts of diet cola and eating huge amounts of chain restaurant food, at least whenever he wasn't playing ball or sleeping. But now he was in Des Moines, Iowa, and he was alone, hungry, and completely out of beer. Pathetic indeed, but at least he was pathetic where no one could see him. A fact he felt he could twist enough to suggest he wasn't pathetic at all. Right.

His recent fascination with beer had come out of nowhere. Billy Rick would sometimes toss him a cool one and they'd throw a few back and Mo's life was exactly the same whether he had a couple or not. Sometimes it tasted okay; sometimes it seemed like work just to finish the last few ounces of a single can. But something profound had occurred in the last few months. Mo became convinced that vast improvements had recently been made to the overall flavor of the beers produced by the nation's major breweries. Same thing with imported beer, they started getting it right as well. And the micro-brewed stuff too, really pretty good. They all were. *Amazing… I get hurt, and they all step up big-time, go figure.*

Mo looked at the clock. 11:21. He couldn't be sure, but he suspected he'd called his dad at home just to say 'hey' about an hour ago, unless it

was more or less than that. Where the hell was his dad, anyway? The
man was incapable of not calling back immediately upon getting a
message from Mo. Hell, his dad sometimes called to say he just got a call
that read 'out of area' on caller ID, and he wanted to make sure it wasn't
Mo, what with him being in Iowa and all. He knew it was just his pop,
ol' D Mo, making an excuse to see how he was doing. It was annoying -
but he kind of liked being annoyed sometimes.

The message he left for his dad, well...Mo couldn't really remember
what he had said, or how he said it. And it was the 'how' that concerned
him now, as in, just how drunk might he have sounded. *Nah, I'm fine, or I*
was fine then. Now? Yeah, I'm drunk, or drunkish. Which is so totally Billy
Rick's fault, always keeping a whole bunch of Buds in a place where they're
allowed to get really cold - which made them taste even better...yeah, when
they're really cold, they do, Billy Rick knows all the tricks.

But now the beer was gone, and Mo Moran was alone, and no one
was answering back at home and he couldn't remember whether he
sounded drunk when he left a message for his dad and what he might
say if he picks up on that, and he still hadn't met a single 'Mo-worthy'
girl since he became damaged goods, and he really, really hated doing
his rehab therapy, and he hated not being part of the team, and he hated
doing every damn thing in his life left-handed, and hated not striking
out hitters, and he hated not playing golf if he felt like it, and he very a
lot hated not having anymore cold beer...just hated it all. Damn...some
beer would be good. But it was all gone. And he hated that he hated that.

Where the hell is my Dad?

Mo turned the dimmer switch to low and changed the channel from
ESPN to ESPN2. Nothing but televised poker. Shit, even a rodeo was
better than poker, and he didn't consider sitting on a cow a sport either.
Then he went from room to room to gather up a couple of partial bags of
Cheetos that Billy Rick had left lying around for easy access.

He was able to find the couch, athlete that he was, even with the
lights down low. He wrapped his fingers around the head of the former-
presidential–candidate-a-phone, and asked himself some hard questions:
pepperoni, or just cheese? before never actually dialing.

Next thing he knew, Maurice "Mo Mo" Moran woke up on the couch at 5:05 a.m. with a tongue that felt like a flap of flannel, a jackhammer inside his head, and a face that was easily thirty percent orange.

Never again, he thought to himself.

Again.

∞

Chapter 17

Even in the dim spill of a feeble streetlight, he detected a subtle shift in her posture when she first saw him pulling up and heard the confirming cadence of 'Feelin' It,' the Jay-Z tune. Relief maybe.

He decided he would describe the woman as uncommonly attractive. That description, he felt, skewed toward sophistication, and would keep him from coming across like a kid at the zoo or sounding drunk on Y-chromosomes. She appeared poised yet wary as she circled the Impala to the passenger side. The way she moved, the manner in which she opened the door and entered the car, reminded Danny of the swift but unhurried grace of an ace waitress at a crowded diner.

Danny had done a few minutes of Internet research on hip hop terminology, and so he felt he was now as qualified to call Cindy Young flat out fly as anyone with whom he's shared the bangin' sick freshness of Jay Z. Danny wondered if he was hearing the lyrics right...damn, guess ya just say what comes to mind. Cindy said she wasn't all that jazzed on "the Jigga's" music, but was confident she could recognize his "beats" anywhere and that she appreciated "Jonah's" hustle in running it down. Danny scrambled his face to look pensive, but it was nothing more than misdirection, a way to make staring look like thinking. Cindy took the look as one of curiosity and told him it was a long story. Danny would have hung on every word had she cared to share why she'd know "the Jigga's beats" anywhere, just to keep looking at her.

And so Danny had to work to steal peeks as they made small talk on the drive. Was Cindy's stun-gun beauty a cover? Something disguising an alcoholic edge or coke-hag past perhaps? Sexual slavery or other forms of abuse? Who knew. Most all of them had mind-boggling back stories. He took his time weaving through streets framed by part-time neon, loose siding and crumbling brick, no longer feeling the need to hurry or gawk at the dolled up and dressed down characters indigenous to the fringes of downtown Milwaukee. Between stolen glances he decided there was nothing shopworn about her, only a lucid and seemingly very lovely young woman. Polite and subtly fragrant, she spoke without a single uh, um or ah. As if she could hear his thoughts, she sustained a long exhale without embarrassment and said, "I'm so ready for this."

"Tomorrow is the first day of the rest of your life," said Danny, turning sub-doofus on a dime. Rainbows, butterflies and astral dreams might not be far behind if he kept talking.

"That would be today," said Cindy, glancing at Danny, a lot like he was doing with her. "Today… would be the first day of the rest of my life."

"Of course, but…you know" said Danny, "tomorrow would actually be the first full day…maybe…?"

"You presume…" The word, "presume," made Cindy's lips protrude – a fleshy and inviting destination - and it was at that moment that Danny felt a throbbing between his legs. It took him by surprise, as always, and he reached down to quell the source of his sensation. This time it was Cindy who rearranged her eyebrows, raising them briefly as she watched Danny bring up his little cellular flip-phone. Danny gave her a quick, flat smile before checking the caller ID. It killed him to see it was Mo Mo. He'd have to get back to him in the morning.

∞

Later, Danny felt both satisfaction and regret when he let Cindy off at the now-familiar front door step. From the car, he watched her go up six steps, two at a time. Jungle cat material, he thought. He heard her knock in the arrhythmic cadence of a preset code and watched her wait. She turned to face him and somehow smiled using mostly her eyes. And then she gave him a single, slow, nod. Danny blinked hard. Spooky.

Pulling away from the curb, Danny Moran could only come up with back-to-back chucks, which was very rare. It meant the intermission after the first chuck was potent enough to produce another. Not common. By definition, a chuck was supposed cover everything in one syllable, one sound. He chucked often, as did a lot of folks, and why not, they were versatile, economical, and sometimes strategically ambiguous. Rapid successions of two or more chucks are not, of course, chucks at all. That amounts to chuckling. Not uncommon at all. Danny decided Cindy Young was indeed uncommon. The back-to-back chucks just confirmed it, just as the visits from his internal butterflies confirmed something else about his relationship with Molly.

Out of habit, he turned up the stereo and the sounds of a quite different song from Jay Z jumped all over him. He immediately turned it off and drove home to the soundtrack of the city becoming the suburbs. His thoughts kept pace and made the transition with him.

∞

Chapter 18

On the morning of his last crack at winning the Wisconsin State Open, Danny Moran jerked his car out of his garage and was on the street before his garage door had whirred its way back to earth.

He whispered a blow-dart "dammit" at the digital dashboard clock for confirming just how late he was according to his plan. He was out of his neighborhood before most had even fetched their local dailies from their driveways, yet he felt...behind. He had wanted to get to The Hill Farm good and early. Now, considering how well he had been playing of late, he was left with getting there good.

When alone, Danny generally drove under two powerful influences: his favorite music and/or an assortment of daydreams both regularly scheduled and spontaneously constructed. Molly, literature lover that she was, often linked her husband to a quote from Proust: "If a little dreaming is dangerous, then the cure for it is to dream not less, but more." Refreshingly, Danny could not agree more. He reveled in the stuff that made him feel happy, heroic, or needed, if only in his mind. Like, for example, helping his kids succeed in achieving their goals, or winning the Wisconsin State Open, or single-handedly plundering a sleeper cell of terrorists that roused the wrong cock when they messed with a man by the name of Danny Mo - all of this from inside his Chevy Impala while munching on lightly salted almonds and a Diet A & W. Whatever, triumphant reverie was the goal, and the closer Danny came to his goal the faster time passed. Danny often joked that he had become so good at daydreaming that real life achievements were almost redundant.

Immersing himself in uplifting music and custom made-dreams from behind the wheel had a downside, of course. On the freeway he too often drifted from his lane, sometimes cutting off other motorists as well as driving…obnoxiously…slow. Other drivers often dealt with this by activating their horns or mouths or middle fingers. Danny would respond with one long nod as if he understood, and that was usually that. If anyone wanted to push it further, Danny disarmed them with a *mea culpa* shrug. Everybody moved on, nobody got hurt, and Danny went back to his privately-owned parallel life.

Driving to golf tournaments - the important ones - was an altogether different ritual with its own dynamic. Danny would operate in silence, lost in the management of all things Danny, his uneasiness unmoved by the quiet. And so it was now as he made his way to Crusty's house to pick up his friend and caddy before heading to The Hill Farm for the first round of his last State Open. Danny could be rather aimless at the wheel in this state too as well as a bit heavy on the gas pedal. Not that he noticed. He'd just stare indifferently at anyone cussing, honking or gesturing until one or both moved on. He just didn't care why their lives sucked.

As competitive as he was, Danny rarely swore in anger – audibly anyway - on the golf course. It was a credit to his dad, Lawrence "Curly" Moran, who had ingrained in him that cursing one's own performance was either "weak, a waste, or window dressing." Ol' Curly Mo claimed that investing emotion in failure was "like freezing tainted meat," that it was just "negative energy that takes up space and is a threat to spoil the good stuff around it." As a kid, Danny wasn't sure he got all that but he wasn't gonna risk disappointing his dad by messing around with bad meat.

These days, if, for example, Danny was late in getting to the course due to one of his morning spats with Molly over some toast-crumb, kitchen-sponge, or refrigerator-shelf violation, and if on top that, say a usually reliable shoelace snaps while rushing to tie his golf shoes in the parking lot while his group was stalling for him on the first tee, *perhaps* then…an intense and commaless F-bomb avalanche might come barreling out of his mouth, though usually in whisper format. Nevertheless, in a near supernatural reversal of the standard electrical circuitry wired into in the minds of most competitive but rarely televised golfers, Danny simply refused to drop audible bombs on the golf course.

After a few beers with the boys at The Aftermath some years ago, Danny was prompted into addressing what he called "Coarse course Language," delivered like one of his stylized business-type summations, one of his freefalling only partially put-on soliloquies that were part of the package for certain clients of MOS. It was entertainment and substance at once when Danny Moran - "the enlightened conman" as a college professor once called him - got into the zone.

Al Kerlin, a crass journeyman amateur who also played out of The Old Barn had tried to pin him down. "So, Danny...people were askin', why the hell you don't curse on the course? And christ almighty don't be tellin' me it's some Irish-Catholic thing. Wilgus says 'maybe it's cuz the son of a bitch don't hit no shitty shots, dude's got nothin' to piss and moan about.'"

Danny cocked his head until he achieved the little neck crack that was supposed to make it worth the effort. "I don't know about that, AK. Everyone gets bad breaks...but there are some things that are important to understand." Danny took in another slug of beer and contemplated going off on the subject. "And those things...? Well, it goes a little like this..." And go off he did.

"For those of us flying under the wild blue psychopathic yonder, there's a part of the brain that allows for a pretty controllable level of internal dialogue. This includes profanity management, as well as the will to resist saying things to your wife like 'would ya shut your pie-hole, Honey,' or when you wanna tell your son that his brain must fit his head like a BB in a boxcar, you know, the things that come to mind when you're a little worked up but we internalize for the greater good. Now, for the golfer, over time - could be four holes, four rounds, or in some cases, forever – but for however long, all the cussing you keep inside will bang repeatedly against a cognitive membrane whose resistance varies from person-to-person. In civilized culture it's called the 'Decorum Membrane.'" Danny did the quotation gesture with his fingers just comically enough to get away with it.

"The Decorum membrane, not unlike the hymen of a young woman in love, eventually gives way when stressed, from the banging that I mentioned, and it does so not because of the relative preventive thickness of the membrane but because of the part of the mind that has both allowed and empowered the banging to go on unregulated.

"And when it goes, gentlemen, it's gone; the polluted inner dialogue erupts like a stomach-turning burp or seeps out like noxious fumes. Something called "vanity profanity," ironically enough, which really amounts to a primitive and rather feeble way to tell everyone, 'I'm too good to suck like this, ergo my anger.'

"I got your ergo right here," Crusty interrupted.

Danny ignored him. "My dad called it 'window dressing.' And sometimes it's nothing more than reflex, a habit, or simple laziness…but if it goes unchecked for too long? You can end up with a lifestyle where quick-draw vulgarity drones on like an endless disco beat at the gayest club in hell until you die and find out for sure. But you wanna know what it really is? I'll tell ya. Pissed off profanity – talking the kind that's born of anger or frustration, not the kind that strains for comical effect – well, it's really nothing more than how people act out once they're too old for it to be socially acceptable to scream or cry or pout in public; I mean who couldn't use some more bitching in their life? Usually over petty things, just to accentuate one unfortunate moment in the lives of people who're way too spoiled to know just how freaking lucky they are."

Across the table, Danny had noticed Crusty's 'here-we-go-again-with-this-shit' body language. A sure sign he was amused. Danny continued. "And whether this all manifests itself in primal club-tossing tantrums or some form of demon-driven bitch-screech or both, there is no escaping the fact that there are dark forces hatched from the hell-bent will of countless spirit-world henchmen who have but one unearthly aim: to ambush anyone who's ever craved to play better golf. The desire to swear will forever stir within you, tempt you, seduce you. But…who wins is up to you. And, gentlemen, there ain't an ounce of conventional sense to any of it… I've played with potty-mouthed priests, all black and white and sure of what's right and I've played with gosh-oh-golly cops all draped in blue. Go figure."

Danny had been sitting with five others at "the big table" at The Aftermath. Along with Kerlin, the topic's facilitator, there was Crusty Sindorf, Carter Slane, and two of AK's buddies who played out of The Hill Farm. Danny finished off his pint of beer with a hearty draw and then set off to finish his little speech with another celebrated crock of what-the-hell. "That I do not curse on the course is my choice. That's how I was raised and it's based on things I've come to believe. For some damn reason the subject is often brought up by others as if it were a big deal. It isn't, nor should it be, but I will tell all of you this…" Danny waited a beat, cleared his throat to humanize his dramatic pause, and continued "…I have no interest in conforming, I have no interest in becoming one of those who brandish their seven to ten words of weakness in angry moments as if it's the most honorable of all failings, never once stopping to consider the psychic waste that's created when people further trample the well-worn path of least resistance just to participate in the useless ritual of freezing tainted meat."

"Thou shalt not freeze tainted meat," said Carter, solemnly.

Only Crusty and Carter actually understood what Danny was getting at with his pyrotechnic linguistics and the tainted meat thing. They nodded as if their friend had just cleared everything up. Kerlin and his buddies were dumbfounded and looked it.

"Tainted meat? Wha' the fuck is wrong with you?" Kerlin had asked, looking around.

"Takes ups valuable space," said Crusty. Then, almost snobbish, "What's the point of preserving bad shit?"

"What?" A high-pitched cartoon voice came out of one of the Hill Farmers.

"Excuse me, but…uh…why would anyone risk letting bad shit spoil the good stuff?" Carter said this like it should have brought total clarity to an eight-year-old.

Whether it was the fear of disappointing his dad or a mishmash of influences in his formative years that led to such resolve, the fact remained that Danny had quashed the impulse to curse at an early age, and rarely gave in to it again, at least audibly. Just a part of being who he is by what he doesn't do. Danny once explained this to Crusty.

"Sure, Dannymo, good for you," he had said. "Me? I'm just happy I don't give a shit about my worldwide ranking in opening jelly jars or lighting birthday candles in a single match and shit."

As a kid, Danny developed a little code for adding his own color to things. The code was loosely based on an old joke played on him by his hard drinking and long dead Uncle Leo. Danny didn't exactly recall how the joke was set up, but he never forgot how he was the butt of it. And the more people called it silly, the more a young Danny Moran embraced his little code. When he explained it to Crusty, his friend just shook his head. The code consisted of two nouns – "couch and crown." If he made a bad decision on the course, he said, "Couch and crown stupid!" Or, "couch and crown brilliant" if he was feeling sarcastic. "Couch and crown good" was a pat on the back.

It broke down like this: couch = sofa and crown = king, therefore, "I'm couch and crown stupid" actually equaled "I'm sofa king stupid!" How this differed from 'I'm so fucking stupid' or a stand against contaminated meat is anyone's guess, but the adolescent Danny Moran was always a little different according to his teachers; "unwittingly unconventional," was how one put it. In junior high he and his buddies would mess with their nutty ex-Nam vet science teacher, Mr. Artibissi. "Admit it, Mr. ABC, radioactive isotopes are couch and crown cool aren't they?" They'd then bust a gut trying not to. Danny rarely said couch and crown anything these days, at least aloud, but there were days when it came back to life.

Like today. The long-buried bit of nonsense came back, perhaps to cover some burgeoning early anxiety. He said it several times. Before, during and after breakfast. He was on the verge of saying it over and over the way Jim Rome would. Knew the conditions were right, felt it coming, and indeed the edginess came. He didn't like the way his Frosted Flakes fought the laws of gravity by remaining captive in a kinked bag inside a giant box, and he didn't like how a dozen or so One-a-Day vitamins came flying from the plastic bottle when all you need is one a day, and he didn't like letting little things get to him. But, if he was going to take pride in being top-five in so many trivial pursuits, then floundering at equally mundane endeavors had to hurt a little for those triumphs to have meaning. The fact that his $2.99 bottle of Gentle Head shampoo would run out on this particular day at first seemed an affront to the toiletry justice he felt was due him, yet he had been meaning to get more Gentle Head for nearly a week now and flat forgot. He had it coming. So, yeah, Danny Moran was couch and crown edgy it made his body clammy. And putting the stale old phrase back in play didn't help matters after having gone on record all these years with his 'Decorum Membrane' bullshit. Then again, maybe it was precisely that premise that resurrected his childhood euphemism. Whatever, on this day he was putting it into play - repeatedly. Maybe it was just easier to bust it out in an empty house. But then…couch and crown what.

∞

On the morning of the first round of any major tournament that he felt he could win, Danny expected to feel on edge. The degree of which varied, but seeing as this was the first day of the State Open, his holy grail, on a course where he had won before, the feeling was intensified with the juju of expectations. It generally subsided while warming up on the range and then came back fighting to survive like a fin-snagged fish over the first few holes. Then he'd settle in and turn it to his advantage, an edge, the dangerous part of a weapon, until the last putt was holed.

Danny's discomfort was not a simple case of fluttering nerves born of doubt or the fear of the unknown, the so called butterflies; it was much more about expectations, the need to win when he knew he'd put in enough hours of preparation to get the job done.

Instead of butterflies, Danny's game-time goblin was an inner voice. The same inner voice he heard when he struggled on the range. No one knew about it but him. Couldn't explain it, but, absurdly enough, it was delivered in Jim Rome's clipped delivery. The cadence identical. The national sports talk radio host, calling him out. Dry. Wry. Chiding him. Not to blow it. Ambiguous. The words and the tone could easily be

taken as supportive, but Danny knew the sound-alike Rome was
dubious, skeptical. Sarcasm packaged in even tones. He expected the
voice, even planned for it, tried to remain outwardly unbothered by it,
but his inner Jim Rome was as real as the road he was taking now to
Crusty's house.

He knew he would bury Rome - the very sound of Danny's
expectations meeting Danny's reservations - in less than four holes of the
first round. But the guy who called his regular listeners, "clones," never
really stayed dead since "Romie" returned time and again at the
beginning of the big ones.

When he pulled into the short driveway and Crusty took about a
good half-minute to come out of his house, Danny decided Crusty must
have died, overslept, or been kidnapped. When the door budged, Danny
started backing the Impala out of the driveway like a man tired of
waiting. Crusty shook his head; he knew exactly what Danny was doing,
so he volleyed back with his performance of a man struggling to lock his
door. Crusty started for the Impala and then stopped, spun around, held
up his just-a-minute finger and headed back to his house.

He supposed Crusty went back inside as a one-up counter to
Danny's sulky act of backing up the car, but Crusty came out only
seconds later with a small object in his hand. When he entered the car
Danny saw that it was an old green bottle, gunky around the cap with
some indeterminate mud-like stuff dried to the side. The sight of it
would have made Molly seize up and fan herself.

"Morning Crust" said Danny, slightly cool. "What's, uh, couch and
crown crucial about the travel-size VO5?"

"Dannymo." Crusty nodded, put on his seatbelt, and looked straight
ahead.

Danny pulled out and drove in silence. He didn't have anything he
needed to do or say other than let his thoughts tumble-dry toward a
fresher start. Wasn't working though. *Let the matches dry, Danny.* He
drove as if it took great concentration.

After a while Crusty spoke. "Okay," nodding again. "So you're
couch and crowning. Been a while. What's up?"

Danny shrugged. "Nothing."

"Okay."

"What's up with the bottle?"

"Used this crap in the service. Came across it in the basement the other day. Saw it as a sign. Still got a little left. Never dried out...completely anyway."

"Thank God," said Danny.

Crusty ignored the sarcasm. "Used it once here in the States, too, weird stuff, got a strange stink to it, but it works."

"Good," said Danny. "Stinky stuff," he turned to look at Crusty, "and it's all ours."

I'm tellin' ya..." Crusty looked at the vile. "...this junk here, according to the guys in my platoon...it's a crazy mix of shit. Some kind of extract from a plant with a long name, from Tanzania I think it was, it's mixed with a special kind of rhino dung. Whatever, it keeps insects away. Shit was gold in the jungle."

Danny frowned. "So it's gotta be special rhino dung...or it doesn't work?"

"Yep" Crusty looked straight ahead. "Only works if the rhinos fed on those special plants indigenous to Tanzania, as I understand it."

"How does anyone figure that out?"

"Somebody probably noticed that some of the piles of rhino crap attracted insects, and there were some piles they stayed away from. That, Dannymo, is whatcha call the scientific method."

"And you think we might wanna use it against those mutants at The Hill?"

"Maybe - if they show. Be good to have just in case. Only need a little."

Danny shook his head. "Heard the freak-bugs were really bad last year. Maybe they'll stay away. A shame...such a good layout. I've heard they're supposed to be some strain of stable fly, whatever that is, and another guy told me they were Buffalo Gnats or some such."

"Hate the sons of bitches. Reminds me of shit I don't care to remember."

"Sometimes they bite, and sometimes they just…taunt." Danny regretted his words. He knew Crusty still battled some lingering demons from his days and nights in Vietnam. A few years back he and Crusty were in an open field looking for Danny's ball when they startled a pheasant. Crusty dropped and rolled and hardly spoke the rest of the round.

Crusty was still looking straight ahead. "Hate 'em."

"Everybody's gonna have their dryer sheets tucked in their hats and belt loops like everyone does at Branch River and Eau Claire CC… but those things they get at The Farm in August. Not sure what that fabric softener stuff does."

"Yeah… I can just hear the bastards screaming, 'Jesus Christ, they got Bounce, head for the hills…the humans have soft fresh-smelling sheets!" Crusty looked down at his little bottle again. "My captain, the ol' prick, used to say this shit'll 'spook just about anything - including your dark side and your inner child.'"

Danny was driving with less manufactured focus now. The absurdity of the conversation would have rated higher on the amuse-o-meter had he not been couch and crown edgy. Crusty didn't help things a whole lot by changing the subject. "How's Molly and the relatives doing in Chicago? That baby gonna show up pretty soon?" Crusty loved the Morans, but the questions came out as nothing more than good manners.

"Well, Molly is miserable, if you can believe that. Feels there's nothing really wrong with Maddy, says everyone is overreacting. Maddy is waited on hand and foot, and Molly's cooking and cleaning just to keep from having to sit bedside and ask Maddy how she's doing. The first child's' first child is what it is. Molly's sister asked Molly what she thought of Maddy's condition and Molly told her, that as far as she could tell, Maddy is pregnant. Now, well…Molly said there's a little tension in the house. I made the mistake of suggesting she might be feeling right at home."

"Bet she loved that."

Danny chucked. "Another endearment not taken well. Trying to keep it light is all. Help ease what she's dealing with…but it backfired, I guess. It's what we do. She says, the usual, you know 'do you have to make a crack about everything?' which leads to her trusty ol' 'you'd better be keeping things neat while I'm gone.'"

"…ah but ya love each other."

"Nolo contedere. The evidence is overwhelming. We do. An act of pure will sometimes. Makes me kind of wish I wouldn't have suggested that she 'shut her pie-hole' this morning." Danny raised his eyebrows and glanced at Crusty. "Not the best long-distance word choice."

"Ah, the pie-hole." Crusty smirked. "Very graceful, Dannymo. You do use 'pie-hole' more than most men of your learnin'."

"Well, I was trying to get ready for this little golf tournament today. Molly knows this is it for me. Thought she might be wanting to wish me luck, but it was all highly caffeinated griping this morning. Mostly about Maddy's need for attention and how she's feeling trapped with her all day while her sister and husband go to work…which is, by the way, why she went down there to begin with."

"Where's the husband?"

"Molly says he's been away on business, but she's said he's also tired of the drama and fussing over his wife's condition – told Molly his wife was 'soft' and 'so much for having three kids.'…but you know Molly, she can sniff out controversy on a walk to the mailbox."

"Pie-hole, huh?"

"Yeah." Danny chucked, again. "Weak. But Molly's misery is her pride and joy, she circled right back to whether the dishes were piling up and was I throwing out the newspapers – for which she busted me on a recycling charge - and wiping down whatever…you know, hittin' for the cycle. Finally I said, 'I'll answer you…dear…if you'd just shut your pie-hole for a second.'" Danny shook his head and smiled. "I mean, I listened to every excruciating detail about whether there was or wasn't a high protein count in Maddy's urine and how - amazingly - she didn't have high blood pressure at all and how she's been misdiagnosed with something called preeclampsia or Jedclampsia or whatever it's called. Anyway, she hung up on me."

"Okay," said Crusty. "I'm bored now. How 'bout Mo Mo and Rinny?"

"Rinny's loving Boston. Guess her roommate's been running wild but says she's pretty smart about the bottom line, whatever that means. Says with soccer and orientation, getting her books in order, there's not enough time. But that's Rinny, you know…studying before classes even start. Mo Mo's frustrated with his situation…first big setback of his life. Talked to him a few days ago. Sounded tired, hung-over maybe. Got too much time on his hands."

"Seems pitchers practically form a line to get their Tommy John card punched…" said Crusty, "…but shoulders, depending…they can be a tough deal."

"Mo Mo's tough, but he's scared…only had ticky-tack injuries before, and never any arm trouble. Worried he won't have the same pop when he comes back." Danny sighed. "Me too…for him."

"You know as well as I, Dannymo, some do some don't." Crusty, the former minor leaguer was too honest and cared too much to shy away from tough love. "No telling. I've seen guys cut corners with their rehab and come back guns blazing and other guys with stronger arms and a better work ethic do everything right…and they got nothin'. Or it blows up again and they're done. Sometimes it comes down to a sharp surgeon making the right call."

"Amen." The sobering thought of Mo Mo Moran's uncertain future left the two friends silent for the remainder of the ride to The Hill Farm. Danny was grateful for the silence. His reasons for stepping back from competitive golf started with being free to see his son pitch for the Cubs as often as possible; hitting the road for home games at Wrigley and staying home to see him pitch on the road against Milwaukee. When that would happen, now, was anyone's guess. Sure, he had plans to grow his business and travel with Molly to places they'd put off visiting until their kids were on their own. But to see Mo Mo kick and deal, in a big league uniform… The experience would surely transcend his daydreams of it.

Playing catch in the backyard was a parenting ritual among most dads and even some moms, even if it meant dabbling robotically at the activity for the simple joy of shared discovery. And good for them, but Mo Mo and his Dad, they didn't just play catch, they worked at it. Danny testing slightly arthritic knees in a catcher's squat as his son tortured his mitted hand with the increasing heat Mo brought the older he got. Still, the elder Mo, Curly's son, never let on if it stung, simply nodded; pride overriding all.

Danny had instructed Mo Mo to throw only fastballs until he was at least 12, or even 13, to protect his arm. He could blow everyone away on smoke alone anyway. Danny believed that Mo Mo was following that advice until he drove by Lions Park one day on his way to get some Reduced-Fat Wheat Thins and other provisions for Molly. Danny pulled over, parked out of sight and watched Mo Mo playing ball with some older neighborhood kids. Mo was breaking off benders and the other kids were either diving out of the way or doubled over laughing at what they saw coming from the arm of an 11 year old. Danny was mad, and proud as hell, and he decided to let it go when he recalled his own curiosity with the curveball at the same age.

Now Danny was having doubts. Maybe he should have stepped in and put a stop to Mo Mo's childhood curveballs, his yakkers. Surely any kid as talented as Mo would mess around with his "stuff." But maybe, like the yakkers on the range, Danny hadn't paid close enough attention. Was it possible that the first microscopic scission in the labrum of his shoulder was created over a decade before it finally gave out?

Danny eased off on the gas pedal. Ahead, through the jagged spikes of an obnoxious sun, he saw Ol' Norby Hill's green and yellow John Deere tractor at the entrance to The Hill Farm. He was only too glad to set aside the topics that he and Crusty covered en route; nasty mutant bugs, and special rhino dung, and suggesting that his wife shut her pie-hole, and the protein count in his niece's urine, and the inescapable possibility that he may never see Mo Mo Moran take the mound for the Cubs. Heading down The Hill Farm's long drive, he passed the spacious driving range to the left and was surprised to see only a handful of players setting up to hit balls and maybe half the normal traffic one would expect to find on the putting green at this time. Something wasn't right. A large plastic banner on the course's refreshment stand next to the 10th hole declared that Palermo's Pizza was proud to present the 88th Wisconsin State Open.

When Danny turned the corner and headed toward the clubhouse, he took in a scene in mid-unravel, one that couldn't be good.

"…the hell," said Crusty.

There were squad cars, marked and unmarked, as well as an ambulance and a fire truck. All were parked at odd angles, rotating beacon lights flashing. A scattering of players, caddies, and tournament officials had gathered behind some ropes and makeshift barricades. Danny saw Ray Buck, The Hill Farm's head pro with the one cop in view; he was mostly shaking his head. Danny didn't notice a motorcycle cop directing him and Crusty toward an apparently designated area to park. Danny was whistled down and barked back to a place away from the commotion.

"Couch and crown sorry, Officer," said Danny. He parked the car.

∞

Chapter 19

Two expressionless Emergency Response Team members shoved the stretcher into the ambulance as if it were a giant loaf of day-old bread. From their police-approved parking spot, Danny and Crusty could determine little else from the unfolding hubbub between the fire truck and the extended door of the ambulance.

The siren of the ambulance burped a quick sound check test yodel and the way was cleared for it and all but one of the law enforcement vehicles to leave the scene. Two cops, detectives presumably, remained. The fire truck finally lumbered off, its primary purpose had apparently been to lend gravitas to the proceedings as a view-blocking temporary moveable obstruction.

Standing near the trunk of the Impala, Danny and Crusty watched the collection of onlookers disperse... amateur sleuths now, speculating out loud in small groups as they went about retrieving their clubs and heading back to the range and practice green. Much like the resumption of play after a severe weather delay - one where the players in the tournament were being told to return to the course even as heat lightning continued to flash overhead.

"Well..." said Crusty, surveying everything without moving a muscle, "it's more than just a grounds crew accident...too many cops."

"Everyone looks clueless," said Danny. The sirens finally faded in the distance.

"Guess we fit in then."

"They gotta tell us something." The words were hardly out of Danny's mouth when the P.A. system crackled and settled on a hum.

An officious voice came on. "This is Detective Hayden Richards of the Ozaukee County Sheriff's Department and I have a brief statement to make. The unconscious body of a white male, approximate age 45 to 50, was found on the grounds just inside the tree line off the 13th hole by two members of The Hill Farm maintenance crew. He has been taken to a local medical facility for immediate attention. We are investigating further. Special instructions from tournament officials are forthcoming. Thank you and hit 'em good."

Voices went up in the parking lot until Joe Stadler, executive director of the State PGA came on the P.A to announce that everyone's tee times were being delayed 30 minutes and that more direction would be provided at the first and tenth tees, where groups would go off to start the tournament.

"The ol' unconscious body on the 13th hole delay," said Crusty. "Never cared for it much."

Danny was now sitting sideways with his legs out the open door on the driver side of the car. He was reaching down to pull on his golf shoe when he stopped, looked up and raised an eyebrow at Crusty, "You know what the talk is gonna be...no matter what they tell us."

"Nimrod," said Crusty. "The 13th runs along the forest"

"The Hills are alive, as they say." Danny got up from tying his shoes and slammed the door with his usual behind the back dribble action. "Okay Crust, let's try to play some golf. Maybe we start some rumors later."

"Come here, Dannymo." Parnell "Crusty" Sindorf pulled Danny's clubs from the trunk. With the trunk still open, he burned a serious look into his buddy. "Take all the crap that's happened this morning - all your Molly squabbling,' your crappy drivin' and the sleeper on No. 13 - and just dump it all right here. In the trunk." Before Danny could even begin to defend his driving, Crusty slammed the trunk down hard. Unnaturally hard. Danny looked at Crusty, the little lunatic. He was smiling. "Now we go, Dannymo."

"Nothing wrong with my driving, Piecrust."

Danny warmed up on the range so well and so fast that he found it pointless to keep doing it. He also got a feel for the speed on the putting green almost immediately, his shoulder rocking rhythm felt borderline sensual. He ended up spending the rest of his time hitting showy little pitchy chips in a shameless display of touchy feely self-indulgence.

The tournament official waiting on the first tee had a weathered, humorless face and wore a navy blazer as he paced nearly in place under a green tent canopy that displayed the PGA logo on two sides. He had been the perennial starter assigned to the first or tenth holes for the Wisconsin State Open for over three decades running. A PGA lifer who, from behind his neatly organized table of scorecards, tees, and hole-location sheets, insisted on going over all pre-round player instructions and any local rules in excruciating detail. He administered them in the coldest and most dispassionate manner possible; a self-pleasuring act meant to twist up the insides of the nervous and the weak, as if his haughty damning of hopeful souls from the outset was part of a thinning of the herd ritual fashioned after the coldest doctrine ever devised by the Council of Trent. He never bought into the Danny Mo persona, found D Mo's act "tiresome," and said as much to anyone who'd listen. Danny thought it possible the guy's attitude stemmed from having been named Shelly.

But it was evident that Shelly Wilkerson had embraced the day's drama and relished having the chance to spoon feed some special instructions to the competitors. "Listen up now," he said, "there is a stipulated area outlined on the 13th hole that is to be considered ground under repair. The GUR is adjacent to, and includes a significant portion of, a section of the woods in that area. Okay. Now, the perimeter of this area will be clearly marked, not only by a white line, but by a series of yellow cones as well. In the unlikely event that you hit your ball into this area, there will be a drop area from which you must play. You do not have a choice. Now, if you do not play from the drop area, the penalty shall result in your immediate disqualification. Understand, gentlemen, this GUR is not to be trespassed upon in any way; to do so shall result in your immediate disqualification. Okay, everybody keeping up here? And yes, this means if your ball ends up in the marked area, you may not retrieve it. It is likely there will be some people working inside the area from which you are prohibited; they are not to be addressed. It is not your business. We will have someone from the tournament staff spotting further ahead on that hole – this person will be able to assist and/or disqualify players as necessary. Okay. Are we clear? Any questions, ask them now."

Danny smiled at Shelly; obviously the area adjacent to the 13th hole is where they found the guy who was carted away by ambulance. "Riddle me this, Shelly," said Danny, "can a temporary movable earthling that's influenced by an outside agency cause an area of ground under repair outside a marked hazard to be ultimately deemed as, uh…markedly hazardous?"

Shelly shook his head and squinted at Danny as if Danny had serpents coming from his ears. The official broke his stare to glance at his watch. Danny's two playing partners smiled and drifted from the starter's table. Crusty acted as if he were preoccupied arranging clubs and putzing with other caddy-type things. Danny grabbed a Sharpie and jotted something down on the back of a Culver's coupon for a free dairy treat (deep-fried cheese curds excluded) that he had taken from a stack on the table. Shelly then made a point of staring into some higher place above the heads of the 8:16 group and beyond the minds of simple men until he realized he was no longer the center of attention and abruptly announced the order of play.

Danny was up first. He waggled once, stepped away from his teed up ball, and walked back to the table and handed Shelly the piece of scrap paper he had written on. It said:

Shell –
If I leak me a squibber into the GUR on 13 ☹ make sure my ball is properly donated to The Hill Farm's junior golf program.

Q,
d mo
PS I'd be happy to sign it. ☺

Without hesitation, Danny Moran stepped up to his ball and smoked a missile so hard and straight it had to annoy Shelly Wilkerson even more.

The whole bizarre scene of ambulance and cops and announcements and the weird ground under repair for some reason put Danny at ease in the way that distractions sometimes do. He couldn't recall it, but Danny was sure there had to be some Zenny term for it. He did remember reading about the "Zen of Letting," and went on to play well by taking "The Let" with him. His verbal swing key became 'Port-o-Let.' It traveled well, and Danny's rediscovery of his 'Port-o-let' swing-thought really smoothed out his take-away tempo.

Danny went on to play as if everything in his world was in peaceful balance. The sardonic early tournament "takes" that typically arose from the specter of his inner Jim Rome demanding that he "not suck," never materialized. Rome represented *Serious Doubt* within Danny and manifested itself in the clipped and mocking tone for which Rome is known, but in a voice only Danny could hear. *Maybe*, he thought, *Nero finally fiddles for thee.*

And so it was. Danny's uneasy morning must have indeed remained captive in his car's trunk. He fired a bogey-free 68. At the end of play he had the first round lead by two shots over former Mid-American champion and current mini-tour hotshot Christian Vanbuesakossem (known to most as "Boozer," to simplify his 14 letter last name, nothing involving alcohol). Five other players in a bunched field had 71 including Carter Slane. Andy Salamone tripled number 13 and posted 74.

By the time Danny and Crusty made it back to the car, most of the talk centered on the infamous Nimrod's role in whatever precipitated the morning's excitement; that he must have scared the shit out of some poor soul who likely strayed from the river bank running under the County Trunk PP Bridge. The bridge provided a semblance of shelter for some hard luck homeless dudes referred to by the locals as "The Fishermen." Sounded logical to Danny and Crusty, but as Crusty liked to say, "Live by logic, die by logic."

Danny's second round, on a cool and fairly bug-free (by Hill Farm standards) Tuesday afternoon, went just as well as the first. He didn't hit the ball as well as the day before, but rolled it better, posted another 68 and increased his lead to five shots over Christian Boozer. This time, Danny and Crusty decided to have a beer in The Hill Farm clubhouse after handling a few questions from some of the state's golf beat writers and a couple local television network affiliates.

Though his confidence was soaring, Danny was careful to avoid giving in to the feeling. Time and again he'd winced over the euphoric bravado of fools; too many quotes and sound bites from players, Tour pros included, that too often turned into weeping forehead boils a day or two after their utterance. It was Danny's experience that the toughest and most confident players were rarely so needy or self serving. Publicly anyway. Regardless of personality type, the greatest champions seemed to know what *not* to say.

Danny Moran and Gary D'Amato, the long time beat writer for the Milwaukee Journal Sentinel, had come to know each other pretty well. They liked to joke about being "summer friends" after so many years of Danny competing in, and Gary covering, the state tournament scene. D'Amato hung around until it was just player, caddy and writer at a corner table in the rustic great room of the mostly empty clubhouse at The Hill Farm. They sat near the enormous fireplace with its gas fueled flames dancing around a stack of radiating ceramic logs that looked like split oak. As the sun began to set, it was cool enough for the fire to feel kind of good even if it was only August. It reminded Danny of two things: that he was getting old; and the heat was coming tomorrow, in more ways than one.

"Well, nice playing Danny, who's your bet for runner up?" D'Amato said, jabbing an elbow at Danny.

"Not funny." Danny was feeling too good to look fierce. "Take it back Gary…and then ask me something important, like, ah…who's my favorite cartoon dog."

Crusty rolled his eyes and looked at the writer. "That would be Underdog."

"That's right, Crawdaddy," Danny dismissing Crusty before turning to D'Amato. "So, anything to share about yesterday's discovery of the snoozer on 13?"

"Got a name, heard some stuff. Can't verify much."

"You're with friends."

D'Amato looked at his notebook. "A buddy checked with his cop buddy. Guy's name is Trammel Heitman. 48. Guy was drunk. I mean, like, nearly 'never wake up again' drunk."

"Anybody know the guy, I mean, here? Ray Buck?" Danny was intrigued.

"Ray's seen him around. Salamone supposedly knows who the guy is."

"Of course," said Danny.

Crusty's face flashed a look of recognition. "Ahhh…The Pirate," he said. "The eye patch guy, I remember the name, Trammel. I grew up in Michigan, Tigers fan. Guy hangs with Sally's cousin or brother-in-law sometimes. Drunk on days that end in y." Crusty sipped his beer. "Heard he can't see straight without the patch, double vision 24/7. Whatever."

"Yes, seen him around," said Danny, pleased to know who it was. "Saw him at The Farmstead a couple months back. And yeah, he was with Salamone's brother-in-law, guy looks like a bloated John McEnroe, they were polluted that night too."

"Don't repeat any of this, of course." Gary looked around. Danny had the third from last tee time for the second round and now the earlier bustle was dwindling.

Danny nodded and sat back in his chair, tired, content.

"Word has it the guy's pants were down, around only one leg, know what I mean."

"Oh boy," said Crusty.

D'Amato shrugged. "Don't know anything else. Cop said don't go jumping to conclusions, drunks do some weird stuff. He hasn't seen a report or anything. Shop scuttlebutt is all."

Danny sighed. Not much else to say.

"Alright," said D'Amato, getting up to leave. "Gotta go write a story, good luck tomorrow, Danny."

After a minute, Crusty slapped his palms to the table. "So...Dannymo, about my caddy fee." As he got up, he muffled his response to a 57 year old body that had stiffened up during the course of a single beer. "You owe me one Steamin' E."

"With not as much cheese as mine."

"Roger on your damn cheese...but I'll be needin' some more beer to get me to tomorrow." In Crusty's world this was near the peak of living well; multiple beers and a Steamin' E on Danny Moran. Five shots on a field full of young guns and tested veterans. Professionals, amateurs and collegiate in-betweeners. He knew to enjoy the moment; tomorrow would be thirty-six holes. The heat and humidity was expected to arrive around mid-day, an indicator that the mutant gnat-fly-bee brigade would likely be joining the party soon after.

Their waddles became dignified strides after a few steps as they made their way to the car. They stopped before getting in and looked around at the heavy shadowing the setting sun had painted on the undulating face of The Hill Farm layout. In a state of recovery now, it was a big, quiet piece of land that had probably seen more than it ever wanted to.

"I am..." said Danny, staring off, intending to say something about being hungry.

"Dannymo," added Crusty immediately. "You are Danny fucking Mo."

"He's my son, Crusty. We're Morans, not Hills."

They entered the car and settled into their seats like two middle-aged guys happy to sit down again. Danny cranked up a song by The Saw Doctor's, "To Win Just Once." Danny proudly championed "Cousin Leo's band," called them the "craic-heads from County Galway," specifically Tuam, a small town in Northwest Ireland. Danny thought them the greatest band in the world, and Leo Moran was indeed the band's lead guitar player and one of their primary songwriters. Danny was constantly threatening to take Molly to the Emerald Isle and follow "The Docs" around the countryside for a batch of concerts. A tribute to their universal appeal, Molly was all for it, and now, Crusty, a talk radio addict, was giving in to some toe tapping and little head nods as the anthem filled the silver Chevy.

Life was good.

∞

Chapter 20

Fresh off yet another uncanny Steamin' E experience at The Aftermath, Danny dropped Crusty off and circled back to the Pick n' Save a half mile from Crusty's place.

His first few strides through the parking lot resurrected some of the stiffness accrued over 18 hilly holes, but it was nothing a five shot lead couldn't soothe. He entered the store, found the clean smelling aisle, and after storming past the gaudier boxes of powerfully scented and mostly granulated offerings, he went about fondling more than a dozen different plastic bottles. He tried to decipher the fine print listings of active ingredients, but the effort was taxing his tired eyes and he cursed himself for leaving a pair of mangled cheater reading glasses in the car. But he was committed to the fight. He battled the blurry vision of age with squinting eyes and by holding the different products at arm's length and then fine-tuning with an assortment of chicken-swivels of the neck. Finally, bewildered by the sheer number of choices and the similar complexity of the chemistry, he purchased a bottle with overlapping ingredients and similar performance versatility - with Molly's favorite shade of blue breaking the tie.

Back in his car, he checked off items on a mental list of business concerns at MOS. An accumulation of voice mails and emails from clients, friends and dreaded others was inevitable and those related to Modus Operandi Solutions would likely require a solid hour of home office follow-up work. Some of those messages would be short good luck and go get 'em notes from clients and business friends. Other messages would be the drier, detailed and sometimes pointed ramblings of business-addicted executives feeding their need to be heard, many of whom didn't even know, or refused to acknowledge, that Danny played competitive golf. He set the reality of those tasks aside and allowed his thoughts to freefall.

Driving almost unconsciously, he meandered his way through the early evening darkness and a labyrinth of subdivision parkways with French names that eventually fed back to County Line Road, the main road back to his home. A 'Saw Doctors Live' CD still played and rang out in melodic triumph, but at a lower, more fitting volume for night time ruminations.

The darkness, as it will in late August, descended a bit earlier every day now, the first and most subtle sign that another Midwestern fall was rehearsing somewhere not far north. Every year Danny would sense the summer waning at the State Open, but this time the feeling seemed more profound, perhaps because a large part of his life was 36 holes from changing in a way he couldn't exactly predict. Of the four seasons, he felt the rites of fall had the strongest air of transition despite the reliability of its progressions; the changing colors of the leaves and the giant Vees of migratory geese, the sweeping communion of students and teachers returning to the routine of school, and the countless farm families and football teams hustling to harvest their due from different fields – all of them signs of the time.

And whether these signs pointed more toward the yin of rituals starting again, or the yang of other ones ending, it was this week, every year, when all the coming and going first seemed near. That dichotomy – of autumn coming into view as the summer was shrinking to fit the rearview mirror – was like two sides of the same coin, each a harbinger of different images, such as it was when his thoughts turned to his all-time favorite teacher, the one who was also his life's most enduring challenge, far more so than golf, the one who was out of town and had hung up on him the morning before, and the one he could not walk away from regardless of those moments when the idea held some momentary appeal.

Molly.

Danny was not unhappy when he learned that his wife had agreed to go to Chicago to help her sister - her lovely sister, and her undeniably beautiful, unquestionably spoiled, and hypochondriacally-inclined niece with what was reported to be the world's single most difficult pregnancy of the modern era.

Molly Moran admitted to snippets of guilt - guilt in letting her relationship with her niece drift away to almost none at all. It had become easy to do when small gifts and voice mails went unacknowledged, and when Maddy would describe "Rand," her then boyfriend, now husband, almost entirely in terms of his net worth and his many important friends, and when, after so many years of wanting to be a teacher like her "Molly Godmother," she announced at a family reunion that she'd like to be "more than just a teacher." (And then apologized too profusely in the way the self-absorbed do when addressing the less ambitious.) "More power to you, Madison," Molly had said at the time. But then Maddy met Mr. Real Estate, dropped out of school, and began finding it harder to relate to some good and longtime friends while finding it easier to take her family for granted.

Back then, Molly made no secret of her growing disenchantment with what she felt was Maddy's headlong plunge into the material world. In light of that, Molly came to believe that maybe a week or two in Chicago with her niece and sister's family might be a good thing. A chance to start anew, just as a new life was graced upon a family coming together once again; as well as a chance to reinvigorate their once special relationship now, as adults... a bond they both had cherished when a little girl in pigtails and braces used to go on breathlessly about her smart and pretty Aunt Molly, the schoolteacher. And back then, when Maddy said "teacher," she said it as if it said it all.

Danny thought it was sweet when Molly asked if "he'd mind too awful much" if she went. "I know it's Danny Mo's farewell to golf and all," she had said. Shortly thereafter, when he was enthusiastic in noting how very sweet indeed it was - her willingness to go away for a week or more to help her family - Molly peppered Danny with curious comebacks like, "I suspect you're just happy to have me out of your hair for a while." She also claimed to know that he wouldn't miss her and that he'd be "in hog heaven" having the house to himself. The woman wasn't stupid.

The thought made him smile. Through two decades of the rock-paper-scissors reality of marriage, Danny had come to realize that holding a justly earned; "R U F'ing kidding me" card didn't mean the RUFKM card had to be played just to declare a victory where nobody wins. Similarly, Molly's sighs had grown less dramatic over the years, even when she noticed some form of unaddressed debris or moisture on the counter. Wise or simply combat weary – and Danny believed it was a bit of both - they never would have learned such tolerance without the challenge of each other.

Danny pulled the Impala into the garage. With Molly out of town he had nothing going with the butterflies, and despite the sense of tension-free emancipation he initially felt, he discovered that he now wished her home. When in competition for something as important to him as the State Open championship, Molly usually found fewer ways to feel persecuted and most times just let him be. Now, he felt the way he always felt whenever they had left things on bad terms, either before bed or before leaving for the day. "Graffiti on our family photo" is how he saw such transgressions. The unceremonious "pie-hole" exchange that resulted in Molly hanging up on Danny had been their last contact. That was nearly a day and a half ago. Stubborn graffiti.

So the first thing he did inside the house was check for voice mail messages. There were only six, and he listened to them as he went about other tasks. Half-listening to the first two, he pulled his final round apparel from his closet... olive slacks and a black shirt, which, with his black golf shoes, was his traditional final round look. He took the clothes he planned to wear the next day, and headed to the laundry room. There was a message from Marty Archibald; it went on and on with best wishes and plenty of advice, and some confidential updates on "his girls," and how kind Cindy thought Danny had been, and so on. Finally, there was a message from Molly. He listened to her words as he tossed his final round shirt and slacks in the washing machine. He switched the cordless phone to his fresher ear as if the act was a tribute. She was excited, all sweetness and light. No discernable misery.

"Hi honey, maybe I'll try to call you later tonight from the hospital, but it'll probably be some time tomorrow...we're off to have a baby.

Maddy's ready. But in other wonderful news - yesterday Maddy and I had a real breakthrough, about everything, for hours. Over the last day I think all we've done here is talk - talk and cry and hug. Everyone, Rand included, they're all coming together, sharing, opening up. I'm, well…I'm happy." Molly fired off some mind-numbing prenatal facts that would require some translation later. Or not. Danny rearranged his couple pieces of clothing in the washer as if he knew what the hell he was doing.

Her message went on, "And Danny, don't think we don't see that you're leading the Open by five shots at that creepy Hill course. I want you to know, this is your time, you deserve it, I can feel it. Remember now, 'on, under, and until…no one!' I'm chopping the air…can you feel it? Everyone here is pulling for you." Danny actually felt his eyes humidify as he listened. "And you know what, Danny Mo, I'm never going to be apart from you this long again…at least not without taking your robe with me, you know…Oops, I just got beeped, the voice mail thingy, I'm going to get cut off in a second, I better shut my pie…" And then Molly was gone.

Danny laughed his 'Molly-happy-so-Danny-happy' laugh. Molly's tone was rejuvenating. Things had flipped for the better with her family in Chicago and her one at home. It was good to have that graffiti gone. He replayed Molly's message. Danny knew too well that things could flip back at any time, but for now he'd ride the upside vibe of recovery. He replayed Molly's message. Danny grabbed the blue bottle of all-in-one detergent he bought at the Pick n' Save while he listened to the message again. Without measuring, he dumped some hearty glugs of the blue liquid into the machine and then worked some dial settings that he really couldn't read without better light or eyewear. A three-quarter turn seemed about right.

He went to his office feeling revived enough to plow through his emails. Coming from Molly, "on, under and until…no one!" was exhilarating. He was even glad she shoved a little "pie" back in his face. He did not, however, have a clue about the reference to his robe. Molly abhorred the thing. She had long ago expressed her disbelief at Danny's primitive philosophy on bathrobe maintenance. He never felt it necessary to have his robe washed because he only wore it after he showered. Therefore, he claimed, he was always perfectly clean when he put it on and he would appreciate Molly washing it once after purchase, and one final time when he felt his relationship with it was over and the robe was ready for someone new as determined by the folks at, say, the Military Order of The Purple Heart. When Molly countered with how his stick deodorant residue had built up in the armpit area - "caked in the pits" was how she put it - Danny would smile and reply, "Yes, like a fine Cajun skillet, Mol, it gets better with age." That was three robes and nearly fourteen years ago. It was never discussed again. *Without my robe? Molly?* The comment made no sense. She'd sooner picnic in a landfill.

He finally got to bed a little after 11. Mo Mo and Billy Rick had called earlier from their apartment in Iowa. Said they were having a few beers to celebrate Billy Rick's first ever homerun to the opposite field. And, of course, "D-Mo leading the Open," followed by some drunkish "No ones!" Danny didn't hang on long. Still, in that time, Rinny had called and when he called her back he got her voice mail. She sounded great. "Way to go Daddy Mo! No veins. Everything like butter, now. I talked to Mom before she left with cousin Maddy for the hospital, she's excited about everything. Everything is good here. Okay, back to the library. I'll call tomorrow night. Love you."

Lying in bed, Danny was only vaguely aware that the experts on ESPN's Baseball Tonight were going on about the impact that hitters sheathed in elbow armor had on plate coverage and the diminishing returns for pitchers looking to work inside. He had drifted back to his own ball playing days when he suddenly recalled the laundry he had started. He rolled out of bed and was ambivalent about what he saw in the two mirrors he passed walking to the washing machine. The laundry room stayed dim when the eco friendly light bulb showed no sense of urgency so he went ahead and took out his clothes for the next day and laid them all on top of the dining room table to flat dry. He'd do a quick supervised tumble dry if needed and touch up with the iron in the morning.

He slithered back into bed and turned off the TV. His thoughts returned to The Open. He wasn't sure whether to push the replay button in his mind, or the fast forward, but he was absolutely certain that his fingertips smelled especially clean.

∞

Chapter 21

Wednesday. 6:26 a.m.

When Danny pulled up the driveway, Crusty was in his front yard bumping little chip shots over a plastic bowl and off a flat rock angled against a split log. Precisely struck, the ball would bounce back off the rock like a pitch-back net and land in the bowl.

Though caddies were allowed to wear shorts in The Open, Crusty wouldn't think of it. In crisp khakis and a white golf shirt buttoned to the top, he wore a structured baseball style cap that was, always, the color of his shirt and featured an old school big-leaguer brim, neither too flat nor too curved. It was overcast and still cool now, but the forecast had the temperature inching up during the morning and becoming warmer and muggier by the afternoon.

No matter the weather Crusty seemed to rarely perspire and his clothes refused to wrinkle. Danny marveled at that, as did others in the golf community. Danny was a strong and fit 46 and his M.O. was to perspire early and often. Keeping his right, ungloved hand dry during competition on warm or humid days had been a longtime problem for him. A problem that at times crept into his head.

Crusty stashed his wedge just inside the doorway and headed to the car. His yard was as neat as he was. He had gotten the house when his tiny wife of 13 years left him for her Zumba instructor, a tall handsome Greek woman who'd attract, as Crusty claimed, "any hygienic primate on the planet." Though Crusty was tight-lipped about it, the three of them regularly had dinner together.

"Dannymo," Crusty said just before he slammed his door shut.

"Morning Crust," said Danny. "Thanks for being ready."

"You still got that bug shit in your bag don't ya."

"I do. Except I thought it was rhino shit." Danny shifted into reverse. "Might need it today, huh."

"No shit. Smells clean in here."

"Thanks."

"Really clean."

Danny looked at Crusty.

"You sleep okay Dannymo? Crusty was still sniffing the air while he fixated on Danny's face.

"I'm good. Feel really good. Look good too, don't you think. Used Molly's incredibly expensive shampoo this morning and, wow…never enjoyed such lather before. Smells a little foofy.

"Foofy," said Crusty, "that must be it. If foofy means clean. "You look like you're still waking up."

" I feel the perfect amount of tired," Danny decided to come clean since it seemed the theme. "You know, relaxed."

"So…restless night again?"

"Slept pretty well, actually - only woke up twice and went right back. Dream came back, though, right before The Who exploded from my clock-radio with *Who Are You*." Danny leaked out a sigh, the kind he'd prefer to bury.

"Hank, huh," said Crusty. It wasn't a question.

"Yeah…Hank But I swore I heard Daltry singing about Rin Tin Tin…you know Crust? Is Rin Tin Tin a lyric in Who Are You?"

Crusty looked at Danny "Don't know. Just seems that 'Who are you?' is a question that never gets answered."

Danny shook his head. He turned onto County Trunk PP and stayed silent while Davy Carton of The Saw Doctors sang the lines from *To Win Just Once*, which had been playing whenever his car was running since the day before.

"To never have considered losing
As if winning was by your choosing
Bare your soul for all to find
An honest heart and an open mind

"To win just once
That would be enough"

"Ol' Hank," said Danny. "One minute we're having fun or just chillin', next minute he's gone. Dreams. Weird. But I can see him, all miserable, you know, in my mind. Wondering where the hell I am." Danny cringed inwardly at his outpouring.

"Sure it wasn't the other way around, Dannymo?"

Danny made a face. "This was worse...it's usually just me floundering and I can't find him which is bad enough. But once in awhile, like last night...I still can't find him, but I can still see Hank, see him crying. You think dogs actually cry? I mean, this isn't howling. It's different."

"Anyone can do anything in dreams. Maybe Hank's cryin' for you."

"I just said that."

"No...I mean maybe he cries so you don't have to."

Danny looked at Crusty who was staring straight ahead. The color of day was green against gray in Ozaukee County. "Hmm..."

"Or, maybe he cries sometimes just so you can see him cryin'...so you can cry a little yourself. Heard dreams are supposed to balance you out some. Subconscious thing. Or unconscious. Whatever."

"So if I dream of a drunk donkey doin' an Irish jig in a Mardi Gras mask, it means something?"

"Ever make an ass of yourself at a party, Dannymo?"

"Never, Crusty – so maybe that balancing thing is true," said Danny immediately. Then, after a few seconds, he added, "Molly might disagree about that ass at a party thing. But...I'm sure I'm not the only guy to check into a hotel with a baby rattle suction-cupped to his forehead." Danny looked at Crusty, who continued to look straight ahead although his lips had stretched. The story of The Rattler was an all-time favorite of Crusty's.

"Who knows," said Crusty, "some of my dreams would probably get me committed."

On the crowned and curving county trunk, Danny drove through wide expanses of rural scenery, mostly farmland and dense woodlands bought dirt cheap when such dirt was much cheaper and then held by local families for generations. Deep pocketed developers had made only limited progress in securing sizable chunks of it to commercialize or subdivide. Still, it was the differing definitions of progress among the disparate parties that held sway more than sizable chunks of money. And so the road on which they rode would remain serene for the foreseeable future.

Danny felt at peace but couldn't resist occasionally checking his segmented visage in the rearview mirror. No doubt about it, Molly's expensive shampoo had indeed worked some magic, and it had Danny reconsidering the value of PH balancing. Maybe it was indeed time to make a management change at the top. Danny's vanity demon was among his worst, but like his inner Jim Rome voice, he usually managed to get beyond it. Maybe not. His thoughts returned to Crusty's comment on dreams balancing things out.

"So, Crusty, since I'm probably among the best daydreamers of the modern era, you're thinking maybe the misery of my nighttime dreams, like the Hank nightmare... they're supposed to balance out the rapture of my daydreams...maybe bring me back to Earth?

"I should know better than to get you thinking." Crusty looked out the window at a giant farm field lush with even rows of rich soil and low clumps of leafy green things. "But you're not the only jungle cat to bounce around an inner sanctum of eternal return."

"Uh, sure," said Danny, furrowing his brow to show he was thinking. "Where the hell did this come from, Crust...some song?"

"Nah. Just thinking that whatever happens today is what happens today. You keep losing Hank - and yet you still survive..."

"It's a dream for God's sake."

"So is the Open title. You'll be Danny fucken' Mo no matter what happens. You will still believe you can go down basement steps faster than anyone..."

"Top-five, Over 40 division."

"There ya go"

"Modesty requires the truth."

"That's right, and whether you win or lose today, you'll still be the same ol' nutcase. Just sayin. Maybe it's good to shed a tear on occasion, but you don't need to win today. Be great if you do."

"You'd get misty too if you knew Hank like I know Hank."

"No doubt," said Crusty. "But I know you...you'll never stop looking for him, will y..."

"Of course not," was Danny's reply before Crusty had even finished.

Then it started to sink in. Danny had believed he was ready to walk away from competitive golf. He also knew he wouldn't really know until, Hell...who knows, maybe next spring, when the craving to play and compete came roaring out of hibernation like it did every year. When everything reprised... the walking and the talking and the Steamin' E burgers after a five dollar Nassau goes down to the wire and somebody's partner dunks a bunker shot to win the pot and all the bullshit back and forth. Yeah, could be tough. It would be easier to go out as the State Open champ. They drove in silence, each working to return from where the conversation had veered.

Crusty broke the quiet. "Nice column by D'Amato in the paper today. You see it?" Crusty laughed, knowing the answer.

"Might have skimmed it," said Danny.

Crusty recited a line from the article, "Danny Moran, arguably the most popular amateur golfer in Wisconsin golf over the past couple decades, has taken over the open at The Hill Farm as if he was one part Navy SEAL and one part standup comedian – totally prepared and with the guts to get in front of everyone and be perfectly comfortable doing it."

"Embarrassing," said Danny. "I mean…arguably? Who would argue with any of that?"

"No shit," said Crusty.

"None at all," said Danny.

He hit the "seek" button and played "To Win Just Once" once again. Such a damn good song with a sweeping melody meant for singing along. And both men did - maybe not aloud, but in their hearts, and they rode the anthem created in Northwest Ireland the rest of the way to The Hill Farm in south central Ozaukee County in the Heartland of America.

Five shots on the field. Two rounds to go. They drove past Norby's tractor and entered The Hill Farm on a note of triumph.

∞

Chapter 22

"We got us a spitter," Crusty shook his head. "Boozer's a dipper," He took Danny's club and cleaned it.

"Really?" Danny first met Christian Vanbusakossem when "Boozer" was a bony 16-year-old junior champion with braces and no fear. "Snuff used to be big on the mini-tours, but I thought that was like…so yesterday, as the kids say. Maybe not."

When Boozer came up to him at the range Danny didn't recognize the kid. Besides looking quite different than he used to, Christian was now barely distinguishable from countless other young mini-tour pros and hotshot amateurs biding their time until they, too, were ready to go down swinging in the Darwinian jungle of play-for-pay golf. He had wrap-around shades resting backwards on a sweat-stained Taylor Made cap with some kind of chain necklace, presumably of precious metal, and a wannabe goatee framing a lower lip bulging with dip. Boozer was spitting routinely enough to confirm that dip was indeed critical to becoming the spitting image of anyone wanting a spitting image.

"Mr. Moran, nice to see you." Boozer grabbed his shades before taking off his cap and extending his hand. "Good playing."

"Chris? Thank you. Nice playin' yourself." Danny was impressed by the pre-round intro. He stepped away from his spot on the range and shook Boozers hand. "In your mini-tour uniforms it's hard to tell you kids apart."

The freshly minted pro turned his head and produced a sound-only spit. "What can I say? The ladies dig the look." He smiled, full wattage, specks of smokeless tobacco polluting otherwise perfect teeth.

"Maybe guys too; I mean, look at you."

Boozer didn't know how to take that, so he spat, laughed and spat again.

Danny took a step toward the kid and delivered the standard pre-round good-guy line. "Well, good luck today, Chris, gonna be a long one, let's have some fun out there."

"Absolutely, Mr. Moran." Boozer turned to head back toward his spot on the range. Off to Danny's right, players in carts or with caddies and a few spectators milled about inside a congested, polygon-shaped courtyard of sorts penned in by the first tee, the range, the putting green, the tenth tee, the 18th green and the clubhouse.

"Chris," Danny called out to the kid, now almost ten feet away and walking with his back to him. Marty-like.

He stopped and turned back, "Yes, Mr. Moran."

"No more Mr. Moran today, okay?"

"Yes sir."

"Call me Danny. Or, if you prefer…Sir Daniel James Moran is fine, too."

The kid smiled, "You can call me Boozer," he said, and headed back to his spot.

"Polite," said Crusty. "Between spits."

"Yeah…now," said Danny. He waggled and then flushed a five-iron. Towering, falling right. Butter. "At some point today, we'll see if it's real or not."

Danny headed to the 10th tee to start his final 36 holes. With split tees for the 66 players who had made the cut, the leaders would go off on 10 for their third round and then the first tee to start the fourth.

The third member in the final group with Danny Mo and Boozer was a guy named Stuart "Nice" Johnson. A quiet and slightly built guy in his mid-thirties, Johnson rarely posted a high score nor did he go exceptionally low. Even after more than decade of competing alongside him, Danny found Nice Johnson a hard guy to know. Nice rarely spoke except to compliment a fellow player's shot. It was almost always a hushed, "nice." If a joke was told on a backed up tee on a short par five or long par three, Nice Johnson didn't laugh really, he just smiled and said "nice."

He had circular, rimless glasses and hit the ball shorter off the tee than most every top, non-senior amateur, averaging maybe 245 yards. Danny knew that Nice Johnson was some kind of engineer and was rarely one to speak first, but there was not a speck of evidence to contradict that he was indeed anything but quite...nice.

So the final round of the Wisconsin State Open began with three players in the final group in their 20s, 30s and 40s, and two of them amateurs, which was rare. Shelly Wilkerson cared little for any of them. In fact, Shelly cared little for anyone who wasn't from the era of nostalgia-enhanced legends ala Marty Archibald - most of them dead, infirm or ceremonial performers only. He believed most everyone else were just imposters with no idea how good the old guys with old equipment on slow greens were in his day, back when the same handful of guys won every event, usually shooting a handful of shots over par over 72 holes.

"Just under the wire fellas, 20 seconds from a penalty of two each," said Shelly as the three players, apparently taking Danny's lead, arrived simultaneously at the tenth tee.

"Didn't realize we cut it that close Mr. Wilkerson," said Boozer. No spit.

Danny didn't play into it. He knew Shelly's threat was just another player-marginalizing piece of self-serving tripe and his expression suggested as much. No rise out of Johnson. He was looking at his shoes, or the ground. Shelly went about delivering instructions but his mustered-up authority was mitigated by the collective disinterest of the actual achievers he was talking to. There was nothing new other than the fact that the yellow cones and yellow police tape had been removed from the wooded area off the 13th hole. There were maybe a dozen spectators hovering in the vicinity and none of the players knew any of them well. The gallery for the Open on the final day was usually sparse until the afternoon round.

Nice Johnson hit a nice tee shot, Boozer boomed his, and Danny mashed one a couple yards past the strong, flexible kid. It was meaningless to the bottom line over next 36 holes, but for Danny, satisfying nevertheless. There was still plenty of thunder in the old man's bat. With temperatures in the low 60s and under overcast skies, the air was chilled further by one of those premonitory breezes off Lake Michigan that hints at changes to come. At the moment however, Danny could not have been more comfortable. For the first time he caught a whiff of a clean smell, no doubt the source behind Crusty's mention earlier. Had to be either Molly's shampoo or the detergent he bought. Didn't matter.

On the course, in the heat of competition, the mini-tour version of Boozer turned out to be a self-talker with a habit of cursing himself over the smallest imperfection. A wedge pulled 15 feet left, even if it was pin high, was a "fuckin' yank job"…punctuated with a spit. A chip shot on line but a little short of the hole was worth a "fuck me"…and some spit. In between the showy self-loathing he returned to the blueblood politeness he demonstrated on the range. It was classic vanity profanity; the affectation perfected by performers who want others to believe that their very best is but a barely-met standard and so-so is another one of Satan's practical jokes. Couch and crown trite in Danny's view, but like Boozer's whole look, it was hardly anything new.

Stuart Johnson had never won a meaningful amateur tournament, yet his overall consistency was uncanny. A ton of top-tens; qualifying medalist for the state match play a couple of times; an impressive string of club championships at a good country club track. Over the years Danny had played with him so many times in state competitions that Carter Slane once claimed Crusty Sindorf was becoming jealous of Nice Johnson. Bellied up to the bar, they were into a few cold ones and in giddy anticipation of Steamin E's at The Aftermath. "Get one thing straight," Crusty had famously replied, "I am jealous of no Johnson - hell my wife went off with a woman."

And so it went. Danny Mo made no birdies and one bogey but after a thin 3-iron second shot bounced up perfectly, eagled an easy par five and turned at one under for the nine. Boozer was even and Johnson was two over.

The back nine was not all that different for the three except there was no eagle for Danny and Nice Johnson had the rapture of chipping in twice to shoot one under. Danny made a birdie and a bogey and Boozer made nine straight pars, apparently even par for nine holes was a plight the kid enjoyed complaining about.

As the group approached the 13th green and took no more than half of the allotted five minutes to find Boozer's tee shot, which had clearly ricocheted backward off one of two side-by-side hickories, Shelly Wilkerson came riding up in his cart from the woods near the previously sealed off "location of interest" area on the other side of the fairway. He informed the Boozer-Johnson-Moran group they were "not yet in violation of the prescribed time set forth in the pace of play guidelines for stipulated tournament rounds conducted at this particular course" but that they were "trending poorly and officially almost 75 seconds behind. Just an FYI."

The group including the caddies kept walking toward the green still 50 yards ahead. Most of the small gallery had already moved up to a spot near the green. Boozer said "We'll pick it up a bit, Mr. Wilkerson." He spat. All sound, no fury.

"Hundred bucks, Shelly?" said Danny.

"Hundred bucks what, Moran?" Shelly lurched forward in little stop-and-start bursts of the cart's accelerator trying to adjust his speed to that of the walking golfers.

"If we don't have to wait on the 15th tee when we get there, I'll give you a hundy. If there is a wait…you leave us alone for the rest of the day."

"Look Moran; I'm just doing a job. A job I take seriously, and it's a job for which I volunteer my time." Shelly took a deep breath. "You don't have to be grateful but you better respect the fact that without due enforcement these rounds would go on longer than a Jerry Lewis Telethon."

"And apparently we'll 'never walk alone,' said Danny. "We're the final group, Shelly, we aren't holding anybody up. You want the bet?"

"And if I refuse? Not that I…"

"Then you still gotta leave us alone," interrupted Danny.

A suppressed-laughter snort escaped Nice Johnson and it caught everyone off guard. It was as if Marcel Marceau suddenly shouted, "Eat me!"

Crusty snapped his head a quarter-turn like a guy who hears a noise in the dark, uncertain whether to believe Nice Johnson really was the oinker. Boozer lost control of a chuckle and it spilled into contagious laughter. His caddie, an acne-scarred beanpole of a kid, tried to hold his laughter in but the effort made his shoulders bounce. Nice Johnson's 40-something caddie looked a little confused but smiled at the sight of the laughing golf people.

Shelly Wilkerson's nostrils flared slightly. "No problem." Shelly said it like he was happy to say it. Then he sped away, no doubt on his way to the 15th.

Crusty said, "You okay, Johnson? What's with that hog noise come out of you?"

"Nice one by Danny," said Nice with an uneasy half-smile.

Boozer spat. "He take the bet or not?" He spat again. Classic bookend technique.

"Don't know, but you can bet he's gonna put the cattle prod to every group on 15." Danny looked pleased. "In any case, maybe it won't be quite as backed up for us when we get there."

Boozer looked at Danny. "You da' man…" Spit. "Sir." Spit. A dry one. Habit.

When the final group got to 15, there was no one on the tee. No doubt due to Shelly's heavy-handed brandishing of his ever-present weaponry: stopwatch, radio handset, and dogma. There was no sign of the group ahead over the rise in the fairway, nor was there a spotter in sight. Two of the three players in that group were riding in a cart and had been moving along well all day. Still, there was always a wait on 15 in tournaments at The Hill Farm.

Danny nonchalantly scanned the periphery and found what he knew he would. Lurking behind their group, some 80 or so yards away and partially shielded by a couple of arborvitaes, was Shelly Wilkerson.

Nice Johnson, the short hitter, had the honors and so there was immediate hitting, no waiting.

Nice teed up his ball and walked behind it as was his routine. When Danny heard the distant sound of a cart, he knew it was Shelly coming to, at minimum, gloat. He kept his head down, waggled his driver, and acted oblivious. The sound of the gas-engine cart engine grew louder. Danny was working on a line for Shelly, something like "Ah, here's our 100 dollar escort now," when he heard Boozer laugh.

Though no more than 80 yards away, Shelly had to travel a serpentine cart path to the 15th tee. Almost the same amount of time it took Paul Williamson, a top player from the La Crosse area playing in the group ahead, to come barreling over the crest of the hill and down the dense forest line to the left of the fairway on his way back to the 15th tee as well. Williamson braked and popped out of the cart. "Lost ball," he grunted. "Sorry." When Shelly came over the rise to the tee area in time to hear Williamson say it, Danny put his hands in the prayer position, flat against the side of his cocked head. Mr. Sleepy Guy, waiting to play. The nostrils flared again as Shelly sized up the situation and roared away in his cart. The group exchanged snickers.

Williamson turned away from his teed up ball. "Something funny about me losin' a ball?"

"Yes and no, Paulie," said Danny. "Tell ya later...but you will not be Shelly's favorite from now on."

"From now on?" Wiliamson smiled. "Funny." Then he smashed his golf ball right down the middle - central standard - where most reloads go when the first tee ball goes all coastal, postal or fugitive. After that, the pace of play picked up and everyone in Danny's group found a rhythm that's all too rare in tournament golf.

And so after three rounds, Danny Moran's lead at nine under par was now six shots over Christian Vanbusikossem, eight over Stuart Johnson and another mini-tour player named Charlie Delsman, both at one under par for the tournament. Delsman had flown back home late the Sunday night before the Open after a fourth place finish at a Hooters mini-tour event in Georgia. Sleep deprived, he had opened with a 78 and had fought his way back to where he could be considered, technically, a contender.

Danny had his usual Hill Farm lunch; a slew of breaded chicken fingers that looked like little first basemen's mitts, all aligned in a row on the plate with an extra helping of The Hill Farm's life-changing honey mustard that, as Danny had long proclaimed, would make junk mail edible. Crusty had the Klement's double bratwurst that he immediately debunned and sliced into coin-like pieces. Then he tossed his sausage currency on a mountainous garden salad and tried to remain calm.

They sat down to eat at a corner table in the clubhouse and said very little. A steady stream of players came up to them with congratulatory comments with a whole lot of "way to go" back slapping that varied in sincerity and decorum. With 18 holes to go, anything could happen. Danny had made up almost as much ground in a couple of his wins over the years, and almost every great player has puked up a big lead at some point in their careers.

Andy Salamone was having lunch at a long table with five others not too far away from Danny and Crusty. He could be heard, loudly and deliberately. "What - you guys forget how Norman spit the bit in the final round at the '96 Masters?!" Then he made a show of looking around the clubhouse before leaning forward as if he were passing on the Da Vinci Code and other things that could only be whispered. The guys at his table were the chronics; cart-driving, bet-making journeymen, Golfing Jesses who tended to gravitate toward each other at tournaments and post-round. Not as well known as Salamone, they nevertheless pleasured in the act of busting his chops about his classic rock hair and faux-gushing over the so-called honor of being invited to sit at his table. At the moment, however, it appeared as if Sally's back-up band was plenty interested in whatever the big man was passing on to them.

Danny looked over at them. "Salamone must've played well the way he's holding court with the boys."

Crusty, chewing, shook his head. "You know what I cannot believe, Dannymo?"

"Huh?"

"That bratwurst salad hasn't caught on." Crusty swallowed. "Don't even need dressing, really."

"Let me have your bun if you're not gonna use it," said Danny. "Make me a chicken finger mini-sub." Clearly satisfied with their culinary improvisations, they reveled in the welcome silence between bursts of premature congratulations.

Heading for the range after lunch, Danny noticed it had warmed up and it felt good on a body that had stiffened from sitting in the air conditioned clubhouse. It was routine these days, the stiffness after a round of golf - or even after an especially enthusiastic Rattler for that matter. As Danny had proven over the years, he hadn't lost much power in his swing, but he gained significant appreciation for the need to loosen up. It wasn't that long ago when the process seemed optional. Now, getting loose was as vital to his game as his spine and its supporting cast.

Getting loose for the fourth round wasn't a priority for Boozer or Nice Johnson. Johnson had spent his time between rounds near the putting green, eating dried fruit and granola bars and working on what had been working for him all day, chipping and putting. Boozer left The Hill Farm for lunch and returned with ketchup on his goatee and carrying a tub-sized paper cup that looked big enough for trout to spawn in. On the side of the tub it said THE ONE TRUE MONSTER MALT!!!

"Me and my caddie are takin' a cart for the final round," he said. Then, after a long burp, he pointed to the tub o' malt, "Still got about a quart left."

The wind remained a factor on the front nine holes for the fourth and final round of the tournament. As anticipated, the temperature continued to rise. The size of the gallery remained small. The Hill Farm was a demanding course to walk and it had a notorious reputation for weird bugs. With the specter of Nimrod and the aura of the interbreeding freaks that once inhabited the land, the place still gave some people the willies... or the "Hillies," as Danny and Mo liked to joke. Some of the Hill Farm regulars actually believed the flies had their ancestral roots in the land itself and that they may have assimilated with the earthy "Hilldren." The feeling being that, when the body-washed, deodorized, shampooed and conditioned golfers along with the herbicide- and fertilizer-friendly grounds crews took over the overgrown land from the unwashed, inbred, cow-humping Hills, the flies simply freaked out from the exposure to their new chemically-treated reality, and these under-the-influence bugs simply went about exacting annual revenge with a seemingly arbitrary plague during certain stretches of the summer.

The first hint that the freak-flies would be showing up *en masse* occurred on the third green and fourth tee, two areas ensconced in trees and protected from the wind. After birdying the second and third holes, though, Danny was momentarily indestructible, willing to swallow a couple dozen of the bastards and spit their stingers out one at a time if necessary. Back-to-back birdies are flat-out dope. A panacea, as some have claimed, for migraines, Machiavellian business practices and even erectile dysfunction according some senior net division competitors providing the birdies are, of course, "natural." Anyway, no way would the alien flies or the mind-numbing pace of play get to him this day. Not with a big lead getting bigger, not with Crusty on his bag, and not with his hair holding up remarkably well in the wind and increasing heat. Despite its ridiculous price, he would remember to sing the praises of designer shampoos with burdock root to Molly after the tournament.

The lead was now seven shots with nine holes to go. Nice Johnson kept making pars with his deft short game. Boozer had dropped a couple shots to par and his slumping body language spelled resignation wrong; he wasn't going to catch Danny Moran. The local papers had focused on how the State Open had been wrenched from Danny Mo's grasp by way of dismal providence and *force majeure* over the years; and that perhaps this would be the year that Overdue Justice would even out the tough luck ledger and that shitty fortunes would finally be proctologically retrieved. Such magical balancing sounded a little like socialism to Danny... good solid golf seemed a safer approach to winning. He'd have to stay focused as Charlie Delsman, the Hooters

Tour vagabond, was playing well in the group ahead and was now in second.

The tenth hole brought about a delay due to crossover logistics – a tradition in tournament golf featuring 36-hole finishes – and a ruling a couple holes ahead of them related to a player hitting the wrong ball. Two players in the same group had marked their balls with one black dot centered above the Titleist logo and got confused. Go figure, thought Danny, might as well include "white, with dimples" as identifying characteristics. In any case the final group was forced to stew for nearly fifteen minutes on the tenth tee.

"Two hours 35 minutes for nine holes in a threesome and we still ain't made the turn." said Boozer. "And the old man's bent out of shape over, what, 75 seconds with us? What time do you have, Mr. Sindorf?" He did not spit.

Crusty checked his watch. "4:15, Master Christian."

"Daylight's burning," said Boozer. "Don't want Nimrod jumping out of the dark on the forest holes. I usually piss in the forest on 15, see if he's around." Laugh, spit, laugh, spit.

Crusty looked at the kid and remained expressionless.

Danny was preoccupied with staying loose and fending off some of the flies that seemed fixated on his hair. He wondered if it was the fragrance that seemed to attract them. The heat was beginning to intensify as the wind died down. The forecasted front had finally arrived and seemed ready to impose its will on the final nine holes of the Wisconsin State Open.

When it was time for the final group to begin their final nine, a small bird appeared out of nowhere and hopped on to the tee box. It came unusually close to Danny before it stopped and peered up at him. Danny noticed the bird's big eyes: kind of vulnerable, or afraid. Not that he had a clue about that stuff since he wasn't exactly a naturalist, but for moment a feeling of sadness hung in the air. Danny stepped up to his teed-up ball, but before he began his swing, the bird suddenly elevated, suspending itself, hummingbird like, though it was too round to be a hummingbird. The rapid flapping seemed like equal parts labor and grace and the bird used this action to land on Danny's right shoe. Again the thing looked up at Danny. Reflexively, Danny softly moved his foot as if to shoo it away, let it get back to its comfortable suburban digs, but the bird tumbled awkwardly toward the rocks that horseshoed the slightly elevated 10th tee box. It righted itself and hopped to a stop, took two more tiny hops, then turned around and looked at Danny still again. Then the bird took a grasshopper-like flying hop over the rocks toward an area of tall grasses, small trees and bushes. Gone.

He looked around; most of the gallery had gotten a head start and were already down the fairway or near the green. "That was weird," he said.

"I'm afraid that bird isn't long for this world," said Crusty.

"The proverbial broken sparrow," said Danny, who had no idea if it was a sparrow or some other kind of small bird with wings and feathers. "Defying Darwin."

"For now," said Boozer.

"That bird was hung up on you Dannymo," said Crusty.

"What could I do?" Danny felt foolish talking about it. "I have no problem if it wanted to follow us on the back. But it can't hitch a ride on my shoes."

"Owl snack," said the caddie for Nice Johnson. He had been introduced as Clell, Stuart Johnson's half-brother. Also a quiet sort who had made it clear right off the bat that he didn't know the first thing about golf. "Just here to carry Stuey's tools and stay out of the way" he had said. Clell looked like the type who might know what owls eat.

After a brief moment of silence, Danny shook his head and then swatted at some flies near his head. Everyone backed away from the tee markers and Danny went through his pre-shot routine. The sun was bringing an intensity it had not shown for the last three days, and the clouds had bunched into continental bodies of bright white and deep gray and made the remaining sky look bluer than before. Danny shook off the incident with the little bird, wiped his right hand on his right buttock, and slapped a thin, heal-job tee ball that nevertheless found the fairway.

"Catcher in the Rye?" asked Crusty, winking. "It'll work." The trusty caddie put his head down and bolted ahead of Danny, showing he was either focused on the task at hand or looking to put some distance between him and the flies drawn to Danny's burdock-leavened hair.

Danny missed the green just right, misread the lie, fluffed a chip onto the green but well short of the hole before falling into a state of otherness and somehow rolling a 14-foot putt that plopped in for par on the last roll. It was embarrassing, but he got over it.

"One of those 'not-a-single-decent-shot' pars," said Danny. "Never happens when you need one."

"Don't think you need much of anything at this point," said Boozer as they walked off the 10th green. He spat once, but only after making sure he was completely off the green, having had his chops busted for such a violation earlier by Crusty.

"Not that I'm paranoid…" Danny flicked his hands over and around his head, "…but they do seem to be picking on me."

"You are the chosen one," said Boozer. "But then…you're Danny Mo." Danny sensed there was a hint of something else behind the kid's smile.

Danny dug into his golf bag on the move as Crusty resumed his stride up to the 11th tee. He pulled out the little green bottle with the military-grade plant extract/rhino dung potion as Crusty put down the bag. "Is it time?"

Danny opened the bottle and his face twisted up. He gave it back to Crusty.

"Bugs are gettin' bad…for everyone…and this here shit…" Crusty looked down at the bottle and then at Danny, "…big advantage."

"They're supposed to get worse closer to sunset," said Danny, like a guy thinking out loud.

"Oh it's gonna get worse," said Nice Johnson's half-brother caddie, Clell, a rural looking guy, and a guy who looked like he would also know the behavior of mutant flies as well as what owls snack on. "Soon enough."

Everyone looked at Clell. He was looking into the forested yonder, oblivious. Danny thought the guy might be tuning his brain to the insect wavelength after logging off on the bird frequency. Kind of fascinating, thought Danny. Kind of.

Danny Mo set it all aside and quickly played a stock seven-iron to a back left pin on the uphill par three 11th. Despite it being a back left pin, Danny played his trademark butter cut. He wanted to let his ball drift safely to the middle of the green, but he pulled it. Just a little. The ball was laboring, trying to work to the right and toward the pin. To help it, Danny made a couple of crossover steps to the left as he tracked his ball, as if the movement of his body could influence his ball to move right. But it was all out of his hands.

His ball landed just over a deep revetment bunker -- known locally as the Hotel California ("you can check in anytime you like, but...") -- that guarded the left side of the green, popped up and appeared to stop on an isthmus of sorts between the bunker and the green. The spectators standing nearby sagged slightly. Danny assumed immediately that his ball was held up only by the longer untrimmed grass lining and overhanging the cavernous bunker. After Johnson and Boozer played serviceable shots to 20 and 30 feet respectively, Danny uncharacteristically charged up the hill to the green to check out his lie.

He slowed as he got within twenty feet of his ball. It was as he feared. Because of the angle of the bunker, he had no place to stand in order to play his next shot. He looked at Crusty. "What would you do here, Crust?"

"Me...I'd backhand it with a putter." Crusty shrugged. "Just block it on."

Danny slapped at some flies that weren't there just to feel a little more persecuted. "Not a bad idea. I'm leaning toward goin' lefty with a flipped over Lazarus. He pulled his sand wedge from his bag. "Little bump and run."

"What I'd do if I was you," said Crusty.

Standing over the ball, Danny felt a little lost. He was uncomfortably warm now. His final round outfit, the freshly laundered black shirt and dark olive slacks felt heavy on him, a little different, kind of slimy. He took an awkward stance on the left side, glove on the low hand now. For some reason the flies had momentarily backed off. Perhaps they were regrouping, saving their energy for a later attack when they could mess up an easier shot.

He delivered a wristy little chop at the ball and caught it flush, about right for weight but a little left of his aim. He had wanted to play safely right of the hole, but his ball, at the mercy of the sandy soil, clumpy grass and the laws of gravity hopped left in the direction of the flagstick, but was losing steam fast. In what seemed like slow-motion, the ball bobbled along the ledge of the bunker, little hops becoming bobbles then a roll. Danny attempted to will the ball onto the green with the body language lean of The Heisman Trophy…until…he…lost…his balance and found himself airborne. Athlete that he was, he spun in mid-air to face the green and stuck the landing in the bunker with Lazarus held horizontal across his chest rifle-drill style. With the sand nearly seven feet below his take-off, it was jarring. Danny allowed a big knee bend and a hop-step, but before he could designate his recovery top-five worldwide, he saw his ball land in the bunker right after he did, some 20 feet ahead and about a yard from the deep face. Because the pin was back left, he wasn't dead, he had an angle at it, a little something to work with. It was good bad news.

Crusty raised both arms in triumph ala Bela Karolyi. Boozer and Johnson rushed over to take a look. Danny casually walked to his ball, took a quick stance and waggled Lazarus. He felt warm, like he was rushing things, and decided he better walk up the slope to the green, size up the shot. He felt a twinge in his back when he took on the incline, put it out of his mind, but felt it again heading back down to the bunker. Danny was working up a good sweat after hustling up to the green from the tee and then again from the bunker. Again he felt like his clothes had taken on some added weight. He took his stance, opened the face of Lazarus wide, risky wide, and made an aggressive swing that took but a sliver of sand. The ball popped up and tugged to a near stop after two hops before trickling out. And though he, as they say, "tore the legs off the ball," he left it two feet from the hole.

Boozer proceeded to miss a three-footer for par and uttered "Stick a fuckin' fork in me," the chorus of the quitters' national anthem. Danny felt a quick spasm from bending over to attempt his two-footer, then backed away, stood up straight, then back down to find where it hurt least, and knocked it in to save bogey. Nice Johnson, who had never won a championship, but committed doggedly to every shot, watched Danny with admiration. "Nice work, Danny," he said louder than usual.

Danny busted his tee shot on number 12 despite his concerns about his back. It had hurt crouching over the two-footer for bogey more than from the act of belting the tee shot. Not unprecedented, he decided, backs were funny. The flies did regroup with some seemingly choreographed chaos as Danny stood over a simple eight-iron shot from the first cut just off the 12th fairway. The tension in his grip and forearms increased slightly and the ball came out hot, settling at the back of the green. Danny was closer still to calling upon the rhino dung.

Setting up to putt, his lower back reprised the spasm thing again. Danny muffled a chuck. Putting? He found that bending way over felt the least bad. Holding his putter with his right hand on the metal of the shaft, he lagged his 50-footer to a foot. He looked funny doing it but with a six shot lead with six holes to go, looking funny was fine.

Danny's back held up through a solid butter-cut tee shot on 13, but he felt lucky; his right hand had started to perspire even more. No commercially available chemical, lotion, or powder, nor any amount of toweling or repeated swipes against his slacks had ever prevented Danny from the feeling that his right palm was what he called "beading." Like the glass coasters on their nightstands, once the waterworks began, it not only wasn't going away, it generally got inside his head.

Walking down the 13th fairway, Danny recalled playing in 90-plus heat and humidity at Nagawaukee Golf course in the State Public Links Championship several years earlier. He had been tied for the lead with Tom Halla, a local legend from the Waukesha County village of Lannon and known to some as The Lannon Cannon, with five holes to go when the beading got so bad his right hand became a five-finger faucet. The heat was oppressive in the still air on the 14th tee that day and there were two groups backed up on the reachable downhill par five. The tee box there sits atop a large hill with a spectacular view of the tree-lined fairway and the shimmering blue of Pewaukee Lake in the distance. Danny's dad, Larry "Curly" Moran called the autumn view from 14th tee at "The Nag" the most postcard perfect vista in Wisconsin golf.

Then, and to this day, Danny carried some of his dad's ashes in a small vial in his golf bag since he died seven years ago, and he always made sure to sprinkle a pinch of his pop on various holes at all his favorite courses. With help from some of Danny's friends serving as benevolent operatives, Larry Moran had also been scattered over many famous courses around the world. Augusta, Pebble Beach, St. Andrews, Pinehurst, Merion, and Whistling Straits were just some of the hallowed grounds his dad never got to see in life, but had since become a part of as his ashes found their way to various resting places around the world.

On that hot day in the final round at The Nag, Danny quietly pulled his dad from his golf bag and attempted to sprinkle a bit of him on the 14th tee. He had done so on the day before too, but for the final round, the rarely used "back-back-black" tees had been put into play. This time, however, Danny's dad wouldn't come out of the vial. Could have been the humidity, Danny wasn't sure, but he gave a little tap to the vial and then a whole bunch of Curly Mo came gushing out and into his sweaty right hand. Danny couldn't shake his dad completely off his hand, so he just kind of used him as rosin, like a baseball player. And why not, Curly Moran was a semi-pro baseball legend, a third-baseman, the Brooks Robinson of the Wisconsin baseball scene. Danny went on to birdie three of the next four holes and won the tournament.

He had used his dad as a drying agent a few more times after that when the heat was on. Danny didn't care what others thought, but kept it quiet nevertheless. "Just my dad giving me hand," was how he rationalized it to himself - and to Crusty, Carter Slane, and Mo Mo. Not that his dad's ashes always led him to victory, but they always helped him get a grip on things. Like always.

And it was his dad's willingness to offer a helping hand – to his family, or anyone who needed one – that was the theme of the eulogy Danny had given at Curly's funeral. It had taken just over four months -

diagnosis to death – for Lawrence Moran, and watching how the cancer destroyed such a powerful and athletic man so quickly put Danny in as much pain as he had ever known. Still, there was never any doubt that he'd speak at the prayer service the night before the funeral mass. In contrast to his commitment to pre-tournament practice, preparing remarks for anything was never Danny's style. He had gone to the lectern amidst the silence and the sniffles with no notes and uncertain of how to even begin; a million thoughts clamoring to be the one sentence to break the dam. He looked at everyone, no one in particular, and took a deep breath. To his surprise, he opened with a statement that came from who knows where.

"There have been better baseball players than my dad, the Major Leagues are loaded with incredible talents, but I don't care where you go in this world," he said a little shakily, "I would wager with anyone...that my dad was the single finest pepper player in the history of baseball."

Danny continued, "With the bat in his hands, he never missed. You could throw the ball over his head or in the dirt or way outside or right at him...it didn't matter. He'd reach out with one hand on the bat, or up high, or go down for the short-hop off the grass and he'd always slap it right back. He might've popped one up or fouled one off on a terrible pitch, but he never, ever, missed. If he did, I never saw it."

He went on to talk of the vacations they took as a family at a cottage 40 miles from home. How they stayed close enough to home so they could drive back and Danny and his brothers wouldn't miss their little league games. You didn't miss games; you were there for your team. He spoke of how he and his brothers would play their pepper games behind the cottages, and how his dad would reward them with ice cream at the snack stand for catching 25 in a row, two scoops for 50 in a row. All the time, every time, Curly tapped it back, never missing, and at the same time teaching his kids not to miss either, their ballgames or groundballs. And a lot more.

"My dad went years without missing a day of work doing a tough job he didn't care for," said Danny, "but someone had to fix the power lines. And he never turned down the overtime, which the company always seemed to need, sometimes going months without a day off. He didn't do it out of loyalty to the company; he did it for the time and a half and double-time pay, to provide for his family, so his kids wouldn't miss out on the opportunity to be all we could be... so that we wouldn't have to fix power lines someday -- climbing poles, and towers, and crawling into dark places. 'Be more than me,' he'd say." Danny paused after that, regrouped and said, "We'll...I'd be proud to be half the man my dad was."

The grief had made him repetitious, almost as if this was his last chance -- unreasonable as it was -- to tell his dad the things he should have said when he was alive. As if somehow God lets all good people listen in at their own funerals. He went on for almost 20 minutes. But the theme was clear. Curly Mo didn't miss anything. The list was endless: ballgames, birthdays, recitals, Sunday Mass and the steal sign. And Packer games, "unless he was working," and "the catcher - if he dared to block the plate with Curly coming hard."

Danny came to the finish. "But I keep looking back at those pepper games we played, thinking how my dad never missed. And how it foretold before I could fully understand, just who Larry Moran was, the kind of man he was. The man I came to know best as I too became a man. He was, simply, the man who never missed – that's it." But that wasn't it. "Most of all, Curly Mo never missed a chance to help his family. Or his friends, or the friends of friends...people he never knew. He was the king of never missing, and he never missed what mattered most."

It had been a montage of sights and sounds for Danny that evening, and so it remained for the days that followed. But what he had said that day with the assembled mourners, he said to the ones who already knew precisely what the son was saying about his father. The son looked at his mother, Amanda, her head held high, comforted completely through her faith, the one who Curly had always called "the strongest Mo of all."

Danny had blinked back tears. "We are people of faith, and we know Curly Moran is doing fine now, his soul is safe with God...but the man who never missed a single chance to lend a hand to all of us, and I can honestly tell you, when I think of all the crazy little sayings my dad had, the one phrase I heard as much as any of them, was a simple one,

one not so crazy. It was actually a question, but really, more of a statement. It was simply this…'Need a hand?'…that's it. 'Need a hand?' And what good hands they were. The hands of the man who never missed. So, today, it seems somehow profound when I think about how much that man is gonna be missed…" Danny then walked away from the microphone but repeated it aloud and then to himself "…and missed, and missed, and missed…" As Danny left the lectern, the friends and relatives of the Morans broke into spontaneous applause, an ovation that Danny joined as he turned and faced the easel holding the large photo of his beaming father; one last hand, if you will, for the man who was willing to lend one, any time, any place.

∞

Danny and a flock of the freaky flies reached his ball on the fairway on 13 and had to wait on the group ahead. Delsman had holed a 30-footer for what Danny believed was a birdie. He looked at Crusty who was keeping more distance between them as the day went on. There was no longer any doubt that Danny was the flies' object of desire.

"Keeping your distance, aren't ya Crust?"

"Not at all, Dannymo…you are no more the lord of the flies as anyone else, I'm right here with you. You want the rhino shit?"

"No. I want something else." Danny went into his bag and pulled out the vial containing his dad's ashes. "My right hand is beading."

"Why not," said Crusty. "Curly'd wanna be part of this."

"Oh, he is." Danny said quietly, as if to himself. "Always."

With his dad in hand and his grip feeling much better, and with the thought of his daughter saying "butter-cut," Danny played a beautiful looking nine-iron from 144 yards. He posed, pleased; his finish in perfect balance as he watched his ball cover the flag. Until it disappeared over the green.

"That's couch and crown…impossible!" Danny quickly looked at the bottom of his club to confirm what he already knew. Nine iron. He handed the club to Crusty and then rapidly waved his hands in all directions near his head like a silly fellow fending off a pillow attack from a gay flirt.

"Bad time to flush one Dannymo," said Crusty. "Let's go find it."

Danny found his ball directly behind a tree that was three inches in diameter. He summoned Bill Linneman, the scorer and rules official for the final group, to determine if he got any relief from such a "young and impressionable tree."

After Linneman said, "Sorry Danny," Danny proceeded to chip his ball onto the green, but 50 feet away from the cup. Bending up and down to find some comfort, Danny bent way over again and managed to again look funny, but three-putting is rarely funny, which he did. Danny's six shot lead at the start of the hole was now down to three ahead of Delsman.

Danny short-sided himself with his approach on the 14th -- and chunk-chipped it from some clingy rough, right into the cup. His ball would have gone at least 20 feet by the hole had it not hit the pin. Birdie. Right on top of a Delsman bogey. The flies rioted with impunity, clipping his head from behind after the chip-in. This time the birdie-fueled force field of invincibility buckled and Danny grunted the word "die." His lead was back to five going to the 15th hole, and with Delsman's group still waiting on the tee…Danny decided the time had come.

"Gimmee that bottle of yours," he said "They've called for backup. Molly's shampoo ain't helping. Looking this good just isn't worth it. Not here, not now."

Crusty had the green plastic bottle in his hand, having sized up the situation following the chip-in. "Here." Crusty looked directly into Danny's eyes. "Dannymo, listen to me. The first 30 seconds you're gonna feel like you might puke. You get through those 30 seconds, you'll be fine. The stuff works."

They went up a hill on the cart path to an area next to a red brick building with restrooms and some beverage vending machines about 70 yards from the 15th tee. Danny went into his golf bag and pulled out a tube of sunscreen and squirted a pile in his left hand. Then he poured the eye-stinging plant and rhino extract on top of the suntan lotion. Crusty's potion was a brownish lotion with chunks of something he didn't want to think of. Danny was proud of his idea to add sunscreen to mask the odor, but it was about as effective as a drop of Old Spice in a loaded barf bag. The smell was shocking at first, but slightly familiar, too. Danny was in survival mode now, his focus was all about overcoming the flies and his beading hand and capturing the elusive Open title. He rubbed has hands together and quickly slathered it over his face and neck and arms. And then he whipped up another batch of coconut and crap and ran it through his previously luxurious hair. The stinky stuff still stunk enough to make Danny a bit nauseous and perspire even more. But he withstood the assault of its first wave and bobbled his head like a boxer who survived a couple good shots in the early rounds and was now ready to get it on.

Danny and Crusty sat on the benches by the restroom, happy to have the temporary solace. "Tell me, Crust, how's my hair?"

"It's bad, I can't lie. But without the distraction of its TV news anchor perfection it sorta brings out your eyes." Crusty did not smile. "But, uh...Dannymo?"

"Yeah?"

"Between you and me..."

Danny waited.

"Your hair is bad, you smell like shit, and now you've got your dad all over your face."

Danny laughed in resignation. "Well, guess what. Break out the other vial because all this lotiony stuff's made my hands slimy."

Crusty pointed at the bag. "It's your bag; and he's your dad."

Danny got up from the bench, grimaced, wiped his hands on the grass and his bag towel, and retrieved Curly from his bag. He poured a healthy portion of his remains on his hands and rubbed them together.

"Dannymo, I know you loved your pa, but..."

"Look..." interrupted Danny, pointing toward the fairway of the 18th hole. It was a couple hundred yards to the side and behind them, but they could see it from their perch on the hill. Carter Slane was walking down the fairway as Andy Salamone rode alongside him in a cart. Sally appeared to be talking non-stop. They both had dryer sheets sticking out from their hats and back pockets, as did dozens of other players, using them to fend off The Hill Farm flies. "Poor Carter...Salamone got a lot to say today, huh?"

"Who gives a shit," said Crusty, reflexively. "Not Carter, that's for sure."

"Do I still smell like shit?"

"See...you're getting used to it already," said Crusty. "Noticed something else, though. When you pointed. Lift your arm again."

Danny lifted his arm. "Your arm pit is foaming." Crusty almost smiled. "I thought I noticed something earlier. Lift your other arm."

Danny lifted both his arms higher and looked at his pits. They were covered with white foam, like dish soap or shampoo lather. "What the..." Danny looked at Crusty, his mind working. "Ah, I think... I'll bet... Last night, after I dropped you off, I bought some detergent with fabric softener and washed the clothes I'm wearing. I mean, I'm not sure those fabric softener sheets really work, but...the detergent's got some of the same chemicals. Thought it couldn't hurt, maybe turn out to be a brilliant strategy. I knew the stuff was concentrated, but I think I might've poured it on a little heavy. Could've messed up the rinse cycle or something too when I set it. You know...I wondered why when it got warmer...why my shirt felt so slimy, and heavy, and when I wiped my hand on my pants it felt kind of slippery too. Molly usually handles the wash." *But I fold and sort.*

"Don't take this the wrong way Dannymo, but..." Crusty grabbed the sweaty placket of Danny's shirt near his chest and rubbed his hand back and forth. The action worked up more suds and its whiteness was conspicuous against his black golf shirt. Crusty laughed, "I think I could shave with that."

Danny laughed out loud. No chuck. Big, hearty laughs. Crusty laughed louder now, too. Two older gentlemen wearing shorts and sneakers with high white socks had come by to use the restroom so Danny quickly put his face in his hands to smother his laughter. When he looked up, Crusty was laughing even harder. He could only point at Danny's face.

"Your face…" Crusty was almost doubled over. "…now it's really covered with Curly. I mean, you black, brotha."

Danny was laughing so hard it took a moment before he was able to get out, "What better war paint is there, Crust…than The Main Mo? Huh?" Danny started calling his dad "The Main Mo" when he was a groovy teenager. It stuck because Curly enjoyed using it himself. Danny and Crusty laughed until it seemed possible they might swallow some of the airborne bugs, and trying to stay quiet just made it worse. When they had finally regrouped, they each popped a couple Advils before easing their way down to the 15th tee.

Danny chucked. "Damn, Crust, my belt's pumpin' Barbasol…the hell, I know the stuff was concentrated but…"

"Well it's time to get over it, Bubble Boy," said Crusty with a laugh. Then he turned serious and picked up Danny's bag. "Now we go."

The 15th hole is a par five that can be reached in two with a tee shot that carries or bounds over the crest of a hill and avoids the forest on the left. It requires a risky shot off a downhill lie over a crossing river gulch some 30 yards wide and maybe another 30 yards short of the green called E-Kah-Tah Creekway and 25 yards in front of the green. The E-Kah-Tah empties into the much larger O-Kah-Tah River which runs parallel to the entire length of 15th fairway, about 40 yards to the right of the cart path. The area between the cart path and the O-Kah-Tah River is partially wooded with smaller trees and strips of bushes breaking up some spotty but playable rough. A stretch of high natural grasses guards the remaining territory leading to the river bank and where only the most improbable slices go to die.

With a five shot lead and four holes to go, Danny decided to hit a three-wood off the tee and then lay up short of the gulch from a level lie. He wasn't crazy about his current three-wood, but every time he considered replacing it, he'd pull off a shot that suggested the problem wasn't the club. Still, he didn't love it like he should and pulled his tee-shot into left rough, short of the crest, and close enough to the forest that Nimrod was likely to be either tempted or repulsed by how Danny smelled now. Danny loved talking like Nimrod Hill was real and rather amused that there were those who believed the man-beast existed. Of course, those people would no doubt be amused by Danny's blackened face and his attempt to take on conspiratorial flies with soap suds and an unseemly concoction of Tanzanian byproducts.

Danny selected a six-iron to lay up short of the river. Holding on a little too firmly to the club, he caught a flyer that strayed more right than he wanted. His ball would be in the rough, but, provided it missed the cart path, not in danger of reaching the trees and bushes. Boozer went for the green in two, fanned it into the gulch, and then glared at Danny, scrunching his face as if the assault on his sense of smell contributed to his whiff. "You smell like shit," he said.

"Might be that shot you just hit your smellin'," said Crusty, not missing a beat.

Danny and Crusty, Boozer and the beanpole, Nice and Clell, and Bill Linneman and his walkie-talkie headed to the area where Danny's ball was expected to be. It wasn't immediately visible, but neither was there much immediate concern. Most of the spectators had gone up ahead to the far side of the green to watch Delsman and then wait for the final group. The rest of the small gallery had remained behind with Danny. The confluence of events left no one in a position to see Danny's shot land, though Boozer would have been in good position had he gone straight to his perfectly struck tee ball. He didn't. He and his caddie had carted off to the edge of the forest so the Boozer could, as promised, relieve himself, proudly, in defiance of Nimrod. With Danny playing it safe and plenty of room right, it really shouldn't have been a problem.

But golf is full of problems that shouldn't be. Danny and Crusty began to grow more anxious the longer Danny's ball remained out of sight. It simply wasn't where it should have been, where it had to be. Crusty was incredulous that someone associated with the PGA section wasn't there to spot, as there had been for the first three rounds. Linneman, WSGA Director of Rules and Competition, was informed by radio that the spotter on 15 had been driven batty by the insects and Shelly Wilkerson was supposed to have replaced him.

Danny and Crusty were at a loss. They came to believe…well, they didn't know what to believe. The five minute clock was running. Boozer wandered around casually, mostly looking straight ahead and holding his nose, not enough neck swiveling to suit Crusty. After watching him drift apathetically in the general area for another 20 seconds, Crusty, his voice dripping with seethe, said, "You might as well get in your cart and go take your drop, kid cuz you ain't gonna find shit."

"Sure." Dry spit, dry spit. "Whatever you say," said Boozer, and he and his pipe-cleaner caddie went ahead toward the drop area that was near the E-Kah-Tah Creekway some 40 yards away. Crusty's attempt to motivate Boozer backfired in one sense, but the kid going up ahead to take his drop and play his shot would provide a little pace of play PR.

That's when the earth reversed its rotation and Nice Johnson took charge. "Alright, we still have two minutes. Clell, you check the other side of the creek and see if Danny's ball hit the cart path and kicked forward left, maybe it ran across the bridge. Danny – let's go check the bushes by the river. Could have hit something or kicked funny. Crusty…check back along the path, could have hit the path and off one of those trees."

Crusty and Danny looked at each other. Neither had ever heard Nice Johnson say that many consecutive sentences on a golf course.

"No way it went over the river," said Danny. "Not like it was hooking back."

Crusty nodded in agreement.

Nice Johnson shrugged. "One crack in the asphalt, or a stone…"

"Best I check," said Clell.

"What the hell do we know," said Crusty, his eyes darting everywhere.

Danny would have been touched by whatever had come over Nice if he hadn't been couch and crown edgy at the moment. Where the hell… It didn't make sense. Competitive golf was all about so many unsolved mysteries, and disappearing balls would be the fattest chapter. Maybe Shelly took it; he was supposed to be spotting, wasn't he? Maybe he wasn't late after all…or maybe he was just living up to terms of their bet.

Nice and Danny Mo found a few balls that weren't his. They each went separate ways on narrow paths that led to the rushing river some 20 feet below them. Nice Johnson was bobbing past branches and weaving around trees and fighting through the brush for every ball he saw in order to identify it. The man was committed. Danny could not believe the turn of events. The 15th at The Hill Farm -- of all holes. The flies, and now mosquitoes and a few bees, were all around and banging into him like bugs fooled by a window. Even if he found his ball here, it wasn't gonna be good. As usual, they had checked all the areas that wouldn't be disastrous first, but…nothing. Danny felt like the temperature had gone up 10 degrees.

They were nearing their final half minute before the ball would be deemed as lost when Hillbilly Clell yelled back to the group. "Got 'er! I think…a little scuffed she is, but I think I got 'er." And sure enough, he did. Crusty went ahead to verify. As Nice had suggested, Danny's ball had to have hit the asphalt path and scooted across the river on the E-Kah-Tah Bridge, just a short pitch from right of the green. Danny's metabolism quickly regulated and he immediately designated Nice and Clell as honorary Mos for life.

Then, Nice Johnson suddenly cried out. "Danny…come here." He sounded panicked. "Danny! Ahh…damn."

He was 30 yards away, concealed by the woods and bushes. Danny, drunk on the euphoria of a found ball in big tournament at a key moment, took off like a farm boy after a runaway calf, hurdling underbrush and then plowing through some bushes and other greenery until he got closer to his new best buddy, the little guy who solved an investigation he wouldn't have. Danny saw him through some natural grasses that were shoulder high to Nice. Nice looked different.

"Danny, I lost my glasses. I was squeezing through these branches and one of 'em snapped back in my face. I can't see…gotta find 'em."

"I'll find 'em," said Danny. "I owe you one, buddy."

Just then Bill Linneman yelled, redundantly, that Danny's ball was up ahead. That Johnson's caddie found it.

"Hang on Billy, we got a problem." Linneman didn't respond -- he was probably in mid-drag on still another cigarette. Danny circled around a clumpy island of tall grass and a couple of bushes near the river bank and worked his way toward Nice.

"Careful Danny, my glasses have no rims, they're hard to see…they're almost invisible. We may never find them."

"Did you hear them land?" Danny asked. "Could the glasses be stuck on a branch?"

"I don't know, one of these branches over here," he pointed, "hit my face and they were gone. I'm blind as a bat without them."

"What's going on?" It was Linneman, trying to get through the brush.

"Stu lost his glasses," said Danny, over his shoulder.

In the congested parts of the vegetation, the heat was stifling. Any moving air was created by humans and bugs. Danny felt the fervor of the flies, probably because they had the humans where they wanted them now, in their lair. Danny was almost to Nice Johnson, who was tentatively moving about with his hands forward, feeling for branches and the like. Without his glasses, Nice looked like he had Sharpie dots for eyes.

Boozer yelled from his position in the fairway ahead. He somehow thought it useful to paraphrase what Clell and Linneman had already yelled. "We found the damn ball! It rolled across the bridge." He had no clue as to the delay.

Crusty, from somewhere unseen, yelled back. "Hey Boozer…shut the hell up for the rest of today…okay?"

No reply.

Linneman was fairly close but sealed off from Danny. "Ah, Danny, we really do need to keep moving. The group ahead is long gone. Shelly's gonna raise holy hell."

"No -- he's not," said Danny as he stepped over a stump. "We get five minutes to find a lost ball, don't we; shouldn't we get at least that to find someone's eyeglasses?" Danny had no idea if that was true, but it felt right. The thrum of the river current reminded him of how fast and powerful the O-Kah-Tah actually was.

"It could be argued as undue delay," said Linneman, unconvincingly, as if to no one. "Rule 6-7." Billy Linneman knew the rules of golf better than whatever trick a one trick pony knows.

Suddenly Johnson let out a yelp that cut through the water's roar. In that moment, born of some inexplicable instinct, Danny reached for him just as Nice stumbled over a fieldstone he obviously couldn't see. His tumble took him to the steep bank that descended to the O-Kah-Tah River rumbling with purpose 20 feet below. Stuart Johnson's desperation grasp on the tall grass gave way just as Danny caught hold of his forearm.

Danny held on with all his might, but down low, in the heat of a confined area walled off by bushes, his hand had become moist again and the act of grasping Johnson's perspiring forearm made his grip slick. Nice Johnson had a slight build, but even at probably 150 pounds it was enough for Danny to feel him slipping away. The flies joined the party by banging against Danny's face and head and then flying away, either to pass the baton or do it all over again.

Danny saw a flash of fear in Nice Johnson's now tiny looking eyes; he too sensed there were mere seconds before he'd go tumbling into the river. Nice kicked for some footing on the dirt bank, but it was crumbling away and useless. Danny sensed Nice couldn't swim, and willed himself to pull harder. He was pretty sure that plunging blind into a river from 20 feet in the final round of a golf tournament wasn't what the little engineer had in mind when he took command of the reconnaissance mission to find Danny's ball.

Danny's arm was now taut with tension, painfully so. His back was spasming something fierce. He pulled – convincing himself that he would be top-five worldwide, over 40, sweaty-hand division - but the pulling only made for more slithering. It didn't help that Nice was trying to grasp Danny's forearm at the same time, making it wriggle. "Relax your arm Stu…let your hand relax!"

Danny was willing his prone body to somehow anchor itself into the earth, but he knew it was a matter of seconds before he'd lose him, and worse, he'd have no choice but to scramble after him in the river. Maybe if he could reach down with his other hand; his gloved hand, he could do something. But just as he felt Nice sliding another inch through his right hand, Danny felt another body come crashing through the foliage and another hand appeared. The new hand clamped on to Nice Johnson just below where Danny's hand had been. Danny felt his load lighten and together, the two hands pulled Nice Johnson to safety and plopped him next to the rock that tripped him up. As Danny had sensed, the other hand belonged to Boozer, who, coming from further down the fairway had a clearer and more direct path to where they were. He had arrived just ahead of Crusty.

"I knew something had to be up," said Boozer. Spit, a blank. "Not that I expected a scene from Indiana Jones."

They took a few seconds to catch their breath. Danny slowly got to his feet and tested his back. "Let's get the hell out of here," said Crusty.

Nice Johnson was still a little shaken and just laid atop the tall grass next to the woods and bushes. "I can't finish without my glasses," he said quietly. "We have to find them or I'll have to DQ myself."

"We gotta look for Nice's glasses." Danny said it, and meant it, but couldn't believe he was in this position. His back was yelping in pain. It wasn't good.

"Mr. Moran," said Boozer, "with all due respect…"

"I know. I stink."

"Yes, that too, but you look like you just went through a car wash…without the car."

Danny looked down, his shirt and now his slacks were more white than dark; the suds were taking over. The increased perspiration and all the friction with the ground and with the bushes and branches had turned Danny's shirt into some kind of special effect.

"It's a long story, Booze," said Danny. "Thanks for the hand."

"Yeah…thanks guys." Nice was lying on his back and talking to the sky. Then, as he rolled on to his side he said "But I gotta find 'em."

Linneman had finally arrived at the bank ledge and had no idea what to do. So he lit up a cigarette. His radio crackled and he pulled it from his belt, held it to his mouth and said, "Uh...I'll get back to you."

Nice Johnson was back to the search, crawling on all fours, but it was pointless. Crusty cleared his throat, and with his eyes directed Danny to where Nice had been laying. Boozer and Linneman noticed as well. Nice Johnson's glasses were a little easier to see with one lens cracked and veining in all directions.

"Stuart," said Danny as he picked the glasses up from an area of flattened brown and green natural grass. "We've got your glasses."

"What's wrong?" Nice was blinking at the group like he would be clear on everything if he kept it up. "Are they busted?"

"They're busted," said Crusty. "Half busted anyway."

Danny put them in Nice Johnson's hand. He put them on.

"I think I rolled on them trying to keep you from the piranhas," said Danny.

Nice said nothing. It was obvious he could see nothing without tilting his head to use the one working lens most effectively. One cracked lens had a way of making a guy look younger and more helpless than he was. Harry Potter after a clash with Voldemort's henchmen.

"Let's go," said Nice.

And so Crusty led the group single file through the high grass and huddled trees and bushes as they hurried back to the industrialized world. Danny trailed behind and could see from the way Nice Johnson was stumble-bumping into things that Harry Potter was screwed. And from what he could hear coming over on Linneman's radio, Delsman must have eagled the 15th and an official sounded absurdly confused trying to explain the riverside events over the radio. And he could feel his back throwing a tantrum inside his sticky soapy shirt. And his own nose was telling him that he smelled bad enough to be fairly glad his shirt was soaping up with every step. And when he went to tuck in his shirt and found enough suds for a good start on a sink-full of dishes he had to chuck. His lead was three shots now, with four and a half holes to go. Danny Moran heard Crusty Sindorf's words in his head. "Now we go."

∞

Chapter 23

Crusty stopped, let the clubs drop, and turned back to check on Danny who was dragging his richly lathered ass with unusual delicacy as he brought up the rear. After escaping the mother of all golf ball cluster-hunts, and after surviving bug-infested natural grasses and deciduous trees with spring-loaded branches and a river bank that fell steeply to the inexorable current of The O-Kah-Tah, both men were relieved to return to a civilization more closely mown.

Crusty stood on the cart path and studied the movements of his good friend who, at the moment, was leading the Wisconsin State Open by three shots. Danny Moran walked evenly with his head held high despite the suds and soapy residue that clung to his shirt, and his dung-moussed hair that horned out and down like a jester's starter cap.

"You're hurtin' aren't ya?" said Crusty. "You're smooth walkin'."

"Ah, smooth walking..." said Danny,"...sure"

"Your shoulders ain't rollin' like usual, and your ass -- hell it's...I don't know, more low key." Crusty face was stone. He knew how to keep Danny loose. "You're movin' more like a nervous groom than some African cat."

"My buttocks are like molded boulders, as if sculpted by some ancient Greek dude, and you, Crusty, can kiss my Irish arse." Danny words trailed off as he squinted hard at something ahead.

"All the same, I'm not seeing the heaving, the undulation..." Crusty stopped and turned to see what Danny was fixated on.

"Well, stay on it," said Danny, still staring. "Now what?"

"Well," Crusty's tone had already gone hard. "Speaking of asses."

Shelly Wilkerson had materialized once again. He was 70 yards ahead, sitting in his cart and waiting near Danny's ball just short and right of the green. He checked his watch, crossed his arms and turned his head toward the long-vacant 16th tee.

Crusty and Danny stopped to watch Nice Johnson who was working on playing a wedge from about a hundred yards out. Nice was swiveling his head trying to find the best way to play with, essentially, one good eye. He shifted his broken glasses so the one good lens balanced on the center of his nose. Normally Nice Johnson played very quickly, but now he was taking his time, contemplating several alternatives, all of them awkward.

Danny cocked his head toward Shelly. "What do ya think is up with the ROG Nazi?" *(Pronounced "rogue," stands for Rules of Golf.)* "Can't believe he'd even think of messing with us now."

"Who gives a shit," said Crusty. "And he better not give us any."

"Shelly never has liked you much, Crust."

"Nada shit..." Crusty exhaled loudly through his nose. "And look who's talkin'...he can't stand your, ah...molded boulders..."

Danny casually swatted at some flies near his head, mostly out of habit now, like Boozer's sound-only spits. After the episode in the brush by The O-Kah-Tah, the mutant flies didn't seem so relentless anymore. Maybe the flies knew they had blown their chance to put away the final group when they had them cornered in the brush and sealed off by the river. Perhaps going through the motions was all they had left, their collective bug spirit sagging, apathy taking over, content now to shirk the dogma that had been driving their back nine jihad against the golfing infidels. The term "bug" was becoming an impotent verb instead of a lone constituent in a proud swarm of winged-bullies bent on cultivating a culture of fear.

Time to just play.

Considering the condition he was in -- back howling, shirt sudsing, hair surrendering and everything stinking -- the flies were bound to seem less a factor. They had to be reeling. Danny had come to accept that he was representing the human race, that it was time to put the onus on D Mo himself, and that it must be he who prevails in the war of wills for the sake of second-millennium mankind. On some level he knew his characterization of the mindless bugs was merely his mind working to survive, but if he could empower unworthy insects with organizational skills, then he should be able to just as easily emasculate them; show them to be the hit and run pussies they are. He would entrust it all to his mind and his buddy's dung. The notion of Crusty's resourcefulness prompted another thought that had taken root in Danny's brain, and while it wasn't the time to think about it now, he'd be cross-examining ol' Crust about it later, when the round was over.

Nice Johnson hit his wedge shot solidly. After making contact, he dropped his club and grabbed his glasses with two hands and held them in front of his face with one eye shut and watched his ball stop 12 feet from the flag. Clell looked like he might clap but didn't. Then Nice returned his glasses to the normal but now 50 percent useless position and resumed walking.

"Nice one, Nice," enthused Danny, a little relieved.

The little one-eyed Johnson beamed. "It's gonna be okay." As if he knew Danny felt bad.

As they crossed The E-Kah-Tah Bridge, Danny caught Crusty sneaking peeks at his so called "smooth walking." The pain in the lower right side of his back was intense now, a dull knife tearing instead of cutting. Danny anticipated that Crusty was going to say something. "You know Crust, something isn't right. I mean…what's wrong with the picture here?"

Crusty looked around. "Pick something. Seen it all today, including some stuff too fucked up for the theater of the absurd."

"Something is missing," said Danny.

"Gee, let me see…" Crusty made a show of thinking hard, "…maybe Natalie Gulbis juggling the GI Joe Collection while sucking the salt off a pretzel rod."

"Now that you mention it, there is that," said Danny, laughing. "But look around, four holes to go. No Gary. No media at all. Where'd Billy go, for that matter?" Danny turned and looked back, and it hurt him to do so. Linneman was in his cart well behind the group, talking on the radio, no doubt trying to explain the riverside scene and justifying why the final group had fallen so far behind. When they got to Danny's ball it was still being guarded by Shelly. Crusty handed Lazarus to Danny and then held his ground, staring at the old man.

Shelly looked at Crusty first, then at Danny. At 75 years of age, the crotchety old man still seemed full of the vinegar he pissed in.

"Gentlemen, we need to talk."

"Of course, Shelly," said Danny. "It's what you do."

Shelly ignored the comment. "Very well then...I've been listening to Bill on the radio go on about an expedition to find a golf ball that was nowhere near the river. Did you know your little Easter egg hunt took almost nine minutes?"

Danny looked at Shelly like he was Lucifer himself. Boozer and his caddie and Nice and Clell all came to listen in. Linnemean could be heard coming toward them in his cart. He was just getting to the bridge.

"Whatever, Shelly." Danny had no use for this. "How about you get out of the way, and let me play," Danny looked down at how his ball was sitting, "without delay." *Great, now I'm Dr. Seussing, what next...?*

"Tell me, Gentlemen. Did Moran..." Shelly stared at Crusty, "or his caddie...identify the golf ball in the allotted five minutes?"

No one said anything. Danny was stunned. "No. Johnson's caddie found it. We had some issues in the brush by the river. Took priority."

"So I've heard," said Shelly. He raised his eyebrows and slowly cocked his head like he hated to lower the boom with an unfavorable ruling, which of course, he relished.

"I got your allotted five minutes," said Crusty.

Shelly's smile straightened out with the arrival of Linneman who was shaking his head as he cruised to a stop, cigarette in mouth. "Problem, Shelly?"

Shelly recounted the fact that neither Danny nor Crusty had "identified" Danny's ball within the allotted five minutes. He quickly added how "bad" he felt. He didn't get any further.

Stuart Johnson said, "Neither did I."

"Neither did you, what?" asked Shelly.

Nice J. looked at Danny. "My ball was in the fairway, exactly where I expected it to be, but I didn't, technically, ID it in five minutes. You penalize Danny; you've got to penalize me."

Shelly held up his right hand, fingers splayed. "Five minutes is all anyone gets. You want to read rule 27, or shall I read it for you? All of you."

Danny, Boozer and Johnson began to talk at once.

"Shelly. Everyone…just hold on." It was Linneman, and smoke came out with his words. "27/5.5 in the Decisions on the Rules of Golf book covers this."

Shelly huffed. "Decisions aren't rules; they're cockeyed amendments to what should be a straight-forward constitution."

"Shelly, please don't get going on this again." Linneman looked weary.

"Yeah, well, whatever happened to play it as it lies, the course as you find it, and count 'em all?" Wilkerson said it defiantly, but there was no doubt he was taken by surprise. "You get five."

"Shelly," said Linneman, "they need a ruling on 18 fairway."

Shelly held up his radio. "I have a radio, Bill. I'd have heard if I was needed on 18." He clicked the radio off and placed it on the seat next to him.

"1998 British Open, Birkdale," said Crusty. "O'Meara in the hay."

Linneman nodded, twirling an unlit smoky treat in his fingers like it was perfunctory foreplay. He had tried to shield Shelly from embarrassment.

Nice Johnson spoke up. "If the ball believed to be the players is located within the allotted five minutes, the player is allowed a reasonable amount of time to identify it." Everyone looked at Johnson. Nice nodded. "Something like that."

"Which includes as reasonable," said Danny, who thought he may have actually violated the rules, "any time required to rescue a fellow competitor from a steep bank above a dangerous river."

"Providing he saved your ass first," said Crusty.

"Molded boulders."

The hard old man looked at the people semi-circling him. Boozer and his bean-pole caddie, Clell, Nice and Crusty were muffling their amusement. He opened his mouth to speak and then shut it. He refused to even look at Danny.

Then Shelly started to cave in. Moments before he had sat with his arms crossed and his chin up. Now he was stone still, looking smaller, sitting in his coveted official's cart, the lines on his face deepened by the angle of the light. Shelly didn't flare his nostrils or narrow his eyes; he just looked down and away. Danny felt something like self-doubt radiating from the old man who still wore his blue blazer in 80-plus degrees. It was entirely possible that in a quiz on the 60 defined terms and the 34 rules including subsections and the 23 page index and all three appendices that comprise the 162 page booklet called The Rules of Golf — Shelly might score higher than anyone in the state. But rarely does one set of rules truly address fairness.

The ever expanding Decisions Book was the USGA's and the R&A's attempt at recognizing fairness. It was designed to provide further clarification to the sometimes wacky situations golfers inevitably encounter but aren't specifically covered in The Rules of Golf, stuff that would seem hypothetical if they weren't based mostly on actual situations. The Decisions Book had grown to over 600 pages; so it was a challenge for most to keep up, providing they were able to dead lift it to begin with. The Book would, for example, cover how a player would get free relief should a ball end up next to a poisonous snake, but not if it was found in a patch of poison ivy. The USGA ultimately refutes that they are in effect picking your poison by pointing out that it was the player that hit it there.

At the moment, however, Shelly Wilkerson appeared to shrink, and the silence was uncomfortable. Boozer's eyes were wide, the bean pole was ready to do what anyone else did, Clell held Nice Johnson's putter with two hands at his waist as if it were a rifle, Danny was working his back in hopes of finding some magic twist to make it better. Bill

Linneman held up a finger as he held his radio to his ear. He was about to speak, but Shelly beat him to it.

"Well," said Shelly, "you guys are now two holes behind and Moran is here crowing and we haven't even got to the point where…"

"Okay Shelly." Linneman put his radio down. "They do need you at 18. Actually they need you near the clubhouse. Follow me." Linneman and Wilkerson drove their carts to a place away from Danny's ball. Whatever Linneman said, it got Shelly to speed away and not look back.

Danny's curiosity about what Billy told Shelly was overpowered by the pain ripping through his lower back. He walked up to the green just to get refocused. He came back and grabbed Lazarus, his 57.5 degree wedge, opened it up to over 60 degrees and took a couple practice swipes. He had short little pitch to a front right pin. No bunkers, no mounds. Not hard.

"Carry the fringe," said Crusty as he stepped away. "They've grown a little grabby."

Danny flexed his knees to help his back. He sliced under his ball aggressively and it came out softly, the ball landing on the seam where the fringe met the green and shot forward. It barely missed the hole and then rolled a good 25 feet past. When Danny tried to set up to the first putt, his back hurt so much he broke into a sweat around his neck and up the back of his scalp. He wondered what it would have felt like without the Advil. He ignored the half-ass flies and, bending over at nearly a right angle, decelerated on a shovey stroke and left his birdie putt over three feet short of the cup. He marked and stewed.

Nice Johnson looked in need of Red Cross assistance; his light-colored clothes were streaked with grass stains and dirt as he once again balanced his good lens on the center of his nose. Then he rolled his putt in for birdie. Danny now thought Nice might have an unfair advantage going with one lens.

Danny, still annoyed, stepped up to his dicey par putt. With the sun coming more from the side now, the longer shadows made the green look grainier. The small gallery had crept closer to the action. The ones who had hung on the periphery during the adventure on the river were doing their best to explain how much they didn't know after the others had asked them what had taken so long. At the same time, those hanging greenside were informing the fairway-goers about Delsman's successful eagle putt. "Sixty feet, easy," as Danny had heard someone say. They obviously were not through cross-examining each other and the whispers, especially the "s" sounds, were louder now with the wind dissipating. Danny stepped away and smiled at two of the whisperers. Both apologized profusely, but each seemed mildly pleased to be part of the show.

Danny Moran still had a three shot lead, an otherwise healthy margin that suddenly didn't feel like it. That's when his world flipped and his thoughts suddenly came streaming in fluent sarcasmese. Jim Rome had come to the party. Late. *"Nice lag, Eldrick,"* Rome said, *"If that's three feet then I'm Darko freaking Milicic."* Danny's central nervous system was pumping snark now and garnishing it with mocking sides of snide. *"Incredible. You want a couple scoops of truth? Closing is dirty freaking work. No one's suggesting you lack 'nads, D Mo. You are a legend because you've always nutted up when your neck detects the dragon's breath…but this is it, the balance of your Elway Ending hangs, and, frankly, I see a whole lot of squeamish going on."* It was unprecedented, Rome resurrecting himself late in a round like this, in the final round, much less Danny's final final round. It was always early go only. Three or four holes and out. Now, Danny had three holes and change to go. Then more words, at fluctuating volume, *"Okay. Quiet, Clones. Hide the ham sandwich Mama, this I have to witness."* Then it was just Rome growling, *"eeeerrrr, eeeerrrr, eeeerrrr…"* No words.

Danny stepped away from his ball for a second time. Three-plus feet for par still waiting on him. It wasn't going away. Anyone there could've heard some "Oh-ohs." He heard Rome say, *"Re-set. Never good."* He pulled out his heavy, oval-shaped Celtic good luck coin to re-mark his ball and start his routine all over. He was glad Shelly was gone. Danny slowly squatted down behind his ball. Marked it. Picked it up. Looked at it and blew on it for some reason. His back screamed. Romey teased. The freak-flies buzzed. He wiped his damp hand and then lined up his ball with the d mo imprint upside down so it looked like ow p. Rinny's idea, said it stood for "O What a Putter." Danny picked up his lucky Celtic marker from behind his ball. One side of the coin had a four-leafed clover and said *"A man's fame lasts longer than his life,"* and the other side was in Gaelic, *"o'l siar e' agus na' lig anear e'."* Danny's uncle had given him the coin and claimed the line translated to 'Drink it back, and never let it up again.' On cue and in his way, Rome went off again and repeated the line three times in succession in his trademark playful cadence. *"Drink...it...back and...never-let-it-up-again."*

And so Danny did just that, in a manner of speaking. Primal instinct took over. He let loose with a blast of internalized profanity that was beyond crude and so vulgar both he and Rome could smell it. Rome battled back. *"Great. The man just came hard with a barrow full of big-league reek. Perfect. D freaking Mo just trying to smoke me out. Trying to bury me in god knows what. No question. Dude. Is. Serious."* If Danny's lips were moving he did not know it, but his Decorum Membrane rose to the challenge and kept it inside and unheard. No couch and crown anything now and he felt completely alive. The streak of blue served its purpose and power washed a psyche mired in a momentary flight of lunacy after an unheard of experience that was the first five of his final nine holes of competitive golf. Danny thought his last blast of profanity had pulled the plug on his Inner Sarcasm and drove lead vocalist Jim Rome into the graveyard of irrelevance for good, but instead he heard a fading *"Rack 'em! I'm out."* Danny was pretty sure he smiled, but he most certainly stepped up, leaned over, and poured the three-footer in the heart. To bury the putt for par while smacking back at the host of The Jungle from the Premier Radio Network helped to put the jungle cat back in Danny. From deep within his world, Danny heard he distant strains of psychedelic sitar intro to Tom Petty's "Don't come around here no more." He knew that Rome was history. Just knew it.

His reverie receded when Linneman informed Danny on the way to the 16th tee that Delsman had birdied 17. The lead was now two. The better part of an hour had passed since he holed out on the 14th hole and Danny couldn't help but laugh a weary laugh. He'd have to keep his lower back from messing with his brain, but the fact remained that Danny could barely swing. He bunted his driver on the 397 yard 16th and was actually out-driven by Nice Johnson. Everyone was looking at him now, and he knew he must have looked like someone on Survivor. He had 174 yards to the green… choked up on his 19 degree hybrid and then managed a swipey little slap-fade to 30 feet.

Despite his discomfort, Danny felt the coming of a familiar next-level type of focus, and it brought with it a rugged sense of well-being. He did, however, notice a few extraneous things. The media had arrived at the 16th green at the same time the final group did. Danny caught Gary D'Amato looking at him and then writing in his notebook. He knew the writers would have to know a little of what had happened from Linneman's reporting, but it was strange that they all showed up at the same time. Danny went into his nearly right-angle putting stance and easily two-putted for par despite the feeling that he looked like a crane. While he waited with the others to putt out, he looked over at the par three 17th. 206 yards over water. All carry.

Normally a 3-, 4- or 5-iron, depending on the wind, he went with his moody three-wood. Flushed it. But the ball did not move left to right at all. With his back downright angry with him, Danny couldn't get his body through it enough to cut it. The flip with his hands actually made the ball draw and it landed mid-green, 40 feet left of the pin. It didn't stop rolling until it got to the tacky fringe at the back of the green and came to rest against the long bluegrass rough collaring the green.

After the shot, Danny's back screamed like the tortured creatures of the evil moor. His body convulsed. Crusty looked concerned. Danny took a few steps, shaky-legged, more of a wobble, like someone with the flu, each step an accomplishment. His eyes actually watered and he hated that. Flies bounced off his head and he felt an odd form of freedom to let the bastards know that he didn't give a shit what they did. He was sweating from every pore and the extra suds were now but reminders of how many things he didn't know.

Then, as he neared the 17th green, something went off in his hair. The sound of fury and chaos, and suicidal insects with nothing to lose, infighting over strategy perhaps, turning on each other. At least two, possibly more, were trapped in mid-conniption in Danny's gooey hair.

"Damn, Crusty," said Danny, trying not to grunt. "I think there's a turf war going on in my hair." Danny put his hand on his head and the creatures went insane. The sound was sickening, like a psychotic dentist turning a souped-up drill against his skull. Danny went to a knee. He bent at the waist to relieve some pressure.

"Holy Christ, Dannymo." Crusty was at his side.

"Get my Erin Hills cap out, Crust." Another fly got into Danny's hair but it didn't stay. "The hell…"

Crusty reached into Danny's golf bag and dug around. "No cap Dannymo."

"Probably in the trunk. Damn"

Crusty pulled out a tan colored Gore-Tex bucket cap. It was extremely wrinkled and had a who-knows-how-old half-empty bag of Sweet and Hot flavored beef jerky tucked inside it. "How about your rain hat?"

"Give it to me." Danny immediately pulled it over his head. As he did, his armpits released a flurry of soap suds that either fell to the ground or floated off. Danny checked his chest and foam was forming there too. He stood up straight.

Crusty took in the sight of Danny Moran. White foam clinging to dark clothing, face streaked with dark smudges from his dad's ashes, all topped off with a wrinkled light brown bucket cap. When Crusty tried to utter his trademark "Now we go, Dannymo" he couldn't do it without laughing.

"So I look like Carl Spackler, big deal. Come on…now we go." Danny was again awash in the liberty that comes from finally belly-flopping into the last pile of pig slop required for full membership to the swineherd.

Crusty was still laughing. "Dannymo, you know I love ya…but you've gone straight past Carl Spackler and right to Crazy Guggenheim." Like an older brother helping his kid brother after a bit too much to drink, Crusty walked side-by-side with Danny to his ball.

The lie was bad, bird-nesty. Danny had over 50 feet to the hole; the green was banked severely back-to-front so the putt would break sharply to the right. He was away. He took Lazarus and very little time to blade the ball onto the green well left of the hole where it nearly stopped at the crest of the slope above the hole. Then it rolled, wobbled actually, another 10 feet, as slow as a ball can go, down the slope. The gallery cheered it on, every creeping foot added to the legend of Danny Mo -- not simply for the greatness of his short game but as a man with an amazing sense of occasion. The ball stopped six inches from the cup. The hooting and clapping was prolonged and heartfelt. Boozer and his caddie clapped too, and meant it. Nice Johnson stared at Danny with his one good lens balanced on the bridge of his nose and appeared to be in awe.

Danny was relieved. One more hole to go. The long and difficult 18th. Linneman told Danny that Charlie Delsman had parred 18 to finish up. Danny still had a two shot lead. Even though it was downhill, he had zero confidence that he could get to the 451 yard finishing hole in regulation. He was beyond faking he was fine. He started to feel like one of those marathon runners who lose most of their ability to function but somehow stay on their feet while the security detail and the medics have to point them to the finish line. Danny didn't care. When someone yelled something loud in support of Danny, he nodded and even made an attempt to give a tip of his crinkled bucket cap but couldn't really even make out anyone's words other than Crusty's.

"Almost there, Dannymo." Crusty handed him his driver. As with the wedge from the collar, Danny took almost no time. He connected solidly with a half-swing but he was weaker now and it hurt worse than even 15 minutes earlier. Luckily, the ball rolled a long way down the hill because it carried no more than 180 yards. He had no idea where Boozer and Nice ended up with their tee shots.

Danny was away. 211 yards to the middle of the green, pin up nine yards and five from the right, 202 to the hole. A bunker short right protected the pin and was 188 yards to carry. Cattails and some boggy wetlands were well left. Downhill, deduct one club. Blown-up back, add four.

"I'd normally say that the bunker don't kill ya, two shots up and all." Crusty was looking hard at Danny. "Don't think you need to be playin' out of a bunker right now."

"I lay up, Crust, I leave a dicey pitch off a downhill lie...I could still end up in the bunker." Danny put his hand on the head cover of his 19 degree hybrid. "Crust?"

"Yeah."

Danny looked at the tree tops as if studying the wind which did not exist. As he did this he whispered, "Could you take this club out of the bag please."

"You got it. I like it." Crusty raised his eyebrows.

Danny waggled his hybrid, his Shaq-toe. At 19 degrees and weighted to get the ball up quickly, it had the loft of a five-wood and the length of a four-iron. Most everyone on every tour had gone to them, and on the Champions Tour long irons were like land lines now.

"One more full swing, Dannymo," said Crusty, his voice with a whispery rasp to it.

Danny thought his caddie seemed more emotional than usual. He shut out the sirens. The dull knife that was tearing at his lower back seemed wired to his eyeballs. He kept blinking, trying to soothe them. He had hoped this moment could have been, well, maybe a little more magical. He had imagined coming down the final hole in his last competitive round, comfortably ahead, a montage of memories flashing before him. Yet, there was something to say for what it would mean to survive this day, with Crusty at his side, and the unconscious eye-patch guy delay, and Shelly's antics, and the riverside rescue and the random snatching of Nice's glasses; even the lost little bird on the 10th tee, which seemed like a week-old dream now, added to a memorable three days at The Hill Farm. Like his lucky Celtic coin said, "A man's fame lasts longer than his life." For the guys in the final group, the stories would live on forever.

Had it not been for his experience in a lifetime of competitive sports, Danny wouldn't have believed he could swing even one more time. But he believed, at the moment of truth, he would get through it somehow. He waggled, *Port-* he swung *–o-* he nutted it *-let.*

He got through it - stayed with it to hit it high.

"Oh be right, Honey," said Crusty.

"Crust," Danny said matter-of-factly as the ball reached its peak, where it seemed to become the brightest thing in the sky, "whatever happens…that's all I've got."

"Be so right." Crusty was begging.

Danny dropped the club and put his hands on his knees and watched like an outfielder trying to look ready. The ball was covering the flag and as it descended Danny saw why Crusty was begging. The ball slammed into the front wall of the bunker. The shadows made it hard to see if it had plugged or not. The gallery behind the green slumped, then, almost in unison, shuffled to their left to see what the lie looked like.

Boozer and Nice Johnson eventually played from the fairway. All sights and sounds of them doing so were a bunch of kaleidoscopic light and color and disembodied voices with some floating suds and bubbles thrown in to complete the psychedelic preface to the end of Danny Mo's triumphant ride to the finish line of one hell of an amateur golf career.

The lie was perfect, on the upslope of the band shell bunker to a tight pin. There was maybe six feet between the bunker and the fringe of the green and another 10 feet to the hole. If Danny could wrench it out, he could two-putt to win. The lip of the bunker was eye-high and the slope of the green ran away hard. A safe explosion shot landing on the green anywhere near the pin would end up in the middle of the green, 40 feet away minimum. The thought of trying to two-putt from 40 feet, now, all bent out of shape, seemed like starting all over on house of cards.

Crusty's eyes were alight. "Alright…you got that pouty lip there…don't mess with it. Nothing cute now. Just get it out. Two putts and I'll buy you a beer." He picked up a rake. "Tell me something, Dannymo."

"What?" Danny had already begun to take his stance.

"Can you swing at it at all?" Crusty was above him on the patch of grass between the bunker and the fringe. Intentionally slowing Danny down. He took his time walking around to the side of the bunker.

"We're gonna find out," said Danny. "I honestly…" He didn't finish. The gallery had grown. There had been some laughter about Danny's appearance but now the people cheering for him grew silent. Danny's only two thoughts were 'sand first' and 'shallow.' He surprised even himself when he went right into the swing.

His back exploded more than his bunker shot. As Danny carved out a thin sliver of sand under his ball, it popped up and over the lip, and through the emergency alarms Danny could almost hear it sizzle with spin. The ball carried the slender panel of rough and landed perfectly on the fringe and hopped forward. It was equal to or greater than what he could have done in perfect health. But as Crusty would tell him later, the ball hit into the grain of the fringe, bit, and stopped on its second hop, still on the fringe. A collective gasp could be heard. Anyone who has ever played golf at a decent level knew Danny had just hit the type of shot that is sometimes referred to as "too good."

Danny, however, never saw the end of the shot. He had gone down as if shot. Crusty had just finished whispering "No way" when he jumped into the bunker like a paratrooper with the rake still in his hands.

"I slipped is all," said Danny. Danny didn't even bother brushing at the sand plastered across half his body. Against his soapy, sweaty, black shirt, the sand stood out and looked like the black and tans he enjoyed so much.

Crusty knew he was lying. He started raking while looking at Danny's face. He knew his horse was done. He could swing no more.

"Ten-footer, Dannymo. Perfect." Crusty raked now in earnest as the spectators cheered Danny's effort.

Danny realized that his putter was in his hand. He assumed Crusty must have put it there. He stood near his ball looking at his feet, breathing audibly. When it was his turn, he went into a bubble of silence and focused. Two putts and The Wisconsin State Open, finally, would be his.

He discovered that leaning in the direction he was putting, with all his weight on his bent left leg and with his right leg perfectly straight hurt the least. It looked ridiculous. The bucket cap felt itchy all of a sudden so he threw it off and it went in the bunker right where Crusty had just raked. Crusty smiled. Danny could make out nothing from the murmuring spectators and fellow competitors ringing the green. He had to hit the quick left-to-right putt through a few inches of sticky fringe and yet avoid knocking it five or six feet by the hole.

Danny never bought into using the toe of the putter for fast, downhill putts. It was a variable that led to over-thinking the force he would need to apply to an intentional mis-hit. He got the ball barely rolling with a short stroke and watched it trickle. Shouts and cheers and what might be construed as true love came from many in the gallery, and all the rest watched in silence or faked it altogether. Before he hit the putt, Danny would have been thrilled to have a one-footer or less. Now, he wanted it to go in and end it all in style. The ball rolled slowly, breaking slightly. It was, once again, seemingly perfect. But the ball caught the high side of the cup and curled to the right and stayed out, no more than four inches from the hole.

Finally.

The crowd cheered in an almost reverent way. There were some hoots and plenty of "Way to go, Danny Mo!" platitudes offered, but the applause was impressive and sustained. Danny smiled at the lip-out; his sense of relief was immeasurable. He took one step and felt the pain rip all over again. He didn't care.

For the first time, he took a good look at the crowd, most of whom were still clapping. Marty Archibald was there. The Great Man had come to see the younger man carry the torch; one he might suggest was first ignited by "Ol' Arch," himself. He was one who wasn't clapping, but he was nodding with a satisfied smile. With him were Cindy and a few other women who looked vaguely familiar to Danny. Marty winked. Carter Slane was laughing and clapping. Danny saw Charlie Delsman clapping softly but sincerely, and Andy Salamone going through the motions with soundless claps as he whispered something to Gary D'Amato who was politely nodding and writing in his notebook. Finally, he noticed Witchy elbowing her way to get a better view and create some space for the shorter Orsman. Collectively, it was the kind of applause rarely seen in a state event, but such was the popularity of Danny Moran and the collective understanding about a cherished championship that had for so long escaped him.

Danny, quite unintentionally, did a bit of a Marty impression as he walked toward his ball. The one tough hombre limp was all his for the moment and he did it without shame. Danny decided to mark and let Nice Johnson hit his four-foot putt for par first and then finish. Danny dug in his pocket and it hurt just doing the digging…but not nearly as much as when he bobbled his lucky ball-marker taking it out. The heavy coin hit the green and rolled into his ball. It moved the ball a quarter inch at the most.

Danny froze. He wasn't sure what the ruling was on a marker coin hitting a player's ball. He thought he read once that accidentally moving the ball while marking it was simply a matter of moving the ball back at no penalty. Danny stood still. He could feel Nice Johnson's two eyes through one lens burn into him. Nice knew the rules pretty well and his Cyclops stare was disconcerting. Not everyone saw it, but the celebration had quieted while the chatter and confusion rose. Bill Linneman didn't see what happened, blocked by Danny's torso and his molded but now sand-covered boulders. When the official circled around into view, Danny still had not moved.

"Billy, I dropped my coin and it hit the ball." Danny noticed Crusty holding the flagstick; his head was twisted completely away from the people and toward the marsh.

Linneman worked his entire hand over his face moving from the bottom to the top and back down. His face flexed then popped back into place. "Danny, were you going to mark the ball?"

"Well Billy, what did you think I was gonna do with the coin I use for marking my ball?"

"What I mean is, were you in the act of marking it?"

"The act?"

"Danny, were you attempting to place the coin behind your ball?"

"That was the idea, yes, but I fumbled it. When does...the act...begin?" Danny's mind was swirling. Crusty came over to listen. He looked sick.

"At what point did it leave your hand?" Linneman did a slow blink. His hands felt for a pack of cigarettes in his front pocket but he left them there.

"I'm not sure I ever had control of the coin, Billy. I scooped it out of my pocket with my fingers, you know, standard method...probe, capture, clean and jerk. I admit, my fingers are a little clammy and my pants are a little soapy and the coin went sailing just as I brought it to the open air."

"Danny...if you're saying you were not in the process of marking the ball. If, in fact, you bobbled the coin while retrieving it from your pocket, you would have to incur a one stroke penalty and you would need to replace the ball to its original position." Linnemans's voice cracked as he said it. He had watched Danny Moran battle through so much for this, and now... this. "I'm so sorry Danny."

The message was clear. The Decisions book giveth, and The Decisions book taketh away.

"Then it's a penalty on me." For an instant Danny's body seemed to deflate to the size of his bones. But he kept his head up. "Not your fault, Billy." Crusty's throat was pulsing in an attempt to hold back the untamed forces of his inner crustiness. Danny went to his ball, moved it back, and marked it. His vision went all white from pain. The gallery had begun to figure it out and those who hadn't were being told. They were talking furiously and Nice Johnson didn't even wait for the buzzing to subside before knocking in his par putt.

Danny replaced his ball and tapped it in for double bogey and a round of 74. Delsman, with the help of his eagle on 15 and the birdie on 17 shot 66, the low round for the tournament. They both had finished at seven under par. The Wisconsin State Open calls for an immediate sudden death playoff in the event of a tie after 72 holes.

Danny recalled Crusty's rhetorical question after the bunker shot -- the one about someone being serious. He sat at the scorer's table now, dazed and throbbing and in total disbelief. He signed his card without checking it. He trusted Nice Johnson's scoring skills and it was indeed correct. Crusty had gone to get a cart for the playoff. As he left the table, Danny Mo felt the truth coming to bear. His customary optimism could no longer airlift him out of a dream on fire.

Danny appreciated that he was given some space. His friends were sneaking peeks at him, but Danny could do nothing but endure his time as a macabre curiosity in the freak-show side of golf. He heard Salamone laugh heartily and then say "Jesus Christ." Danny looked over at him. He had obviously showered and changed, his hair wet with ringlets. He saw Carter quietly say something to him. Sally stared at Carter and then walked over to Marty Archibald.

Crusty was at the wheel of the cart and coming toward him. His buddy's posture was upright, but Danny noticed subtleties in body language that only close friends can know. Crusty knew what he knew; the use of a cart at this point was nothing more than a downfield block for an already tackled back.

∞

Danny sat motionless in the passenger's seat. When Crusty started up the Impala, "To Win Just Once" came roaring over the speakers and Crusty immediately turned it off.

"This tournament will be remembered by everyone for…hell, who knows, pick your sideshow," said Danny.

Crusty said nothing.

Danny let out a long breath of air. "What a day."

"It was, Dannymo, and no one will ever convince me you're not the goddamn champion."

Danny awkwardly flipped his plaque over his shoulder and onto the back seat. Even that hurt. The plaque bounced back off the backrest and tumbled to the floorboard. Hopefully, thought Danny, upside-down.

The plaque was awarded to him for being "Low Amateur," and he was exactly that. It was the fourth time Danny had been the best of the amateurs in The State Open.

He started laughing. "Can you even believe that?"

"It'll go down in history, that's for sure," said Crusty. "You probably shouldn't have even tried another swing."

"Gotta go down swinging, Crust."

"Like in the bunker on 18," said Crusty. "Thought we might have to carry you out right there, but no…Danny Mo rose again."

"A cakewalk compared to Calvary I presume."

"Roger," said Crusty. "But even the Carpenter didn't have to deal with Shelly Wilkerson."

∞

Danny Moran had stepped up to the tee box on The Hill Farm's first hole of the playoff and summoned the remaining will within him. He would not let Crusty tee his ball for him even though Crust offered to do it. As he stood over the ball, it was as if he were in the middle of one of his Hank dreams where no matter what he did, he could not find his damn dog. He had, with a grunt, gotten the club back; how far he did not know, when it all collapsed into the searing end and a body shutting down for its own protection. Danny knew something had ruptured or herniated or whatever happens when a back blows up. His driver hit bottom, a good half-foot behind the teed-up Titleist in an explosion of grass and earth. Danny had let go of the club and he watched it cartwheel before looking to see where his ball had ended up. Not that it mattered.

It was only 100 yards or so to carry the marsh, the same marsh that was to the left of the 18th hole, and not at all in play from the first tee. After Danny's playoff tee shot, it still wasn't. His ball had tumbled forward about 40 or 50 yards and stopped on a muddy down-slope short of and directly behind the cattails that circled the marsh. There was no shot from there -- short of going backwards.

After his hideous spasm-slash of a tee shot attempt, Danny wasn't quite sure what to do. This was, like the previous nine holes, new territory. Delsman had yet to hit. The mini-tour pro looked at his shoes, stunned as anyone. Danny took a deep breath, he heard himself chuck but had no idea if it was audible. Then…he walked after his ball. The spectators around the tee remained for the most part, eerily silent. Danny worked hard to walk as proudly as he could, even as each step was still another edge working against tattered nerves. Head up, he looked only forward. When he got to the ball, he thought of calling out to Delsman that it was, in fact, his. Just to be funny. But he did not. He bent down, hands on knees, and looked at his ball sitting on the packed mud. From his view, the **d mo** was upside down and the **d** was obscured by a chunk of mud. It read, **ow**.

Danny picked up his ball, wiped off the mud, and looked at the d mo one last time. Two-hundred feet away, over a hundred people were watching him. He felt not at all self-conscious and neither did he feel some quixotic need for the limelight of tragedy. He was at once both crushed yet convinced of his own resilience, even as his every movement now shook him to his core. The blows that the game often delivered to the competitive golfer could be devastating, but Danny knew that devastation was a relative term when in the context of anything considered a game. Still, the whole thing just sucked. He casually tossed his ball over the cattails, toward the center of the marsh where it would forever lie in a swampy grave that it, too, did nothing to deserve.

∞

"Something I gotta ask you, Crust."

Crusty raised his eyebrows and glanced at Danny who now had the passenger's seat reclining nearly all the way back.

"The rhino crap. It was gnawing at me. Wasn't really rhino crap, was it?"

"Why would you say that?" Crusty ignored the turn-off to his house. "I'm taking you home. Carter's picking me up at your place."

"Great," said Danny. "Now, what up with the dung?"

Crusty sighed. "Told you about my captain, the one who gave us the stinky shit to use. Well, one of the things guys back then worried about in the jungle and the fields was different animals giving away our position. Gave us some stuff that was supposed to cover up our human scent. Turns out he had no idea if it did a damn thing, but it made guys feel a bit safer, like we had something working for us."

Danny laughed a tired laugh.

"What?"

"So you thought as long as I thought it was a special blend of extract that no one else had...I'd have an advantage, at least in my head."

"You did the same damn thing, Dannymo."

"What?"

"Dousing your clothes with that detergent," said Crusty. "Same thing."

Danny stared at the car's roof. "So what was it? Why'd it have to stink so much?"

"Ah, just some sulfur and nitrogen and a bunch of junk...some vinegar and some actual bug repellent lotion you can only get in Canada. Seemed the worse it smelled in Nam, the safer the guys felt. Added some Absorbine Jr. just to lube it up, make it bit more contemporary and weirder."

"What was I thinking, the whole idea's absurd," said Danny, shaking his head. "You keep saying the guys felt safe, how bout you Crust?"

"Ahh...I don't buy into that junk."

"But I do?"

"Yeah." Crusty smiled and passed a hay-bailer on the county trunk. "You are Dannymo, if you believe it, you pretty much achieve it. You're so damn certain you have the edge in everything it almost don't matter whether you do or not."

"...as long as I believe it."

"Roger."

"And your crap seemed exotic enough for me to buy into it."

"Those damn flies are a plague," said Crusty. "And it is a fact about those plants that certain rhinos eat and the bugs leave their crap alone.

Dung studies are a real science. I mean they track 'em by their crap. Rhinos...they do...seriously."

"You're a beauty." Danny lolled his head slowly from side to side against the head rest.

The two rode in silence. The crown of the sun continued to loiter above the trees beyond the passing farmland and the effect was enough to make a mountain range of the clouds and cooperating shadows. After a spell, Danny said, "Got me thinking, Crust."

Crusty said nothing.

"Think it might be time to let my Dad's ashes rest in peace." Danny took a deep breath. "You know, it was an accident the first time Curly stuck to my hand at The Nag. But, let's face it, I won because I took fewer shots than The Cannon and everyone else that weekend... it's not that complicated. Mighta made too much out of Curly giving me a hand."

"No doubt." Crusty shrugged. "And let me repeat...for 72 holes you took fewer shots than anyone else this week too. Don't you ever forget that, Dannymo. Stupid fucking rule."

"Get me home Crust. We need a few beers."

"Roger."

∞

Chapter 24

With the help of Parnell "Crusty" Sindorf, Danny leaned against two ice packs wrapped inside a dish towel while jack-knifed in a chaise lounge on the backyard deck off the Morans' suburban home.

It was still warm and the remaining light was indirect. In minutes Crusty brought up a block of ice from the basement freezer, put it in a plastic garbage bag, covered it with a canvas dropcloth and smashed it into chunks and chips with a crowbar, then dumped it all over a cooler filled with bottles of Killian's Irish Red. He had already asked Danny twice if he was okay. Danny had no idea if he was checking on his back or his overall welfare. It was probably one of each. That done, Crusty went inside and brought out the phone and placed it on the small table next to Danny.

"Molly'll be calling, right." Crusty gave a quick twist to his face that said 'shitty job.' Golf may not be life and death, but for tournament golfers in families close enough to share in it, the lowest moments often went deeper than the heights achieved in triumph. At the same time, it was the nature of such sharing that softened the former and intensified the latter.

"She'll call. Probably my mobile number," said Danny, his jaw tightening as he pulled his little flip-phone from black slacks that still showed evidence of soap and sand residue. "She may know the results already if she has access to the internet. Probably putting in her time at the hospital. I'll know what she knows in one second by her voice. Same with Rinny and Mo Mo."

"When's Molly comin' back?"

"Friday."

"Couple days." Crusty squinted, calculating the logistics. "I'll take you to that sports doctor buddy of yours tomorrow morning."

Danny chewed on that. "We'll see how I feel."

"You gotta go."

"I know, Crust, but I'm not helpless. I could drive if I had to."

"Carter said he's got some news." Crusty changed the subject; a sign that it was decided. He would help get Danny around until Molly returned Friday. He took a slug of Killian's. "Some bizarre shit Salamone told him."

Danny polished off his beer in three chugs, and did a fruitless double-check. Not even close to one of his top-five worldwide type records, but it had to be close to a personal best. He looked over at Crusty sitting in a patio chair across from him. Helluva guy, he thought, the Crusty one. Along with Carter Slane, he was one of Danny's two best friends. Probably count Marty in there too, but in a more avuncular way. Danny had known Marty for over 30 years, Carter since college, and Crusty for about a dozen years.

Crusty Sindorf was as unpretentious as the old crowbar on the deck next to his patio chair. He had put in 25 years in the service, where he learned one million things, it seemed, including water mains and hydrant repair. He'd won numerous military tournaments in more countries than he could remember, and never told a soul at The Old Barn. Danny, of course, then told everyone once he learned about all that from a service buddy of Crusty's. After he retired from the service, Crusty looped for less than two years on the PGA Tour. He agreed to caddie for the kid of a colonel he despised but frequently played with in Europe, "just to see my own country for awhile." He walked off his tour caddie gig for good on the 13th hole of the final round of what was then called something like the Shearson Lehman Hutton Andy Williams San Diego Open.

Seems Crusty had come to despise Blair Stetson as much as he did the kid's old man when he felt the kid changed completely in his second year on tour. The first year he was relatively humble, worked hard, and had an adorable girlfriend. The next year, the kid - tall, blond, and maybe too good looking for his own good – was no longer intimidated. He got comfortable. His work ethic suffered, but he was off to a great start on the west coast, having benefited from the previous year's experience and just knowing the courses better. Then, Crusty claimed, Stetson started "sleeping with every other local weather babe, car show model or steakhouse waitress who threw herself at him." The kid dumped the sweet little peanut that Crusty loved, went out and got himself some genital herpes and spread it from California to the Gulf Stream waters.

The story of the day Crusty walked off into the sunset was a folk legend among caddies, mostly old timers, who enjoyed passing it on. The account went that a bleached-blonde masseuse in a mini-skirt was walking along with the Blair Stetson group and whenever possible, made a point to position herself around the green opposite the kid. On 13, he asked Crusty to squat down with him to, presumably, help read his putt, which he often did. With Stetson leaning over his shoulder he whispered in Crusty's ear, "Check out Tiffany in the orange mini. Got no panties on." Sure enough, the blonde squatted down as if to watch the action and flashed Stetson, Crusty and the entire pre-horizon hemisphere behind them.

Crusty, no doubt in his droll way, said "Well, BS...looks a little crusty to me." Then he stood up and walked off the course, leaving Stetson to explain. It was something Crusty said he had planned to do at some point as the kid became more and more short-tempered and full of himself. "Of course I enjoyed the view," Crusty had said, "But that chick's beave gave me the opening, so to speak, that I was looking for."

"You know what kills me about this game, Crust?" Danny turned the phone so he could see the ID screen easier.

"Nothing, Dannymo." Crusty smiled, got up and handed Danny another beer and sat down again. "You may claim you're retiring from competitive golf but after all that shit today... ain't nothing about golf that'd ever kill you. Lightning maybe."

"You know what I mean." Danny took a swig. "In the final round I hit four ugly shots on the 10th hole and made par. On the 18th, I hit four shots as well as I could and made double bogey."

"Nothing new about that," said Crusty. "Timing… that's what bloodies the psyche."

"I know." Danny exhaled, a staccato-styled release to counter any perception of a sigh. "Just keep thinking if I hadn't messed with the detergent, maybe I don't bobble the coin. Can't believe it, me, top-five worldwide at marking my ball…any angle, either hand, in and out, never step in anyone's line…then, when it mattered most, I let it slip."

Crusty polished off his beer and reached for another. He knew Danny was going through the process of coming to grips with another state open slipping through his fingers. "Maybe you leave the laundry strategies to Molly from now on. She's disciplined; know what I mean…assignment sure."

"Be good to have her back," said Danny. "And if that sounds needy, it's only because I am."

"Yeah, sometimes there's peace and quiet…and other times, it's right out of a bad movie. You know, it's quiet… too quiet."

"True enough." Danny sensed Crusty was speaking from experience.

They sat in silence for awhile, drinking their beers. The temperature dropped as the shadows stretched and the evening breeze was enough to make the bugs seem downright neighborly. The setting, Danny's mind-body bummer notwithstanding, was the antithesis of the Hill Farm finale.

"Gonna have to work through my gullibility over that cosmic dung-free goop of yours, Crust." Danny laughed as he said it.

"When it comes to golf, people just want to believe in something. Copper bracelets, therapeutic magnets, those bright colored graphite shafts or putters that look like cattle-branders…you name it. It's all about believin'."

"I guess it was only a matter of time before medicinal animal feces took its turn as golf's placebo of the week."

Crusty eyes sparkled. "Not really like me to bait and switch like that."

"No," said Danny. "But, damn if I didn't think it was kinda actually sorta working."

"Even if it actually worked, with the stench, it's 100% unmarketable," said Crusty. "It was more like hypnotism."

"Whatever," said Danny. "Probably not a big market for stuff to combat mutant gnat-flies."

"No stink, no faith." Crusty's eyes invited Danny to think.

"Yeah, I know...no buy-in, no efficacy."

"Dig the business terms, Dannymo," said Crusty. "But it's all about believing, ain't it? Crusty grabbed two more beers. "Since you brought it up earlier...you think your Dad's ashes absorb better than other stuff...really? Course not. You think you couldn't work magic with a new wedge if somethin' happened to Lazarus? Sure you could. Gonna have to soon. How lucky was your lucky coin?"

"It wasn't the coin," said Danny, "it was the clerk."

Crusty released a small burp out his crooked grin's upside.

Again they sat in silence, going into deeper thoughts and the coming gloaming. The smells from a nearby barbecue reminded Danny that he still had things to look forward to. Carter Slane came strolling around the side of the house holding a six pack carton holding four Red Stripe beers, another was in his hand. "Danny, Babe... I talked a little with Billy and Nice Johnson...I mean...shit, man."

Danny could only shake his head and take another glug of beer. After 36 holes, beer generally delivered greater flavor and a serious increase in its power to enhance and/or medicate.

Carter looked like he could cry, even as he laughed heartily. The owner of a chain of dry cleaners, he'd suffered through a divorce that stunned everyone in their circle. It was five years ago, and losing Christy ate him up. The resulting dark period, however, took the wrapper off a new-found compassion in him. "Took someone beautiful for granted and it woke me up the hard way," was how he put it. Crusty had been way off in putting the over/under at six months of next-level sensitivity before the cool and casual Carter came back. Danny, too, thought Carter would heal, and then feel his way back to the shallower waters of everyday suburban comfort. But the transformation seemed soul-deep now, and a testament to the responsibility he accepted for letting his priorities shift to fit moving targets. And it cost him Christy Slane. She was an under-the-radar champion for social justice and asked for very little in the divorce settlement. Told Carter she'd forever pray for his happiness and then went off to some missionary work in West Africa before taking a job at a huge Cancer Center in Houston. Crusty liked to say she was one Y from being Christ – one letter, one chromosome." Danny agreed, and kept to himself that his longtime best-ball partner's adorable wife was easily top-five worldwide in the Elfin Nurse category;

Carter sighed. "Danny, my brother, when you walked to your ball in the playoff…even without knowing all the details, you know, the shit you'd been through…I was moved, man…I mean, you walking back with that little smile, everyone clapping and cheering…I was, like, hearing that Chariots of Fire song in my head. Felt the tears coming. Proud of ya, man."

The phone next to Danny rang. Gotta be Molly. The caller ID read "unavailable." He let it go. Telemarketers, for sure.

Danny shook his head. "Probably the only guy ever to have a three inch putt to win and then…not win."

"Hell, that's almost a better story than winning, Dannymo," said Crusty. "So Carter, what's the big story?"

"You guys hear anything yet?"

"No, they gave me my plaque and we got the hell out of there," said Danny. "Gary did mention that there was some news about the guy they hauled out Monday. I wasn't really catching everything at the time. Told him to talk to Nice or Booze about my round…or Billy Linneman for that matter. I told him I really had to get to icing my back and I'd talk to him later if he needed anything. Thought maybe it might be him who just called. Him or Molly."

Carter nodded, pulled up a chair and sat down. "Well…according to Salamone, and I mean this is some wild shit…but…the cops think the guy they found passed out on Monday might actually be the infamous Nimrod."

"The hell you say," said Crusty. "The twerpy little drunk with the eye-patch...Trammel something..."

"That's the guy, the guy with the eye-patch. Turns out Salamone's brother-in-law, remember him? Used to caddie for Sally? Guess he knows the eye-patch guy." Carter took a swig of his beer. "Because the brother-in-law bought weed from the guy. The eye-patch cat was his dealer."

"Ah, Puffy Mac," said Danny. "Those guys just won't go away. Molly and I saw him and the eye-patch guy at The Farmstead. Beyond properly drunk - both of them."

"That's the M.O.," said Carter. "Turns out, or so I've been told, the eye-patch guy had an arrangement with Norma Hill to grow some weed on the Hill's land, some remote area of the woods by some, like, half cave or something. Had pretty good cover from the sky, some solar power, slick little operation. And dig this, eye-patch guy supposedly had a little humpin' sumpin'-sumpin' going with ol' Norma."

"Well if that ain't an image meant for flushin' from your brain," said Crusty. "She was two and a half times the size of Eye-patch."

"And let me guess," said Danny. "Sally got the word out - said he'd say more when he finished playing today."

Crusty sniffed. "Bet he thought he was keeping the writers from covering Danny Moran's march to victory." After a marathon march covering over 12 miles, the weary caddie laughed without joy. "Prick."

"So, Sally gets all this from Puffy? The pothead?" Danny was on his third beer. Or fourth.

"That's just it, who knows what's true," said Carter. "Anyway...the story goes that old man Hill found out about the weed patch and Norma's involvement with this Trammel guy, the eye-patch dude. Sally says it was Eye-patch blackmailing both sides until all three wanted the other two dead. I guess Eye-patch had been in jail for something else a few years back and then came back, ran into Sally's brother-in-law, and started talking some crazy shit about ol' Nimrod. The guy either assumed the role of Nimrod, or, according to Sally, confessed to some details that sounded like the guy could actually be goddamn Nimrod.

Sally's brother-in-law spilled it all to Sally -- who, by the way, loves this shit -- trying to save his job after failing another drug test at work. Guess he works at Sally's company...or Sally's daddy's company, I should say." Carter finished off his Red Stripe and sat back in his chair.

Crusty was doing his little oval shake-nods. "So Norma was boinking the eye-patch guy, Norby discovers it somehow, maybe through a blackmail threat, this sex for farmland deal or whatever the hell, but...are you saying Eye-patch actually beheaded Norma and stuck a whiskey bottle down her throat?"

"Pretty much what Sally is saying, or that maybe Eye-patch had somebody do it. Guy knows a bunch of ex-cons and freaks I guess," said Carter. "Puffy claims Eye-patch was drinking more and more and sayin' weird shit about the Hills and what he knew. He'd get plowed on Puffy's tab cuz Puffy needed access to his weed. Anyway, the eye-patch guy then started claiming he knew Nimrod...then he started sayin' he was Nimrod...how he'd trap some game, you know, wildlife...and slice 'em up and leave the carcasses around the course to keep the legend growing. Braggin' how he'd never been caught. Guess it made him feel important."

"I don't get it," said Crusty, "how does all this come unravelin' just because the Eye-patch guy is found passed out at The Hill Farm?"

Carter smiled. "Good question. Guess the cops checked out some places in the forest Puffy claimed Eye-patch told him about, found all kinds of shit... knives, tools, fertilizer, even animal traps and stuff. Supposed to be close to the end of that overgrown dirt road, whatever they call it, the one supposed to be, like, haunted, crawling with spiders, the black widows. Whatever, I haven't heard about any actual charges yet."

"I'll repeat," said Crusty, "Sally had to be getting' an erotic charge from all this, holding court and bein' the go-to guy, while stealin' the spotlight from Dannymo."

"Well, this had to be his lucky week then." Danny thought about it. "He had to know something about this for awhile. I mean, that's a lot to go down in three days, you know, from the time they found Eye-patch ass-up in the woods off of 13."

Carter nodded. "Exactly…so when Puffy told Sally that Eye-patch could be Nimrod, Sally said he thought it was bullshit at first, but…in the interest of justice, Sally leverages Puffy to do two things: claim he just now came into this information, and…just for jollies, call Trammel's bluff, have his Puffy-in-law get Eye-patch as fucked-up as possible and offhandedly suggest he make a big Nimrod scene with some dead creatures strewn about The Hill Farm the night before The State Open. You know, so that the incredible legend of Nimrod could just explode. Sally, the concerned citizen sleuth could claim he just found this stuff out and then come forward whenever he felt like it…if at all." Carter was shaking his head; he too had walked 36 holes and looked exhausted. "But, I don't think anyone seriously suspected that the eye-patch creep had actually lopped off Norma Hill's head. Anyway…it seems Puffy got Eye-patch so trashed the guy passed out peeing in the woods on 13."

"This kind of shit," Crusty huffed, "is right in Sally's wheelhouse."

"It's an amazing story," said Carter, "But I'm more amazed Sally couldn't resist telling me everything…he was so excited walking down the 18th…the big boy couldn't help himself."

"Pretty sweet deal he was going for," said Danny. "Credited with solving the mystery of Nimrod and the murder of Norma Hill, while uncovering a drug operation and - the ultimate cherry on top - me blowing up in my final tournament."

"Yep" said Crusty and Carter at the same time.

Carter added, "Talk about hittin' for the cycle."

"Somebody give me a hand," said Danny "I gotta whiz."

Carter laughed.

"Never mind." Danny started to get up; Crusty and Carter were there in a second to help him. "Alright, I'm okay. Gonna use the tree."

Danny walked uneasily by himself to the tree some 30 feet away. Danny had his back to the deck and relieved himself. He looked up at the branches and the leaves of the hickory, the same one in which Molly had been stranded some four months ago. Danny couldn't look at it anymore without thinking of her up there, marooned. Still a few weeks or so until the leaves would be turning colors before setting sail for his gutters. Still time to get some screens. As he was zipping up, his back still to the deck, he said "You know…if it's true, Eye-patch probably couldn't keep it inside anymore. Cops will tell you it's human nature, people want to tell. They actually want to confess."

"Well," said Carter. "Why don't you ask for yourself?"

Danny turned around and, sure enough, Ray Radtke, a pretty high ranking local cop had come around the corner of the house. Danny knew Radtke enough to say hello. Recalled that Ray's son had been a decent high school cornerback and had an unrequited crush on Rinny when she was a freshmen or sophomore. Danny's first thought was, "A cop, why not?" It was a 'why not' kind of day.

"Hi Ray," said Danny. "Want a beer?"

"Have a place we can talk, Mr. Moran?"

"I'll take that as a no on the beer." Danny felt the beer kicking into a safe-at-home glow. "How about we step inside, Officer Radtke."

Crusty was filling in some of the blanks for Carter about Danny's adventure on the 15th hole while trying to not seem nosy about the presence of the cop.

The two men entered the kitchen, Danny struggling with the two steps up. Radtke said, "Sorry to just walk into your backyard like this. I rang the doorbell a couple times."

Danny could not care less about Ray Radtke walking into his backyard. What he cared about was something in the man's eyes, something about his manner. Radtke continued walking toward the foyer near the front door, as if he needed to be near his escape. Through the door window, Danny could see the unmarked car in his driveway behind Carter's Jeep Grand Cherokee.

Ray Radtke turned to face Danny Moran. At some point in his career he had been trained to do many things. This was one thing for which no amount of training helped a whole hell of a lot. He went right into it. "We received a call… I'm afraid I have some bad news, Dan. Your wife was in an accident today. She was leaving St. Michael's Hospital just outside of Chicago in a white Toyota Camry between 4:15 and 4:30. She collided with an ambulance and was pronounced dead on the scene. No other passengers. I'm very sorry."

It was the horror of an unknowable sadness that enveloped Danny then, and it not only sucked the air out of the room, it began ripping out handfuls of his insides with the sharpest, crudest talons reality could deliver. They were scraping at places so deep within him there was nothing he wouldn't have done to keep them undiscovered. There simply was no good in the world that was greater than this was bad. The events of the day lost all meaning in an instant, something belonging to someone else in another life. Danny tried to breathe but was washed over by waves of grief so devastating that the sum of all his nightmares and fatalistic daydreams – those sick fears of having the worst happen to his family — were rendered to nothing more than the wetness that remains on cement after the rain. And the waves kept coming, and then coming harder, until it was one merciless battering.

Danny sat on the floor the moment he told Ray Radtke it was okay to leave. Reeling, now, he almost said thank you. In fact, he may have. He was given a piece of paper with a number to call in Chicago. He had crushed it in his hand.

He hadn't moved, just sat with Carter and Crusty in his living room and could only recall them doing and saying things that good and loving friends do and say. He was struck by their struggle, by their desire, by the depth of their will to do what they could. Danny felt their awkwardness, and their lack of inhibition, in letting him know they would do anything to help him for as long as forever. But it was as if he was watching them in a movie. The waves kept coming. There was nothingness in everything now.

The kids. He needed to tell Rinny and Mo Mo. The thought brought a wave too big to brace for. He didn't fight it; just submitted to its indiscriminate pummeling, a brutal invasion of his most guarded places, until the relentless currents of reality owned his ass and slammed whatever remained of him into a new life on a foreign shore where Wheat Thins were Wheat Thins and the only socks to sort now, would be his own.

He needed to be alone.

∞

Chapter 25

Baby steps.

That's how Mo Moran felt about having refrained from even one sip of beer for, as he told Billy Rick, "going on four days." He'd have to make it through the rest of the evening and then another full day after that to actually total four days, but he figured "going on" gave him some leeway. To Mo, such statements made him more accountable. The key was announcing it the world, even if only by way of Billy Rick. However misleading, it gave him a goal, and he would need to achieve it to make his claim true lest he be seen as less than honest. Mo had told himself there was nothing wrong with putting the truth on layaway as long you live up to the terms.

Alone in his apartment. Again, he had nothing to do and the rest of the day to do it, other than calling his dad, hopefully to congratulate him. After returning from another nerve-torturing shoulder rehab session, Mo checked the Wisconsin PGA's website and saw that Danny Moran had a six shot lead after 54 holes. Later, about the time he figured the final round scores would be posted, his laptop screen suggested he "refresh" or "try later." He did both, repeatedly, fruitlessly. Nothing. The site was down. Pissed him off.

He called home but got his dad's voicemail, which now ended with a self-amused quasi-Dennis Miller-ish, "So…what do you say, my friend?" after having shelved a twist on Jim Rome's "have a take" with "leave a take," which Danny aborted after 10 days because Molly abhorred it. He hung up and started to call his dad's cellphone but decided against it. Final rounds took forever. Maybe they had rain. Whereever D Mo was, he was no doubt with Crusty. Mo loved Crusty, who was like family, but hell, his dad had always talked about "winning the State Open with my boy on my bag." Never happened. Still, caddying for his dad brought

him a lot of attention from adults and gave him insight into how good
men compete as well as measured doses of the reflected swagger that
even humble champions emit, plus the memories of road trips, coming
through "at cheek squeezin' time," chewing on gnarled strips of beef
jerky, the trophies and the laughter and the countless burgers after.
Father and son talking long after their food was gone, in no rush while
nursing the birth of new memories from the day's events and free refills
of diet soda. And then talking some more.

Going to tournaments together had been their thing since he was 11,
pretty much until baseball became his more important thing. His dad
had always made him feel he was crucial to "their" success. Even later,
as he made his way through the Cubs' farm system, Mo missed looping
for his pop in the big ones... the State Am and the State Open.

Not that caddying had always been an unqualified blast. When he
was younger there were times he'd find himself traipsing up and down
hot, hilly, mosquito-infested courses with acres of sand and no shade.
When things went bad, Mo seemed to get madder than his dad,
sometimes *at* his dad. Lately it was Rinny or Crusty on the bag and that
was fine, better than fine, it was right. Still, it bothered him a little when
he first began to feel...replaced. That he felt little tugs at his heart over
such an irrational sense of caddie infidelity felt small, but it was the
truth. He didn't really want to interrupt anything now with a phone call
if his "sub" was right next to D Mo celebrating, at long last, the State
Open championship; the one title to have escaped a man who had nearly
everything and nothing, really, to prove.

No. He'd rather get his dad at home, where he was assured of
getting the full story via Danny Mo's verbal high def and without the
'aw shucks' humility of his dad's public persona. And home, ironically,
was where the father and son could talk without being so paternally
correct, so typically father-son. In those times, it was just D Mo and Mo
Mo, a couple of jungle cats, guys who compete, guys who get it. Same
reason Mo couldn't wait to tell D Mo about his victory over Iowa's long
drive champion, Randy Ride, a couple months ago, before the shoulder
went to hell.

But damn, he wanted confirmation, some good news. He tried his Mom on her cell; she might know something by now. No answer, just her voice greeting, her cheery "flight attendant" tone.

Mo logged on and tried again. The site still showed results through three rounds. He called The Hill Farm Golf Course and got a recording stating they were closed for the Wisconsin State Open. He sighed and half-heartedly began reading an article in the August issue of *ESPN The Magazine* about a statistical analysis of the projected workloads for, and its potential impact on, the bullpens of teams within four games of a wildcard spot. It was practically an Excel spreadsheet. He fell asleep.

∞

The phone rang, waking him. His dad. Mo listened - and then everything started unraveling at a sickening pace. It was bad. The worst.

Mom. Ah… Goddamn.

He hung up, and broke down. And sat. Sat and sobbed until he…just sat and thought. Then he packed – or at least went about stuffing things in a couple of nylon duffle bags. Stumbling through the apartment, he howled at the walls; questions, declarations, begging. Didn't finish most of it, or any of it, at least not out loud. He made sounds he'd never made before, those of misery and anger, but mostly of sadness. Jagged fragments of hurt melted down to a slurry that plumed up through his throat until its edges scorched the inside of his face and transformed into tears. As the hot gush eventually cooled into sludge, it became heavier and retreated downward, taking with it his heart and everything else.

After a while spent half-slumped against the wall, he worked at getting it together, grinding internally, more thinking. He left a note for Billy Rick, his roommate and best friend in pro ball.

> **BR ~**
> **My mom died**
> **Car accident in Chicago**
> **Headed home,**
> **Mo**

He had five and a half hours of driving ahead of him. With his shoulder on the mend, he wasn't supposed to drive long distances, doctor's orders. Right. He got in his car at 8:23 p.m.

And so he drove,and fast, though it didn't seem like it. He felt the strain of just trying to see, as if the world now existed on the other side of a sheet of gauze, thin and transparent at the center but thick at the edges of his periphery. A gathering haze of grief threatened to close in on Mo from every direction at the speed of life. Despite leaving the note and the fact that he knew Billy Rick was playing the last of a three-game series in Omaha, he called his roommate's cell. The mundane task somehow let him breathe infinitesimally easier, induced him to settle down a little, a comma's worth of respite from a fusillade of emotion. Writing the note had worked the same way. He steeled himself and left a message about letting the trainers and everyone know. His voice sounded like someone's shaky imitation of his morning-after voice.

384 miles to go.

He replayed his dad's words. How Danny had said them, the softness in the voice. He thought at first maybe the final round had gone bad, but his dad had never been one to mope over botched tournaments. If anything, D Mo dealt with his on-course mess-ups with a mustered-up brightness and self-deprecating humor and moved on quickly. But Mo never asked about the tournament and his dad said nothing of it. The phone rang and he heard his dad like never before. Hushed, trying to sound strong, but without his customary crackle. Different. Two words and Mo knew it was bad.

And so he figured his dad had probably won the damn tournament. It would figure, the way the world had been working; something pretty good gets paid for with something pretty bad and something great gets paid for with something as bad as it gets. Earn a pro contract, cruise through the farm system, then the shoulder blows up and your mom dies. Yeah, bet he won, and what the hell did it matter.

Once he got beyond Des Moines, everything looked how everything would look for the next four hours, at least until the relative incandescence of Greater Rockford. The stretches of nothingness were monotonous, interrupted only by the peripheral flicker from anonymous clusters of gas stations, fast food joints and motels with vacancy. Then again, through the blinders of abject misery, a Woodland caribou could have been laughing in the act of lighting its own farts in the passenger seat next to him and Mo wouldn't have noticed.

Images of his mother came alive within range of his inner eye. Like any form of torture, it was one after the other. Mostly of Molly in serene moments, or when she'd lift everyone's spirits with her twist on motherly mirth. Mo learned early on that when his mom was at peace, the odds of real-time family happiness increased. She controlled the house with her moods; claimed her worries and concerns "are what keep this family from total anarchy." Mo knew the rough definition of anarchy at an early age, and one of his sweetest childhood highlights was making his teacher, Mrs. Cavallini (a former Alice in Dairyland beauty queen) laugh out loud when he used it like it was perfectly normal for a third grader to describe chocolate milk shooting through Howie Dettloff's nose as "total anarchy."

He forced himself to think of the times when his mom was rigid and demanding and the main source of tension under their roof. Ironically, it was Molly Moran's inexorable battle against domestic anarchy that could turn ordinary moments into miserable ones, even if such stories became family classics years later. Often, it was a young Mo Moran who got that ball rolling.

He was 13. His mother had reprimanded him after he erupted into a laughing jag over an insensitive joke that had Mo Mo mocking the speech of a stroke victim. The more Mo laughed, the madder Molly got and the louder her scolding became. It was then the son of Danny and Molly Moran uttered a stupid line he'd previously reserved only for prissy tattletales. He told his mother that she "took the 'n' out of fun." Whoops. Not that he really meant it, but for about 18 months of his life he actually thought it was clever. That left F U, and left a chagrined Maurice Moran banished to his room to reflect on things.

When his dad came home and got the story, he dutifully supported his wife regarding Mo's FUN minus N formula. But just when he was about to deliver something of a "Listen up, boy" lecture, his mom

suddenly decided it was the perfect time to jump all over his dad for
being the reason their son was turning into such a smart ass. Mo never
forgot how his dad raised his eyebrows and, while still looking directly
at Molly, asked him what the joke was about. How, through thickening
tension, a flustered Mo reluctantly tried to dignify the slurred speech
required for the tasteless joke. And when his mom sensed his dad may
have cracked 1/32 of a smile at their son's feeble attempt to satisfy a no-
win request under enormous pressure, how it all blew up into a
Saturday Night Live skit in funnier times.

It was one of those times when his mom would fume to the point
where she'd fire away with sharp questions for which she demanded
good answers and then tell anyone who dared reply to "be quiet, I'm not
through." When she eventually slammed the guest room door in the
firestorm of "The Moran Family's Stroke Joke Debacle," the large mirror
in the foyer had heard enough and committed suicide by jumping off the
wall and crashing into the antique chest of drawers under it before
smashing onto the hardwood floor where the glass exploded into
eleventy gazillion pieces. Mo Mo had just "helped" his dad hang the
now-deceased mirror a few weeks before, and after the thing offed itself,
his English teacher mother loudly flunked his dad for crappy
craftsmanship. "Looks like I'm not the only one who can't find a stud in
this house!" she wailed. Then, in a hushed, hissing voice, she said,
"You're so half-assed I don't even know how you use the toilet." Mo still
laughed at the memory, how his dad looked at all the mirrored shards
and collateral damage before shrugging, all matter of fact, before
suggesting "We need to Molly-proof this place."

Those so-called tough times hardly seemed tough at all now. Over
the years, the Morans busted into some family laughing jags over such
transgressions, including Mo Mo's inappropriate laughing jag over The
Stroke Joke he should've never told. They'd always glue everything back
together with good humor and once again become the mighty Morans, a
family greater than the sum of their parts. "You'll be stronger where the
scars remain," his dad would say when any of the Morans (or,
embarrassingly, their friends) whined about anything. In fact, he said it

about almost anything imperfect, temporarily broken, or inconvenient. To him, it was always fixable. Until now.

His folks had instilled the notion in him that they were one lucky family. Good times, tough times, all times. Whatever -- everything was a blessing that would surely come in handy down the road; "everything…" his dad would say, "…is an opportunity." Despite some counter-intuitive carping, Mo Mo had witnessed his mom and dad, in different ways, show they had indeed learned from certain missteps. It was a compliment to the kids that the parents believed their kids would usually get it, and so a compliment to the parents as well. The stuff of life that plays out over time, without panic or fear, with trust in each other, they came through every challenge, better. Eventually.

Mo vaguely recalled sharing those thoughts with Billy Rick not too long ago over a few beers. Actually, it was as Billy Rick would say, "a few-few beers." Nine sounded bad.

He would need to refuel. He had envisioned making it to the Iowa 80, The World's Largest Truck Stop (according to the sign), but he stopped well before he got there and filled up. And, conveniently, since it turned out to be before 9 p.m., also bought himself a twelver of Miller Lite. He didn't feel like eating and felt no guilt; he only had room for memories and the comforting pain of them. Nothing else. The beer was for later. He figured he'd get home at around 2:30 a.m. and was concerned his dad might've depleted his inventory. Right.

Mo Mo pressed on through the night. And in the pressing he found he was leaning forward, crowding the wheel a la the elderly, as if there was something in the lean that would get him home sooner. He looked at the beer in the brown bag. He asked God for a sign, anything that would give him the okay to have a cool one. Did he not deserve one or two for God's sake. His prayer was answered when he saw the sign "MOLINE, NEXT EXIT." Mo-line. Pronounced Mo-lean. His sign. He'd made the trip enough times to know it was coming. He drank, and drove. Later, he saw another helpful sign, for a Mo-tel. Another beer.

Then another, a sign for Mo-tor Vehicle Assistance, or some such. Another. More leaning forward. More memories. More. Mo-re.

The beer felt good going down for a guy feeling so bad. For a while. Then it felt like...nothing. No effect. Overridden by thinking. Remembering. Feeling. Mo merged with the hum of his car. He had no use for the radio. In his mind, music would've had no meaning, or maybe too much meaning. He wanted the quiet, the hum. Bloomington-Normal came and went, Rockford just before midnight. He felt he was among the better drinking drivers of – as his dad liked to say – "the modern era." The paranoia helped him to bear down. He had another beer. No stop signs on the interstate. Must be okay.

The forward lean turned into rocking, back and forth, a rhythm best described as consistently random, his movement again deluding, as if it could both expedite the trip and disperse pain. He thought of his dad alone at home. Rinny would be arriving tomorrow... actually later that morning. By the time he was through the Marquette interchange in downtown Milwaukee he had tears running down his face. Traffic was light; the dreaded freeway construction project wasn't a factor at two in the morning. The familiar surroundings amplified everything. His body leaned and released, rhythm quickening; everything about him aching for home.

Awash in white noise and sailing on the concrete of I-43; Glendale, Fox Point, Brown Deer, the further north he got, the more alone he seemed. Even with the window down, his car held despair captive. He was minutes from home now; his need to take a leak was excruciating, his bladder had been begging for relief since well before Beloit nearly two hours ago, a near mind-over-matter miracle after knocking down "a few-few beers." Just get the hell home and let it all out. Everything.

That's when the red rooftop lights violated the darkness and fell in behind him.

County sheriff.

Shit.

Mo checked his speed... he was going 77. His empty wasp-waisted cans were poised and quietly waiting to testify against him in the brown paper bag he had requested at the gas station over four hours ago. He knew he was busted. And whatever consequences awaited him now, none came close to the delay this would mean in getting home.

And so with his chest pounding from the sudden burst of the sheriff's flashing lights, and his heart heavy with sorrow while a thousand thoughts taxed his ability to reason and torrents of Family Past pooled and merged with his now painful need to piss, the pressure from all of these things building into an act of evil alchemy intended for weakened and tender places: his shoulder, his heart, his bladder and his smoldering brain, Mo Mo Moran knew something would have to give or rupture, like the breaching of a dam designed for lesser loads, and that everything inside him could explode and drift like a damp mist across the city where he grew up. And just ahead, a mere pitching wedge away, was his exit, yet hardly an outlet for anything now.

"Nice sticker." The approaching Milwaukee County sheriff's voice had an ambiguous tone that cut through the night like the angled beam of his flashlight.

Mo said nothing, sat still and looking forward, stewing in the clamminess he felt from everything turning to shit. *Sticker*? He was certain the stickers on his Wisconsin plates were current.

"The Cubs?" said the sheriff. "Seriously?"

∞

Chapter 26

"In my darkest hours, I have always counted on my faith to do the heavy lifting, but faith, like my back, can falter too." Danny had said, finally, "If you know what I mean."

Right. Even he wasn't sure what he meant. He'd been there before, frozen in front of everyone with no idea of how to begin. Curly. This time, looking out at the overflow of mournful souls packing the pews and horseshoeing the back end of the church, Danny felt disoriented. Exhaustion and doubt had ganged up on him, and with them came the confusion that chipped away at an otherwise long-standing acceptance of God's will. At last he got a sentence out. That usually did it. Usually bought him a few seconds to come up with something better.

With the rupturing of his L5-S1 disc and the devastation in losing Molly, he had barely eaten or slept in three days, but for little nibbles and involuntary naps. Danny could feel himself start to hit The Wall. Whether one actually smacked into the metaphorical wall or was rendered useless by its looming, an irrefutable truth remained: when The Wall goes up, people go down.

"Half-way between dread and dead" was how he had explained it to a counselor. His thoughts went back to some wretched stretches of his life; to those sleepless nights when his brain kept cycling, thoughts turning over just so they could circle back and roust him again, like a laboring engine that wouldn't shut down. They took him to where he could at least sense the wall ahead. Many times right before dawn, he'd decide to call it a night and begin battling his way into a new day with long walks and a whole lot of coffee, anything to kick-start what he hoped would be a dead-on impersonation of his so-called "real self." If not dead-on, then at least close enough to get him through the day's objectives and back to the evening when the sleep would come easy early. But it was never too long before he'd awaken again, as if poked, and start the thinking all over again.

St. Cecelia's was silent but for sniffles, coughs, and noses being blown, sounds that might have echoed in the medium-sized church had the building not been with filled with people and humid with grief. Everyone was waiting for Danny to again speak. Those who knew him well would guess he was floundering, or so he believed, which only made the moment worse. Unlike when he eulogized his father, when the words came as if heaven sent, he was coming up empty now. And empty was exactly what he was.

He had screwed up earlier, before leaving for the church. He'd resisted at first, then relented at last, and accepted a shot of Jameson's Irish Whisky from his freshly divorced and still miserable brother, Jimmy, who was staying at the house for the funeral. He'd not bothered to hide his irritation with his self-medicating brother who kept offering him a "wee wan," and finally blasted his brother's whiskey nips as "juvenile." Danny had preferred to deal with his present bleakness by keeping busy or appearing to be. He dragged himself around the house, futzing with whatever, checking on the funeral mass and burial details, and other arrangements already handled by his mother, Manda, with help from Rinny. But he hurt so badly and the Vicodin for his back wasn't doing a damn thing. The fact was, he'd never been big on pills that masked symptoms. He preferred they treat something, like swelling or heartburn. Or heartache.

So, in a weak moment and in complete contradiction to his earlier contention he did a damn "wee wan of Jame-O's." Couldn't hurt, he thought, couldn't hurt anymore than the hurt ravaging him already. He did not admit aloud that the shot warmed him in a pleasantly weird way for a few minutes. Then, just before heading to the church, his brother handed the bottle to him again and without thinking he took one more slug. This time an irresponsible gate-crashing double glug right out of the bottle, not a wee wan in any way.

Feeling dazed and filled with emptiness, Danny never doubted his ability to address the hundreds who had gathered at the memorial service for Elizabeth Margaret "Molly" Moran. He had a lot to say --

needed to say -- about the love and respect he had for Molly. Earlier in the day, during visitation, he felt his weariness had actually worked for him; helped him get through the grind of greeting one person at a time for hours. It was the lone upside to the melancholy freedom in being too crushed to care how he was supposed to do anything.

The combination of a spirited one-two punch from whiskey and very little food and two pain pills and very little sleep had become a legitimate threat to any semblance of Danny Mo's ballyhooed control. It was on this shifting foundation that Danny began his eulogy for his wife by uttering a statement he didn't totally understand himself. And the effort to reason it out on the fly, one of Danny's greatest attributes, did nothing now but intensify the unwelcome prickle across his scalp and empower the perspiration slaloming down the canal bisecting his back. He was clammy and cold at the edges, the feeling that usually (and did again) gave way to the freaking butterflies. The same ones he endured on his nightly drives home, when the closer to home he got, the more anxious he became over what Molly's current mood might mean for the evening.

Danny squinted at the congregation. Everyone waiting for him to continue. *Uh, Danny?* A moment ago he had been sitting in the front pew with Rinny and Mo Mo on either side of him. Danny was to follow his cue, a nod from Father Tom. When the time had come, Rinny had put her hand on him and asked if he was okay. *Do I look that bad?* He set aside his cane and willed his way the eight or ten steps to the front of the church and up three carpeted steps to the lectern. There was a milky whiteness at the periphery of his vision, he didn't have the spins but felt a little lightheaded. He knew he was in trouble.

Eventually he spoke again.

"In my darkest hours, I have always counted on my faith to do the heavy lifting, but faith, like my back, can falter too," Danny had said, finally, "if you know what I mean." *Huh?* He hoped no one - NO ONE - would realize or acknowledge that he'd repeated his opening statement.

"I...Molly...jeez...disregard what I just said..." Danny had a little grin, the helpless sort. He quickly, almost sadistically, glimpsed the eyes of Rinny and Mo Mo in the front row; saw the ache in them, all made worse by having to watch their surviving parent choke like a talking tree in a kindergarten play.

Being aware of this floundering kicked up his metabolism. His stomach was doing somersaults; his last real meal was the plateful of chicken fingers between rounds at The Hill Farm. He knew now that he should have grabbed a sandwich or something after the visitation at the funeral home before heading to the memorial at Saint C's, and he damn well should have stuck to scoffing off the Jameson's. His senses had become untrustworthy now, and a Tampa afternoon had broken out inside his dark suit, and he was pretty much falling on his face in front of a whole lot people pulling for him to get it together, to find a flash of the Danny Moran they all knew, heard of, or read about. But he cared little about saving face now, he wanted more than anything to do well by Molly, to make good on his suspicion that God, in some way beyond all comprehension, somehow filters out the grief and lets all good people listen in on their own funerals, wakes or memorial services. There was so much he wanted to say, but he'd entered one of those dreams where you just can't do what you want to do, no matter how easy, meaningless or hard - like finding your dog and going for a cool one together at The Aftermath.

The Wall had taken dead aim at the man behind the lectern. Still, he regrouped enough to say, "Molly...my sweet and crabby Molly..." Did he actually say "sweet and crabby?" It was a phrase that he had repeated to himself hundreds of times over the past three days, an inner mantra he found comforting in its familiarity. One he had repeated throughout their marriage as he worked to understand his "sweet and crabby Molly," and their differences... the ways to make two people with different outlooks but overlapping values become greater than the sum of two peas in a pod - to have something better than those couples who, because they had everything in common and nothing to say, finished each other's sentences.

He had intended to champion the literacy campaign Molly had started in the surrounding school districts. How she had promoted her love of books and how contagious her ideas were and leadership had been. How her program had become a template of sorts for reading programs around the country, and how she had influenced so many kids of the X-Box Playstation, Cable/Dish/TiVo –movies-on-your-phone generation to actually develop an affinity for books, despite about a billion gigabytes of initial resistance. But he felt the thickness of his tongue and the dryness of his mouth and knew he wouldn't stand a chance in hell of pronouncing "the Advancement of Adolescent Literacy." He thought about comparing Molly to a challenging book, the kind that took some work and patience, maybe talk about the rewards that came from things with many layers, with depth, with surprises, and wit and meaning and thoughts… that stay with you forever.

Instead, his mind scampered to an easier, folksier way to say the same thing. He wanted to tell everyone how they used to spar, the kick they got from absurdist debate. Molly was wired to detect human and mechanical flaws and Danny would counter with the full force of his inner Pollyanna and they'd fight to a tie. Danny always claimed a tie, since "everyone knows the tie goes to The Rattler."

Danny heard coughing in the congregation and it snapped him back to the moment. He hadn't known panic much in his life, but holding onto the lectern now, this was feeling like the real deal. The filing system in his brain was broken. He was lost. He was transfixed by the bright blue carpet on the alter of the church. The swoops of the vacuuming pattern made the grain in the fabric seem to move. *Say something, Danny Boy!*

And so he tried a final time.

"Molly didn't approve of the satisfaction I derived from beef jerky so much. Preservatives, you know…and way too much sodium…but…I told her that they named my favorite flavor after her…Sweet and Hot. It's not easy to find good Sweet and Hot jerky." The word preservatives came out as pruh-zerver-divs, and he felt like a hick. Some titters emerged from in the pews but they seemed presoaked in both sympathy and sadness. Danny's voice was shaky and he had taken to swaying.

"Molly was…and I say this, uh, lovingly… but she was like a good batch of jerky sometimes. You know, sometimes tender, sometimes hard and tough, but worth the work...but..." Bonehead, big-time. Danny focused on the blue of the carpet now. So blue, he thought, so very brilliant. "I'm sorry...got sidetracked...this blue carpet reminds me of Boise State's blue football field...in fact. Well, I'll tell ya...one night Molly and I were laying in bed; she was reading and I was watching some late-night college football on ESPN, Boise State was playing...and Molly glanced at the TV and was fascinated by that blue field they have...she said it was a 'pretty blue'...and let me say that the blue was, like, the same blue as my bathrobe...and Molly always hated my bathrobe. She... " Danny looked up could see faces, and some hands going to faces. He thought his mother might have been blinking back tears.

Danny swayed just enough that he needed to take a half-step to regain his balance; he was too warm, swampy under his dark suit. His face was glazed and his fingers ice. He tried again. Words weren't coming... He was shaking his head, long shakes, as if tracing the arc of the vacuum swoops on the blue carpet.

Suddenly, somehow, Rinny and Mo materialized next to him at the lectern. Rinny took the mic and said something. The siblings then tried to lead him to the side door. In three steps Danny whispered. "I kinda hit the Wall. I should just sit down." Father Tom appeared with a cup of cool water. Sipping it helped. He made it back to the pew with Mo Mo's help and sat down, too exhausted to feel self-conscious. He knew Mo Mo had to have noticed his overall dampness. Danny's eyes, which had been itchy and dry standing in front of everyone, were now moist. He was done.

As he sat, head down, he worked to regain his senses and felt better with Mo and Rinny next to him...except Rinny wasn't there. His mother had moved down the pew and was next to him now. But he could hear Rinny's voice, or was it Mo's...it was Mo's "Dad...you okay...want to get some air?"

Then he did hear Rinny's voice, louder, coming from speakers. She had taken over for her father. And as he watched and listened to her, he felt himself improving, as if his daughter's strength was transmittable through the PA system, through her bearing and presence. She looked like her mother.

Rinny sweetly chronicled life as a Moran with stories and observations about her mother, how she treated each person in the family differently, "according to their idiosyncrasies...what was best for each of us...never once caring if it was popular or not. She loved us all too much to worry about being buddies or being 'cool' in our eyes." Danny knew exactly what she meant and marveled at his daughter's command of the Moran family dynamics. Danny lowered his head again and took a quick, quiet crack at saying the word "idiosyncrasies"...as a test.

"You sure you're okay?" Mo Mo was looking at his dad like he might be cracking up before his eyes. "Sinker at the knees?"

"Sshh," said Danny, a warm finger to dry lips.

Rinny took a deep breath and placed her hands gracefully on the top of the lectern. Danny was reminded once again why Rinny was someone he wanted to be more like.

"I can confirm my father's claim," said Rinny in a confident voice. "From time to time I have heard my dad call my mom 'Sweet and Hot,' and I always thought, 'oookay.' But I never knew about the connection with Beef Jerky. What could I have been thinking? I'm sure most marriages have things known only to the two of them in it. That's probably one of those. But sometimes one spouse keeps a secret or two from the other. I know of one I'm hoping my mom would want to share with my father now. I mean, she probably intended to anyway. I had stumbled upon my mom's secret accidentally and respected her request that I keep it private." Rinny paused and looked at her dad; she looked as though she would break into tears. And then she gathered herself in a way her broken-down father couldn't. "I believe it is the right thing to do."

"About two years ago when I was 16, my dad was out of town at a golf tournament, and I was staying over at a friend's house. Mo Mo, of course, was down south playing ball. Early the next morning, maybe 5 a.m., I was awake in my sleeping bag on the basement floor at my friend's parent's house…and, I just wanted to be in my own bed. So I got up and went home. As I walked to my room, I saw the door to my parents' room was slightly open. Mom was lying in bed, and I could see someone lying next to her in Dad's blue robe…I learned today that this blue would be called Boise State blue, I guess. Needless to say, I was shocked."

Total silence. No one sniffled, coughed or moved. The church had become much smaller in Danny's mind. He could feel people looking at him. Rinny looked at her father again, now she did have tears in her eyes. Rinny took a deep breath. "I barged right into their room. My mom sat up instantly. I looked at my dad's side of the bed and there…right next to my mom…was my dad's robe stuffed with a couple of pillows. Half of it was under the covers, and half propped against his TV watching pillow."

Danny didn't know he was holding his breath but sure felt the release.

"My mom…" Rinny's voice broke, and she sobbed for a few seconds. "My mom saw me looking at my dad's robe, and just said. "You're home early, Honey; want some breakfast?" Rinny wiped away some straggling tears with the heel of her hand. "Later in the day she told me that whenever my dad went out of town…she made what she called her 'Dummy Mo.' That she was more comfortable being alone with his smell near her and that if I ever said anything she said she would, quote, 'just die.'" Rinny looked out at the congregation. "But not before she killed me first."

People laughed, and some tears flowed. Rinny had lifted everyone in the church. Smiles of compassion brought light to the darker places of these survivors of sorrow, if only for the moment. But a moment so welcome, so needed.

Again, tears were streaking Rinny's face. she looked at her dad, with tears welling in his eyes as well. "And even though she made a big deal about how her Dummy Mo didn't snore…I know Mom could never love anyone more than she loved you, Daddy."

After the memorial service, easing his way with his cane toward the back of the church, Danny couldn't help but notice people were looking at him like they did when he walked back to the tee after his hideous tee shot in the playoff at The Hill Farm. Building upon his fuck-ups, he thought. It was the first time the open defeat three days earlier had entered his mind. He didn't even glance at the newspaper the next day or since.

Rinny and Mo were on either side of him.

His rescuers.

His kids.

When they reached the church foyer, Danny saw Molly's niece, Maddy, who had come up from Chicago against her doctor's orders. She was holding her five-day-old baby. The five of them came together in a long, wordless hug.

Life goes on.

∞

Chapter 27

"So," said Mo after about a half mile of silence, "Jerky, huh?"

"Yeah. My bad. Your mother told me that no woman wants to be compared to dried meat. Go figure," said Danny, "but I think she liked the Sweet and Hot reference. Not that she ever let on."

Mo drove slowly through a residential area that led to Green Bay Avenue and back home. "A guy just doesn't think of his mom as hot."

"Try using the wrong kitchen sponge."

Mo chucked. "The color code system's still in play, huh? What is it…yellow, dishes; green, counter; blue for floor and miscellaneous?"

"Yellow is dishes, for sure. The green and blue I always got mixed up. On the off chance I'd make a little mess on the counter or kitchen table, hell, your mom would look at me and I'd flat choke…never wanted to make a non-yellow choice when she was watching." Danny was reclined all the way back in the passenger seat of Mo's car and looking at the roof. He was getting used to the position. Rinny, Grandma Manda, Maddy, and baby Elizabeth were in the car ahead of Danny and Mo.

"You think she's watching us now?"

"No."

"No?"

"No," said Danny, "I just don't think Heaven would be all that heavenly if she could see us falling apart."

"Seriously? You don't think Mom would've have gotten a kick out of seeing you sweat, you know, like Crusty says, 'steppin' on your uh…self,' bumblin'and stumblin' a bit tonight, going on about beef jerky and the Boise blue robe and all?"

"Might've for a moment, but in the end your mom would've been dying right along with me up there. She wanted everything for us. You know her shoulder starting hurting after your injury?

"No way…" Mo was disbelieving.

"Doctor didn't find anything." Danny shrugged and left it at that. "But, yeah, I screwed up tonight, shouldn't have done the couple nips of whiskey. Dumb."

"Well…" Mo took a moment. "…I screwed up, too, driving back from Iowa."

Danny carefully repositioned himself into a reclined position that looked just like the reclined position he had previously been in.

"I'm serious," said Mo. "I screwed up."

"What?"

"Driving back, bought some beer, got pulled over for speeding, right before getting off at our exit."

"Beer? Driving?"

"Shouldn't have. Did. Long story lopped, I didn't want to dump even more on you so I called Crusty from the station. I passed the field sobriety, breathalyzer was borderline but I was fine."

"What's borderline?"

".08 once, .076 a second time. I was fine and they knew I was fine, other than feeling worse than I ever felt in my life…they knew about Mom. Crusty talked with a bunch of the cops, must have taken care of things. He brought Carter to the station and it worked out. I'm lucky, won't happen again. Got me for speeding and the open intoxicant thing. Cost me $399.20"

Danny was about to ask Mo if the beer made him feel any better, but stayed quiet. Felt his moral authority had been compromised by his pills n' whiskey performance at the memorial service. True, he hadn't gotten behind the wheel of a car, but it drove him wiggy thinking how he had failed Molly. Twenty-five years of indelible memories, then 25 more ripped from the Moran family planner. Molly deserved better. Danny wanted to be pardoned. Partial absolution, at least, for his final words to Molly. *"…if you'd just shut your pie-hole."*

He'd said it over the phone. She was in her pre-upset upset danger zone and he knew it. The household tension over a so-called troubled pregnancy had been taking its toll as the week went on. Her nagging about keeping things neat was his wife's way of venting, her default setting. Molly's rigid commitment to order had nothing to do with her fundamental nature, those deeper qualities that inspired him to work hard on their marriage and why he had slugged through counseling to better understand what he could do, and more importantly, what not to do. *Let the matches dry, Danny.* Molly Moran would never have wanted her husband saddled with a "shut your pie-hole" send-off, but for the rest of his life, that's what he was going to have to live with. Rinny's revelation about the existence of a Dummy Mo had proven to be all too true. There were indeed two dummies.

"Well, Mo," said Danny, "no one needs to hear about dumb behavior right about now, you and me both."

"Thanks."

"Remind me to get all over you another time."

"Deal."

They drove in silence until Danny asked Mo to stop at the Piggly Wiggly. Death had filled his house with the living, and those guests were quickly depleting his supplies… supplies were his responsibility now. For a moment the two of them sat in the store's parking lot, thinking. They watched a mother and two freakishly helpful kids load groceries into a mini-van two spaces away. Danny and Mo waited, still disbelieving of the wheel-jerk turns their lives had taken. Father and son. Jungle cats. De-clawed, injured and exhausted. Danny made some small talk. "Lot of people from the Harbor."

Mo nodded. "I assumed the folks I didn't know either worked with Mom or were from the Harbor."

"You meet Sam Bursinger?"

"No idea."

"Probably pushes 320, bad comb over."

"Oh, yeah, met him," said Mo. "You ever see a good one...I mean, have the words 'good comb over' ever been uttered...before now?"

"Sarcastically, I'm sure. But a valid point."

Mo gave his dad a double-take. "What about Tubby?"

"Says the folks in Rock Harbor are up in arms, at least the ones that know about it." Danny sighed, and then spoke as if he was sorry for bringing it up. "Loren Ferguson reportedly wants to build a world class golf course along Harrow Bluffs."

"Wow," said Mo, evenly. "It would be spectacular, the view from those cliffs."

"And pricey, though Loren's got it." Danny shrugged. "Sam exaggerates everything, anyway. Says the Harbor will revolt if he somehow gets his hands on that land."

"Doesn't he have like, a million dollar mansion on the bluffs already?"

"Probably worth four times that. According to Sam, he'll gut it and make it a clubhouse, or just tear it down. There's a lot of DNR stuff to get around before anything could happen. Sam says Fergy would buy out the other two properties along the bluffs. He thinks he can pull it off with the right number. Sam kept bugging me about what I thought."

"Tonight?" said Mo. "The guy peppers you with that tonight?"

"People are awkward, don't know what to say but wanna say something." Danny knew the feeling. "I asked how things were back home. He jumped on it."

"Well, what do you think about your old stomping grounds becoming a golf course?"

"Exactly Sam's words," said Danny. "I'll tell you what I told him. 'Not much,' my exact words. You know, I just don't have the energy to process that stuff right now."

"I know." Mo looked around the parking lot. The mom got behind the wheel of the van as her son, who couldn't have been more than 10 or 11, held the door for her and closed it once she was buckled in. The kid even gave the door a little post-slam love tap. "Remember how you used to give me '*the look*' if I didn't get the door for Mom?"

A tiny smile worked across Danny's features. They sat in silence until the sound of the van pulling away rose and fell. "Alright, can you run in and get a bunch of lunch meat from the deli counter, a few loaves of bread, a few cartons of orange juice, couple dozen eggs, butter, couple big vegetable and fruit platters and anything else that's pre-cut, ready to eat and on a tray, maybe some bacon…and some cheap shampoo." Danny reached for his wallet and it hurt like hell.

"I got it," said Mo Mo." Breakfast stuff, lunch meat, trays, platters and shampoo."

"Cheap shampoo," said Danny. "Nothing with burdock root."

"Yeah, okay, keep the doors locked and don't talk to anyone."

With his good arm, Mo slammed the door. Danny got through some knotty spasms in his back to sit up. He watched his son walk away from the car and toward the doors of the store, disappearing inside but not before slipping a full-on blitz from three little kids storming out the 'in' door. Mo never broke stride, nimble as anyone with a wounded wing could be. *Top-five worldwide*, his dad thought.

∞

The blur that life becomes for the living as they come to grips with it ending too soon for someone dear renders the passage of time both meaningless yet mandatory for survival. The conventional feel-good wisdom about "living in the moment"-- probably espoused by people feeling good at the moment of their espousal -- would have crushed Danny by now had he attempted to comply with such advice. For him, it had been three straight days of too many faces, too much talking and too many thoughts spliced onto an endless reel of personal cinematic scene clips and soundtracks and other movie trailer ways of honoring the dead. Tear-jerkers and romantic comedies, most of them, much of it overdramatized by shaky memories and tongue-tied slices of fond nostalgia. So too were there snippets of horror and suspense, but in the plainer and more painful sensibility of a documentary, where things turn out as they do, not how one wants. He wished he were indeed only

watching it instead of living it, but he knew now he had been damned to
the reality of both. Such was the nature of Danny's inner life and how
certain customary behaviors influenced his views on new worlds
unfurling for Maurice, Corinne and him. Everyone meant well, he knew
that, but he wanted the formal, ceremonial part of Molly's death to end.
And he wanted his kids to know the world would be good again. And
once again he needed some time alone. Soon.

Danny had asked for the burial ceremony to be kept small. Had he
not been proactive in limiting the numbers, he felt like the several
hundred who had come to the wake, memorial service and funeral mass
would've come to the Twelve Apostles cemetery so as to not fare poorly
in some unspoken *how-much-do-you-really-care-about-the-Morans*
competition. Not that first place was so prized, but no one wanted to
bring up the rear. And while the circumstances were tragic and sad, and
many friends and family had come a long way to pay respects and
provide support, all the meals and activities seemed to have become a
celebrated social happening for some on the periphery. This too was
wearing on Danny, and it bothered him that he was annoyed, like it was
a crime against a good percentage of his heritage, a blight on his
Irishness.

He had long hoped his own death would one day bring folks
together for food and drink, with laughter and stories and any kind of lie
that might put him in a better light. He even had some "perfect" songs
picked out. Molly had seen this as just more DJM indulgence. At the
moment, however, when he saw folks who had come to the funeral from
upstate and the UP going about laughing and making plans for dinner
and to take in a Brewers' game, he felt a sliver of irritation knifing
through his common sense. He was the crabby one now, and yet on
some level he knew that his kind of crabby was merely the selfish
teenage son of Sadness. He knew he'd grow out of it, just as he knew
he'd never be the same without Molly.

Danny had insisted on bringing his black trench coat to the burial
though there was no threat of rain. It was noon, warm but not hot. He
had held his coat in his lap on the drive over, folded at his side during
the Mass, and it was now draped over his arm as he stood around the

coffin at the cemetery. The trench coat had been a gift from Molly for his birthday four years ago. It tapered to the waist, then caped out a bit and down low, below the calf. Molly called it a "duster" and Danny felt like he was channeling his inner private eye when he wore it. The first time he put it on, he checked himself out in the hallway mirror and for some reason said, "D Mo here, everyone relax." When Molly rolled her eyes and shook her head, Danny made "everyone relax" into a mandatory catch phrase any time he felt he was dressed cool and looking good. "Dashing," as 'Molly-in-a-good-mood' would put it.

And so the burial was limited to those closest to the family. Molly's never-married best friend growing up was there, as were two dear friends from the Advocates for Adolescent Literacy program, which the three of them had started together. The wake had been closed casket as the accident had been a comprehensive horror. As it turned out, Molly was at fault. The ambulance had had the right of way. Molly's niece had gone into an all-evening and part of the next day labor and delivery, and Molly had stayed up the entire time. She had received a phone call on her cell phone at the approximate time of the accident. Fumbling through her purse for it? No one would ever know.

At the grave site, Rinny and Mo Mo stayed at Danny's side as if the three were connected elbow-to-elbow, like a tight front line of foosball figures. The smell of freshly cut grass permeated the air as summer delivered an ain't-dead-yet sense of revival to southeastern Wisconsin. Two dogs watched from behind the chain link fence maybe 50 yards away and three backyards apart along a row of modest ranch style homes that abutted the cemetery. They were exchanging what Danny assumed were conversational barks. The same cadence, over and over. Border collie one bark, labradoodle two. Silence for awhile. Then, right back to the border collie one, labradoodle two. Danny thought he may have been losing his mind. One high bark "Jeez" two lower barks "us-Christ." One bark "Sue," two barks "per-star." Danny thought...could it really be a canine rendition of that ol' Jesus Christ Superstar song? Was his mind was playing tricks on him? Earlier, inside the church, the lighting and the sound system seemed different. This was a church he'd been inside hundreds of times and now he was seeing and hearing things in a way he never had before. When he had looked at the carpet on the alter, it looked dark, not Boise State blue, but when he went up to receive communion, it looked all Boise State again.

"You recognize that?" Danny whispered to Mo.

"Recognize what?"

"Listen," said Danny. In the distance…one bark, two. Bark -- bark-bark. "Hear that?"

"What?"

"That."

"All I hear is some barking."

"Exactly. Recognize it?"

"You're scaring me, Dad."

Danny hummed the melody to Superstar. "Hmmmm…hmm hmm." And again. "Hmmm…hmm hmm. Can you hear it now? Your mom played it a lot when you were young. You kids would sing it too."

"Ah…I remember mom singing Christmas carols - and *Danny Boy* when she was liking you."

Father Tom began the burial ceremony with a prayer. Danny looked at Mo. "Never mind," he whispered. Maybe he was cracking up.

The Pastor talked with confidence about life and death. That death was not the end, but rather a rite of passage to a better life, to eternal life, a life in full union with the Lord. It may have been boiler plate stuff but Danny found it comforting. He knew in his heart Molly was at peace. And he knew everyone in Heaven would soon be enlightened as to the importance of color-coding kitchen sponges.

Rinny had contacted a friend whose older brother was a multi-instrumentalist in a popular regional rock band called Sonic Plaid. She had been assured that one of the instruments he played very well was the bagpipe. Danny had loved the idea, but so too had he seen bagpipers over the years show up at events late and drunk and sound like fighting pigs when they finally did play. At the end of the final prayer, when the coffin was lowered into the earth, the Sonic Plaid dude, a pony-tailed guy named Ollie, appeared out of nowhere and performed a version of Amazing Grace that touched Danny in the magical way that only music can. And he was not alone.

His back in full protest now, Danny stood very near the grave site as if he needed…well he didn't really know what he needed…entirely. Molly's parents were long-deceased and her remaining family came by group-by-group before departing. Embraces and silent affirmations were exchanged more than any feeble stabs at philosophical final words, and still the dogs engaged in their prayerful three-bark soundtrack melody. Ollie mentioned his affinity for Labradoodles and headed over to the fence with his pipes to hang out by the two note wonder.

Finally it was just Rinny, Mo Mo, Danny and his mother Amanda. Danny's brother had volunteered to drive some older out-of-towners to the Moran home where the final scheduled funeral function would finally wrap up. Manda Mo had quietly handled so many of the details the past few days that Danny actually had to pretend he was properly harried with it all. They looked down at the casket, now recessed in the earth. Somebody would be filling in the remaining emptiness later. The four Morans looked at each other. There was nothing left to say. This was it.

A watery-eyed Mo Mo couldn't resist breaking the silence. "Ollie likes you, Rinny." He was nodding at his sister.

"Oh, Mo," said Rinny, between sniffles.

Mo looked past everyone. "Well. It's us four and Ollie over there. Pretty much the five you'd expect to be here to the end."

"Probably waiting to be paid," said Danny, who decided Ollie was having a conversation through the fence with the Labradoodle. Maybe negotiating a deal for a backup singer.

"I took care of it, Honey." It was Manda, and of course she did. "He refused, and I insisted."

"Mo may be right then, Rin. Is he Catholic?" said Danny, reprising Curly's customary first words when any of his kids dated anyone even once. Manda smiled.

Danny let out a long sigh, easy to do in his exhausted state, but also an indication that he had something to say. Rinny, Mo and Manda looked at him. "Well, my dear Mos...had I known about this earlier...but...feels a little...I don't know..." Danny aborted his attempt at coherence again and unfolded his black trench detective-guy duster. Inside, lining the coat was his blue robe with a flattened pillow inside. Manda put a hand to her mouth. Rinny insta-sobbed before insta-recovering. Mo swallowed hard and nodded. All were blinking back tears.

Danny tossed his blue robe on top of the casket and it slid a little to the side, on the corner, where it caught and stuck. One arm pit turned partially inside out, the chalky whiteness there evidencing years of accumulated deodorant rings. The four Morans stood in a row, arms around each other, looking down. Ollie must have thought it a good time to play An Irish Lullaby, bagpipe style. Softly, from a respectful distance, as the dogs watched in silence. Too-Ra-Loo-Ra-Loo-Ra.

"I think," said Mo, quietly, looking at his sister, "Mom would approve."

∞

Book II

Chapter 28

At times, the memories of Molly were vivid enough to mess with his metabolism, other times they were like old photos stored in a musty book buried at the bottom of one of those junk-filled closets that everyone tries to avoid.

Danny sat back in his chair and shoved off to gain clearance from his desk. He was at his office, but his mind was elsewhere. Memory was a terrible thing to waste, he figured, good times and bad. Seared in his brain forever, though, was the recollection of when everything got turned inside out and ripped apart. Thirty years of love and worthwhile frustration, twenty-five of those years married. During times of strength he vowed never to forget the lessons of that period. In weaker times he found himself praying to the Patron Saint of Amnesia - St. Whatsername.

Churning out words on his laptop had been part of some hunting, pecking and venting therapy. Blasts of rambling prose and esoteric verse were attempts at flattening out the soul-jarring ruts he encountered on the unpaved roads to the so-called dumps. Writing had been his outlet, a flotation device for those moments when he sensed he was adrift in deep waters, where any hope of rescue came only through the passage of time.

He wrote almost nothing about Molly, yet she was at the center of why he needed to write. She was gone and he was reeling. A story as old as time. Death and divorce were supposed to have a lot in common, but it was Danny's feeling that while the shooed-away honey bee may suffer pain or embarrassment, it was better than the splatter of the windshield. He had started down the "miss you, Molly" path a few times only to detour almost immediately. So powerful were his feelings of loss that trying to write them down bordered on discounting the existence of God. Faith didn't come with vouchers; the living and the dead couldn't just redeem coupons for assurances that they were in fact dearly loved and terribly missed. But since Molly was into coupons, he chose to believe that "on earth as it is in heaven" would hold sway. He hoped so anyway.

And so he had plowed through sludgy stretches of time by writing, for hours, a quarter hour at a crack. Survival. An outsider would have observed a man who alternated between possessed bursts of two-fingered typing and impassively staring. Mostly staring. But so too would the observer sense the whirring of whatever internal machination was working to turn over the rocks that buried too many truths, or pedestalled others to naked light. And it was those very rocks that sometimes crushed him as severely as when Ray Radtke first delivered the tragic news he'd never talk to Molly again.

Back then, during the darkness, his brain would nearly fry from the grind. His forehead would get warm, his heart would clutch up, and breathing became a conscious act. He had labored through those moments as if the simplest action had to work against a jacket of tar. A bad place to be, but too often he flat-out felt too moved to move. It was through sheer will that he freed up two fingers and typed. Trying to breathe, trying not to sigh, trying to think one minute and trying not to the next. He sometimes varied his trying, but like some imponderable dream, it was way too much and all too trying. Impossible really, but for better or worse, committing to the effort was an instinctual act for Danny Moran. Time and again, in the form of professional marital advice going back some seven years, it had been suggested that he be the one to let go, to not try so hard.

The rush of abstractions related to these obsessions would slow down just enough to deliver the false hope that they might actually stop, at least long enough to unclench his heart and free his breathing. Sometimes the thoughts seemed profound, sometimes crazy, but regardless of whether he cultivated either, they, like the clock, maintained a pace he couldn't control. Back then, in the abyss, time was not what he needed it to be.

For the first time in the nearly three years since Molly's death, he clicked on a document titled, *Time,* and read some of the vaguely remembered words he'd created then and resurrected now on the laptop screen before him.

Behind Me Like a Friend

Me and time aren't
worth as much as
time and me are
For I need time behind me

Behind me like a friend
How much, and when
Much more, and soon
I want this time behind me

Now is, as is
And as is has
everything happening now

A blessed man cursed, a hollow time or worse
Yet good that bad was let to live, once left behind at last

I need this time behind me
To summon up at will
At last, behind me like a friend
A promise showing promise
of being free and me again
The same yet changed, with clarity gained
from clues now luminous from a reexamined past

With now becoming then, but behind me like a friend

I look ahead and all around
Inward, out, backward, down, the places I have been
Granting wisdom enough at last, to look behind me first

Danny let those words from years ago work into him. He cringed at how he wrote as if talking to himself, as if to immediately mock the notion of him writing poetry. Even going so far as to title it. The idea of writing words no one would read was weird. He was pretty sure that writing *Behind Me Like a Friend* had a more profound influence on him then than it did reading it now. Still, reading it, he sensed the smoldering remnants of burning ghosts and the vanishing tracks of spirits soaring off to freedom redefined. Like the scent of blue jeans worn to a bonfire, he knew he had been there. He looked at another effort.

It Is Time

There comes a time when time is what defines us
Forever it is...
sliced up, consumed, or wasted
However it is...
time remains an autocratic entity
Whomever it is...
Everyone gets it equitably.
Whenever it is...
there comes a time when time rolls on without us

Danny was dumbfounded. It was not unusual for him to ponder whether the stuff he wrote would ever have meaning to anyone else, but what was clear to him this time, with *It is Time*, was borderline bizarre. Though the words were in verse form, comically enough, they were nothing but a recycled version of how he often addressed the utilization of time in business environments. He had some clients that would recognize it. When he wrote it, he hadn't noticed, or maybe he did but needed to lose himself in the familiar. And *It is Time* sure as hell had been lifted from the Modus Operandi Solutions breakdown of time management, of how employees are to be evaluated by their use of time, and how those who consistently misuse time may unfortunately have to be terminated. The title was actually contracted into the heading *It's Time!* for the PowerPoint and Process Improvement Summaries that Danny put together for his clients. A distinction without a difference? Not really. No mas or Know mas? Exactly...ish.

He saw now that the passing of time had seemed to defog his view, and he didn't know whether he should be embarrassed or proud. *Just writing what I know,* he thought. *Just like Jay-Z, Feelin' It, Yo.*

Over the years Danny had half-joked about one day writing limericks for all occasions. The Original Limericks of Danny Mo (OLD MO Co) would be his way of scratching a creative itch in his later years. He had a folder full of them. Maybe put them on greeting cards someday, he thought. Now, looking at his curious ramblings on time, it seemed like time to put such wacky thoughts to rest. The limerick thing seemed like something only the Danny Mo from years ago could do.

He looked around his office at MOS. Orsman was out ill and Witchy was watering the plants. Fixating on the concept of time had been a brief predilection of Danny's after Molly died. Grief therapy, it was called, and he'd attended a group session. Once. When he was overloaded with thoughts that had no place to go. Writing helps, he was told. At the time he figured he was too busy thinking to write. He never went back to the group, but for a period of time he typed voraciously and backspaced neurotically. What many writers do, according to Molly, who knew such things.

Spooked, he read some more of his own three year old words. No poetry this time, just rambling.

So, what the hell am I thinking, saying, and/or really believing? Seems to me that TIME is a generous tightwad. Maybe God signed off on it to see if we'd be beggars or choosers. Whatever - I'm a beggar now. As the man said, I need to get some time behind me. Selfish. Uncomfortable. Hate it. DANNY MO? Hell, I'm DAN EMO! Truth? I feel like screaming FUCK from time to time. More than in the past. Just for a shock to the system. My system. Collateral damage

*for the greater good. Gotta love those contradictions. Always have. Face it. The
F-bomb is only truly bomb-like if it's rarely dropped.*

*A 'fuck' in anger is weakness at work, it does nothing but empower
negative shit for future reference, timestamps the shit. "Freezing tainted meat,"
my dad would say. The Main Mo knew his shit.*

*So people are telling me it takes 1000 days to mourn a loved one. Did they
all read the same book? 1000 days. Sure. So on the 1001ˢᵗ day do you suddenly
laugh out loud at a Seinfeld rerun? Now that I think of it, Seinfeld maintained
that the F-bomb is nothing but a cop-out, at least in stand-up. Calls it the easy
way out. Molly, hell, she could fire off F-bombs like a stiffed hooker. Maybe why
I willed myself not to. More than some fear of freezing bad fucking meat. Moral
high-ground bullshit? Great. Way to keep your fucking powder dry. That'd be
me, no doubt. Hated it so couch and crown much when she fucked it up good.
Molly knew it. Still, I'd kill right fucking now to hear her scream it for our
neighbors and half the city to hear. Like the time the rabbits ruined part of her
garden. How about you let it go, D Mo, you stubborn fucker.*

Danny daydreamed for a spell, then returned to his words and read
one more sentence, further down…

*I took the fewest shots and lost The Fucking Open. Ah, hell…the fucks ain't
helping.*

…and then turned off his computer.

He hadn't remembered much of what he wrote then, what he called
his MFP, his Mourning Fog Period, just that he did it a lot. He
remembered promising to never forget his learning, the stuff that got
through the Mourning Fog. Like his servitude to time. How time was all
that could heal him. But a minute doesn't seem a minute when one needs
it to pass quickly, and neither is it when one wants it to last. Yet every
single one is exactly 60 seconds. Danny was about to call it a day, when
his office phone rang.

It was Witchy. Marty Archibald was on his way back to see him.

∞

Chapter 29

Marty Archibald's one-tough-hombre limp was as pronounced as ever, his face was tanned and his eyes sparkled. He put his practiced half-smile into play just to assure a watching world that he was holding up okay. That he had become the oldest state senior amateur champion in Wisconsin history eight days earlier only punctuated his affectations.

"Hey Champ," said Danny. He pulled a chair closer to the front of his desk for Marty. "Nice column by Gary this week. 70-70 at the age of 70. Great symmetry. Great achievement."

"I'm quite fortunate, Danny." Modest Marty mode, then a mischievous grin. "Almost forgot how it felt to play a good honest competition. Under pressure, yet by the rules, you know."

"You bet."

"Yes I do." Marty sat down and looked around. "Heard Salamone was none too kind to me — torchin' my rep at The Aftermath."

"Shocking. You grabbed some of his spotlight." Danny walked back around his desk and sat down. "Crusty said Sally was barking big-time. Usual crap — gives you your props, then blows you up as the single-most iniquitous cheater of this, the steroid era."

"What's new?" Marty fondled the jewel case of the CD he had brought with him. "You would think the cheating thing would be old news by now. He's playing great…but it's gotta be driving him insane to keep emptying his wallet into mine in our little games. Wants to up the stakes now, asking for a five-hundred dollar Nassau, minimum, next Thursday. Or, if I prefer, thousand, thousand, thousand. Something worth his attention, he says."

Danny smirked. "Mr. Big Shot on Daddy's dollars."

"He's thrown that high stakes shit at me for years, ya know," said Marty. "I just laugh."

"And tells everyone you won't play him for any, you know, 'real money.'"

"Don't matter. I don't mind bleedin' him of 50 or a hundy at a time."

"You got his head," said Danny, "so he's pricing you out of his life."

"Could be. But he's playing too good — and he's been around long enough to know the odds eventually turn."

"You're tempted this time aren't you?"

Marty brushed Danny's comment aside. "Gotta be something to it, you know, the way Sally's game took off almost the moment you quit. Pisses him off when I mention it, too." Marty grinned. "And so I do...often."

Danny shrugged. "I'll stake you to half."

The only sound was the buzz of the fluorescent lighting above and the distant strains of Witchy's radio. Marty's mouth slowly widened. "Danny Moran."

"Go ahead." Danny relished sounding like the Dirty Harry of golf bets. "Call his bluff."

"The Barn from the forward tees — why not go crazy once."

"Thou, thou, thou." Danny wondered what had come over him.

Marty was nodding. "He's got it. The house really needs a new roof. City inspectors are on my ass. And bothering Sunya, too."

Danny turned his head until he heard a crack. "Well then...do what you must."

"Let's get it on." Marty leaned forward in his chair with just a hint of a grimace when another man would have moaned or possibly passed out. "Now...on the subject of doing what ya gotta do; here's the CD for tonight. The song is written down."

Danny looked at it. *B.O.S.S. Crooked I.* A yellow Post-it note said, *Dream Big.*

Marty put his forearms on the front of Danny's desk. "Cindy asked if you could be available a little later than what was arranged. She's had her hands full lately. By the way, she was disappointed you couldn't make her birthday party." Marty laughed. "Gotta be impressed by a woman who doesn't act all depressed at turning 30."

"What can I say? That pup you left on my doorstep picked a bad time to puke in three different rooms." Danny looked at his computer screen. "How much later?"

"I'll let you know. She'll be watching for you two."

"Whatever. I'm getting better at tiptoeing out of the house without waking up Hank."

"Hank gets jealous?"

"He does," said Danny, shaking his head. "Gives me the sad puppy dog eyes if I don't pay enough attention. Unless Mo is staying over, then I don't exist."

"Then you get jealous, huh."

"Nah...I understand Hank needs to see other people."

Marty changed gears again. "Heard Mo drove back-to-back par fours at the County Open last week. Ten and 11, was it? Bet no one's ever done that."

"No one that I know of. Still kills it for a kid off two shoulder surgeries." Danny sat back in his chair. "For anybody, really. Haven't seen anyone any longer than Mo. At least, nobody was back when I was playing. If he ever gets his wedges to behave..."

"Mo Mo doin' okay? Don't see him much, always seems in a hurry when I do." Marty squinted.

"He's okay. Thought about throwing for some semi-pro team, but decided to jump into golf instead. Probably throws back too many beers from time to time too, but..."

"May he who hasn't tossed too many back at some time cast the first empty... "

Danny smiled through a pensive look. "No, I know..."

"What?" Marty leaned back in his chair.

"Mo." Danny was silent for a moment. "He's heard all the talk about you cheating."

"Ain't talk, Danny, that's pretty much the truth. Of course, not like people say, but the possibility that I might try to pull something is more valuable than the act," Marty laughed. "But I suppose it was inevitable. Hell, other than cheatin' spouse gossip there ain't no gossip like cheatin' golfer gossip. I can tell by the way some people look at me. But...I could give a rat's ass."

"I know." Danny hesitated, and then relented. "I just play dumb and tell him things aren't always what they seem. I've been tempted..."

"Got it." Marty nodded slowly. "But I appreciate you keeping your promise, my friend. Someday you'll be able to tell everyone. Sooner than you may think."

"What, you win your seventh Senior Am and now you're up for the big hitchhike to heaven — or do you have an ascending cloud already booked?"

"Ready anytime, you know that. Joy awaits." Marty closed his eyes for a couple seconds. Joy Archibald had been dead for over two decades. It visibly dawned on him that Danny's wounds were quite a bit fresher. "Jeez Danny, I'm sorry."

"Forget it, Marty, got it pretty much behind me now," said Danny. "No more talk of dyin', okay?"

"Well it's never totally behind you, Danny, but, anyway, you know the kind of guys who want me dead. No escaping that."

"That's why I've got this, uh... Crooked I CD, Mart. I'm here for you. We don't have to cover this every time."

"I know, but seriously, it's getting a little spooky. And now I'm really worried about you...so is Cindy."

"Don't think anyone wants to risk the wrath of Marty's girls. Make that, Jonah's girls."

"True enough," said Marty Archibald, nodding, a dollar bill-sized shingle of his combed back silver hair pulled away from his otherwise sparse dome, a bobbing, matted plank floundering in no man's land. He stood up to leave.

"Call me later," said Danny. He noticed Marty's pate was sweating; probably what sprung the shingle free. He watched the old man head for the door. Before Marty could turn with one more thought, Danny preempted him. "Oh, and Marty?"

Marty stopped in mid-gimp but did not turn; no doubt a little disappointed that Danny flipped him on his routine. Marty turned his head enough to let Danny know he had his attention.

"I know I just yanked my clubs out of hibernation, played some twilight nines is all, but...I wouldn't mind playing along when you play Salamone for all the dough."

Marty proceeded with his slow dramatic turn. Somehow he was able to remain standing. He was smiling. "You mean it, Danny?"

"Actually, I'd love to." Danny felt another surge of a familiar feeling inside him, just as he felt it earlier, talking his friend into taking the big stakes game with Salamone.

"We were each gonna get a guy, so..." Marty eyes were blazing, "I'll tell him I got me a guy -- just won't tell him who." Marty shut his smile down in a second to great effect. "Perfect," he said quietly.

And with that, the old warrior shuffled his way out of the office. Danny heard Marty say goodbye to Witchy as if he was certain there was no way she could be anything but awestruck.

∞

Chapter 30

The Steamin' E burger had made a comeback in Danny's life. He had taken more than a two-year break from them after Molly died, perhaps because he equated The Aftermath's reliably blissful signature sandwich with a small measure of fulfillment.

That and simple logistics.

He had pretty much gone underground during his Mourning Fog, staying at home just about every night (unless he was helping Marty and his girls). Having stepped away from golf and therefore The Old Barn, the regular post-round visits to The Aftermath had come to a halt, and thus enforced his abstinence from the pleasures of the E. It had been a time in his life for doing without.

Returning to The Aftermath after emerging from the darkness proved to be as natural as when he decided to start reading the sports page again. It was as he remembered it. It was good to see Kai, the creator of the Steamin' E — who remained as coy as ever about the meaning behind the letter E. Kai had two replies to such inquiries. "The E stands for a word that speaks to a universal truth about our most cherished moments in life, perhaps even about life itself," he would say when he was feeling philosophical. "Edible," was his eye-wink reply when he wasn't.

Danny sat at the bar with Crusty on his right and Mo directly to the right of Crusty. Mo was focused on Lexi, a rock climbing, parasailing, twenty-something waitress whose personality was equal parts sparkler and welding torch. Mo had found her pretty enough, but darn near perfect when she pulled a ponytail out the back of her ball cap. Today it was a retro, politically incorrect Milwaukee Braves cap. The three men had just played a quick nine holes before sunset at The Barn. Crusty hit it short and crooked and shot one over par; Danny hit the ball great,

putted bad, and shot three over; and Mo hit it nine miles and to every
field, rubbing his shoulder after every bad shot. If his shoulder was a
magic lamp he'd have been cited for genie stalking. Their Steamin' E's
were on the board.

"So, the match tomorrow...Marty lose his mind?" Crusty kept his
voice low. Apparently Mo wasn't supposed to know about it since
Danny had quietly mentioned the match to him at the course while Mo
toiled in a bunker. "He think he's calling Sally's bluff?"

"Maybe." Danny thought for a moment. "Maybe he had some help."

"You fronting the cash, Dannymo?"

"Said I'd put up half if he doubled Sally's high roller minimum."
Danny stirred the straw in his diet cola, "that'd be a $1,000 Nassau...so
as to not, as he put it, 'waste his time.'"

"You losin' your mind too?"

"Early and often," said Danny with half a grin. "I'll cover Marty if
necessary. You know, if he goes down in flames, which wouldn't occur
to him as a possibility."

"Still buzzed on his victory, ain't he?"

"Marty gets buzzed just being Marty."

Crusty nodded. "He'll be amped to have you along tomorrow."

"Be interesting to see how Sally reacts when he finds out." Danny
sipped some of his soda. "My presence won't affect his game if he's
playing good, and obviously he has all year. But he's always been a guy
who could melt down if he gets off bad with me watching. Used to
anyway."

"Sally don't know yet?"

"Not as far as I know." Danny lowered his voice and looked over at
Mo, who was still shoveling charm in the direction of Lexi, who kept
circling back to him after each order or delivery. "Marty wanted to, in
his words, 'spring it on him' tonight. You know, have him sleep on it."
Danny chucked, "Just Marty bein' Marty."

"I take it Mo don't know either."

"You know what he thinks of Marty, and his…ways." Danny shook his head. "Rather not get into that again unless I have to."

"Got ya."

"Plus, he suspects Marty's fondness for hookers and all that."

"Ah, true enough." Crusty smiled and glanced over at Mo, whose conversation with Lexi had intensified. "But hardly the truth."

Danny nodded and looked at Mo as well. His son casually rubbed his right shoulder as he spoke to Lexi. The shoulder rub had become an unconscious habit, but only when he was talking, or after a bad golf shot. "Still, hard to blame him."

"Someday he'll know, Dannymo." Crusty remained expressionless.

Danny glanced across The Aftermath and his expression lightened. Two guys from The Old Barn known as Baggie and Boots were locked in a ferocious dice game. Danny wasn't even sure what their real names were anymore, since no one at the Barn called them anything but their nicknames, even on the scoreboard for club events. Baggie was a germaphobe and always had plastic sandwich bags in his pocket, ready to draw. He would unfailingly place one over his hand or hands before touching anything frequently touched by other people. He did this even when he handled the flagstick or carried a bucket of balls to the range. And, when he grabbed and slammed the dice cup.

Boots' nickname evolved in the convoluted way that esoteric quirks get reduced to their simplest form. It went like this: Boots always marked his golf ball with the minimum coinage required to cover the distance of the putt; a nickel for 5 feet or less, a dime for 5 to 10 feet, a quarter for 10 to 25 feet. Boots would stack a dime on top of the quarter for 35 feet or under, and so on, always enough to cover the distance of the putt in total feet. And, since boots cover feet, well, that is how Big Joe Stippich became "Boots."

Danny had just pointed at Baggie in acknowledgement, after Baggie had waved to Danny with his bag-free hand, when he noticed the appearance of Marty near the door. Marty smiled an odd smile, something like relief on his face. He worked his way toward the bar with a little more purpose and a little less limp than usual.

Marty went through the motions with some nods and half-hearted slaps to the backs of other patrons on the way to the bar where Danny, Crusty and Mo – and now Lexi – were gathered. He shook hands with Danny and Crusty, and turned toward Mo to do the same, but the younger Moran never turned away from Lexi. She was Mo's world for the moment.

"Was hoping to find you guys here," said Marty, politely inclusive. "You ready for tomorrow Danny?"

"It's not about me, Marty. I'm just there for air cover."

"What does that mean?"

"No idea," said Danny, "sounded good."

"Well it sounds useful, especially these days," Marty's gaze was unusually nonspecific. "Anyway, I left a message for Sally to meet me here if he could."

Crusty smiled. "Talk some trash, maybe?"

"Just wanted to confirm our foursome for tomorrow. He hasn't been here, has he?"

Crusty shook his head. "No…you'd be smelling the aftershocks of his cologne if he had been."

"He probably won't show." Marty signaled for Kai who came by and greeted Marty warmly. "You still got the gruel going, Kai?"

"The Big Bowl?"

"Yes sir," said Marty. "The gruel of life, for however long that is." Marty loved Kai's cheesy potato soup.

Marty was the only male in Danny's circle who shunned the Steamin' E Burger. Yet, Marty claimed that Kai once told him what the E stood for, but was sworn to secrecy. Kai denied — maybe with too much enthusiasm — that he had ever told anyone.

Marty took a deep breath and barged in to Mo and Lexi's world. "Hey Mo Mo! Hi, Lexi." He gave Danny a quick look and nodded. Apparently The Great Man had been ignored long enough.

Lexi turned and smiled for Marty before excusing herself to get back to her job. Mo didn't change expression. "Hello, Marty," he said, rubbing his shoulder.

"Hear you're back to bombing it like nobody, or whatever your dad says."

Mo shrugged. "Hittin' it okay, when the body cooperates. Doesn't seem to wanna always."

Danny cringed inwardly. Marty was 70 and playing with replacement parts and his son's self-pity had him about to make an enlightening crack, but Marty was already into a reply. "You look fit and strong, Mo Mo, but I guess only one person can know what we feel like underneath our own skin. And I will tell you, son, some folks fool ya with their body."

"Okay," said Mo, suspicious, "I can buy that.

Marty's eyes locked on Mo, who was momentarily Lexi-less, the server having gone out on a beer sortie for Boots and Baggie. "You have a moment for me." It wasn't a question. Danny flashed back to what he'd shared with Marty about Mo's impressions of him when he stopped in at his office a few days earlier.

Mo glanced at his dad for a split-second. "Um...yeah, sure?" If ever an eye-roll could have been detected without being visible to the naked eye, Mo had pulled it off. The body language disappointed his dad; Marty wasn't stupid.

And the old man, for all his injuries, was still a bull. He stood before the two Morans and Crusty, all of whom had turned away from the bar when Marty arrived. Marty started talking. Fast. "You know, Mo, when I was a kid of maybe 12 or 13, growing up in a small town a few hundred miles north of here, there was this kid who lived right across from us. He was enormous, way bigger than everyone else. Redheaded guy named Cliff. Clifford Lubberman. Used to shove all of us kids around, threatened to beat us up all the time, on the playground, the school hallways, down at the creek where we fished. Did I mention that the kid was really big and scared the shit out of me and everyone else?" Marty didn't wait for a response from Mo. "Anyway, Lubberman would just come up and stand over you... and stare."

Lexi arrived with Marty's soup. Steam rose from the big bowl. "Thanks, Honey. Just let it cool on the bar there. Perfect."

Danny was certain now that Marty wasn't quite himself, something was off. He had not heard this story before, which in itself was amazing; he had assumed he heard them all, probably twice. This was the type of story Marty would normally have taken his time with, and digress all over the place.

Marty looked back at Mo. Kai came over and dipped into Marty's soliloquy. Lexi had returned to Mo's side. Marty cleared his throat, letting everyone get settled. "Okay, anyway, Lubberman had a one-armed step-dad that he hated. I mean, he just hated the guy. Whined all the time about how during the fall his step-dad would come home from work and force him to split logs behind their house. And, though he hated fall and log splitting chores, he liked bragging how it made him stronger and tougher than everyone else. All us Archibalds could hear the log splitting, like clockwork, every night during the fall, a constant BAM...BAM...BAM, for about an hour, sometimes two. Clifford claimed someday he was gonna beat his ol' step-dad to a pulp.

"Now the step-dad was kind of short and mostly bald, with glasses, and he was, of all things, a freaking florist. Lubberman was embarrassed by that. Was always going on about, 'Why can't he get a decent job at the paper mill like everyone else?' And remember, back then no one knew much about stepparents, divorce was taboo, he was the only step-anything we knew of in our town – this was the 40s, you know. So we just assumed he was a nasty ol' bastard who picked flowers, and was raising a nasty ol' fat kid that wasn't really his. My brothers and me would be out playing by the road, and the guy would drive by in his sky blue pick-up truck. We used to wave to him, but he'd just honk his horn at us, so, you know, hell with him." Marty paused for moment, memories from over a half century ago made his eyes sparkle.

Danny furrowed his brow, a way of encouraging Marty, curious where this was going. He turned to see if the Steamin' E's were imminent, as if looking at a closed kitchen door could provide a clue. He glanced at Mo, whose expression made it clear that he was now playing the role of whichever saint had established a reputation for patience. St. Mannequin, maybe. Crusty was leaning back in his bar stool, motionless, his pilsner untouched since the start of Marty's story.

"A strange thing about Lubberman, even though he was a bully — hell, I remember him shoving Ernie Pfaff into the creek and taking his creek chubs, well, actually Ernie told me later that he intentionally fell into the creek cuz he was so scared he peed himself and was embarrassed — but Lubberman never went far enough to get in any real trouble with the teachers at school, maybe because it turned out he got decent grades." Marty said this like it was a big revelation. Danny thought Marty was acting more like Marty now.

Danny wasn't pleased to see Mo toss Lexi a quick wide-eyed eyebrow lift — the international expression of "big whoop."

Marty was nodding, as if his simultaneous existence in two places several decades apart was one of the benefits of aging. "One day after school, it was November but still pretty warm, I had to deliver an Advent wreath. Lubberman's mom had ordered it from my mom, who was in charge of selling them for our church -- two and a half bucks a pop. I cannot tell you how much I dreaded having to cross that road. Just the scary sound of the pounding, the maul hitting the wood; and the rhythm of the sledgehammer hitting the wedges and the wood splitting like my face would if Lubberman decided to haul off and crack me one. I don't scare easy but I was scared shitless."

Marty glanced back at the kitchen door; he took a deep breath and picked up the pace as the coveted Steamin' E's were on the way. The cook, Ricky, was bringing them… Lexi and Kai were preoccupied listening to Marty.

"I went to their front door, rang the bell, and nothing. Knocked, and nothing. Lubberman's mom wasn't home. I sure as hell didn't want to go around to the back, with that psycho step-dad crackin' his whip. And Lubberman, you know, a young and heated Paul Bunyan, and me with my Advent wreath, and ribbons having to ask for two and a half bucks. I

was ticked. I'd catch hell if I came home without making the deal. So I
went sneaking around the far side of the house which was protected by
bushes. The sound was really loud now, BAM...BAM. I mean, my heart
was pounding. I came to the corner of the house, and took a look, and
couldn't believe my eyes. The bald one-armed step-dad was in overalls
and a tight tee shirt. He was raising the sledgehammer with his one arm
like it was nothing, and BAM the log split into pieces. He grabbed
another log; rolled it over, buried a big maul into it a few times; stopped;
and set another wedge into the cavity. All the while big fat Lubberman
was watching, not happy, pouting. His step-dad asked him if he'd like to
try again. Lubberman was sulking that his hands were sore, while his
old man, this flower guy, held the hammer out to him. His arm was fully
extended and as big as a man's leg, with muscles on muscles, probably
cuz it had to do the work of two. Then I see Lubberman sobbing. Yeah,
sobbing! Lubberman took the sledgehammer and swung it at the wedge
in the center of the log and missed not only the wedge but almost the
whole log. And he just dropped the hammer, said 'I told ya.' And the kid
was half crying, half-hiccupping and spouting that he had homework to
do. I'm thinking 'what the hell.' His step-dad smiled and said something
like, 'Well, then go back in the house and study — just thought you
might want to try your hand again now that you're getting bigger.'

"That was when I decided to walk toward them. They both turned to
face me. It was dark but there was a lantern lit, and I could see
Lubberman had tears in his eyes, and slime coming out of his nose. I told
them I had been watching from the side of the house, just to rub it in to
Lubberman. The kid turned even redder, and he walked straight into the
house."

Ricky placed the Steamin E burgers by Mo, Crusty and Danny, but
none of them turned around.

"I'm just about finished here." Marty was looking at Mo. He leaned
his butt against the back of a chair and continued. "So the step-dad says
hello to me by name, first and last, and asks if I want to take a crack at
log splitting. I had never done it, but after seeing Lubberman's pitiful
attempt I jumped at the chance. I don't think I have to tell you I always
had good eye-hand coordination and pretty strong hands, so I willed

myself to bust up some wood. I wasn't great, but I got better fast and was relentless. I had the guy with an arm of steel encouraging me until it was time to gather the pieces up. We hauled the wood in a wagon with the sides built up. Took it all to the big pile on the other side of their house and stacked it. He said a wheelbarrow didn't work too well when you're flying on one wing. Then he said neither does steering and shifting his pick-up truck. That was why he always honked his horn when we used to wave to him. Even when we didn't, he still was sayin' hello.

"Then, as I was leaving, we walked by the window of his house. I could see Lubberman sitting at the kitchen table with his school books, and drinking chocolate milk. His step-dad — think his name was Thorson, but anyway — Mr. Thorson told me, winking as he said it, that Clifford always seems to have too much homework to help out much with the wood but didn't mind too much as long as he got his grades.

"That was the day I turned Lubberman into Tubberman in my own mind. From the time he saw me walk by, and I saw him through that window, we never looked at each other the same way again. It dawned on me that he never really picked on anyone close to his size, not that anyone really came close. He was busted, and he, for the most part, left people alone after that. Anyway, it was great, and I almost forgot about the Advent wreath. Mr. Thorson picked it up and asked what he owed. I told him two-fifty. Then he did something that I will never forget, something amazing. He pulled his wallet out, and with his one hand, performed what seemed like a magic trick. Just try opening a wallet with one hand, and pulling out some bills, and then sorting them with your fingers until you have three singles held between two fingers while putting the other bills back into the wallet with the other two fingers. As quick as he did it, it was done. Wallet closed, back in pocket. The whole wallet thing was over in less than 10 seconds, never used any other part of his body. I actually laughed. He told me you just go with what you got. I never forgot that, or the strength in that dude's arm. Learned a lot that day."

Marty looked directly at Mo Moran and repeated, "Sorry for getting carried away, but I think a lot about how things are. Really. I'll leave you guys alone. Wish Salamone would show." Mo nodded, and then worked his head like a dashboard bobble-head before he finally looked away. Danny noticed Mo reach to rub his shoulder as Marty stared at him, but covered it with a scratch. Marty walked to the bar, grabbed his bowl of soup and took it over to Baggie and Boot's table and sat down. No one said anything for a half-minute or so.

Danny watched Mo turn toward his Steamin' E on the bar. Lexi was next to Mo, and said something that made him agree, albeit grudgingly. Crusty looked at Danny and said. "Well there ya go," he said.

They picked up their E's as one might an infant, careful and smiling, before biting off a limb.

Danny, Mo, and Crusty strolled toward their cars, which were parked together in The Aftermath's lot. Marty had left quickly after finishing his "Gruel of Life," convinced that Salamone wasn't going to appear. It was a darker evening than most, but the parking lot was lit well enough by four light stands, and some atmospheric landscape lighting. A black Escalade came barreling too fast into the parking lot, went past them, stopped too quickly, then backed up to the three men.

Salamone's window came down, cigar aglow, of course. "Is that Dan Moran I see, or the ghost of Danny Mo?" He grinned.

"Probably a little of both, far as your concerned." Danny kept walking for a few extra steps, making Salamone shift back in order to crawl forward, and along in his car.

"Ah." Salamone kept his smile in place.

"Probably haunt you forever, Sally, trying to figure it out. Maybe we learn something tomorrow at The Barn. Thought I'd play along. Been a while since I played 18 holes in one day."

"No fucking way, Moran. Thought you were done with this goddamn game." Salamone looked amused, then glanced at Crusty and Mo, who were lagging behind.

"Ceremonial appearance. Just for fun." Danny stopped. Crusty and Mo did too, and Salamone's rolling vehicle overshot them, and he had to back up six or eight feet. Sally grunted as if throwing the 'lade into reverse took great strength. Danny was pleased with his puppetry.

"Well, you can referee then. The old man tries to cheat just about every time I play him. Gotta watch that guy." Salamone loudly worked up some mucus. Danny moved a little closer to the Escalade giving Salamone no angle in which to spit.

Danny noticed Mo shift his weight, maybe from the sheer energy it took to bite his tongue. Danny bore a look into Andy Salamone. "You really believe that to be true, Salamone?"

"Damn straight. I mean, if it's for money. I don't mind telling anyone and everyone. And I do. I don't know what he does with you, Slane, or Sindorf, but he's been pretty sneaky with me, and some of my buddies — all us guys he plays for decent cash."

"You mean guys like Dailey, Barber, Menzel, Jumbo Larson?" Danny, leading the witness on cross.

"Exactly." Salamone looked at Danny as if had just figured out a simple exercise. "Pretty much stealing, if you ask me."

"Don't hold back, Sally." Danny drilled another squinting stare right through Salamone's skull. "May as well tell the world if that's the way you feel."

Salamone shook his head, like everything was now beyond him. Mo had a similar expression going. "Whatever," said Salamone, who then took off, too fast, for the other side of the parking lot.

Mo was quiet on the drive back home where his car was. Then he looked at his dad. "So, big match tomorrow, huh?"

"Guess so. Marty and Salamone. I'll just be… around."

More silence. Then Mo spoke again, this time looking out his window, away from his dad. "So, was that one-armed lumberjacking florist story supposed to inspire me about getting over my shoulder?" He had his hand on his shoulder but wasn't rubbing it.

"Could be."

"Or it could be about a whole lot more too, huh. That's what you're thinking, isn't it? Something I was supposed get out of all that?"

Danny shrugged. He turned onto the street that led directly to their neighborhood. Danny hadn't taken any of his infamous "shortcuts." Hadn't since Molly died. No point in it.

"Seemed Marty was trying to tell us all something tonight, Mo …" Danny pulled into his driveway. By rote, the two Morans looked at the picture window. Hank's head had already popped up from the backrest of the couch and the dog would soon be wasting a lot of motion waiting for the men to walk in the door. Mo was staying at home until his lease kicked in for a place on Milwaukee's lower east side. Then, almost to himself, the elder Moran said, "And maybe hiding something else."

∞

Chapter 31

"Okay Hammer…" Danny was halfway out the door. "I'm off to The Barn, back later with stories I'm sure. Pick up after yourself will ya."

Hank gave his "you can't be serious" look. It was Henry's expression whenever Danny said 'see ya later' before leaving the house without him. Incredulous was the pup that there could be activities of any merit that did not include him.

It was nearly three years ago when Marty and Cindy brought a young yellow lab to his house -- a gift of life for a friend dealing with death. Danny was touched, yet his first concern at the time was for his wife's purported allergies and thus how this would affect his standing at home. "Molly's gonna freak," he thought. In truth, his inner voice never arrived at the word "freak." He knew it was just ahead, all ripe and ready, a one-syllable multi-purpose word waiting on the other side of a synaptic cleft, but…it went away. Like Molly had. Reflexes die hard, and closure is a dawdler with a rather loose itinerary.

Over time, however, Hank (or Henry or Hammer) seemed to sense his master's pain and, in his loyal dog way, helped make Danny's life better. Like almost everything, it took time. Hank made his role as friend look effortless, primarily because making no effort whatsoever came naturally to Hank. Danny wasn't sure at first whether to actually name his new pet, "Hank," and mentioned as much to Crusty.

"And you wouldn't name him Hank because…why?" is all his befuddled friend had said.

Hank was as self-centered as any starlet, yet he made everyone who gave him some attention feel glad they did. He wasn't particularly tough, though he barked and strutted about as if he were. Something in his bloodline, probably. And so it was that Hank was happiest hanging with people who pampered him in the lifestyle to which he had become accustomed.

"See ya later, Henry Mo," said Danny, looking down at his now dismissive dog as he closed the door to the garage.

The Old Barn had undergone some changes in the years that Danny was away. Motown was history. The firm, flat, semi-dormant practice green that was Danny's private haven for short game practice had finally been concreted into a cart staging area. The greens superintendent, Red, had impregnated Phyllis, the big-boned half-his-age cart girl, and they were now engaged. Somehow, Red had kept his job. The yellow barn had been painted red, perhaps as a nod to the super, who some at The Barn now called ViagRed. The little plaster farm family toiling at the side of the golf course driveway had simply disappeared. Some said they were kidnapped, part of a high school prank, while others believed they had defected to a farmer's market with real crops in a smaller town.

And so Danny was relegated to the new putting green, now the only putting green, which was cradled in the bosom of the L-shaped pro shop and clubhouse. He could feel the looks and overhear some of the comments from other Barnstormers, repetitious scuttlebutt that Danny Mo was "back," whatever that was supposed to mean.

Danny checked the Coca-Cola clock on the side of the snack hut near the tenth tee. It was a few minutes before one, and their tee time was at 1:20. Salamone was coming from the range in a cart and was headed toward the putting green. He passed the practice bunker where Crusty was blasting away. Neither bothered with a glance toward the other. Marty was nowhere to be seen. It didn't feel right. Marty always got to the course early on any day he played -- and even earlier on days when he simply hung out and chipped and putted and shot the bull. This was especially true when he arrived at The Old Barn all baggy-eyed after coming straight from an evening downtown.

As far as Danny was concerned, there were only three acceptable excuses for not showing up for a tee time without a phone call. One, the player or an immediate family member suddenly became dead. Two, the player or a member of his immediate family were in an accident or admitted to the hospital due to physical ailment or mental breakdown. Or, lastly, the player found himself behind bars and could prove his one allotted phone call went to an attorney. Danny went to his golf bag to check his phone, which was set on mute. Again, no messages. Not good. Danny's thoughts flashed to the night before at The Aftermath, how Marty seemed a little off from the time he arrived and until midway through his story about Lubberman and the step-dad with the arm of thunder.

"The hell, Moran, where's the shameless holy man?" Salamone stepped from his cart. He looked smaller to Danny, but his breasts bounced and bobbed and eventually, to the naked eye anyway, came to rest.

"Don't know."

"You think maybe the whole thing got to him?" Salamone raised an eyebrow. "The stakes? Though I'm guessing you're helping out there."

"Glad to keep you guessing, Sally." Danny dragged his three balls with his putter toward a hole further away.

"Is that right?" Salamone bristled.

Danny didn't respond.

"Except at The Hill Farm," Sally snorted. "It was me got you guessing there."

Danny casually went about rolling a few putts. Salamone had played whatever hand he felt he had with the passed-out Eye-patched would-be Nimrod guy debacle, and had indeed known something no one else did. And while there was a buzz about the unconscious body delay back then, after everything played out, in the grand scheme of things, all it really added up to was a momentary boner for Salamone, Danny Mo's unrelated nightmare notwithstanding.

"Admit it…you know I had you guessing, Moran." Danny could tell Sally was happy, maybe even relieved that Marty no-showed. Obviously the man had been waiting to claim some sort of mind game victory -- minor as it would have to be considered -- for manipulating the media at The Hill Farm and holding court with them while Danny Mo built his lead, and then turning them loose in time to see him fumble it all down the sewer. "You don't think maybe I had a hand in setting up the little dope-growin' drunk, do ya, Dan…putting ol' Nimrod away and the whole damn legend to rest? Timing is everything. I mean, could it have played out any better?"

Danny nodded; fully aware this exchange involved the leftover oats Sally never got to sow in Danny's presence a couple years back. In reality, Danny's tragicomic flameout in the Open at The Hill Farm -- immediately followed by the news of Molly's death -- had, in golf circles, watered down Nimrod's newsworthiness and thus dimmed the spotlight Sally sought. And, really, Danny did not fritter away anything. With his back having gone haywire, he made a bunch of solid pars between the time he saved Nice Johnson's ass from the mighty O-Kah-Tah River and the moment of the correct but bizarre coin marker ruling on the 72nd hole. The rules of golf had worked in the favor of the eventual (and slightly sheepish) champion, Charlie Delsman, and to some degree, Andy Salamone. Big Andy would have been good and giddy over how the final round of the State Open had gone down at The Hill Farm. It was one of those times when the world seemed unjust at best and Godless at worst. Still, Danny suspected the whole deal turned out less fulfilling than Sally might have hoped.

"Never been one to wonder how low you might go Sally…but, hey, whatever blows your skirt." Danny smashed a four-footer into the back of the cup. The ball popped up and then dropped in.

"Information is power, Moran. You of all people know dat." Salamone dropped three balls from shoulder height so as to make the thud of their plop seem bold enough to go with his veiled reference to when a tipsy Danny shared some of his findings with Sally about his dad's company. "Now…do you have enough power to tell me if Marty's gonna show up today?"

"Don't know," said Danny. "Do know he was looking forward to it."

Salamone smiled. "The guy tells me he'll be at The Aftermath last night, gotta talk to me, but he no-shows, just like now. What's with the old man, huh?"

"As you know, he was there earlier." Danny looked directly at Salamone. "And, right now, I think you're ecstatic Marty's not here. The guy has your head."

"Bullshit." Salamone spat. "Goddamn con artist. And you, Moran, look bad just being his friend. I've said it over and over, the guy acts like he can't even bend down to mark his ball but he sure as hell can bend the shit out of the fucking rules."

"That right?" asked Danny. It might not have been a brilliant comeback, but the edge to his nonchalance added unspeakable value. "You'd be the guy to know what looks bad."

Salamone seized on it as if Danny was complimenting him. "Yeah, Archibald's the worst. And you know what?"

Danny ignored him, squinting as he scanned the parking lot looking for a sign of Marty's merlot not maroon car pulling in.

"He don't give a shit if anyone thinks he cheats or not." Salamone over-laughed. "That's what blows me away. I mean, he don't fucking care."

Danny turned toward Salamone and smiled. "Two things, Sally, he knows what you're telling everyone, and no, he does not care what anyone thinks… especially anyone who'd believe you."

Salamone beamed at first, and then retreated into a partly cloudy look. "Whatever." He lumbered off, shaking his head, to be by himself at the far corner of the new green. The move gave him time to think. The big man then wheeled to face Danny, albeit from a safe distance. "Maybe you oughta talk to your son, then." He tossed his three golf balls down hard enough to make his jewelry jingle and then raked them closer.

The mention of Mo Mo bothered Danny Mo. The idea of Salamone and Mo sharing an opinion on Marty was far more digestible when Danny didn't know that Sally was aware of Mo's position. Mo was passionate in his beliefs and, hell, word does get around. It wasn't like Mo believed Marty was a cheater because of Sally's relentless carping on it -- Mo had seen evidence enough with his own eyes -- but the perception of a loose alliance was nauseating to the elder Moran. Danny allowed himself a quick daydream, one where the whole issue with

Salamone, his pals and Marty Archibald played itself out. He looked
over at Salamone who had joined a conversation with some others he
would normally ignore. Danny wondered if somewhere inside the big
man's hypocritical heart there might be a fraction of doubt as to who
knew what. Probably not, he decided. Sanctimonious blowhards usually
live as kings of their own snow globe worlds. Danny picked up his balls
and left.

Driving home, Danny went through a checklist of possibilities.
Knowing Marty as he did, none of them were good. Marty had been one
of the last functioning civilians to resist carrying a cell phone, but these
days he brandished it freely and often, proud almost, that he now
belonged to a group as exclusive as, say, water drinkers. It was
important nevertheless that people be able to reach him when needed.
Any of his girls could call at any time from any part of the city and
Marty would come to the rescue. When he was double booked or having
a body part replaced (most recently his hip), Danny was the one to step
in. Now, Danny's calls were going straight to Marty's voicemail. He
knew full well the dangers Marty faced in his downtown activities.
Danny faced them, too, when he partook in them. Marty wasn't one to
downplay the danger — in fact it was his style to trump it up — but
neither did he ever back away from it. Scorned pimps, delusional
"boyfriends" and everyday lunatics were around every corner. He was a
marked man, and he almost seemed to enjoy the fact that he was so
marked. His girls would tell him things they knew or heard and Marty
would soak it up and spit it out like so much gristle. As with most things
involving Marty, what was real and what was show were almost always
both at once. And Danny believed it was, in part, due to the fact that
Marty Archibald was not afraid to die.

Without really meaning it, Crusty had asked Danny about playing
once the big match had been postponed. Crusty said he was going to
snoop around and see what he could uncover. The ex-soldier had
contacts in all walks of life and he always seemed to know plenty of
people who knew people who were useful to know – "shady but
honorable" was how he described some of them.

Danny had called Witchy at the office to see if she had heard from Marty. She had not, but said there was something she needed to discuss with him ASAP, whenever that was to be. There were plenty of others needing his attention too, but that was the norm on days Danny took off. He would get to them. But now Marty was missing, and regardless of whatever legal criteria is needed in order to classify someone as "officially missing," there was no greater litmus test for something amiss than Marty missing a money match with Andy Salamone.

Danny returned home and went straight to his office; still no messages from Marty. He called Cindy and Sunya, a women nearly Marty's age and perhaps Marty's closest friend. Neither could be reached. He left voicemails and then left the house and drove to Marty's. The house was dark and Marty's car was gone. He called The Old Barn. Again, nothing. Bill Smith, the clubhouse manager, said he'd call if Marty showed or he heard any news.

By the time he got back home, Mo's car was in the driveway. His son was in the doorway urgently motioning for his dad to come inside.

"Ah yeah, Marty's in the news. Not good. You better get in here, quick." Mo turned and hurried back inside with Danny on his heels.

A young television reporter kept brushing back her long dark hair with her microphone-free hand as she battled a Bad Hair Breeze and was talking about a shooting on Milwaukee's near north side. "...body was found in an alley behind a dumpster off 11th and Cherry, a high crime area frequented by gangs, prostitutes and drug dealers. A woman believed to be in her early twenties was reportedly also shot and left for dead near Archibald's body; she is in critical condition at Froedtert Memorial. Police believe the shooting took place much earlier, possibly before dawn, and the two were not discovered until later in the morning by an employee of Waste Management Systems. There are unconfirmed reports that the shooter, a male, approximately 40- to 45-years-old, was injured in the incident. His condition is not known. Again, the victim, Martin J. Archibald, age 70, of Brown Deer, was pronounced dead at the scene. Reporting live from downtown Milwaukee, this is Katalina Aranda-Enriquez."

Danny sat down. He could feel Mo's eyes on him. Hank was uncomprehending at the lack of attention.

"I'm sorry," said Mo. He reached out for Hank, who found the effort half-assed. Hank then went to Danny who was equally unfocused, and then went into the middle of the room and after a single tight circle, settled on the floor.

Looking out the window of the family room at the backyard, Danny took a deep breath. "I think he felt something like this was coming." He turned toward Mo. "I know what you're thinking. And you're right; Mo…the girl is probably a prostitute…or was." He wasn't in a hurry to say anything more.

Mo shrugged, not knowing what to say. He sat down next to his dad on the couch.

Danny knew how it looked to Mo. He could see the wheels turn, how much his son wanted to extend sympathy with a hint of 'I told you so' at the same time. Marty the cheater, downtown with a hooker in a back alley, wrong place wrong time. All true. "He was ready," said Danny. "And he was a hell of man, Mo. Trust me."

Mo nodded out of respect for his father. Not sure what to say, he sprawled onto the floor next to Hank and gave the dog some quality strokes. Danny felt a little better seeing the two have their mutual thing. The phone in Danny's office started ringing. He let it go.

∞

Chapter 32

It wasn't the Coco Puffs that made Mo's stomach clench most mornings; he was a devout consumer of the chocolaty breakfast cereal if not, technically, cuckoo for them. The morning paper was the culprit. Sports section. Box scores. Again he felt his midsection tighten and wondered once again if he had it coming.

"Mo Mo" Moran should have been playing in the Major Leagues, too. Plenty of friends had made the bigs, a fact that made it tougher. People were appropriately sympathetic — a promising baseball career blown up by injury. Three years and two surgeries, and a big fat adios for Mo. Yep, he should be hurling for the Cubs by now. But the shoulder went. Triple A, in the middle of a no hitter no less. Ripped it pretty bad, rehabbed pretty hard, came back pretty much on schedule. The Cubs' brass had been impressed at first. But they didn't know. Couldn't know. Mo didn't know either, not with any certainty. But he was pretty sure it was his own fault for not getting to The Show - and it didn't have anything to do with throwing curveballs as a kid.

Less than a month before Mo's scheduled return to the mound -- albeit in a simulated game -- he fell asleep at the wheel returning home after a free outdoor concert by a U2 tribute band in West Des Moines. It was only for a second, he believed, that he nodded off. Whatever, he awoke and through his panic yanked the wheel left as hard as he could. He heard a click and felt the tug in his shoulder. Something bad, no doubt. The sudden tension in his body, the abruptness of his response, working the wheel, away from some bushes on the bad side of the ditch, beyond which was a drop-off to a dry riverbed, and back toward the road. He didn't have time to feel much because in the next instant he was twisting the wheel a second time, this time to the right, just as hard, to avoid the sign that warned of a "Soft Shoulder." The adrenalin surge had swayed him toward believing that the five or so beers he consumed at the concert had played no role in his unfortunate nighttime nap on Riker road.

The car had absorbed only a few scratches and Mo left the scene as if nothing had happened. It was but a momentary delusion, he knew that now. He had been proud of his commitment to not drinking while driving…but drinking, and then driving, well, it was only a few. It was always only a few until you get to six, a couple few, and hell, "I've been so good." The irony of the statement was in its tense. He was never really much good again. Not on the mound anyway. The arm that earned him a professional contract and maybe saved his life with quick reactions was never the same, more than likely injured again in the act of avoiding a different kind of catastrophe. Reflex. Instinct. Of course he used his right hand to work the wheel. That left Mo with powerful *what ifs* to chew on. The most fundamental of them: what if he had made different choices that evening? He'd be with the Big Club now, right? Along with some of his buddies from three years in the farm system and other guys he used to get out on a regular basis. Sure he would. He'd be a Cub.

He never said a word about it to anyone. Mo drove home, went to bed, slept soundly in an actual bed (and right through rehab therapy the next morning). By morning he had almost forgotten what had happened on Riker Road -- until he brushed his teeth and showered. Didn't hurt that much, but the arm was not right, made an odd clicking sound. Time passed, doubt grew. But he would suck it up, eat handfuls of anti-inflammatory pills and manage to make his return to the mound as scheduled. In his first two outings he did okay in short stints, claiming all along that he didn't care to air it out yet. But it eventually became clear that he wasn't the Mo Mo Moran the Cubs drafted in the 3rd round right out of high school. Not even close. Finally, even before a shellacking before the home fans, the club ordered more testing. The team's medical staff found the shoulder was damaged, labrum again. Perhaps not as bad as what led to his first surgery, but…not good. After the second surgery, even with Mo's guilt-driven rehab intensity and an increased focus he had dedicated to his departed mother, Mo Moran never regained the hop on his fastball. Most of his velocity came back, but the movement didn't. It was then he felt his shoulder begin to hurt in direct proportion to his inability to get guys out. The hitters were getting in their rips, like they knew what was coming. Was it really pain or just something in his brain and did it really matter? Even when it didn't hurt, he rubbed his shoulder at weird times now, like when he missed a fairway or said something stupid. It was reflexive, but it looked bad and he knew it.

And so he figured if he kept checking the box scores he would eventually come to grips with his lot in life and admit it was he who had done himself in as a future Major Leaguer. His discomfort his penance. Recently, when the vibrating ridges at the side of Interstate I-43 startled him from a groggy state while driving home after a 36-hole day at Blackwolf Run in Kohler, he allowed himself a moment of redemption. Proof. That a guy like him could actually nod off driving even when he had *not* been drinking. So how could anyone suggest a few beers are what lulled him into the ditch. The games people play.

Mo reloaded the bowl with Coco Puffs and milked them good. He glanced at the folded top half of the front section of The Milwaukee Journal Sentinel and casually flipped it over, but not before shoveling more Puffs into his mouth. When he looked back and saw the headlines running the length of the bottom third of the paper, he stopped chewing.

Overlighter's Salvation House Loses Angel
Hall of Fame golfer contributed time, money and compassion

There was a picture of Marty Archibald from probably 20 years ago. Mo could not help but think of his dad. He knew Danny was out walking Hank and had read the paper already, yet he had left the paper casually on the kitchen table. Not even a note pointing to Marty Archibald's page one story/obituary.

Marty Archibald was well known for having won over 60 amateur golf tournaments in his forty-five plus years of competitive golf, including this year's Wisconsin State Senior amateur title. He was known for doing things his way and never giving up.

What isn't well known is that for over the thirty years he lived in the Milwaukee area, Archilbald had volunteered his time, donated money and demonstrated an endless compassion for people on whom others had in fact given up.

"If ever God had granted an angel to the downtrodden women of our city, it was Martin Archibald," said Sunya Williams, Director in Residence for The Overlighters Salvation House, a progressive, multi-faceted halfway house and rehabilitation center for women trying to get off the streets.

"He took up the torch first carried by his wife, our beloved Joy Archibald. It was one way in which he chose to honor his wife, and why it was so easy for him to offer his service and his love. Joy died 22 years ago. She was my best friend, and we started Overlighters together. It was with the help of Martin that we've made a difference to this day, in our third decade."

Archibald bravely operated in some dangerous undertakings. "He had no fear. He would go into the worst parts of the city just to take a box of sandwiches to a teenager with a couple kids, a girl who may have cursed him for trying to help her the week before," said Williams. "He only asked to stay anonymous, so we called him, 'Jonah,' which is his middle name. He wasn't into accolades. He joked that that was what golf was for…the accolades and the extra cash. And it was through Jonah's promise to Joy, that he would donate his winnings from wagers on the golf course, that we've been able to do a little more than we could had such a promise not been fulfilled."

The article went on extensively after the jump. It covered his remarkable amateur golf career, how Marty loved to gamble, how he loved the action, and how it led to Joy's idea that he donate every dollar he won on the golf course to The Overlighters Salvation House. The story noted how Jonah would often read the newspaper to a couple of women who had had been blinded with a screw driver by a psychotic pimp. How he even looked after other women, and their children, who never quite made it to or through Sunya's "Life Skills" programs for starting anew. How he fixed the roof, made soup and sandwiches, gave rides or arranged transportation for those in need of safe passage to OSH. And there were some touching tidbits on just how corny his jokes were and how much everything about the man would be missed by so many.

It went on. There were details on how Marty met his wife while in the service stationed in the Philippines, and how the feisty, sweet and selfless and aptly named Joy, at 19 was already a crusader against organized factions selling young girls into sexual slavery – the sex trade being a serious issue in the Philippines going back well over half a century. How Marty arranged to bring Joy Dimalanta to America, who in turn brought her passion to fight the good fight in the toughest streets of her new city. And there was this line:

> *Joy Archibald died at the age of 41. She was a passenger in a one vehicle accident. The car, driven by her husband, had swerved to avoid a deer and hit a guard rail.*

Toward the end, the article touched on what seemed a perfunctory wrap-up of how Marty died some three days earlier. It was heavy on the fact that details remained sketchy, but Mo, as he read it, felt that maybe there was more to be told. Finally, the piece ended with information on what was to be a "burial service only" later in the week.

Mo sat back in his chair. His Coco Puffs had gone soggy from inattention. He wrestled with the new information. Obviously there was a side to the old man that Mo had not known. He knew now that his dad knew everything reported in the paper and probably more. That was clear from their enduring friendship. Should have known, thought Mo. It was affirmed by his dad's statement about Marty's character immediately after learning of his death. Mo understood all that stuff. But, for all the good that Marty had obviously done, the ball kicking/foot mashie cheating part of the equation still gnawed at him. Mo was a competitive sort and he didn't like to be wrong. He tried to account for that, but a golfer cheating? Man, that remained a little too far to the dark side of the Robin Hood rationale for his taste. In a game of honor, can the end still justify the means? If only…

His dad startled him when he came in from his walk with Hank. Hank went gaga over the day's first interaction with Mo. Mo gave him some silent but sincere one handed love.

"Morning Mo," said Danny with a flat smile and a touch of ventriloquism, as if speaking for Hank. "How are you?"

"Good, really good." said Mo as he carried his bowl of soggy Coco Puffs to the sink and damned the remains to the disposal. He reached for his shoulder but caught himself and kept his arm moving like it was a necessary morning stretch. It was quickly repeated with the other arm. *Really good? Sheesh...*

"Good," said the older Mo like the invigorated dog-walking morning person he was. "I can feel it."

Mo felt his dad's X-ray vision trained on him. His voice took on a little ersatz urgency, "Gotta get in the shower," he said. Like the morning person he wasn't.

∞

Chapter 33

"I'm sorry about Marty, Danny." The woman on the phone was compassionate though she despaired over death less than most. "You two were good for each other."

"Well, he went out kind of how he thought he might."

"He wasn't afraid, was he? The obituary didn't mention a church celebration of his passage to eternal life."

"Tomorrow. Just a short, no frills burial service, I guess." Danny played it dumb. "His request."

"Interesting...well, he was a kindly old rooster," she said. "So Mo knows the truth now?"

"Partly. We haven't talked much about it. Just letting things come about organically." Danny sat at his desk in his home office, watching out his window as a squirrel snatched pieces of loose newspaper that had blown into the yard and snagged on some bushes. The squirrel had been busy for awhile, tearing the paper from the bushes, bunching it up, putting a corner of it in his mouth and taking it up the oak tree. "All things in time."

"Certainly." Amanda Moran, along with Crusty and to a lesser extent, Carter Slane, had known of Marty's covert inner-city stewardship. Anyone else who'd known had since passed away. "Anyway...I know you haven't wanted to talk about it - but the controversy over The Majesty is getting downright ugly up here. More so than ever."

"Bound to happen. You can't build a lemonade stand these days without someone feeling victimized by the height of the counter."

"That may be, but it seems everyone thinks they know how *you* feel about it," said Manda Mo.

Danny switched the phone to his fresher ear, reminding himself again to hold the phone more gently. The squirrel was working faster now, running the newspaper up the oak tree to a place too high for Danny to see. "Truthfully, Mom, even after I found out about it, I really hadn't given it a lot of thought."

"And now?"

"Don't know." Danny's voice was flat. "I got some calls and emails from some folks up there a couple years ago, a few months after the funeral. Didn't want to get involved. Seems the arguments began well before anyone had any specifics. Next thing you know it's a referendum on who thinks what about whose family. You know, 'if you're not with us you're against us.' It's nothing new. Loren Ferguson runs Rock Harbor; much of western Door County's economy depends on him and he's been good for the area. Sure, his hotels, restaurants, and the resorts, and the agency, will all benefit. But so will other businesses. He's the devil for building a golf course? Not sure I want to get involved."

"You know," said Manda, "there are the folks here who think we need more pottery, knick-knack and peanut brittle shops more than a fancy golf course, and then there are the environmentalists who may or may not care about knick-knacks. Loren has said almost nothing for the last year other than 'wait until you see it when it's finished.' He's done a good job of keeping out of sight."

"Smart man," said Danny. "Let everyone else do the talking."

"Are they ever...outwardly nasty, some of them. It's become an obsession with some people."

"Half The Harbor must work for him. That could be part of the reason for the uproar," said Danny. "A little competition can drive folks from their comfort zone. Can't hurt."

"I'm sure the tax dollars from The Majesty won't hurt, either," Manda said.

"No, it won't, though the tax thing always gets a little cloudy with golf courses." Danny watched the squirrel run back down the tree, its mouth empty. "It will help Rock Harbor in a lot of ways, but don't be surprised when the diners and funky shops start bemoaning their tax rate per square foot compared to Loren's course."

"Well it looks like it will be beautiful," said Manda. When Loren announced his plans to build The Majesty, he assured everyone the course and clubhouse would blend with the land, and promised to keep it as natural as possible, nothing ostentatious. Of course, there are groups getting up in arms about fertilizers and chemicals and what have you. Same as they did with that big to-do at the Klinkdale Farm."

"That stuff is exhaustively regulated by the EPA, and I'm sure they've satisfied the DNR with water recharge and runoff provisions and environmentally protected areas...all that. No one's kids will grow hooves or horns." Danny stood up to get closer to the window and searched the ground for the squirrel. He hoped it wasn't run off by other animals unhappy with what it did with the paper. Paper coming from trees and all. "I'd think there's useable property for maybe four or five holes along the bluffs anyway."

"It's been a long time for me; hard to even remember what it's like up there anymore, a hard climb, but now that there's a road maybe... But you...it still rankles me the way you used to traipse around up and down those bluffs on the sly. Used to worry me sick, all those accidents and falls over the years." Manda sighed.

"Yeah, well...we jungle cats are sure-footed. We know our way around."

Manda moved on. "Sam Bursinger is telling everyone he heard Loren bought off some higher ups in the DNR, just like he bought out the two homes that were in the way."

"Ol' Sam won't be burdened by the truth," said Danny. "The guy thrives on controversy."

Manda Mo almost hissed. "I don't care for the man, personally."

"I know, Mom." Danny had heard it all before. Sam Bursinger was inclined to tell certain people he was Danny's best friend back home. Most of the longtime residents of Rock Harbor knew Danny Mo, though most were now friends and relatives seen only at weddings and funerals.

Manda made a "hmmm" noise. "He's telling everyone you're dead set against The Majesty." Then, in a conspiratorial whisper, "He said you told him so when we celebrated Molly's new life."

"I do recall him bringing it up; he asked what I thought about the idea of a new course coming to The Harbor." Danny paused for a few seconds thinking back. "I said something like, 'nothing,' or 'not much.' Not sure. I wasn't thinking real clearly at the time."

"I know, Hon." Manda let the silence hang in the air for a few seconds. "You do understand that she is doing way better than any of us right now, Molly is, you know that."

Danny loved his mother dearly. She was 70 and in excellent health. Still, she addressed death as if passing away was the ultimate upgrade. "Coach to First Class," she'd say. Buoyed by her faith, she had said it for years, even before her beloved Curly had died; but after Molly's accident she ratcheted up the rhetoric to a vexing level.

Manda broke the silence. "Anyway, some folks are convinced that a great golfer like you is going to...what is it they say...you'll be drinking the Kool-Aid and rejoicing in having the latest and greatest golf course in your hometown. Something like that."

"I'm hardly great...people say things like that to suggest another's bias. It makes a tidy point they can support with logic. But logic can make a mess of the truth. Plenty of businesses - and people - have paid a heavy price from being slaves to logic." Danny was lapsing into MOS mode. "Anyway, Dear Mother, this is my official stance on this issue: Let's wait until it's finished."

Manda laughed. "I agree. Now that would fan the flames, you parroting Loren like that."

"Some people need to get a life."

"As always. But you know what, Danny, there are families who've been here forever who no longer talk to each other over this. The Kriers had their garage windows smashed in with golf balls just because Bruce's company was doing some of the soil grading."

"Usually that stuff goes deeper than the issue. That's the problem."

"Yes, it is," said Manda, "but each side is somehow claiming my famous golfer son is on their side of the argument. Everyone is always asking, they say, 'not that it really matters but, what does Danny, blah, blah.' At the store, at church, they call me at home, wait around at places until they can approach me. I never thought it would get this weird. I just say, 'no idea,' or, 'ask him yourself.'"

"Well," said Danny, "Just tell people that The Majesty will be a going concern no matter what your broken-down former golfer son thinks about it."

"I'll give you a going concern, Danny Mo, and broken down my eye. Still the best ever from the Upper Peninsula."

"The entire U.P., Mom? That's quite a responsibility."

After saying goodbye, Danny pulled up closer to his desk. Hank had come into his office to continue doing nothing at Danny's feet. He fired up his laptop and Googled around until he found a website for The Majesty Golf Course. He was a little surprised he hadn't done that before, but then again, he'd driven past the site during various stages of development when he'd visit his mom, and hadn't even bothered to drive in to take a peek at the place. The website was still under construction too, but there were some routing diagrams and some before photos contrasted with some touched-up projections of how things would look upon completion. Danny knew the place could be nothing short of spectacular and was impressed by how naturally everything appeared to be integrated into to the land. Land he felt he knew better than any living being. That terrain and those hills had been more than memorized. It was property upon which life began for more than one Moran. Throughout the website there were claims and quotes from the world-renowned course architect, C. Charles Revere, about how little earth was to be moved in shaping the holes, and how "the credit belongs with God and His gift of the glaciers." This from a man reputed to have a God complex to begin with. "The Majesty is a way to pay homage to the land and powers beyond us," was another such quote, set off in bold type set against a sunset shot of the bluffs.

Then, on an illustrated map of the course's projected layout, Danny found what he was looking for. Morgan's Forehead. The Forehead was a tower of glacial rock and intermittent vegetation that ascended nearly 150 feet above the average height of the other bluffs that lined the shore of Lake Michigan's Green Bay. It was the highest point in Door County and was to be incorporated into the par five finishing hole at The Majesty. To Danny it looked as if it would be at the corner of a dogleg. He could envision it instantly. The Forehead had sheer walls on two sides and was tapered half-way up the third. Its peak could be reached on foot on the south side if you knew the trick to it. At the top was a fairly flat and sandy surface that was roughly the size of half a football field, including one end zone. The view from there was an indescribable sensory experience. The Forehead was a local landmark and yet the locals either didn't know or disputed who the hell Morgan actually was, or what it was that tied the dude's forehead to a rock tower.

The majestic butte above the bluff line gave Danny Mo the chills. He had lost track of how many times he'd been to the peak of Morgan's Forehead, but assumed it more than anyone else, even if the last time was over 20 years ago, and it was with Molly.

∞

Chapter 34

Killing a morning mourning Marty Archibald was not Mo's idea of fun.

Though it was still morning, it was already hotter than predicted. Even his hair seemed irritable. "Mo Mo" Moran in the sun without a ball cap didn't feel quite right, like shooting hoops in cowboy boots.. His clothes were sticking to him and he was fast regretting going with his dad's suggestion of "dark business casual" for the occasion.

Mo wasn't certain as to proper church-free burial wear, so he followed his dad's lead. He did that a little more often than he cared to admit. Emulating his pop was nothing new, but the objective was not what it once was. It wasn't anything he wanted to be known for anymore. For years it had been the best compliment he could receive. He loved it when someone said he was "just like your old man." Now, Mo felt a compulsion to establish his own identity, time to spread his wings some. But bouncing back from a wounded right wing, he had still another reason to fly in circles above the home in which he was raised. And so Mo's bum shoulder stepped up again to shoulder the blame for his leisurely move toward independence, toward becoming "his own damn Mo."

The elder Moran had assured Mo it was to be a brief burial service, and that he'd appreciate Mo accompanying him and Crusty to it. Mo's first reaction was a subtle recoil, and he almost mentioned his discomfort with death -- the "you know, since Mom died," angle. But there was something in his father's eyes, a quirky mix of insistence and something on the sadder side of *pretty please*. A look he'd seen more and more frequently from his father. Whatever *it* was, it had shut him down.

And so here he was, sweltering in dark business casual in the middle of a burial service to memorialize a guy who turned out to be an enigma known as the noble cheater. Like others, Mo wondered how many of Marty's victories had been surreptitiously tainted. An otherwise good man who must have come to believe the rules of golf were something not to follow but to overcome.

Marty was to be laid to rest at Resurrection Cemetery. His place next to Joy had been reserved for nearly three decades and the plot had been regularly tended to by Marty himself. Danny had said that Marty loved life but had no fear of death, so confident was he of being with his wife "again and forever" when it came time to give up his "earthly address." It was a faithful position that the younger Mo noticed had grown in the elder Mo since Lady Mo had jumped the gun in getting to that perfectly organized place in the sky. Mo supposed he believed in all that too; but he didn't think it mattered much whether a guy in his best suit decomposed in the ground next to the powdered bones of his wife, or as human jerky in the gullets of ravenous sharks. Or, for that matter, as a drying agent for his golfing son's sweaty right hand.

The side-by-side spousal gravesite thing was more symbolic than anything else. The upside of being plot-mates was the twin-killing in a single Glory Be option, a two-for-one prayer deal for tombstone visitors on the go. The thought had Mo recalling his and Rinny's nightly prayer ritual as little kids. Back then, there was no need to be near anyone's remains in order to rattle off a blessing that covered every dead person they could name, and naming them was the key. After Grandpa Curly and Nanna Mommy, and all the brave soldiers and priests and Cassie, their former babysitter whose parachute didn't open, Mo and Rinny would see who could name more goners. On a good night, they'd rattle off everyone that came to mind — Vince Lombardi, John F. Kennedy, Bambi's mom, Princess Diana, the guy who played the Scarecrow in The Wizard of Oz and other notables in the dead community – before their mother would rein them in. Now, waiting for the burial service to start, Mo worked through these things as he maintained a place in the dwindling shade.

Had they not left ridiculously early (in Mo's view), they would have been late. At least three times Crusty had claimed "Okay, now I know where we are…" Before their wrong turns had become all consuming,

Crusty shared some news from a poker pal who happened to be a Milwaukee cop.

Apparently Marty and the girl were shot by a nasty sucka named Anthony Dumas, originally from Memphis, and died well before being pronounced dead at the hospital. Marty had come to the aid of the girl in the very early morning and ended up squaring off with Dumas. Dumas had been harassing the girl for taking some steps to get out of the street trade. When they found themselves trapped in the alley where the girl had been hiding, Marty started toward the man and Dumas shot him in the stomach and then shot girl in the ass as she turned to run. Marty had gone down hard, but he got up, and kept coming for Dumas, who fired two or three more times.

According to what the girl told cops, she saw Marty fall forward into Dumas and head butt him in the center of his face and then fall on top of him. She said she saw Marty, while lying on top of Dumas, lift his head and look over at her lying on the ground. He reportedly reared up for another butt, and again smashed his skull into the face of the pimp. The girl said she believed that Marty had driven Dumas's nose right into his brain, and must have killed him. Crusty dismissed that, saying those supposed nose kills are nothing but martial arts mythology; mostly the stuff of movies and books. The cartilage of the human nose is both too soft and too short to damage the brain, no matter how redirected.

While Marty had indeed inflicted severe trauma to Dumas with his melon, it was actually Marty's left hand, trapped under the dead weight of his own body that clutched Dumas's windpipe, and wrung the life from the jackal before his own expired above him. Or, as Crusty put it, "Marty covered that shit bomb, and the world's gonna stink a little less because of it. God Bless him."

Resurrection Cemetery was enormous, and haphazardly maintained. It was as if the place was developed in three stages. Some areas were sun-baked brown with burned out grass, while other spots were lush with life and blessed with life-affirming shade from clusters of old trees. In the middle section between the barren flatness and the venerable oaks and hickories were the arborvitaes, which stood in straight or right-angled rows of a half dozen or more like cubicle dividers, creating a sectional sense of order. The rest of the cemetery gave way to a vast flatness that went on uninterrupted by anything vertically organic. Only sporadic patches of uneven gravestones and some small crosses dotted the land that led seemingly over the horizon.

Mo sensed a kind of imbalanced caste system at Resurrection, as if the lackluster land to the south had taken in the poorer souls who were seemingly as much an afterthought as the landscape itself.

But, what the hell do I know about those folks, their families, the circumstances? They did what they did, and now they're dead. What did it matter? Yes, Grandpa Curly's ashes were spread over a whole lot of golf courses, and a couple ball diamonds, which always seemed a much cooler fate than rotting six feet under. But then, fate is a worldly outcome that ends with death. Wasn't the whole lot of it a bunch of post-mortem, style-point crap for the benefit of the living anyway?

Molly Moran's death had indeed birthed a bunch of answerless thoughts on death in her son's mind, and Mo was discovering just how much energy could be spent learning almost nothing about the "meaning of it all." Like father, like son.

The remains of the Archibalds would rest, eternally, on the far north end of the Resurrection property, ensconced against two gradually inclining hills, one of which was thick with shade-making trees with branches reaching up, out, and down at the end like the arms of limp-wristed zombies. There were over a hundred older golf-type guys huddled under the comfort of the temporary shade. No wives, no other women. Mo thought it strange.

On the other side of the casket, baking in the sun's still slightly eastern angle of assault, was nearly an equal number of Marty's girls, and Overlighter-related people, both men and women. Hot as he was, Mo felt some shame for being in the shade on the guy side.

"What's with the guys hogging all the shade?" Mo had asked casually enough.

"A good point, Mo, we really should mix it up a bit." Danny said it like he had been looking for a reason to relocate. They had already greeted most of the guys around them, anyway. Mo knew several of the men from The Barn, and met some others who knew all about Mo Mo Moran.

Mo sagged. He'd been grateful for the shade. His comment was meant mostly to show a little youthful conscience, not initiate real action. He figured everyone had already staked out their positions for the proceedings and he'd be safe, awash in his shady good fortune. But he had to open his mouth. Hell, from where he, Crusty, Carter and his dad were located, they had a nice view of an interesting array of women of various ages and nationalities who had gathered to send Marty off. There were women with Swimsuit Issue bodies who were positively ugly, and others with Swimsuit Issue faces atop massive forms with big asses. Many showed the obvious signs of erosion from bad choices and lives lived too fast. But even amid the high humidity and the conspicuous heartbreak, and a few too many who were overly made up or questionably dressed, there was a sprinkling of comprehensively top-to-bottom, Swimsuit Issue women on hand to honor Marty Archibald. Mo kept returning his gaze to a few of them, as if unwilling to believe his own eyes. However their appearances varied, it was the women who seemed to be suffering the greater loss compared to the men.

Sure enough, Mo's dad took charge and the four of them headed to the other side. Mo lagged behind and was duly impressed that his dad went straight to the single-most attractive woman there. In fact, she was breath-catching beautiful in a what's-your-problem-why-aren't-you-famous kind of way. After a few more glances, Mo thought she might be the finest woman he'd ever seen in real life. The slender, olive-skinned gal looked to be of mixed heritage, and of indeterminate -- though clearly ideal for looking perfect -- age. He turned loose his mother-inherited zeal for locating flaws, but could find none. Mo figured she had to have been pricy to rent if she had actually been a hooker. Most of them probably were at one time, he supposed. She was introduced to him as Cindy, and she had a mannered way that made Mo feel guilty for his thoughts, and, truth be told, slightly inadequate. He was certain now that she had caught him checking her out, but she no doubt had plenty of practice. From the way she lit up when his dad came over, Danny

Moran was obviously very special to her. Mo found that strangely disturbing.

Over the years, Mo had noticed how those of the female persuasion - regardless of age, be they stunning or plain, slender or fervently pro-calorie, or somewhere in-between, often beamed and blushed in the presence of his dad, even if he was only ordering an Alfredo-flavored Monster Malt from a pimpled, roller-skating carhop at Wayne's Custard stand. Mo found that to be both annoying and impressive. Danny Mo had the type of personality that disarmed folks while linking diverse lots together for the greater good. It was his business, yet, since Mo's mother died, it was as if his dad was more frequently lost in thought with less of a need to amuse anyone. Not that he'd become Bill Belichick, but neither did he exude the trademark D Mo persona that made Tom Hanks seem like a prick.

Mo understood his dad's reticence about returning to the world he'd inhabited before Molly died. Mo sensed the whole "top-five, worldwide" shtick was a backhanded form of self-preservation. The addition of some lighthearted significance to the mundane may have helped his dad maintain the "It's the little things that matter" mentality, and thus lighten the family's load when his mom's quest for domestic excellence weighed everyone down.

Even the act of opening impossibly tight jar lids — long one of Danny Moran's go-to "top-five worldwide" claims — had been relegated to relative insouciance. Mo recalled the times when his dad would whisper, guru-like, that the key was to hold the jar with respect, to summon cooperation from the jar with soft hands, and frequently referencing the Arthurian legend of The Sword and the Stone before the lid would finally, slowly, turn in his hands. Mo had thought his pop's dramatics were cool, stupid, or humorous depending on his own stage in life. For his mother, the jar lid thing was just another fertility rite before the raining of the eye rolls.

And in truth, Mo had developed his own variation on the assignment of "top-five worldwide" greatness ratings, though they involved acts he felt were less mundane than his dad's since many of

Mo's most recent amazing feats had him competing in the "one-handed division."

Mo felt awkward making his conspicuous move to the other side of the casket. And, worse, he was now taking a direct facial from the sun. No one else moved to join them, but then why would they? Their stations had been taken. The priest drove past the closest parking area, which was just over the hill, and parked his navy Malibu next to the hearse. Dressed in all black, he began talking with representatives from the funeral services company.

Among the ladies of Overlighter's Salvation House, Mo now had a lovely view of the mostly older men standing in the coveted shade. Cindy had plenty to whisper to his dad, who simply nodded, repeatedly. A woman in total command of the world – had to be the Sunya woman – was actively involved with the priest and the funeral folks. After that group had broken up she came over to Danny and gave him a long hug. Then she handed him an envelope. Danny nodded some more.

The priest began the service with the Lord's Prayer. The ladies were clearly more familiar with it than the guys. Mo loosened his collar, an expression of discomfort more than an achievement of relief. Crusty and Carter were studies in proper reverence, heads bowed and still. Mo was antsy, looking around. The air was an olfactory wapatuli of sorts, with colliding perfumes merging with whiffs of perspiration and sun-scorched vegetation, the whole bouquet spiked with the unmistakable scent of burning incense used in the blessing of the grounds and the casket.

The priest prayed aloud.

"O God, by Your mercy rest is given to the souls of the faithful, be pleased to bless this grave. Appoint Your holy angels to guard it, and set free from all the chains of sin the soul of Martin, whose body is buried here, and lays now with his wife Joy, so that with all Thy saints they may rejoice in Thee forever, through Christ our Lord. Amen."

Mo suddenly began blinking. He stared, closed his eyes, and then stared some more to make sure he wasn't seeing a mirage. No way. It simply couldn't be. Coming over the rise that led from the car park area

was a large man dressed in a three piece suit, his long salt and pepper
hair motionless despite his dramatic strides. Others began to notice, too,
and Andy Salamone had the look of a man delighted to be noticed, and
unsurprised that he was. The hottest golfer in the state was in the house,
so to speak, and he took plenty of time making his appearance. Mo
looked at his dad just as Danny, too, noticed the arrival of Salamone. D
Mo nodded like he might have anticipated this and actually seemed
pleased about it. Just like Sally, thought Mo, to think he might pile up
some PR points from being seen at Marty's service. Salamone looked like
a mafia don but made a show of trying to be discreet as he took his place
in a back row next to Jumbo Larson, another surprise attendee. The
shade had retreated from the casket, and the sun had slowly pushed
Marty's buddies further away in order to stay shaded on the guy side.
After the murmurs from the spectacle of Salamone's theatrical
emergence from over the horizon receded, the silence returned, and
made it seem even hotter.

The priest intoned, "God of holiness and power, accept our prayers
on behalf of your servant, Martin; do not count his deeds against him,
for in his heart he desired to do your will. As his faith united him to your
people on earth, so may your mercy join him to the angels in heaven. We
ask this through Christ our Lord. Amen."

Mo returned to sneaking peeks at Cindy, who had her head bowed
but had now, of all things, taken hold of his dad's arm. He was in
desperate need for a breeze but there was barely that. The service went
on for a few more prayers; the VFW fired their shots, folded the flag, and
thanked everyone who loved Martin on behalf of the president of the
United States. Wolfy Curran from The Ol' Barn sang a credible *Amazing
Grace* a cappella. Mo thought this had gone on longer than long enough
when the priest turned over the proceedings to Sunya Williams from
Overlighter's.

With an air of nobility, she walked to a spot next to the casket. The
excavated gravesite was as dignified as dirt could be, deep where
Marty's earthly form would soon remain forever. Sunya took her time
and smiled as she glanced at both groups on either side of the casket.

"I know it's warm out here, so I will not take much more of your time other than to tell you that Marty left a short letter he wanted read at this occasion. An occasion the man we called "Jonah" feared not at all. He was well aware that something like this could happen. I told him to go away for awhile, but he would have none of it. The man was incapable of backing down. So without any more from me, I'd like to introduce one of Marty's closest friends, and one of our very special friends as well at Overlighter's, Danny Moran. It is with Mr. Moran that Marty entrusted this letter."

Mo looked at his dad, who had the letter in his hands. Danny gave nothing away, but Mo thought he detected *something* in his face. As Danny Moran walked slowly toward the casket, Mo was feeling certain the letter was to be a grand bit of humility from "Jonah," all meant to bring a tear, a smile and a lasting memory of his Marty-ness. And why not, he may have been a cheater, but he certainly had a selfless side, something Mo hadn't expected, and, frankly, wasn't particularly thrilled with. It meant Mo was way off in at least one respect. The tribute in the paper took care of that. It also increased attendance at the service, considering Marty had no known living relatives.

His dad was taking an unusual amount of time pulling the letter from the envelope and unfolding it, and Mo could see the wheels turning as he did it. He'd seen that look before. Earlier he had noticed his dad sneaking some peeks at the letter while the priest was blessing and incensing the casket.

Danny scanned the letter, nodded one more time and placed the empty envelope on the casket. "Alright. Here we go." Mo didn't think that was in the letter, but couldn't be sure.

"Hey everybody, thanks for coming." Danny read aloud. He looked as though he found the opening line a touch funny for some reason. "This letter is the result of things getting a little crazy, make that, crazier, on the streets of this town. Somebody was either going to get me, or, hell, I'm old, for all I know, maybe I went face first into my Spaghetti-Os, but it doesn't matter much now."

"I left this letter for Sunya to give to Danny Moran, because Danny knows my death means there are secrets that can now be told." The son of Danny Mo watched his dad, enthralled. A letter from the grave had an eerie allure. The elder Mo continued reading, "This is my final hole-out, as it were." There were titters from the guys' side. Danny let them subside "I'd like to thank the whole lot of you who bothered to come today. To the 'Ladies of The House,' I love you."

Mo then watched his dad hesitate, eyes still on the letter. After an awkward stretch of silence, Danny read again. "There is something I need to say, and something I need to confess." Danny paused again. Mo saw his dad look across the casket and lock eyes with Salamone. The big man, captive in sartorial overkill, appeared hopeful.

Danny then read aloud some of what was in the paper. Marty wouldn't have known of the article having been already dead. "I loved gambling on the golf course. The action has always been exciting to me whether it's a three dollar Nassau or a thousand. Not that I've ever had one of those but it sounds cool to say, even if I'm having it said for me now." Danny took a breath. "But I want everyone to know this. I made a promise to my wife many years ago, that every dime I made from bets on the course would go to Overlighter's. It may have been only about five or ten thousand dollars annually that I could funnel to The House, but over 30-some years it adds up to quite a bit, maybe even a quarter million. I would like to ask any golfers here today to consider doing something similar, maybe figure something out, like your skins game winnings or something like that. It's up to you. I know Overlighter's could really use it."

Salamone looked as bored as Mo felt about Marty's final fundraiser.

"And over the years, I fought hard for my winnings, as you might imagine, and probably already know. A dollar not won was a dollar that The House would not get. It sounds funny to say, but in my eagerness to help The House and assist in their good works, I got a reputation for, sometimes – well, I'll just come out and say it – a reputation for cheating. That's right, cheating. Cheating to get the money, and I know there were a few people who spread this fact around town, and I know word of this has traveled throughout the state, as well as to anyone who would listen, and many did listen. And yes, I did use the word 'fact.' I'll get to that in a moment. But there are two things I'd like you to know. One: I never, ever, cheated in a golf tournament of any kind. Not even worth talking about, that would be disgraceful. And two: I played in some money matches where I sometimes actually did cheat. A few times I even cheated more than once." Danny slowly scanned everyone on the guys' side. No one was in the shade any longer.

Now Mo was intrigued. Part of him felt redeemed. He heard people coughing and clearing their throats along with some sighs of discomfort. It was definitely an edgy moment and, truthfully, a little sad, Marty confessing his transgressions when he no longer had to face anyone. He didn't have to do it, of course. Mo felt bad for his dad having to carry out this last mission for his friend, the legendary Marty Archibald. His thoughts were interrupted by his father's voice again.

Danny read on. "Andy Salamone, as many of you know is one of the most talented golfers in the state, and without a doubt, is the one who lost the most money through my occasional on-course deceptions. I hope you're here today Andy. I had asked Danny to invite you. That fact indirectly makes you one of the larger individual contributors to Overlighter's in the entire city. Then again, perhaps you've lost some weight from the grief of my passing." Muffled guffaws, mostly from the guys' side, but a few ladies laughed harder.

Mo watched Salamone closely. He was shaking his head, playfully absorbing Marty's jab. The man was fairly glowing, his three piece suit battling his processed puffery. Mo wondered if many guys wore three piece suits anymore. Danny leaned against the casket with his left hand, and looked at the letter in his right. Then he looked up and said nothing. To Mo, he looked a little like a hostage forced to read a bunch of propaganda. He dropped the hand holding the letter to his side. Then, looking directly at Salamone, "Andy, I believe Marty would be honored if you'd be the one to finish reading this letter. Seems his confession, the truth he wants share, is directed mostly toward you. It seems you've been right all along about Marty."

Andy Salamone was already moving toward Danny from his place at the back of the guys' side. With head held high, and waves of premeditated hair staying with his every move, Sally strode carefully on the grass. He made a point of literally watching his step, as if to draw attention to his Versace Black Leather Crocs. When he reached Danny, he took the letter and, inconceivably, gave him a quick but showy bump-hug. Danny quickly pointed to the place in the letter where he had left off and then backed away with no visible shudder from withstanding Salamone's proximity. Mo found the scene surreal. He glanced at Crusty, who stared stonily at the two men by Marty's casket.

Salamone ignored the letter in his hand and scanned the nearly 200 people roasting in the sun. Many of the golfers knew quite well the history of Danny Mo and Andy Salamone, and Marty's place in it all. The people in attendance seemed oblivious to the heat now, no fanning, and few sounds, totally gripped by the convergence of the state's three most prominent golf rivals. That one of them was dead and talking through the other two made it the first and only graveside drama of its kind.

Salamone's first words were his own. "I would like to announce right now, before I leave this cemetery," he looked directly at Sunya, "that I am going to write a check for $5,000 payable to The Overlighter's Salvation House." Subdued applause pattered on briefly then petered out quickly, but Salamone accepted it like a politician pausing mid-speech to acknowledge a misinterpreted hoot. "And I'd like to acknowledge Marty Archibald as a champion, a humanitarian, and by virtue of his comments today, by that I mean his confession in front of all of us, truly a man of integrity. I think this shows us that we are always open to forgiveness in God's eyes should we prove truly remorseful. I guess it's never too late, huh."

Mo had the sensation that he was dreaming, unable to grasp just how farfetched this entire production would sound to anyone who knew all the players in the cast. That included Cindy, whose features had taken over Mo's imagination such that he now felt even the most airbrushed magazine face would pale in comparison and complexion.

"Alright." Salamone finally returned to the letter and began reading. "Andy and I had many good battles for some good chunks of money. I was fortunate to win more than I lost. Quite a bit, in fact. But there were indeed times that I fudged things to some degree. The man is longer, stronger and much younger than me. He graciously allowed me to play from the regular tees. If I had to play from the back tees against him it would be no contest." Salamone could not help but smile as he spoke. "When I think of our battles, and some of the battles I had with a few others, I am reminded of a television western I watched many years ago that has always stayed with me, though I couldn't even tell you who was in it. Two cowboys got into a fight inside a saloon. The fight was pretty even but then the guy in the white hat started to get in more punches and took control of the fight. So the guy in the dark hat decided to grab an empty bottle of beer off a nearby table, and smashed it in half on the bar, then he went after the guy in white, leading with the jagged edge of the beer bottle. Ol' White Hat gave a look of disgust, and quickly grabbed a bottle of whiskey off the bar, and smashed it in half as well. Whiskey went flying everywhere and then the guy in the white had a weapon that was bigger and more dangerous."

Salamone read away. He cocked his head and ad-libbed. "Marty, ol' boy, you were maybe watching too much TV." A few tittered, again.

Mo glanced at his dad, who looked a little too amused, his demeanor a little out of context. Like his dad was playacting a bit. Crusty was still as a stone, but something about him suggested he wanted Salamone to get on with it.

Salamone returned to reading Marty's words. "That's all I wanted to say to all of you. You might have figured that I saw myself as the cowboy in the white hat. I was willing to finish the fist fight knuckles only. But, you see, I did cheat. And anyone who's ever blathered on about my doing so is probably right. But I only cheated against those who cheated against me first, like the dark hat guy with the beer bottle did. It's about trust. Once was enough, such is the price of original sin…" Salamone's voice trailed off as he finally got it. He, for some reason, read another sentence, out of curiosity perhaps, or maybe he didn't realize he was still talking out loud. "Only for the money, only for The House…?!"

Mo saw that Salamone's neck was changing color. Sweat dripped from his nose, and his hair had that dank-scalp wilt now. Then Sally threw the letter down and puffed up again. "This is a set-up, total bullshit! Anyone can make accusations when they don't have to face anyone anymore." Sally looked at Danny Mo with daggers in his eyes. "You set me up, you and that cheatin' son of a bitch. You got no proof, you got nothing."

Danny said nothing. He walked to the casket and picked up the letter. Mo saw Jumbo Larson lumbering up the slope of the hill that led to the parking lot, head bowed. Everyone was rapt, in the moment. Salamone leaned against the casket like he had nothing to hide, trying to look casual but breathing in audible sniffs.

"I'll finish," said Danny, waiting a beat before reading again from the letter. "I know that it may seem easy to level charges in a letter. That it may be seen as in bad taste. So be it. Anyone who chooses to dispute this, fine. You should know there is a website with all kinds of information on it, very detailed information. You can guess who and how many have the link to the site." Danny looked up at Sally. The big man's head was turned up and away. His fingers drummed on the casket as Danny read the end of the letter. "And, finally, I invite everyone here to The Aftermath for food and beverages and storytelling, preferably about me. And one last thing. Please think of what the "E" actually stands for in Kai's Steamin' E burger. No one I know knows. I do. Thing is, I told Kai years ago I'd take it to the grave. But I will risk offering you a clue. Life goes by quickly, no matter how long you live."

Danny looked up and finished, "That's it. Cheers, Marty 'Jonah' Archibald. See most of you again, I'm sure of it."

Mo let his head fall like it was released by a cord just cut. He did not want to have his dad see him smile now; it was a smile born of amazement more than happiness. Salamone had taken his first few steps toward the hill that Jumbo was already cresting.

"Gandhi!" said the woman, a half-shout.

Salamone froze. He had his back to the proceedings now. The priest had bypassed the intended final song, or prayer, or whatever he had planned. The murmurs subsided quickly. When Big Andy turned he looked smaller, wetter and redder. His mouth was twisted, like he'd been fed live bait.

"Check please." Cindy said it quietly, but it was enough for a few other women to back her up.

"Yo, Gandhi, don't forget the check," said one.

"You promised, Sir" said another.

∞

Chapter 35

"Gandhi?" said Mo from the back seat.

Mo hadn't known where to begin once they were back in the car, and Crusty and his dad were unusually quiet.

He waited for some response. No one jumped on it.

The air conditioner was delivering the goods and finally getting to Mo's airspace in the back seat. "Did I hear those ladies correctly? I swore she called Sally, 'Gandhi.'" He sat back, again expecting one of them to offer something.

Crusty looked over at Danny, who stared straight ahead as he drove. When Crusty returned his gaze to the road, Danny looked at Crusty for a moment. When they tried the glance again and got it right, an embryonic grin could have been detected on each of them. Neither spoke, nor did they seem to hear Mo.

"Well, was it wrong?" Danny said it quietly, like it was self-talk.

"Just compensation, Dannymo, the son of a bitch."

Danny nodded once. Nothing else.

Mo listened to the men, feeling invisible. Power lines ran tower-to-tower in nondescript fields along the overly-crowned road that would take them back to places worth looking at. Mo wondered if the electrical field was affecting his brain waves such that the sound of his voice was somehow returned to his head before it could be heard by anyone else. Outside, it looked as hot as it was and the view was about as mesmerizing as any mud field as medium could be. No one said anything until Danny and Crusty were certain the soulless power tower road would take them to the more widely-recognized county highway. There, the idiot-proof signs would breadcrumb the way back to the refuge of the interstate.

Crusty turned back to Mo. "Gandhi, Mo?"

"Yes, thank you, Crust. Thought maybe my voice had slipped into a frequency range that only Hank and me could pick up." Mo waited for a reaction from Crusty, but the man's face was about as blank as Hank's would have been had he been subjected to the same sentence. He moved on. "The Cindy woman, I swear she called Salamone, "Gandhi," before he stormed off."

Crusty narrowed his eyes. "Because they're both vegetarians, into truth, love and civil disobedience for the sake of social justice, maybe?"

"Right," said Mo. "I'm sure she called him Gandhi."

"You know how some of Sally's guys at The Barn call him Big Andy?" said Crusty. His eyebrows ascended slightly. "But he insists that it be pronounced B'Gandhi. Probably makes him feel revered."

"Okay."

"Yep. And when he goes on a streak and makes a few birdies, he likes to say, 'Me hot.' Then he's 'Me hot B'Gandhi.'"

Danny gave a sour look and shook his head. Then he reached down between his legs.

Mo smiled. "And even if that was true, how on earth would Cindy know what Sally likes to be called? Does she play golf?"

Danny checked the caller ID and flipped open his vibrating cell phone. "What's up, Witchy?" He listened briefly. "Went well. Marty signed off as he would have hoped."

Then, more silence. Danny listened. He turned the AC down a notch.

"Of all the times to... no, no... it's alright. Just tell me," said Danny. Then he listened some more. For a very long time.

No one in the car spoke. The sound of Witchy's voice going into Danny's ear sounded like an AM talk radio show faintly coming in and out of the signal. Danny's expression was that of one straining to recall things. Mo could make out very little other than something about Orsman being out of the office.

"Hmmm..." said Danny. And then he said it some more, at different times.

On the expressway, the ambient sound inside the car was of a stir-fry on low. Though the Marquette interchange was still under construction after nearly three years, things moved along smoothly. Mo gave up on hearing whatever was up with Witchy and his dad. He used the time to enter his own inner world.

Mo could see his reflection in the rearview mirror from his seat in back. He supposed the sun had colored his face slightly, something he was able to notice because the question-mark shaped scars on his face tanned at a different rate than the rest of his face. Those scars were courtesy of Andy "Hair Dude" Salamone, and so the sting on Salamone had been sweet. Even right after it happened, as a 9 year-old kid, he harbored no grudge with what he learned was a red-tailed hawk. Just a hawk being a hawk. Now, Mo hoped that Salamone had earned some of his own scars.

And yeah, Marty was okay. The story of the one-armed florist and the weak-tit Lubberman; it was easier to see how Marty had meant it now. Still, there was something troublesome about the whole Marty thing, something he couldn't articulate at the moment. He nevertheless felt something good about the fact that the old man cared what he thought. Made him wonder now if Marty actually did see him and Davy at The Barn way back when. Maybe. He'd never know.

As smoking hot as Mo thought Cindy was, seeing her holding onto his dad's arm was more proof that Heaven sure as hell ain't a place for observing what's happening on earth. His mom might understand, but the view of a major babe on her husband's arm wouldn't have passed for paradise. He knew from Sunya that his dad had helped out at Overlighters from time-to-time when Marty asked him to, but Mo couldn't get past her past. Not that he knew the first thing about it.

Mo had been wrong about Marty. Turns out he'd been pulling against someone who was doing some pretty good stuff. Mo had hoped Marty had a darker side, just so he could be right. He considered how his dad had handled the truth... how Danny never betrayed the confidentiality of his friend, and how he was never overbearing about it with Mo. Danny couldn't talk about it, so he didn't. He must have been tempted. Mo would have been.

Danny eventually ended his conversation on a stern note with Witchy, something about, "taking it up tomorrow," and then clapped his phone shut. Crusty looked over at him. Danny's jaw tightened.

Crusty let it rest.

So did Mo. He had been about to throw out another jump ball, something about the meaning of the E in the Steamin' E Burger, if Marty ever really, truly knew what it meant. And that was the thing, this idea of who knew what, believed this or admitted that, and who cheated whom and when did it start and why did it continue. This notion triggered what was eating at Mo.

Going back as far as Rookie ball, he knew a few guys who were juicing, doing whatever, steroids, Andro, HGH, greenies. A lot of guys did it because others did it first. Hell, even Barry Bonds got tired of seeing McGuire and Sosa become folk heroes and get fatter contracts. At least that's the way the argument goes.

Kicking around the Marty rationale, Mo pondered, taking personality out of it, if people found out that Bonds gave 50 grand to charity for every homer he hit, how would he be viewed now? Beloved like Marty?

And then Mo wondered what the cream and the clear might have done for rehabbing a wrecked shoulder. Or before it got wrecked. The thought made him thirsty for a cool one.

∞

Chapter 36

Amanda Moran did not care for her son's way of putting it, but Danny liked saying how, in the Moran family, "baseball was a second religion twice as studied as the first."

Danny loved baseball. Took to it instinctively from his first days in the backyard with Curly, and continued on to be an all-conference shortstop in high school and to play Division 3 college ball. He remained a loyal fan of the Milwaukee Brewers, though he was plenty ready to commit to the rival Cubs when Mo was drafted by them.

Switching from The Brew Crew to The Cubbies would not rise to the bible-thumper-turned-jihadist level of traitorous behavior as would a Packers fan jumping off the green and gold bandwagon to ride the L with the Bears, but it would be seen as poor form nevertheless to trade shades of blue among baseball rivals separated by only 90 miles. Danny believed supporting the team that Mo signed with was a no-brainer exception to this, but that switching team loyalties because of marriage was a tougher call.

Danny knew the game of baseball as well as he knew anything, courtesy of Curly, semi-pro baseball legend. Likewise, he passed on his knowledge and zeal to Mo and Rinny, up until her conversion to soccer. But in spite of -- or because of -- all Danny knew about fundamentals and strategy and talent for the game, he considered betting on Major League Baseball games to be somewhere between impractical and insane. Gambling on baseball, some claim, was less about how to play the game and more about on which games to play. Danny wondered if knowing the umpiring crew played into it.

It would be hard to know for sure when Evan Orsman first began 'borrowing' cash to bet on ballgames. Orsman's weak shrug in response to Danny's wasted question as to when it all began captured the pointlessness of having it answered. What was done was done. Both knew that what mattered now was what to do next. Danny could not answer that one, and the fear he saw in Orsman's eyes only added to a mess not of his making.

Evan Orsman never played an organized inning in his life. He wasn't much of an athlete, but he had a longstanding fascination with sports and competition from the time he first started falling asleep with the transistorized voice of Jack Buck calling Cardinals' games from under his pillow. He had always maintained that he never was good enough at any sport to even register on the Wannabe Meter, but Danny wondered now if *this* was his way to play, to finally get in the game. When he confronted Orsman, Danny had burned a look right through the man and asked, "Aren't you in a fantasy league or two?"

"Four," Orsman had said. "They're called Rotisserie Leagues, and I've done well."

Their mutual interest in sports was a big reason for a friendship that began back in college. Orsman tracked streams of data on college and professional basketball and football but it was his immersion in the calculus-driven minutia of Major League Baseball where he felt most in his element. Orsman could rattle off pitcher's ERAs for road games at night on three days' rest as easily as he could recite the birthdates of his chubby little kids. Danny had known the guy laid a little wood on games from time to time. What he hadn't known was that, at some point, Orsman had found a new hangout in an old cliché, and that place being the odds maker's proverbial land of fiscal quicksand where even otherwise responsible people can "get in too deep." After hearing Orsman out, Danny was surprised at what he came to believe about the whole affair. It wasn't a case of a guy getting all that geeked on the action, or even a guy having to act on his geekdom. It was simply a case of someone who chose to live beyond his means, even as the means changed, literally, before Orsman's eyes in the books he kept. Orsman tried to overcome his lifestyle-driven deficits by betting, and he needed cash to cover those deficits. At least Danny hoped it was only to cover. He found himself in the odd position of hoping the missing money was used only for bets. Right or wrong, at least in Danny's mind, it seemed less like stealing compared to just taking money to buy stuff.

Orsman and Witchy had control of everything financial for MOS, and Danny had given them that control. But Orsman was the one who transacted everything with the banks and most everything else coming in and going out. Witchy had figured it all out, and quietly fumed that Orsman could think she wouldn't, eventually. She further fumed about not getting to the bottom of it sooner even though no one could really know when it all began. Once she knew the money was missing, she guessed that Orsman was into something based on an increasing amount of curious phone conversations she overheard coming from his office and a humorless edge in him that seemed related.

Danny listened to parts of the story in a stilted come-to-Jesus meeting with Orsman at a back corner table of a local family restaurant, Chuck's Place. It was as if each no longer knew the other. There were, of course, "plays" made to fix the "plays" that were placed to fix other "plays," and so on. While Danny Mo's business would survive, his plans for the rest of his life, if he could even cite a plan, were now as clear as the little pond turned algae-covered mud swamp behind the 17th tee at The Old Barn. And like that retreating pool of muck, he, too, was no longer as liquid as he once was. More than anything, it was his loss of flexibility that grated at him now. He'd have to work up more business at MOS, but the real cost to Danny was that working harder was now mandatory instead of an option of relative importance.

Three years ago, numb from Molly's passing and under-aroused by his prospects with MOS, he had come into what had seemed to be some reliable, real-time investment information at, seemingly, just the right time. As "reliable" as a speculative ground floor deal could be, anyway. He had jumped in with a decent six figure chunk of cash on a speculative venture involving a supposedly world-changing water-treatment technology for potable water. Danny researched it extensively and ran it by Crusty and Carter, both of whom would have far better reasons for understanding water usage *and* investments than he ever would, which resulted in both friends going in with him. Carter had been so gung ho he even went so far as to sell one of his Laundromat/dry cleaning stores just to plow most of it into the private placement offering.

It was going to be fun for the three friends to follow every exciting step, waiting for the right mega-company with deep pockets to barge in and buy the whole damn deal for mega-millions. They were still waiting. The deal still had great promise, but things were going to move at the pace that most homerun or bust deals do. That had been fine with Danny. He had enough money. He could be patient. His goal was to set up his family and retire early, to follow Mo as he turned into an ace for the Cubs. That was a different time.

Danny's access to his cash is what allowed him to make an investment like this, and for that, Orsman had patted himself on the back. For years, even though ultimate oversight fell on him, Danny had become only generally aware of his money's comings and goings. Such was his trust in Orsman. As it was, Witchy and Orsman were each paid a better than market base salary from Modus Operandi Solutions. In addition, they received an equal percentage of revenue, plus, each enjoyed a generous benefits package that had become pricier every year for Danny to maintain. The idea was to feature the 'all for one and one for all' team idea that Danny promoted in his business consults; and it was, by all accounts, a forward thinking program deemed more than fair by his two employees.

With that understood, Danny sat and listened to Orsman spill his fractured thoughts over a couple of untouched bagels and perfunctorily sipped coffee. His friend ran the gamut, of sorrow, resentment, justification, as well as guilt. Guilt weakly put upon Danny, as well as his own. It was an uncomfortable 90 minutes for two guys who knew their friendship would never be the same, if not, technically, over. The litany was predictable, and sad. "Danny, it got away from me. Danny, you weren't working much after Molly passed. Your back was shot, your heart was broken. Hell, all our hearts were broken. Danny, I'm so ashamed. Danny, I just wanted to get back close to even. Danny, our revenue the last couple years isn't much more than half of what it used to be, Lori will be off to school. Danny, you sat in your office for all those months just looking out the window or tapping on your laptop and said you were 'thinking,' and our income was shrinking – that is, if you came in to the office at all. You talked more about Hank's antics than any new business opportunities. Kept saying how clients wanted the old Danny Mo and you weren't sure the old Danny Mo was ever coming back. Danny, while you sat and thought, well, I was wondering what to think."

Danny just sat there and listened. Not particularly original, he thought, except for Orsman's comments near the end.

"Danny, I had gotten pretty far ahead early, and wanted one more play is all. But then, well, let's just say there aren't a lot of Major League relief pitchers I can trust anymore. Couple closers you can count on, sure, but too many middle relievers are good for nothing more than breaking your heart."

The sad irony of that statement kept Danny from a reflex counter about how starters don't go deep into games anymore. And the few comments he eventually offered may have had the heft of righteousness. He made a point of saying them as if thinking aloud about hired help. A courtesy or a way to keep from going off, Danny didn't know. He made it clear that he shared the benefits of MOS's revenue "as an added bonus for highly appreciated employees, not an entitlement that necessarily gets bigger every year, just because…what? The employee wants more? Be different if the employee created a few opportunities that resulted in measurable contributions to the company's revenue instead of, oh, say simply managing that revenue."

After a long period of silence, and the terminated employee battling back tears, Danny told Orsman that he was a good financial guy and that he could easily make more money elsewhere. Orsman hung on his words, waiting to hear, no doubt, if charges were forthcoming. Danny knew it but said nothing.

At no point, throughout the darkness after Molly's death, was Danny unaware of what he was doing. Or not doing. When Orsman made the claim that Danny had let a good year go by while doing pretty much nothing aside from thinking, it was not altogether surprising.

Danny knew all that, he just didn't care. Time had become an increasingly ambiguous concept.

And Danny's ambition, the necessary drive to work the conference rooms and auditorium halls, had also lost the appeal it once had. Danny had fashioned a career out of draping his personality over a combination of creative daring and customized common sense. It wasn't for everyone. A prominent leader in the business community called Danny, "The Dennis Miller of the consulting world, but without all the fucking adverbs." And that was fine with him. Once, it had been fun. Now he had no choice but to tackle a terribly uncomfortable situation involving longtime friends, Witchy and Orsman, without losing a business that no longer excited him, but one he now needed to survive.

A small nonsensical part of him held a sliver of respect for what Orsman had attempted, misguided as it was. The financially prudent Orsman, the Orsman that Danny knew, must have had a fair amount of confidence to take such a risk. Then again you never hop on a motorcycle with a man adrift in a mid-life quandary. And all it took was a fleeting thought about the staggering amount that he had lost to snap Danny back to the consequences of his new reality. The loss was well into six figures and it made forgiveness too hard. Restitution was impossible. Unfortunately, and as telling as anything, Danny sensed that Orsman felt he could still fix everything with just another batch of bets.

Danny's entire life had, again, changed for the worse. Though he was uncertain how much and for how long, it was clear that his freedom to simply wing it, perhaps the single greatest freedom on earth for a guy like Danny Moran, was gone.

He had left Orsman to his misery at the back of Chuck's with no indication as to what he was might do. He left Orsman to ponder the betrayal of trust, the betrayal of the statistics Orsman had counted on, and the betrayal of the middle relievers who Orsman, amazingly, had the nerve to call out as people he could no longer trust. Danny left him with all that, as well as the bill for breakfast. Throughout the entire history of their post-collegiate relationship, Danny had always picked up the check. It was an understanding between The Haves and The Have a Little Mores, an arrangement common in many working relationships and one each had been comfortable with. Leaving the check now for Orsman would no doubt be taken as a symbolic tit-for-tat. Danny did not care a bit.

From his position, it was more like tit for Titanic.

∞

Chapter 37

By the time the first anniversary of Marty Archibald's murder rolled around the following July, three huge parts of Danny Moran's life needed to be addressed: MOS, his mom and Cindy Young.

Those central components aside, there were plenty of other things both more and less important about which he was equally clear. But, with three key things consuming him, with three big slices of his life grabbing most of the market share on his overall fixation pie, he was, as a sentient being, just as clear on the fact that these three things would significantly affect others close to him - and the rest of his life.

He was not clear what he should actually do about what he knew to be true. In meetings and presentations for MOS, Danny found it useful to suggest that "identifying the truth is often easier than taking proper action on it." He would follow up with "knowledge by itself offers little except on Jeopardy." Danny saw this as hard truth learned from long experience and argued such points with an activist's zeal. There remained many a sleepless night, however, when he would have preferred knowing less. So too did he believe that action without knowledge was always dumb, and knowledge without action was usually weak, but it had been the knowledge of his own weakness that had him choking on a psyche-strangling form of apathy he chose to call "reflection."

And so the first of the three weighty matters bearing down on Danny was a decision that tortured him until the truth came with blinders: he was through with MOS. Done. Modus Operendi Solutions had run its course. The horse had nothing left. He closed the doors with three months left on his lease and several matters yet to work out.

The second was that the people of Rock Harbor had become far too divided for far too long for anyone's good. The townsfolk remained as stubborn and fractured as ever on the subject of the now-finished work along the panoramic shoreline and the forested inland terrain that had become The Majesty at Harrow Bluffs. Worse was the rampant unauthorized use of Danny Moran's name by folks on both sides of the fight. Complete fabrications about where "Mr. Pro Golfer" (Danny Mo, a lifetime amateur) really stood on the issue had become the norm. But handling that was hardly the biggest issue.

What was entirely unacceptable was the subtle harassment, the drip, drip, dripping discomfort it brought his mother who still lived in and loved Rock Harbor, but had to deal with the downside of small town life. At church, the grocery store, the Kwik Trip. "Manda, what's Danny think?" or "Suppose Danny's thrilled, huh?" or "Danny gonna say something?" It was nothing at first, but then it was nothing but weird. Danny knew he'd have to talk to some people in his hometown soon. His mom was to be left alone.

Finally, and most mind-blowing, was the third conscience-hungry component he'd have to address. Even as she worked on the safest side of widower-at-large etiquette, Cindy Young had clearly fallen for Danny Mo. He had sensed her interest for months and was sure she was…confused. He acted oblivious to keep from having to act at all, so disbelieving was he that someone so Halle Berry-beautiful might be that interested in him. He dedicated a great deal of time to thinking about what to do about all that. And on that front, he flat out couldn't get enough of where his mind took him. Time and time and time again.

Put simply, he'd had enough of MOS. Danny's professional tools, namely his industry experience, his business insights and his captivating yet principled bullshit, had become dulled from a growing sense of sameness. Something exacerbated by his recent inclination to turn inward. More importantly, those tools had become essentially useless for what was ahead. At one time he had seen himself as top-five worldwide at PowerPoint Presentations and as a guy fluent in both conflict resolution and paradigm deconstruction. Now, there were far more powerful points to consider, ones far different than those he had been pitching so effectively to small businesses over the last 15 years.

MOS had grown into a mildly lucrative business; but just as valuable were the activities he found both self-actualizing and therapeutic for a guy like Danny Moran. For every moment of strained silence inside their Molly-centric home, there seemed to be a countering moment of catharsis available to him through his work. He had made his name as a chance-taking culture-shaking agent of change; a guy unafraid of challenging the same old ways and so-called conventional wisdom that keeps most privately owned companies afloat and dogpaddling for survival, and gets you nowhere. He had plenty of competitors, in all price ranges. Some of those aligned themselves with whatever group-think, buzzword-obsessed consulting movement was taking its turn as the flavor of the day -- but it was Moran the maverick who routinely stirred up sacred beehives and who peppered the untouchables in their ivory towers before bringing companies together with odd twists on the tried-and-true and some unconventional remedies made up on the fly.

Danny Moran was his own brand.

But with the Moran brand came expectations. The buzz in the business community was all about having to experience MOS to truly understand the methods of MOS, which in turn sparked enough conversation to make MOS a word of mouth phenomenon. And with these sparks came the heat and fire that brought so much turbulence to light. The greater the upheaval, the greater the expectations of management, but it took a lot of electricity to shine a light bright enough to reveal the process waste and everyday dysfunction built into the SOPs of so many stagnant companies. Despite many wonderful rewards, people and experiences, Danny's work had become slight variations of the same two stories over and over. Only the names changed, except in cases of abject nepotism, where the last name was often the same. Not always though; the best of family-run businesses often enjoyed something greater than the sum of their enlightened siblings, sons, daughters, cousins, in-laws and "like family" types. The worst of the family-run operations, however, were sewers, places where cash could be converted to acrimony and pumped to where it couldn't be found but smelled the worst. Or -- though outside the purview of MOS -- laundered. The second repeating scenario had become just as old, the one where business owners hired and empowered executives who've been around the block and know it all, the type that can talk the talk and are only too happy to do the dirty work that major stakeholders generally dread the most. Owners can then affect the proper disinterest in any fallout, the increasingly toxic atmosphere and southbound morale – or avoid it altogether. Sometimes it was smart, sometimes it was unconscionable, (and often a shifting dose of both) but in any case, it freed those so inclined, men and women and 'tweeners, to either brandish their planetary testicles to the gang at the club or count their krugerrands in private. The principal of MOS had seen enough of it. And so when Danny, after clawing through the anguish of Molly's passing and the compounding misery of the Orsman debacle, finally went back to test his batteries for his return to the idiosyncratic world of breaking down systems, cultures, commerce and egos, the voltage needed to do the job his way was no longer there.

It was during a presentation to a packed assembly hall of pasta manufacturers when he came to know it was over. Standing at the podium, Danny had been innocently sharing his usual thoughts on time management (a recurring theme because it generally impacted every job), but it soon devolved into a rambling dissertation on his current, slightly more jaded views on time, including taking a confusing stand on the difference between *timeless* and *eternal*. Then, without provocation, he went so far beyond left-field that even the corn covered its ears. In a long-winded and elliptical take on the relativity of time… i.e., time at work, time at home, the perception of time as well as all the time that gets stolen, compromised or lost by giving in to other obsessions including too many thoughts on time, Danny found himself teetering on the ledge. When he finally realized his rant was actually one man simultaneously waxing philosophical while lecturing to himself, out loud, in front of a bunch of noodle-makers no less, he wrapped up his talk with something he wrote shortly after Molly died.

"Ultimately then, it comes down to this: Time is a generous tightwad, and God signed off on the deal to see if we'd be beggars or choosers."

Danny had emergency landed on that familiar strip because he knew he was circling on fumes. To his amazement there were some in the Mac and Cheese and Pre-packaged Dinner Division who must have buckled up for just such a ride and politely laughed, perhaps for momentary release from the pressures of the price-point hell they live in. Others, like many in the Organic and Whole Grain contingency, were pensive, puzzled, conspicuously so. It had been coming for awhile, but it was that day in front of the Spaghetti Brigade that Danny was finally convinced MOS would cease to be a going concern. It was as over as when Elvis covered *Hey Jude*.

Before all that happened, he managed to find a good paying job for Orsman in Minneapolis. A personal contract was executed between the two men with 20% of Orsman's before-taxes salary going directly to Danny over a 20 year period in exchange for Danny not pressing charges and keeping the story of the embezzling bean counter out of the news. The agreement mandated that Orsman get immediate counseling, and that Danny not be paid in full – short of an inheritance that Orsman claimed was possible - before the completion of the 20 year deal. It was a way to thwart Orsman's temptation to go for the quick fix. With interest, Danny would lose about 95 grand in the deal. As part of the pact, Orsman was to continue doing Danny's taxes and provide accounting assistance to Witchy in her new, personally designed, *Witchcraft* jewelry venture. She started selling beaded jewelry over the Internet three years prior and the business was starting to take off. There were plans for Witchy to lease a kiosk to sell her wares at a local mall during the holidays. In addition, she continued to teach tennis on the North Shore. Witchy was fine.

There was still little evidence to suggest that Danny's own gamble on the water-treatment technology stock was going to go one way or the other anytime soon. So, Danny decided to take a job as the Wisconsin rep for Laser Link Golf, a company out of Madison that had developed a handheld laser system for measuring yardage to a specially designed target crystal embedded in each flagstick. That Danny Mo was *Danny Mo* was enough to get him in the door at most any golf course or country club in Wisconsin and he was doing okay - but just okay. A lot of the clubs that wanted the system had it already, but the products were good and the company offered a decent benefits package. It required a lot of windshield time, and so he had plenty of time to think, often about Cindy, which was nice. The new job had also seemed to reawaken something else in Danny Mo. He would pay more attention to that.

As it turned out, Danny had gone from a career that focused on time management by observing a company's systems from different angles to a company with a system that provided the exact distance from any angle in no time at all.

He had, in a way, finally put time behind him.

∞

The community of Rock Harbor in Wisconsin's famed Door County was primarily made up of two groups of people of differing origins: Those rooted in the community for generations and those who had moved to the area for its beautiful topography and/or its resort property opportunities and/or to set up small, artsy gift shop businesses. It was almost half and half if you broke it down by dumping the established lineage and long-time townies in one bucket, and the transplanted entrepreneurs and the regular summer folk they catered to into another. And of those who had invested in the debate, nearly half of each half happened to be at odds over the construction of a world class golf course along the bluffs of Rock Harbor. It had become a heated small town dispute, one with no clear line of demarcation, no easy way to break down allegiances by livelihood or longevity as to who supported what. Yet, somehow, most everybody was mad at somebody, if not for being overly mad, then for not being mad enough.

Whatever was at the heart of the dispute no longer mattered. In the beginning, some three-plus years ago, two groups got the ill will ball rolling. At one extreme was the Environmental Activist Kooks, and at the other were the Environmental Activist Kook Ass-kickers. EAKs and EAKAs. Local barstool philosophers and church-going grandmas alike called them thusly. Both groups were smallish and boorish and loud, and collectively they produced enough toxic rhetoric that many in Rock Harbor found themselves sucked into it simply from commenting aloud on either extreme's latest disruptive protestation or tactic. And since there will never be a more powerful human compulsion than the desire to open one's mouth, even otherwise innocent comments had a way of fostering discussions of motives and allegiances that frequently revealed the underlying sensitivities that can cause reasonable debate to migrate into bias-heavy hearsay or escalate even offhand judgments into fiercer arguments and the inevitable defensiveness that can be taken no other way than personally. And ultimately, and unfortunately, it took precedence over the one thing just about everyone could agree upon: The extremes were bad for business and the quality of life in Rock Harbor. And while the EAKs and EAKSs had become the sore at the surface, too many indigenous to the Harbor had allowed themselves to become the bacteria within. Like the so-called supporters of The Majesty who showed themselves to be more passionate about condemning the condemners than for championing the extra jobs or what was being hailed as an "architectural masterpiece" and "by consensus, the best new course in America." *Beautiful*, Danny thought, *more enemy fixation*. He saw it as a microcosm of modern day American politics in a town of two-thousand-plus.

And so the petty feuds that materialized from the small town jealousies and neighborhood envy of pre-Majesty Rock Harbor soon fed upon itself and came back bigger and more demonstrative with more joining in once they had a bona fide issue to fight over. Boat launch permit rates and liquor license threats and cherry picker wages didn't deliver the same level of pissing match satisfaction that came with the making of The Majesty and the ready-made misery that brings sleeping souls to life provided the players involved were properly dubious of change, growth, or the unknown.

At the outset, most in The Harbor wanted nothing to do with either group of picketing poster children, the so-called Barbarians at The Majesty's gate, and made their positions known regarding The Majesty in more even tones. Some felt the course would be a cash-stealing competitor of the area's existing attractions; others felt it would bring more cash into town for other businesses. Some thought it brought in the wrong type of people; that the type of golfers in search of *The Mighty*

Challenge might frequent restaurants and bars but weren't likely to seek out specialty shops offering handcrafted art, designer peanut brittle or porcelain snow-babies. And the folks who've long cherished such treasures - the gentle folks who had been coming to Door County religiously for years - were likely to see much of the available lodging gobbled up by the seekers of *The Mighty Challenge*, i.e., world traveling golfers. Others, though careful to avoid the E(nvironmental)-word, felt it was a pox upon a magnificent stretch of land better left in a natural state. Still others reveled in the fact that such a course would bring greater attention to the overall beauty of Rock Harbor.

When it was announced that The State Open was to be held later in the year at The Majesty, Danny was not surprised by the resurgence of ill will, the announcement being a fresh stimulus for the little resort town to prolong a long-absent arousal level, all prudence notwithstanding. Manda had told Danny that each side felt they knew where he stood on the matter; and that the most reasonable of those who were against the construction of the new golf course along Harrow Bluffs, now that their battle was lost, only wanted their position recognized and respected after all the acrimony, misinformation and hurt feelings. It was as if he had become a de facto commissioner, and though their desires differed in degrees, most of Rock Harbor wanted Danny Mo to at least take a position and give his reasons and live with the scarlet letter of his choosing, like everyone else in the community. Until then, it would be fair game to blame him for saying nothing.

But Danny spent three years avoiding or ignoring the construction of a world class course and its attendant issues, three years of life in a hazy cocoon constructed of "reflections" on time, on his life, on the afterlife, and especially on the meaning of his marriage. Though he imagined how Molly might have felt about it all (and he really had no idea), the whole damn lot of it now seemed a moot point to Danny.

The course, of course, had been built.

∞

With his Laser Link job now requiring him to visit most of the courses around the state, Danny had little choice but to play more golf. The various head professionals, club presidents and even some course owners delighted in inviting the hall-of-famer to play a round when he came to town. In the interest of business, especially if it was a top course, Danny generally obliged. He would toss out lines like, "I've had more colonoscopies than practice sessions lately." Freed of expectations, he played right around par, sometimes better. Playing carefree golf felt foreign at first, but the mostly positive results had Danny questioning all the time he spent grinding on the range.

He didn't call it practice back in the day. It was called preparation; and it was a love/hate thing, always having to schedule his preparation, then do the preparation, before returning home to whatever mood Molly was in, which may or may not have been related to how long that particular day's after-work preparation session ran. It was an almost irresponsible routine to follow while raising kids, and growing MOS, and keeping up a house, a yard, and still skillfully fold a little laundry while convincing Molly that their lives were blessed even if there were, at times, a few toast crumbs in the sink. At times he brooded over whether all that skin-blistering, dirt-gouging, Rome-doubting, Hogan-aping range time, and the feeling that he'd fail without it, did nothing but create a three-ring circus where memory, instinct and imagery fought for attention inside a mind that was nothing like Hogan's.

It was an old-school work ethic all the same, and it had worked well enough for Danny. His record spoke for itself, but trying to carry the same pre-shot/swing-thought/impact imagery from his preparation sessions to the course brought with it some meddlesome goblins that had to be crushed before any course could be conquered. He assumed they were battles everyone waged. That was golf, the one sport that validated the existence of demons, false gods and metaphysical fool's gold. And so a heretofore unfathomable thought began to take root. Maybe he was the sort who could benefit from starting fresh, where every shot comes from the cleaner slate that instinct relies upon, not unlike his freefall approach to business during the heyday of MOS. Would such an approach translate to the golf course? It seemed counterintuitive as all hell to him, but then he'd never had the guts to try, or more to the point, the guts to not try. But what did it matter? He was not Marty Archibald. He never intended to compete until the day he died. At least not at golf.

When the time came to visit The Majesty, Danny attempted to go about his business as if it were nothing more than his next sales call. The course had been open for only six weeks, and already it seemed there were no new ways to phrase the raves and praise. Representatives from the USGA's executive board had already been to the site three times, twice before the opening and once after. According to Gary D'Amato's sources, the course was on the short list for a future U.S. Open, while the PGA had countered with the possibility of holding its championship along with a Ryder Cup in the later 2020s. But setting aside the spectacle of the new course, it was in truth much more than just another sales call; it was special, it was Rock Harbor. In certain circles, be they friend or foe, it was always news when Danny Mo came home.

Measuring devices of any sort were never intended to be a part of The Majesty experience. But with the general public averaging well over six hours a round since opening, the decision was made to consider Laser Link as a means of speeding up the pace of play. Despite contradictions from some self-serving officials who demand faster play yet rage against devices that provide instant yardage to the flag (IY2F), the fact remains that IY2F shortens rounds. It wasn't just the difficulty of the course that had reduced things to a crawl; it was also the gawk-factor. The place was mesmerizing with its stop-and-stare vistas overlooking parts of the course, and particularly those along the precipitous bluffs and rocky inlets along the shoreline of the bay. Apparently, at $225 per round ($105 for locals) the views were nothing to rush.

Not even the spectacular scenery at Whistling Straits could compare to the sensory delights of The Majesty. Altitude is what sets the two apart. Loren Ferguson, the man and the money behind The Majesty, had been heard to say (allegedly after several Johnny Walker Blues with the course's designer, the famed C. Charles Revere) that he "loved The Straits course, but let's face it, it is knee-high to The Majesty."

When told of the comment, Herb Kohler, the plumbing magnate and owner of both Whistling Straits and Black Wolf Run courses, shrugged and said, "Loren has a great course up there. I have four of them. And they're all embraced by the community."

So sure, Danny was more than curious to see The Majesty. And it was, after all, built on the land he endlessly roamed as a kid. No, he would not engage in any extra preparation. Yes, it would be great, as always, to see his mother. Absolutely, he'd work to uncover the causes and those responsible for the uneasy aura that had settled over the harbor and do what he could to keep his mom from all the bother. And yes, Amanda Moran could, herself, handle anyone in Rock Harbor and God help anyone who thought they could intimidate her – and you can bet there would be no help from God - but there comes a time when a son has to step up. How? That was a good question.

Danny quickly consummated the Laser Link deal with Loren Ferguson and The Majesty's affable head pro, Bap Sandstrom, who Ferguson had plucked from somewhere in Scotland. Danny's tour of the course with Bap and his two assistants was a powerful experience. "Heaven's kid brother," was how Danny had put it, to avoid being redundant. The deeper he got into the course the eerier it got. With minimal alterations to the landscape, other than to address some water runoff issues and to build up certain areas with sand and soil, C. Charles Revere had almost miraculously plugged into the themes of Danny's youth.

Tee box summits gave way to emerald laneways snaking to flag-bearing destinations. Places that had once been objectives in childhood had come circling back to the here and now and became goals of another kind. There was a long but fairly easy downhill par five where as kids he and his brothers had tobogganed at high-speeds with little fear of injury. There was a ferocious uphill par four to an elevated, tree-encircled green that was once the perfect "Capture the Flag" province due to its challenging access and guard-watch sightlines. There was a narrow, forest-lined par three that was neither very long nor very far from his old house (and where Amanda still resides) where his dad had suggested, because of its tight quarters and shade-induced hardpan, as a great place for Danny and his brother to prepare before their *Punt, Pass, and Kick* competitions. Looking out the back pro shop window, Danny loosed a little chuck when he saw the range utilized a cleaved and vertical limestone wall that was maybe 80 feet high and 200-plus yards from the tee line to contain and partially return range balls, just as Curly and the boys had used it for batting practice, albeit several hundred yards further south where the wall was much closer to a makeshift backstop that Curly had fashioned from chicken wire. The concept was simple, really. The harder a ball was smashed, the harder the carved igneous rock shot it back for easy retrieval. Golf balls, baseballs, it didn't matter.

The Majesty's signature-hole, the 18th, was unique beyond words, and that, for Danny, was saying something. Starting from the northern-most tip of an elongated peak called North Point, the par five had everything; panoramic beauty, risk and reward. And it had Morgan's Forehead. The Forehead was, in Native American terms, a monadnock, which is an isolated and unusually cleaved tower of rock. (The German term is inselberg, which means "island mountain.") It was a geomorphic hunk of harder rock like dolomite and quartzite, the stuff that remains after much of the softer, sandier materials have eroded from its walls. Like a solitary skyscraper of stone, Morgan's Forehead was the highest point in Door County. Through glacial circumstance and centuries of unpredictable winds, The Forehead stood high above even North Point and the other ledges of wave-cut bluffs above the bay.

Morgan's Forehead stood sentry at the elbow of the dogleg of the 18th hole. There, it shielded long assaults on the par five green from certain angles and altered lay-up shots from others. In order to reach 18 in two, one had to blast a tee ball at least 285 yards to a firm saddle of a landing area. Less than that and it took two more precise shots to get home. A crooked tee shot brought the risk of runaway inflation to the final score index. The second shot lay-up required a mid- to short-iron to a wide but shallow shelf that called for exacting distance control over accuracy. From there it was a pitch to a green that was "20% firmer than any other green on the course," according to Bap. The other lay-up option was to carry the shelf and a moderately steep canyon to a bottom landing area with a long-iron, hybrid or fairway wood - provided you could play a draw around part of Morgan. Overcook it and the ball would disappear into a hazard of bramble, dirt and rocks or, farther left, the bay itself. As Danny played in on 18, he was almost powerless to look at anything else but Morgan's Forehead. With every step he stared. And remembered. The Forehead held secrets never told, and one that had been long-forgotten: nobody seemed to know who the hell Morgan was. The past and present parallels were sublime and seemingly divinely inspired, and Danny could only tip his hat to C. Charles Revere and wonder if maybe God really did choose the man to design The Majesty.

By the time Danny finished his round, the sun had begun to set and word had spread throughout Rock Harbor that Danny Moran was at The Majesty. From his elevation, he could see some old friends had gathered near the 18th hole while a handful of others he didn't know stayed nearer to the parking lot and kept an eye on each other without saying much. They had the look of people who had nowhere to go, as if they were waiting for something to happen or for others to show up. Danny assumed they were either the over-invested supporters or detractors who'd found fulfillment in argument and conflict and now had a hard time letting go of their baby. Like 9/11 conspiracy theorists or designated hitter/wildcard detractors, their respective positions had become part of who they were. Danny knew the type. At the moment though, it seemed they were drawn out of curiosity more than conviction. Danny saw that as a good thing.

With his light carry bag over his shoulder, Danny turned the corner and hustled to the parking lot. A scattering of cars and SUVs dappled the expansive lot in typical end-of-business-day fashion, but what Danny noticed first was even more locals loitering near the more modest vehicles and mini-vans where the employees parked. He was neither surprised nor concerned. He figured he'd have to rustle up a couple of alpha-locals himself, even if just to offer up a few thoughts on mutual respect and the overall etiquette for levelheaded discourse regardless of what anyone thought and however stereotypically clannish his hometown happened to be. Turns out, the natives were restless enough to come to him.

∞

"So, the prodigal son returns." The hefty man with the (bad) comb-over had pulled up in his Lincoln Continental as Danny was putting his clubs in the trunk.

"Hey, Sam," Danny slammed the trunk shut. "Long time."

"Indeed. Though I've phoned a few times." Sam Bursinger looked around at the dozens who had assembled in the lot. "Don't know if you got the messages."

At that moment Bap Sandstrom's young assistant, a long-hitting collection of cartilage called "Bones" with whom Danny had just played, came wheeling into the parking lot in an electric cart. Bones stopped, glanced at Sam then said to Danny, "I'll give you a ride back to the clubhouse when you're ready, Mr. Moran. Mr. Ferguson said to invite any interested parties as well." The kid looked around at the people in the parking lot, many who were now lingering within earshot. "And he said to make sure you know he does mean everyone, no matter who, or how many. Taps on the house."

Danny was amused. Ol' Loren smelled an opportunity. He had asked folks to be patient from the beginning. "Just wait until it's done," had been his mantra. Good communication was sometimes more about how and when things were communicated than what was actually communicated. A basic tenet Danny had reminded his clients to be mindful of during his days at MOS – and something every bit as fundamental to achieving desired outcomes in marriages, parent-child relationships, or any number of reports from Al-Jazeera.

Danny looked at Sam, who raised his eyebrows. "I don't know that free beer is gonna do, other than invite trouble," Sam said, with a slow, all-knowing blink, "but I'll let these yokels know."

∞

Not only did the Townies in the parking lot come inside the cavernous great room of The Majesty's clubhouse, they also apparently phoned others who called others until well over a hundred had taken up most of the tables. Not a problem on a Tuesday evening, but it confused two tables of office furniture reps who'd trekked all the way from

Arlington, Texas, to play The Majesty. Danny figured many of the non-golfing locals now had a chance to actually venture on to the controversial property without appearing conspicuous. Loren Ferguson looked over his place and nodded, not at all surprised by the materializing hordes.

Danny joined Bap and Loren at the corner of the expansive bar and accepted a glass of single malt scotch that would have gone for the price of a dozen decent golf balls. Bap excused himself for a moment and Loren again looked out at the gathering. Everyone was talking and drinking and depleting the baskets of sweet and salty snack mix availed at every table. "Danny," he said, "when the beer kicks in…well, you know, some of these folks will embrace the atmospherics here as the sun sets, but some others might start… you know…I think it would be good if you'd say something."

"I see," said Danny, looking around. There were some faces he recognized, though the majority of them were unfamiliar. The clubhouse was spacious and all-natural wood, leather, marble and glass. The clubhouse and pro shop were situated in the lower cradle of a giant hillside amphitheater next to the 18th green. The bluffs rose up to the south along with the lone countenance of The Forehead as the focal point. There were enormous windows with wooden vertical blinds facing both the western bay and the southern bluffs so that there was always a minimum of at least one spectacular view available, the setting sun consigned to being one of nature's special effects instead of a blinding nuisance. For 30 minutes the townsfolk had done nothing but gawk and talk. And many drank. Heartily.

"Will you?" Loren's expression was noncommittal. A tech stock cash-out beneficiary, the man was a deal-making, late fifty-something hotel and real estate magnate. He loved golf, and adored good golfers. "Doesn't have to be much. We'll never please everyone, I know that. But, coming from you - how about this - you tell the folks that any registered citizen of Rock Harbor, check that, make that all of Door County, can enjoy our Friday Fish Fry for half price."

Danny had sworn off his off-the-cuffing ways since going off course in front of the pasta people. He sure as hell didn't want to incite a riot, and he had fully intended to say something all along. Bap returned with a cordless microphone but held onto it. Danny looked at it, and then at Loren. "Cheap fish is good, but I do have an idea. You have a place where we can talk, Loren, you and me?"

Being the head golf professional, Bap Sandstrom had been on the receiving end of some anti-Majesty grief, but was just too damn happy being Bap to bother much with feeling bad. The Scotsman insisted on doing an introduction and was off with the microphone before Danny could object. The clubhouse was filled with mostly non-golfers, including some later arriving women gift shop owners who had zero interest in free beer.

After his discussion with Danny, Loren Ferguson remained in his office where he could stay out of it and still listen in on the proceedings.

Sandstrom, his Scottish brogue thickened for effect, quickly went into the introduction he wanted to make though none was necessary. "Rock Harbor's own hometown hall-of-famer, Danny Moran has asked to say a few words. The lad, by the way, shot 76 today. First time he laid eyes on the course. And that, folks, is only two shots off the black tee course record set by the PGA Tour's Jerry Kelly at our grand opening."

Embarrassed at how orchestrated it all seemed now, Danny was relieved no one clapped, for long anyway. He expected neither open hostility nor favorite son hospitality and he was spot-on. He took the microphone and started immediately. Danny knew his spit-fire analogy skills, once his calling card, had oxidized over time. Still, he gathered himself and out of sheer pig-headed will, went off into the wild. "I see we have a variety of shirts being worn here today. Yes, I admit, I'm an observant sort."

Danny looked around and plugged ahead. "I see, what, maybe a dozen shirts give or take, that are the color blue, bluish, or relatives of the blue family. I, too, have several blue shirts, at home. Golf shirts and non-golf shirts. But I see a diverse array of them here in this room. Button-down oxfords, blue pullovers, blue polos… I see a blue blouse, a couple crews, all in different hues, fabrics, styles. And those of you in blue are no doubt from different walks of life. And, in my opinion, you all look pretty good in blue." Danny could not help himself. He had waded in deep. Time to start kicking.

"Well, my friends, in Milwaukee, we embarrassed ourselves over a blue shirt. I'm sure some of you know what I'm talking about. It was to be a piece of contemporary art funded by airline fees and constructed of translucent blue plastic, or acrylic, or whatever. A New York artist was commissioned to do it. Think the guy's named Oppenheimer. Anyway, the shirt was going to be some 30- or 40-feet tall and mounted on the multi-level, glassed-in parking structure at Mitchell International Airport."

Danny saw some folks rubbing their faces or looking at each other. "Now, the giant blue shirt didn't really look like, in the classic sense, a laborer's work shirt. In sketches it looked like a nice, long sleeved blue shirt, something you might see in a J. Peterman catalog. People went wild over the blue shirt. Not good wild, but weird wild. Politics and paranoia ruled the day. Some were people were furious about the blue shirt and felt it was, quote, 'pejorative to the people of Milwaukee.' As if being, quote, 'blue collar' was an insult. Like…bankers and lawyers and artists and writers and teachers and engineers and electricians, you name it, as if those folks don't wear blue shirts. No, we were told that this would play into a long-standing perception that we'd be selling ourselves short as a 'blue collar town.' Well, was it really? Of course not. It was mostly a free pass to be mad about something. It was ridiculous. We're so enlightened that we needed to wash our hands of anything that might reflect upon the doing of calorie-burning work. Wash our hands of something that pays tribute to what many of us, and many of our friends, and, most importantly, what many of our parents did for a living. Our folks, the ones who did whatever it took to give their kids a chance to do whatever we wanted with our lives. Yeah…I'm thinking of my dad. Some of you knew him. Pejorative my Irish ass."

Danny continued. "County government meetings and editorials and radio call in shows, everyone vented their spleens as if this plastic blue shirt would come to life and eat our children. You want to argue that the $220,000 price tag would be better spent on creating jobs or food shelters or election recalls? Fine. People get that. But to call it insulting, well, that's exactly what it was in a different way. And then the art community and other supporters of the blue shirt lost their focus and became obsessed with raging against its detractors instead of oh, say, arguing the merits of publicly displayed art." Danny swept a look over his audience.

"On and on it went, back and forth, sniping and whining and bitching about a blue shirt. You'd think a debate over art could at least have been...artful. Would I have liked it? No idea. What kind of impact would that shirt have made on the rest of the world? Who knows. But what I do know is that we'll never know. It wasn't even going to cost the public a dime! But let me tell ya, from the sketches I saw, I think it looked kind of cool."

Danny reached over to the bar and took a slug of Spotted Cow. "We who hail from Rock Harbor, and, more to the point, you who live here now, are better than that. We gotta be better than Milwaukee and all their backbiting over a plastic blue shirt."

There was an audible sense of approval at that comment. The big city, the arrogance, the crime, the traffic jams and stadium taxes.

"But, us? Rock Harbor? It's embarrassing. When I first heard about this course, it meant nothing to me at first. I had stepped away from competitive golf, and sure it sounded interesting, but it registered neither good nor bad with me." Danny again looked into the crowd. Many of them seemed like they might be with him. "But now it's done, and this course is special, in every sense of the word. I understand the fears that some of you had, just as I understand the excitement that others have for it. But either way, it's here my friends, unlike like the blue shirt that never was. Time to let it go, time to stop using it as a reason to be mad about something."

A voice came from the back of the room. "You're playing in the State Open here next month aren't you, Danny?" Danny recognized the voice but others chimed in with similar suspicions.

"I said I've stepped away from competitive golf. I have not entered the Open."

The same voice came back, "Doesn't mean you can't still get in. You shot the second best round from the back tees." It was Sam Bursinger stepping in the spotlight for a moment.

"I would have had to qualify, Sam, and the Qualifiers have already been held I believe, and I wouldn't try to qualify even if they weren't."

Bursinger stood up, a chore for him. "Danny, I love you, you know that, but why does this course matter to you now? Where were you when this was dumped on us three, four years ago? I left you some messages."

"I was burying my wife, Sam. You might recall being at the funeral. Sorry I didn't plug into your priorities." The room got quiet and Sam sat down, eyes closed and nodding apologetically. Danny locked his eyes on him until the fat man opened his and turned away. "Now, I want everyone to consider something."

Danny slowly walked over to the bar, chugged the top quarter of a replenished Spotted Cow and returned to his spot. The room was silent except for the muffled clang of dishes in the kitchen. Danny began in an even voice, but there was an intensity about it that was unmistakable.

"Here's what I noticed today. Because of the creation of this golf course, there is access to a world class piece of property that, until now, had been only available to experienced, physically fit hikers or climber types. The infrastructure that was installed to create these 18 holes is nothing short of miraculous. Loren Ferguson spared no expense, and now there are places where some of the most spectacular views to be found anywhere in America can be enjoyed by everyone."

"That's just bullshit! I mean it sounds good, Moran, but it's still bullshit." It was a guy sitting up front. His shirt was blue, and there was a Lube n' Go oval logo over his breast pocket with *Merle* embroidered on it. "Who can afford that kind of cash?"

Voices muttering their agreement grew throughout the room.

"Good point there, uh...Merle." Danny was not accustomed to anyone interrupting him when he used his intense-guy voice.

"It's called the Golden Rule," said Merle, dismissively. "He who has the gold makes all the rules." Merle looked proud of himself for having unleashed the old bromide. Some people hooted in approval.

"I agree with you to a point, Merle," said Danny, "and this is why." Danny looked out into the great room. This is what they came for. He had their attention now.

"Mr. Ferguson wanted me to convey a few things to you today. Here's the deal. Every Friday and Sunday evening after 7 p.m. until sunset, and every Monday before noon, everyone, check that, all adult residents in the Harbor community are welcome to sign a waiver and take an electric cart and use the asphalt paths to tour the golf course for a period of time to be determined, but let's say...90 minutes. If you've never had the chance to experience the bay from North Point and the incredible views along those bluffs, well, you can now without risking your life. We all know people who've fallen to their deaths and all the accidents we've had around here. Feel free to bring an older relative or friend to The Majesty, people who would otherwise never have the chance to enjoy the beauty and the views. So, please feel welcome. Take photos, sketch, write poetry, share a moment with a loved one. Mr. Ferguson asks only that you do not engage in any sexual activity on your tour, and if you decide to anyway, please do not get caught. I should tell you he will especially frown on any sexual activity involving wildlife or imaginary friends."

Iced tea shot from either Sam Bursinger's nose or mouth or both. The room erupted in laughter, though a few moaned or disapproved of such nonsense. But the idea sunk in quickly. Nods all around. Even the more negative groups raised eyebrows in grudging consideration.

"And, in addition," Danny wound up for the final pitch as the hubbub subsided, a tack-on offer that Loren had planned to be his primary olive branch beyond the free beer and soda. "Mr. Ferguson is offering The Majesty's Friday Fish Fry for half-price for the people who live in Door County year round, and the deal will be good, he says, forever."

Maybe it was the beer, maybe it was the way Danny hesitated before he said, "forever," but the statement was met with immediate applause. At that moment, Loren Ferguson, Bap Sandstrom and his two assistants came charging through the kitchen doors and began serving large platters of appetizer samplers to every table. As they did this, they made sure everyone knew there was plenty more if needed. Danny did all he could to keep from rolling his eyes, the choreographed delivery of deep fried finger food was almost too much.

Danny figured his mom was now fairly likely to be left alone, unless perhaps someone wanted to compliment her on her son's decision to channel his inner-Bono for the betterment of Door County. He knew there were those who would remain staunchly against The Majesty; misery was a narcotic to the chronically beleaguered. But things were likely to be better now, he could feel it.

Later, old acquaintances and strangers alike came up to Danny, delighted to have the chance to take their parents or an uncle or grandchild or a wheelchair-bound cousin in a cart to enjoy the view from North Point and other locales along the rugged bluff line. Many admitting it was the only way they, too, could enjoy such splendor. The tour idea was Danny's but he gave all the credit to Loren. The fish fry deal had been a bonus. Many also wanted to laugh about the gigantic plastic shirt of blue, and how foolish those morons in Milwaukee were in dealing with something so petty. How the people of Rock Harbor were better than that.

Actually, no different, thought Danny as he drove to his mother's afterward, a sense of well-being coming over him at how the day played out. He graciously accepted the A, his grade, Heaven sent from Molly.

∞

"Grilled Chicken breast," said Danny, "lettuce and fat-free mayo." He leaned forward and put his elbows on the bar.

Crusty smiled as he stared straight ahead at the flatscreen TV. The Brewers were pounding the Cardinals. "An E burger for me, Kai, with a strategic amount of cheese, please."

Kai smiled and headed to the kitchen.

"You watching your figure, Dannymo?"

"Does it show?"

"Oh, it shows, alright." Crusty cocked his head. "What do you call your ass again, your molded boulders?"

"No, other people do," said Danny. "No Steamin' Es for me until I get through the tests."

"First, you actually train for your physical. Now, you're dieting for urology tests? When you going in for those?"

"Eight days." Danny repositioned his boulders on the barstool. "They don't think it's anything to worry about."

"You gettin' good sturdy boners when you need them?" asked Crusty, expressionless.

"On demand, Crust. Thanks for asking."

"How about pissin', good stream?"

"Laser beams," said Danny. "Well, laser beamish."

"You know prostate issues messes with that stuff, Dannymo. I've been there, seven eight years ago."

"Really?" said Danny, "You kept it quiet."

"Stuff happens, when you get to be 50 or so." Crusty looked around the Aftermath. It was a quiet night, a couple tables in use and just the two of them at the bar. "No need to talk about it."

"No, but you sure don't mind talking about *my* prostate."

"If you're lying about your boners, Dannymo, which proud guys like you do sometimes, I got some pills you can try. Don't know what kind they are, ends in a vowel. Doc gives me his samples."

"You asking if I'm getting any?"

".Well, Cindy…gotta believe she moves the needle, as they say. But these pills, Dannymo, they really work. Shirley's got a tiny apartment and her bedroom is a glorified closet. I take those pills and lookout, she's like, 'oooh, Honey, there may not be enough room for the three of us in here.'"

"Sheesh." Danny shook his head. Danny saw Kai take a Steamin' E to another table. It wasn't easy to watch.

"So…are you?" Crusty turned and looked directly at Danny. "You and Cindy…?"

"When it comes to Cindy, I have reasons for keeping quiet."

"The hell is that?"

"It's what you're gonna have to live with," said Danny. "I'll tell you this, though; she is the single most accommodating woman I've ever known. Almost nothing she won't do for me. Like she's tryin' to read my mind. I mean, make me a sandwich or nuke a Lean Cuisine, or vacuum this or clean that. And hand massages, Crusty…never even thought of getting my hands and fingers worked over. Good God man, what a discovery. Ever have one?"

"Gotten handies before, usually my own, but, no not like that…but now I think I need one."

"Plus," said Danny, "she's a great shirt folder. I mean, Ryder Cup level. I'll catch her smiling, like…in the car or as she's doing dishes. Says her grandma used to say that blessings tickle. I can click around from channel to channel, she doesn't mind. Everything is fine with her."

"Impressive," said Crusty. "That go for everything?"

"I will tell you this, her kisses are like, I don't know…they have a feeling…not the *feels like the first ti*me cliché, But more like it might be the last time."

"Why?"

"Just a feeling. Don't care to speculate." Danny said it coolly.

"Got ya." Crusty took a gulp of Rolling Rock as the Brewers scored again to go up 9-1 in the 6th. "Still can't get over what she said about Sally."

Danny laughed. "You mean calling him Gandhi?"

"Yeah…he had to shit at Marty's funeral when he realized Cindy knew some of the cash and carry girls he'd…hired. And how he treated them."

"Or how he asked to be treated…that was even better," Danny clarified.

"So, you like her, don't ya?"

"Well, yeah, I like her," said Danny, "a lot. But all the thoughtfulness brings a little pressure. Probably just me."

"Damn beautiful, she is."

"You know something, Crusty, she's so beautiful it makes me wary. I mean, why me? Why doesn't she go break Mathew McConaughy's heart, or someone like that. Probably could. I think ultra-beautiful people sometimes have trouble being normal. Getting checked out all the time, can't be easy to remain unaffected. The gift cum curse."

"Sure. Why not over-think it?" Crusty smiled. "You might be right on all that, but I never had to worry much about it myself."

Danny shook his head and stayed quiet for a minute. "Sometimes I'll be stuck in a traffic jam, or in the longest, slowest line ever at a post office, airport or Costco, stuff that is normally beyond annoying, but instead, I feel grateful, because I have a few more uninterrupted minutes to just think about her. Her face, that smile, the willingness. How much she truly seems to dig me. It just don't seem right. I mean, she's just…happy…and that makes me happy." Danny made a face that copped to his banality. "Tellin' ya, when she sees me, she just lights up like an angel on a Christmas tree."

"You're turning into Henry Hallmark. And speaking of Henry, she light up as much as Hank?" Crusty laughed a little louder than usual. "I have never seen a dog more crazy happy to see someone than Hank is when he sees you."

"Interesting you say that." Danny smiled and sipped some diet cola. "I mean, that's just spooky."

"What's spooky?"

"It was Marty and Cindy who brought me Hank. As you know, I stayed to myself for quite a while after Molly died. And Hank was just a puppy. I had no idea how much work training a 12-week-old yellow lab could be. But I got into it. Made a point of spending a lot of time with him. Blew off work, didn't visit Overlighter's as often, didn't come here because Hank needed me."

"And you, him."

"I love Hank, no doubt. But, an odd thing about Cindy, she avoids Hank. Sorta jealous, but sorta not. I don't know. A while back Cindy and I were on the couch and a minor case of kissy face broke out, and she suddenly stopped. Said she knew it sounded weird but, she preferred that Hank not be around, like not in the room. I thought it was just when we're making out. But I think she's just jumpy around dogs."

Crusty leaned back on his stool, "Not unheard of to be traumatized by a dog when you're young."

"What I was getting to. Brought it up later and she mentioned stuff about a bad experience as a kid, and even recently. So I just shut the hell up. Wasn't gonna go any further. There might be some things I don't care to know right about now. Know what I mean?"

Crusty finished his beer. "Yeah, she's a hot tamale. You like having her around and you're gonna take your time finding out if she's nutzo."

"That's kind of it." Danny nodded. "She's smart and good, and I don't have to mention the gorgeous thing. Always in a good mood it seems - which is gold bullion to me - but man, she says we're a blessing to each other, and I think she might be thinking, like, long term. So, yeah, I really don't care to know her whole story yet. She's, like, 18 years younger than me."

"Let me ask you this. Did she want to go with you when you went back home last week?"

"Yeah. She wanted to meet my mother. Not sure I'm ready for that."

Crusty grinned. "Did you tell her what happened up there? About how you took the parted sea of locals and brought them together, and then followed it with your fishes and loaves shtick with the appetizers and beer?"

"Told her I helped smooth things over."

"You tell her how?"

"A little. She said maybe someday soon I could show her the beauty of The Majesty."

"And by soon, she means soon, doesn't she?'

"Yeah. I just feel funny bringing her to The Harbor. I know it's been over three years since…but it feels like it's a little disrespectful to Molly. I haven't told her about Stadler's call, either."

Crusty chucked. "Who'da thunk it, the State PGA actually offering a special exemption to an amateur golfer who hasn't played competitively in three years. Goes to show what they think of Dannymo."

Danny shrugged. "I think they offered it to Loren Ferguson first, but he's like a four or five handicap and a 14 when he's nervous, and he knows it. You gotta play this course, it's beyond…"

"You told me," interrupted Crusty, "now get us on it, will ya?"

"I'll see if I can take you and Mo Mo on my official practice round."

Crusty bolted up on his bar stool, a little like a prairie dog. Head doing sharp segmented turns. "Well I'll be god-damned, Dannymo, you're gonna take the damn exemption."

"Yeah. Decided last night. Mostly just to have the chance walk those hills and across those bluffs a couple times with Mo. Like to have one last time with Mo as my caddie. God, I loved those days. When I played there last week, I kept thinking how much I'd like to show Mo where we did this and that as kids. By the way, you two are the only ones who know about this. I have no expectations about anything. Not too concerned about what I shoot. Not even thinking about the cut."

"Yeah, right, whatever. Pretty goddamn awesome, man." Crusty's eyes glistened. "You know, I never thought your last competitive shot should be that fat driver into the muck at The Hill Farm."

"I wanna keep this quiet." Danny shrugged. "Not looking forward to telling Cindy. Better she not come along."

"Well, I'll be there no matter what you say." Crusty reached over to shake Danny's hand. "All I know is Danny Mo is going back home to play in the Open…and playing just about as good as ever now that the D Mo psycho has broken his addiction to range balls."

Danny nodded. "Funny. Now that Molly's gone, I don't burn all that time preparing."

Crusty cleared his eating space and grabbed a handful of napkins. Kai was bringing their plates of food. Crusty smiled. "Maybe Cindy can stay with Hank and develop something one-on-one."

Danny willed himself to avoid peeking at Crusty's sure-to-be gorgeous and gooey Steamin' E burger. "Hank is coming with us," he said. "He'll absolutely love it at my mom's."

∞

Chapter 38

Mo Moran's east side lower flat was a cave of his own creation, with odd ceiling angles, funky half walls and a couple coves he didn't know what to do with.

He had actually come to enjoy rummaging through the 3rd Ward's various creaky-floored and candle-scented secondhand stores offering endless array of orphaned junk. Junk he could use to personalize his pad on the cheap. What he called his "Mo-tif." He had settled on a theme featuring cobalt blue; and though he didn't know if it made any sense, Mo preferred to call it "indigo de la Mo." He stood back near his entryway and took in the spectacle of his fussily-placed glass and ceramic knickknacks, artifacts, table lamps and other crap. It was important to him that it looked like a cool place to hang. Not only did he like what he saw, he was sure women would dig it too, which was the goal from the get-go and exactly why he liked what he saw. His mother, however, would have taken one look and smiled an ambiguous smile.

The time had come to think about taking a real job, and so Mo Moran was leaning toward selling boxes. Empty brown ones. Liner, flutes, and medium. On the street it was called corrugated. The unspent portion of the baseball signing bonus had been invested and liquidity was going to be an issue before long. His friend since childhood, Davy, had talked him into considering the box thing. It was Davy's first job out of college and he claimed to be making good coin, and came to believe that commissioned sales was the fairest deal in America if both sides lived up to their end of the deal.

Once Mo was certain the baseball dream had gone to smithereens and the shoulder was healed enough to swing, Mo committed fully to tournament golf. He finished double-bogey, bogey on 17 and 18 to miss qualifying for the State Open by a single shot. His 75 at a long but wide-open course was enough to get into a seven man playoff for two alternate spots but he hooked his tee shot out of bounds on the first hole, the one semi-tight hole on the course. And that was that. No Majesty for Mo. A day later, still smarting from his finish, his dad called and asked if Mo'd like to caddy for him. Once he got off the floor, Mo had mixed emotions. Stunned, he was, by his dad's decision to return for another Open. Like the reflections of light off his collection of cobalt-colored knickknacks, it had come from out of the blue.

Caddying for his dad had been their big bonding thing until he left for Rookie Ball. To be asked to caddie now, in a tournament for which he had expected to qualify, one in which he harbored hopes of having his dad caddie for *him*, put a different slant on the deal. Probably a little like how his dad got a little goofy when he passed on competing in the State Match Play when MOS was up and running.

But listening to his dad's voice did him in. Danny's words were thick with emotion. "This course, Mo, the design, on a piece of land I know like no one. It's something I can't put into words." Not because the course was already rated among the ten best in the America, he had said, but because "The Majesty reawakened something inside me."

Mo took it all in. With all that riding on his dad's return to Rock Harbor and the State Open, Mo could no more turn his old man down than he could refuse blood to his heart.

He stood near the apartment door now. He imagined he had just entered and was taking in the sight of his living room for the first time. He sat down and looked around. Yes. Looked good from that view, too. He got up, went to the kitchen and opened a 1.5 liter bottle of Pinot Grigio. If he was going to live on the east side, he'd have to keep some wine on hand. He sat down with a nearly-filled pint glass of wine and took an irresponsibly large gulp. He made a mental note to buy some wine glasses, maybe find some blue ones. He got back up and put on a CD by O.A.R, sat back down and let the sound merge with the wine for a minute. Atmospherics were good, not great. A tad too bright. He got back up and nudged the dimmer switch down, not too much, he didn't want to seem predatory. A little nervous now. Who wouldn't be. He laughed to himself, what were the odds, a chance meeting at Azure Island Antiques? Go figure.

The doorbell rang. Mo slammed the balance of his Pinot – an even more ridiculous amount to take at once - and went to the door. The onslaught of that much wine made him light-headed. He awkwardly engaged in some hand-to-hand combat with a series of door locks he hadn't yet gotten the hang of. The bolt-lock's turning mechanism was loose and slightly stripped. He finally opened the door, and even though he had prepared himself for just this moment, the sight of Cindy Young in light blue jeans, black ankle boots, and sleeveless black top, weakened his quads and made everything from his calves to his toes go cold.

∞

Chapter 39

The middle-aged Impala took the heat for the three Mos - Mo, D and Hank.

There was a flipside kind of feeling to a summer road trip to Rock Harbor; like celebrating Christmas in Hawaii, with coconut palms reigning at a Scotch pine time of year. The Morans had come to accept the piles of snow and leaden chill that usually accompanied them on their annual trek north at Christmas. The holiday trip had always commenced the day before Christmas Eve right after his dad got home from work, when the dark was first arriving. By the time they neared Rock Harbor, almost everything beyond the spill of the moon was either relegated to silhouette or total blackness. It seemed for every time they were treated to mild conditions there were two or three trips where they were battered by blizzards or sleety slop that added both danger and time to the trip to Nana Manda's house.

Mo's ritual on those expeditions was to sleep as much as possible in the backseat, on the guy side, regardless of road conditions. Rinny, with the aid of a clip-on book light, would read novels, magazines, or sometimes, psychotically enough, text books. His mother would critique her husband's driving or stir up memories of how they used to sing carols or other classics when the kids were little, threatening a reprise of such days. All the while his dad amused himself with rambling observations and whimsical commentary that had a way of driving his wife to sudden solo renditions of *O Holy Night* just to shut him up. Looking back now, Mo could see that his dad was only too happy to shut up for having made his wife sing. In fact, there was no more certain sign that all was well in Moranland than when his mom launched into *Danny Boy.*

Mo looked out the passenger seat window now and contemplated those wintry three-, four- or five-hour-long trips (depending on the weather) of long ago. He was struck by the contrast of the brightness intensifying shades of organic greens now versus the darkness cloaking snowy countryside then. And maybe, because it is through contrast that growth is measured, so too did Mo now sense the grudging presence of growth, both inside the car and out. This awareness led to a pensiveness not unlike his dad's *mood du jour*, and it bugged him some that he might be perceived as taking one more gallop through a parallel universe, as if he were readily conditioned and genetically wired to be "Little Mo" instead of his "own damn Mo." *Hell with it, I'm the one with the subscription to Psychology Today.* Whatever. Of one thing he was sure... growth wasn't always comfortable.

Mo watched D Mo drive with the same peripheral gaze his dad once did to keep tabs on a young Mo with his temporary license. For the last couple of hours the elder Moran had been almost as talkative as he was back then, if not as spontaneously irreverent, as if it was no longer a mission to prove that fun was more a product of will than anything having to do with luck, wealth or other outside agencies. They were well past Green Bay now, less than an hour away from the Harbor. Hank remained asleep in the back seat, his snoring audible only when they came to a stop. Near Sturgeon Bay on Highways 42-57 they came up on and quickly passed a small rectangular road sign, one of many no longer noticed signs for regular travelers to Door County. It was this particular sign, however, that had become the source of a Moran family tradition. When they came to it his dad would casually point and say, "That, right there, Molly, always makes me think of you." When Molly was well past being amused, a pre-teen Rinny would laugh on cue and say "Tell *me* Daddy, if Mom is getting tired of you." So over the years D Mo indeed began to alert Rinny when the sign was coming up, even more casually. "All kidding aside, Rinny, Honey," he'd say while referencing something going on in the news, weather, or sports universe - his way of stalling for as long as necessary - before suddenly pointing, "that right there, always makes me think of you." Mo, usually half asleep or faking it altogether, thought it was so off-the-charts stupid that he couldn't help

but laugh at the fact that his dad continued to do it. The small
rectangular sign stood at a crossroad; it was white with small black
lettering across the top that read, *County Trunk*. Under that, and taking
up almost the entire body of the sign was a bold, black, capital U.

County Trunk

U

When they finally did pass the crossroad that was County Trunk U,
neither said anything. Mo allowed himself a direct glance at his dad,
who glanced back and smiled briefly before tightening his jaw and going
back to his latter-day inscrutability. They had touched on Danny Mo's
return to competitive golf, if it could be called that, since that area was
well tilled before they ever got in the car to come north. It was simply a
case of a hall-of-famer accepting a special exemption to the Open at the
last minute. Simple as that. But this particular exemption was clearly
earned on the merits of an extraordinary body of work, and maybe just
as much in recognition of an unceremonious defeat by way of a bizarre
rules breach three years earlier, a crash and burn story that would be
told in certain circles for years.

Mo sometimes wondered if the crushing end to the Hill Farm Open
hadn't occurred on the same day his mother died, that, maybe, Danny
Mo would have found some dark reward in his highly-publicized string
of bad luck in the Open over the years, something nearly as fulfilling as
the title would have been. Danny Mo as the battle-weary protagonist in a
tragic tale of contemporary Shark-bitten folklore. When he needled his
dad about that a while back, Danny Moran looked at his son as if he had
completely failed as a father. After a solid ten seconds of staring at Mo,
he stood up, shook his head and said, "What is it, Mo, Scientology?
Something in your *Psychology Today*? What is it?" Then he walked out of
the room.

Before arriving at his grandmother's, Mo wanted to wiggle into the
subject of Cindy. He knew his dad had befriended her to some degree
through his work at Overlighter's. After Marty's funeral, D Mo had gone

on about all the reading she had done and the counseling to which she was fully committed; how he admired her courage in overcoming a miserable upbringing and some admittedly bad choices that were, if not inevitable, then unsurprising considering such an upbringing. He had said little else about her. It had seemed to Mo that she was leaning on D Mo at the cemetery, maybe a little more than a friend might lean. Still, Cindy no doubt provoked all kinds of thoughts, including a desire to see the very best in all that she had become.

It was a chance meeting at the antique store. He came around the end of an aisle and there she was, fondling a candle holder. Her immediate smile was like a tiny taze to the heart and a near-teenage moment rolled into one debilitating moment. While she small-talked about Danny being in Door County and how she'd never been there and was it really like the Martha's Vineyard of Wisconsin and so on, Mo was able to recover enough to speak. He told her he had recently moved to the East Side and she said it would be fantastic to have him as a neighbor. He had been holding a funky blue glass marlin at the time and said he was trying to decorate his place and that he wasn't very good at it. *Poor Mo Mo*. But the pathetic angle worked perfectly. She said she'd be happy to give him a hand and he said he would really appreciate that. She seemed sincere, like it mattered that Mo think well of her.

When she came over later that same day, Mo would have been pleased to do nothing more than sit next to Cindy Young. Happy just to count her eyelashes, maybe luck into some incidental contact, something harmless, a clinking of knees perhaps. As it was, they ended up having an absorbing conversation, even if it ended a bit bizarre.

Mo would be the first to confess that conversations are always more absorbing when the words come from the mouths of major babes. Bright, engaging ones anyway. Like Cindy. Someone who made Mo wish he could, even once, find a way to protect her from just enough harm to revel in whatever kind of honey-tongued thank you she might care to offer.

Not that he was sex-on-a-stick, but Mo understood the effects of attraction from screening applicants for supporting roles in the Maurice Moran Experience. He'd dated his share of smitten women who became wide-eyed and mesmerized when he was merely trying to make conversation or ladies who rewarded uninspired sarcasm with a little too much laughter. Mo understood. Those women believed Mo Moran was on his way to becoming a Big League pitcher, so of course he was amusing. But when Cindy sat with him in his blue room, she did so with no such expectation. And perhaps it was that sensibility, that lack of pretense on top of all her beauty that had Mo fighting off his inner nerd and periodic bouts of tongue-tied ineptness in her presence. When his small talk turned clumsy for a spell, he mentioned how thoughtful it had been for her and Marty to bring Hank into his dad's life. Cindy had smiled at that, and immediately replied in a way that sounded rehearsed; how she had never gotten over her fear of dogs after having been mauled by a German shepherd at the age of seven, and how she suffered a seriously torn foot after a gruesome bite from "a very bad man's pit-bull" a decade later. Now, even the smallest dog could make her uneasy. It had been Marty's idea, she said, to help her confront her fears by gifting a puppy to Danny. For a moment she started to elaborate further before suddenly stopping, and asked for a small glass of wine. When Mo returned with it, she said, "I really shouldn't…" and never revisited the subject of dogs.

The way Cindy talked about his dad, it was clear she held him in an exalted place. She thought him kind, funny and "so good, so dear." But so too did she seem delighted to be with the man's son, at Mo's place, under the pretense of home décor management no less, not much more than a five minute walk from Overlighter's, where she was a counselor in residence. Sitting on the couch, Mo stayed easily five chicken-shit feet away from Cindy, enough distance so that looking at her would be nice. And safe. No chance for misinterpretation or a sudden involuntary lick. When their conversation touched on life's various misfortunes and the essence of redemption, she would touch his forearm or knee, or lean toward him to emphasize a point. He tried to freeze time, to think, to keep his imagination a good distance from what could barely be called 'developments.' Fat chance. He felt something. Based on keen observation, various magazine articles and personal test results, Mo was convinced there were no retractable instincts in honest men, and that few men could resist entertaining the possibility of Cindy's warmth meaning something more.

After Mo poured another glass of wine for Cindy ("just a tiny one"), and he himself well into his Pinot, he innocently addressed just that point by sharing his admiration for Cindy and the how it seemed everyone at Overlighter's sincerely desired to help each other. But his voice cracked as he spoke, adding emotion, and it had the effect of making his message a little too potent. Not so potent that a naturally mouth-watering woman might suddenly beg to have her willing body bent over a $650 Micro Suede outlet-store sofa sleeper for mutually satisfying purposes, but apparently enough to compel a teary-eyed Cindy to peer deep into Mo's eyes, sparking an electric moment of face exploration and freefalling inevitability. The two of them fell into an inexplicable, head-spinning, can't-be-happening, movie-scene-in-the-mind kind of kiss before Cindy gently broke the embrace, took one hearty breath for composure, offered up a half dozen *I'm-so-sorry's* and, after working the door locks without a hitch, left his apartment in a rush.

Okay then, thought Mo. The whole WTF experience left him with shaky legs and a lot of questions. He then contemplated those questions while sitting alone in the dim of his *indigo de la Mo* until he heard another bottle if Pinot calling his name.

∞

"Deep thoughts?" His dad's voice was quiet, but it brought him back to the moment.

"Uh, yeah, like father like son, I guess," said Mo.

"Ah…

They rode in silence for another minute. Mo looked at his dad. The man remained fit, and still looked younger than his 49 years, but the lines and signs of a capsizing life were starting to show on his face. "You think you'll ever remarry?"

"Wow," said Danny, smiling quickly enough to make sudden crow's feet come and go, "No idea. Have to get back to you on that one. I will say this, marriage is generally considered only after serious dating. Or some reality TV show competition."

"Doesn't seem like you're getting out much. And I don't mean your salads with Witchy."

"Maybe I'm just discreet," said D Mo. "Everyone has someone I'm supposed to meet. You have someone, Mo?"

"You mean someone for you to meet, or someone in my life?"

"Exactly."

Mo chucked and played along. "Hard to say."

Danny shifted the focus. "Guess Rinny's pretty serious now with Jesse."

"Good guy, that Jesse," said Mo. "It'll be nice to have Rin up here for Tuesday and Wednesday's action. Pretty cool of Crusty to go down to get her from the airport."

"Very cool, said Danny, "but I wouldn't count on Wednesday."

"I don't know, D. I got a feeling you're gonna make the cut. No expectations, no pressure, butter fades all day, this land is your land, all that."

"Don't beat balls like I used to, just my nightly nines and some chipping and putting. Having the family together for a couple days is what matters. Your grandma is thrilled. Wednesday would be nothing but a bonus. No illusions."

"I'll bet Mom would have even come to this one." Mo looked out the window. "Course, she'll be there in spirit."

"She'll be with us." Danny came to a stop sign in Egg Harbor. "She's always along. Just a little quieter."

"I could give you some driving tips," said Mo, straight-faced. "If you ever did want to settle down again, would you want someone just like Mom?"

Danny Moran looked at his son and said nothing. Hank stirred in the backseat like he was about to demand someone's attention, but then resettled himself, satisfied things were under control and that no one was eating anything without him.

"Didn't mean to put you on the spot," said Mo. "I'm sure it's complicated."

"I'm about as settled as a single guy can be," said Danny. "Who can say. Not me. Your mother and I were pretty different for having so much in common. But the differences we had were ticky-tack. Made things interesting."

Danny drove in silence for a few seconds, his right hand draped casually over the wheel. He did not hide that he was chewing on a thought. "You know, Mo, looking back…without the challenge of your mother, I mean…I was on my toes, never could take too much for granted. If it all had come easy, she probably would have felt invisible. We went through a little of that, but I know how I can be. Without the challenge, I fall asleep. Heck, maybe that's just how we rolled. Not perfect, but maybe right. I believe your mom knew that all along. Dwelled on it quite a bit after she died. But hey, life's short, I'll know for sure soon enough."

Mo looked at his dad. "Well, I'd like to go on record that I know Mom dug your shtick. Loved to roll her eyes, loved it." Mo was quiet for a beat. "I think she owned you with her eyes."

"True. The eye-rolls got a little old, but her eyes could change the weather either way, especially when she smiled. Would've preferred we focus on what we had going for us, more than, you know…what we didn't. We were blessed with good health, great kids, slightly sweetened whole grain breads, a back-up sump pump and fat-free Western Dressing and a Saw Doctors concert just about every year, plenty of friends, chip clips… all kinds of things. The good beat the bad but good. I don't deny we had some bathrobe management differences, and jars returned to the wrong shelf, the kitchen sponge stuff and some recycling offenses. But you know what, over time, I did eventually come to realize that I'd been living a life pretty much void of refrigerator rules. What your mom called anarchy. I did improve my focus. I learned my shelves and sponge colors. I didn't alphabetize the spice rack like your mom did, but I eventually got with the program. I was coming around."

"Anarchy." said Mo, remembering. "Well, everyone has flaws. Rinny and me would talk about it and we figured Mom's main flaw was trying to fix all yours. I mean, who has that kind of time?"

"Funny guy." The senior Mo inserted a CD into the player. "I sometimes thought we actually clicked *because* of our flaws. Two people rub up against one another, you gotta catch on something, don't ya, to make a click? Well, we clicked alright. I think that may have played a role in Carter and Christy's divorce. She worked so hard to please him, he fell asleep, took a blessing for granted, and she burned out and went to help people who appreciated it. Frankly, if things were always smooth...I think that's a little unnatural. You'd never know where you were, the days would run on, never forced to think. That's growth deferred indefinitely or forever in some cases. The other side of it is just as bad. Seen a lot of them over my years helping businesses, big shots who crown themselves kings of their worlds, home and work, control freaks that rule by rank and financial leverage and anger easily, but they soon discover that the kids have grown, or escaped, and a whole lotta life is out of their hands, you know. Some try to reinvent themselves before they die." Danny shook his head.

Mo looked out the passenger window and nodded... "So, whatever happened to Christy? Always thought she was cool. Great looking for her age bracket."

"Ahhhh," said Danny, smiling as he weighed his words. "Carter says she's working at the MD Anderson Center in Houston. Huge cancer clinic. And, I agree, she is a beautiful woman."

"Amazing how some crazy relationships work out and others that seem so solid just...end." Mo sighed. "I remember Mom telling me and Rinny, how when you left so ungodly early on weekends to golf, you'd set the coffee maker somehow so the coffee was still hot when she got up. She liked that."

"No kidding?" His dad seemed genuinely surprised. "I...well...so she did notice."

"Of course she did. Said it gave the coffee a burned flavor, but I think she dug the thought."

Danny smiled fast and recovered.

"So, are you saying you'd have to find someone slightly flawed if you were to settle down again?"

"Well, Mo, you just said everyone's flawed, which you know even without your *Psychology Today*. But that's like saying everyone has arteries. Danny considered his next words. "There is one woman I've been seeing. Knew each other for a while, before, you know. We just kind of started doing some under-the-radar things, but…things happen. She's bright, good-hearted, and quite attractive. At first I thought she wanted the relationship to go full steam ahead, faster than I wanted, then she suddenly backed off a little, not sure why. But it's fine, she's pretty young." Danny looked at Mo and winked. "And she's got a thing about Hank."

"A thing?"

"Don't know. She's just not comfortable with him around."

"Is it Hank, or all dogs?" Mo felt his scalp prickle.

"I haven't wanted to get into it yet." Danny masked a sigh. "But it can't be Hank. Hank is the prancing prince of love and naps."

Despite the crack about Hank, Mo thought his dad looked a little flustered. "I would think Hank is a non-negotiable issue."

At that, Hank had heard his name enough and did an awkward, tail-chasing three-sixty in slo-mo before performing a self-gratifying stretch. He sat up in the center of the back seat and put his head forward between the two men, letting them know he was now ready to receive some love. He stretched into a suggestive pose that implied just under his neck was a strong choice. Mo massaged there. His thoughts were elsewhere.

Danny hit the play button for the CD player. "First song on The Docs CD. Tune kills me." D Mo took a deep breath "About life pickin' up speed as you age, and then changes. Cousin Leo's north of 40 now. Davy, too."

Mo was flabbergasted. *Cindy, damn. Dating? Talk about don't ask, don't tell.* He grabbed the CD's jewel case to cover his discomfort. The album was called The Cure, by The Saw Doctors, of course. The E-Streeters of Ireland, his dad called them. Mo read the title of the first song. "Out for a Smoke?"

"A metaphor," said Danny. He turned up the volume slightly.

Mo knew that meant his dad wanted him to listen.

> *There were times when I'd turn back the clock*
> *I'd love to start again and get it right*

Mo sat back and made a point to listen intently. He had to admit, he'd always kind of liked the brogue that The Saw Doctors refused to Anglicize or bury.

> *With the evenings getting shorter*
> *I wonder can we forge another dream*
> *Gather up the pieces and assemble one more winning team...*

A minute later, his dad turned it up again and nodded.

> *Trying to get the balance right*
> *the health the drugs the lovin' and the beer.*
> *It's gone beyond a joke*
> *I'm goin' out for a smoke*

Mo glanced at his dad, who was just letting the little nods wane. Mo wondered if that line about balance was meant for him. Then he looked out the window, but not because there was anything he cared to see.

∞

Chapter 40

"This is it, huh."

Mo took "it" into his hands. They were on the far right end of The Majesty's unique range with the rock wall backstop. "The magical three-wood. Man, you hit this thing good yesterday."

"Yep," said Danny. "Went to Henry's shop after I played here the first time, did some testing on two separate launch monitors, got the data, and he built it on the spot." Danny looked at the club lovingly. "Prototype. Made for the Majesty."

"Longest State Open course ever, and you're attacking it with a three-wood."

"Only on certain holes, Mo, we covered that. The down-slopes on four, maybe five holes are a fit for my three-wood carry range. It's wider there. You get that forward kick, the ball goes just as far, or farther, than if you carry the slopes with a driver. And I can hit this one a little higher too, it's perfect for the 12th."

"The parachute hole. Carry is what…220, end of the world is 260?" Mo handed the new club back to his dad. "Which I found out."

"I told you – 260 max. You went all happy-go-Jacky."

"Hey, sometimes it just goes."

"It's the angle of descent that matters there. Ball has to come pretty much straight down. Watch." Danny teed a ball up and hit a smooth three-wood straight up into the sky. They watched the ball carry high and ricochet back off a tree above the face of the enormous dolomite wall before dropping down in several bounces like a repelling stone.

"That's the one," said Mo, "The parachute drop."

The Morans had played a practice round at The Majesty just before sunset the night before. They started late and were able to fly around in a cart, just the two of them taking in The Majesty before finishing in the dark. In fact, they played 17 and 18 in virtually unplayable darkness. Mo had been amazed at how his dad instinctively knew the lay of the land after only one practice round. And even more amazed that his dad's hyperbolic advance billing did not do justice to what he saw before, during and after the sunset. Viscerally stunning. The Majesty held vistas that flat out affected him physically, a little wooziness in his midsection, a spike of weakness in his legs, not unlike the feeling he had when he opened the door for Cindy three weeks ago.

Looking down the line of golfers warming up on the range, Mo battled a bolt of competitor's envy. He recognized some of the players from his reentry into competitive golf, though perhaps fewer than expected. There were guys he competed against years ago in the few junior events he'd entered, as well as a handful of veterans and journeymen he knew from his days as his dad's main caddy. The mini-tour types were mostly oblivious in their bubbles of concentration as they went about their pre-round rituals and range-time pantomimes. Slotted in chatty bunches were the just-happy-to-be-here guys looking to share laughs with other glad-handers and I'm-not-nervous-either types. Same ol' same ol'. He couldn't wait to be part of it. As a player. He just hadn't put it all together yet. In golf *or* life.

Mo was not surprised that probably 80% or more of the players were using carts, considering The Majesty's steep elevation changes, and though he was impressed with the proximity of the greens to the tees, it was going to be a hell of a hike. He was relieved Mo' Nature had whisked in some cooler weather. He knew his dad would walk until the day he couldn't; but anyone walking in yesterday's heat might have been spotting the field a shot or two shots a side.

They had their spot on the range. That small but coveted piece of land his dad had, in effect, left behind for his son to take over and begin his own quest to become a champion in this sport. But for now Mo watched his dad stripe a handful of butter-cut four irons that landed consistently next to a shadowed area near the base of the limestone wall at the back of the range. It was apparent that D Mo had his soft fade neatly in place. After so many years of grinding on the range, for Danny Mo, maybe less *was* more.

Mo knew all about Shelly. Even before The Hill Farm episode, which was thought to be the last time his dad would have the pleasure of charming the ROG Nazi. Only now Shelly sat in his blue coat under the canopy at the starter's table instead of standing or pacing in place. Shelly had had a stroke and could no longer speak, but arrangements had been kindly made to maintain his presence at the Open. Apparently he still had his faculties about him, although even those who said so said it was tough to know for sure. Standing next to him was a much younger and extremely tanned guy also in a blue PGA sport coat, a perennial State PGA administrator type by the name of John G. Schmitz. He preferred JG over Schmitty, but Danny had always called him "Schmee-G." This time Danny called him "JG" as he approached the first tee with his new three-wood.

JG shook Danny's hand, then slapped a hand on Danny's back and darn near gave him a neck massage worth 60 bucks retail. "Danny Mo, I've missed you man."

"Well…" Danny smiled but had nothing more to say but "…okay."

JG jumped back in. "I'm just giving Shelly a hand here. He's still sharper than me at these things."

"Good for you, JG," said Danny, "you make Shelly proud now." Danny glanced at Shelly, and Mo, who was taking it all in, detected something in the older man's eyes. Mo half expected Danny to add "…and DQ somebody," but Danny said nothing further.

One of Danny's playing partners was one of the state's top pros named Rick Fischer, otherwise known as "Pig." Mo got a kick out of Pig. Call him "Fish," and it was obvious you didn't know him. It was a common enough nickname — there are "Pigs" aplenty in high schools, fraternities, and rec teams in every sport — but Pig Fischer was driving range/nine-hole golf course ramblin', gamblin' pro, and his nickname had nothing to do with slovenly habits. He earned his name from replacing almost every noun he spoke at a golf course with the word "pig." "I killed that pig," or "You see that pig suck back?" or "Ah, I fatted the pig." Of The Majesty, he said, "She's one ferocious pig, ain't she?" Even when he ordered a burger, it was "...and put little cheddar on that pig, wouldya?" Post-concert comments were along the lines of, "Damn, those pigs could play." And while Pig Fischer embraced his nickname, the Pigman was also a tantrum waiting to happen. His blowups were legendary. Called it "getting his pig on." Gary D'Amato quoted the guy as saying "sometimes I have to lose it, to get it back."

Danny's other partner was a good friend, a fellow hall-of-famer a few years younger than Danny named Bob Gregorski. Twenty-five years ago, Gregorski was an all Big Ten golfer at University of Wisconsin, and then went on to have a cup of coffee on the Space Coast Mini-Tour in Florida. After his stint in Orlando, he came back home to get a law degree, regained his amateur status, and then went through women like chewing gum until he dumped an exotic dancer named Daryl to marry a Titleist rep named Candi. He had no known nickname and to this day answered to..."Bob."

JG went over the pre-round details and handed out hole-location sheets affably and quickly. Both Bob and Pig, who were sharing a cart, leaked their tee shots to the right, which prompted a "cart golf" comment from JG. Shelly burned holes into JG with his stare, as if to say, *"Nothing friendly you greenhorn son of a bitch."*

Then it was Danny's turn. A flutter of emotion came over Mo hearing his dad introduced on the first tee and watching him walk casually to the right side of the tee blocks, just as Mo had seen him do so many times growing up.

Danny calmly went through his routine without a sign of nerves, and, using his new three-wood, ripped a low bullet right down the middle. After picking up his tee, Danny walked back to the table without expression and politely extended his arm to shake Shelly's hand. Shelly sat there, looking at Danny before turning away. Danny shrugged and handed his club to Mo.

And so the two broad-shouldered Morans began their side-by-side march on The Majesty. Before leaving the plateau of the championship tee box, Danny turned back toward the starter's table. Standing off to the side of the tent canopy, JG immediately gave Danny an 'I'm pulling for you' fist pump. But Danny wasn't looking at him. He was looking back at Shelly sitting firmly upright at the table. This time the old man stared back and slowly lifted his hand.

Mo thought his dad seemed touched, and watched him give Shelly his big, slow nod, the one Mo knew so well, and a peace offering if there ever was one. That's when Mo saw the old man's hand slowly turn, and a bony middle finger go up, just as slowly, as if inflated. Then, surreal in its suddenness, as if the old man's hand had been zapped with a high-voltage charge, he thrust it forward, his finger fully erect and proud and shaking with new energy. The look in Shelly's eyes, however, was not one of craziness, it more or less suggested he could die happy now. One freaking shot into Danny Mo's return to both golf and the stomping grounds of his youth, and Ol' Shelly was flipping off the hometown hero with the bird of his dreams. The two Morans turned away and hoofed it toward the first fairway. Danny smiled at Mo, who was outright laughing. "Now we go," he said.

Coming to the 18th hole, after five hours and change, the sun was fixing to kiss the bay. If the view was a giant promotional shot for Heaven, Mo was certain there would be a rush on general goodness. Despite some shaky putting, Danny was three over par, birdie for 74, par for 75, and probably pretty good on a ferocious pig like The Majesty. He had hit the ball well all day, mostly little butter fades with the irons, solid with the driver. He worked it both ways off the tee with the big stick, but was particularly precise with his new three-wood.

After some internal debate, Danny went with the driver off the 18th tee, got it pretty good, and his ball ended up directly in the shadow of Morgan's Forehead. Danny was still long enough for a man pushing 50, but by way of Mo Mo and others, he knew there was a whole new dimension to how the young guys bombed it now. Pig and Bob belted long tee shots as well, but again lost them slightly right, and had to lay up. Mo aimed the Quick-shot Laser Link gun at the flag and reported a reading of 244 yards. The 18th was a hard dogleg left, downhill. Danny asked Mo for the "Shaq-toe," his trusty 19 degree hybrid. From where he was now, the green sat some 70 feet below. Even with the help of the extra altitude, Mo, Pig, Bob and Danny were all incredulous when his solidly-struck shot hit the center of the green and bounded forward like a frightened forest creature.

"Wow. What a slab of concrete," said Mo. "They've all been firm, but that was…unnatural." Danny shook his head, and handed his hybrid back to Mo. They headed toward the cart path that would take them around the gulch that cut across the fairway almost 370 yards from the back tees.

"Knew it was hard, but…" said Danny, matter-of-factly, "Loren said it was the firmest on the course." He'd been told it had something to do with the Niagara Escarpment, an underground ridge of compacted rock that runs 600-plus miles from somewhere in Iowa, through the Green Bay side of Door County and Michigan, and all the way to Niagara Falls. Ferguson reportedly spent a fortune getting grass to grow on that part of the cliff line, especially the 18th green. Rerouting the water runoff almost blew up the whole design, but Loren had his heart set on how his finishing hole should be.

"It's unreal," said Mo, taking it all in, the shimmering bay far below, panoramic views north and south, a blend of rock and pines and colors, and the clubhouse, understated but regal in a rustic way. "I think your ball jumped the back bunker into the junk."

"Really? I figured the bunker was my safety net."

After Pig and Bob's wedges bounded, and barely stopped at the back of the green, they all fanned out, searching the dry heathery grass and cliff ferns behind the green looking for Danny's ball for going on three edgy minutes. The guy named either Frank or Fred, a volunteer official, had joined them after first apologizing for not having a clue. He was spotting, but was on the clubhouse side and was forced to peer into the setting sun. Pig kept saying "I saw the pig come in here," pointing. Confused that his confident porcine mind might be letting him down, he kept repeating "the pig has gotta be here." Finally, it was Pig who found the pig, and it was not good.

Sizing it up quickly, Danny pulled Lazarus from the bag Mo had left unattended while engaged in the hunt. He gouged it out of a stony area mixed with some desperate undergrowth, and directly into the bunker. From there, he splashed it to six feet below the hole, a great shot considering the limited amount of green he had to work with. Then he missed the putt. Bogey. 76.

On the way to the parking lot, Mo checked the big scoreboard from a distance, and did some quick math. "Near as I can tell, you're tied for like, 30-something-ish. Not too bad. You didn't even seem nervous coming off a three year layoff."

"Would've been more nervous if I had prepared like I used to. No expectations, no doubts today."

"Solid ball striking for an old man. If a few putts drop...?"

"Fly balls good, grounders bad." Danny shrugged. "Let's get home. Rinny and Crusty should be getting to town about now."

The three minute drive to Manda's house went by too quickly for Mo. Felt good to sit. Inside, his Grandma Manda had a giant crock-pot simmering with shredded turkey breast, and maybe seven side offerings: beans, fried potatoes, various slaws, salads, and chips. In the family room, Rinny was going through the legendary family photo album that had grown to the size of a microwave oven.

When Rinny heard the guys entering, she jumped up from the couch and skirted the coffee table with jungle cat grace. She ran to her dad and brother for a lengthy group hug. While still in the love scrum, Mo blabbed about his dad's solid round, how he was well under the cut line, and was striping his three-wood tee balls, sweet "baby fades" with the irons, etc.

Though Rinny had been away getting two degrees in three and a half years, and was set to start law school at New York University the following week, she corrected her brother. "Butter-cut, Mo," she said, "Butter-cut."

∞

Chapter 41

Mo came quietly up the steps from his grandmother's basement and saw his dad standing in the living room. Tuesday morning, just before sunrise, Danny was already dressed and staring at a picture on the wall. A photo of Danny's parents in their backyard a couple of years before his grandfather's cancer had been diagnosed. Curly had one leg propped on a stack of wood, arms resting on his knee, Manda at his side with an arm around his shoulder. By the honeysuckles, it looked to be late spring or early summer. If Danny had heard Mo coming into the living room, he did not let on.

"Morning D Mo." Mo joined his dad and took in the familiar picture.

"Hey," whispered Danny, who put a finger to his lips. "What are you doing up?"

"You have a monopoly on insomnia?"

"In this family, yes."

Mo shrugged. "Just thinking. Like you say, no off-switch for that."

"Women?"

"Maybe."

"Someone you like?'

"Sure."

"She like you?"

"Maybe," said Mo.

"Beautiful." Danny kept his gaze on the photo.

"Grandma hasn't changed much at all, has she?"

"The woman is timeless. And look at your grandpa." Danny stared at the photo as if viewing it for the first time. Mo let the silence hang.

"Just look at him, Mo. Ol' Curly was the strongest guy anybody around here knew. Big shoulders, his hands, and look at those forearms. Oak branches."

Mo had heard his dad talk of his dad this way before, but the emotion was resonating now with a force of its own.

"Remember…" Danny took a deep breath. "When he got really sick, he made it clear he didn't want us to come and see him in the hospital, you know, seeing him deteriorate. Said to call. Remember those phone calls, Mo?"

Mo nodded, recalling the failing voice of his grandpa, asking how his little jungle cat was doing. Little seven-year-old Mo would tell his gramps he couldn't wait to show him his fastball. That's when Grandpa Curly would summon his old voice just to say "You bet. You go right at 'em, Mo Mo." It was his way of saying goodbye before Mo handed the phone back to his dad. Mo was sure they were the last words he heard his grandpa say.

"Don't think I really grew up until he left us." Danny cleared his throat as quietly as he could. "Used to call me 'the one and only Danny Mo.'"

"Just like, 'No one!' huh?" Mo did a short karate chop.

"Yep." Danny nodded. "Loved that."

They stood there a moment, "Well, you know what Grandpa used to say," said Mo. "You go right at 'em today."

Mo was a little startled to feel his dad's arm around his shoulder. It wasn't D Mo's way. He was a handshake, eye contact kind of guy. Mo sensed that Danny wanted his eyes off-limits for a moment. They heard movement in the kitchen. When they looked, they saw Manda quickly turn away as if she hadn't been watching.

"Breakfast's coming right up, Boys. Parnell's up, and I heard Rinny stirring, too."

The Majesty. 7:40 a.m. Mo dropped his dad's clubs at the range, and before he could even get his towel wet, D Mo told him to go show Rinny and Crusty around a little if he wanted. Danny assured Mo he could get loose all by himself. Danny's range routine had changed in that he no longer had one. There were 40 minutes to kill before his dad's 8:24 tee time, and Mo did feel a nagging need to use the clubhouse restroom.

Mo joined Rinny and Crusty, who were busy checking the scoreboard, and they all headed to the clubhouse. Rinny and Crusty bought some coffee and sat at a table overlooking the 18th green. Mo snatched the sports section from an orphaned Milwaukee Journal Sentinel, then headed to The Majesty's sparkling locker room. He checked the scores, and noted that as his dad had requested, Gary D'Amato made no mention of Danny Moran's first competitive round in three years. Salamone had a 78, and Zane Williams, a former All-American at BYU, finished with an eagle to shoot 68 and take a two shot lead. Mo had heard he was a decent but kind of weird kid, and reportedly, scary long. Mo was wired with a Whatever circuit in him, and figured if Williams was scary, then he, Mo Mo Moran, would have to be terrifying.

Mo felt immeasurably better when he emerged from the bathroom stall, but the feeling was short-lived when he saw a slouched Andy Salamone washing his hands at one of the sinks. Salamone looked up and saw Mo in the mirror and smirked. The man still had those puppy-tits, but Mo had to admit, Salamone looked to be a little fitter than in the past.

"Hey there, Little Mo." Sally stood straight up to dry his hands. "Back as your dad's beast of burden, huh."

Mo had seen Sally around at The Barn and The Aftermath, mostly from a distance. "Hello, Gandhi," Mo smiled. "Or do you prefer, Big Gandhi?"

Salamone huffed. "Don't go there, Kid. First off, those women are whores, whores who will say and do anything for money. That's what whores do, got it? And the old man's letter from the grave was a load of grandstanding bullshit. Just to let you know."

Mo seethed as he thought of Cindy. "Well, you sure did a great job of defending yourself." He took his time soaping his hands. Mo's facial scars from the hawk's talons were made prominent by the bathroom's fluorescent lighting. Mo wondered if Salamone noticed them now, if ever. "Now that I think of it, defending yourself never has gone very well for you, has it?"

Salamone was so eager to reply to the funeral contention that he may have missed the meaning of Mo's last comment. "You don't understand, Kid. The old man got something in his fuckin' head, and he never let it go. No reset, no do-over, no fresh start no nothin'…and don't think I didn't try. It started with me hearing shit about him, me not trusting him, so maybe I did what I felt I had to do, too. And he did the same. But it didn't have to be that way for-fucking-ever. No, Grandpa Marty had his goddamn stalemate, just the way he wanted it. He wuddent gonna play it straight, no fucking way. He loved it the way it was. Pissed me off so fuckin' much I couldn't see straight."

"A lot of ways to step on someone's throat, ain't there, Gandhi?" said Mo. His mind flashed quickly to when his thoughts weren't too different than Sally's. Marty the Cheater. Now, Mo could see it. Once the old man saw the weakness, Marty flipped it, made it Cheater versus Cheater when Sally lost his stomach for it. Like "Jonah," unarmed and 70, squaring off with a punk-ass pimp in a central city alley. A *you-want-some, come-get-some* kind of warrior, happy to beat you by any set of rules you want, or no rules at all.

"Big fuckin' deal," said Salamone. "Drag someone in the mud, and make saint in the process. Crock-o-shit."

Mo raised his eyebrows. "I think you might be gettin' the hang of it now, aren't you? Except it ain't a stalemate when you're the one peeling off the bills. Don't worry, it all went for a good cause. You can feel good about that, and if you trash those women again I'll stuff your head in the toilet I just used. And I assure you, that's one toilet you don't want."

"You think you even matter, Little Mo?" The big man's nostrils flared. "Shit…you probably didn't know I wrote the damn check for five grand, just as I said I would. And besides, I've given more to those whores than that old goat ever did." Salamone's eyes were darting. "I told the ladies of the House to keep quiet about my contributions or they'd stop, and sure as shit, they never said a word. Like I say, anything for a price. Cash is king with whores."

"I wouldn't know," said Mo. "What I do know is the man's been dead over a year, and he still has your head. He must be pleased, lookin' down."

Crusty walked into the restroom just as Mo finished, and immediately picked up on the vibe. He stopped by the door.

Salamone was already going back at Mo. "You think life's so crystal clear there Kiddie Mo. Well it ain't. You'll get it soon enough you ever get out on your own. Hell, I heard you almost made it here as a grownup, an actual player. Too bad you gagged on the last couple holes at the qualifier, huh?"

The two men were facing off now, maybe five feet apart. Mo stared at Salamone, and Salamone back at him. The 6'4" Hair Dude had dropped probably 25 pounds, but still had at least 40 on Mo. Salamone working out? How quaint.

"How 'bout I lock the door for a minute, Mo?" Crusty reached for the lock and snapped it loudly into place. "Not that you'd need a whole minute to pop this parade float."

Salamone turned as if to see who was there, but of course he knew, just as he knew Mo wasn't going to do anything, especially with his back turned. So he laughed his false bravado laugh. "Why it's the little piece of crust, what nobody wants."

"Let's get out of here," said Mo.

Crusty stared at Salamone for a several seconds while Mo waited and watched. "Okay," said Crusty. "Now we go."

Putting remained iffy at best. But if Danny Mo hit it good on Monday afternoon, he took it up a notch to very good on Tuesday morning. The three-wood strategy was paying off in fairways hit, which paid off in reliable, ball-compressing iron shots that worked ten- to 12-feet left-to-right.

After a flushed six-iron from 181 on the 14th hole, Mo could not resist commenting. "You're doing it again, that little sideways shuffle, D Mo, walking your butter-cuts closer to the pin with that little crossover step to the left. That's heyday Danny Mo."

"My inner-Faldo at work," said Danny, pleased. "Now that I'm hitting it almost as short Sir Nick." Always a long hitter, Danny had backed off considerably after his back injury, and from getting more time behind him. Still, he could reach back for some extra thunder when called upon. "D Mo" had a look of on-course contentment that Mo hadn't seen since he could hardly remember when. In fact, Mo wasn't sure he'd ever seen that look. It was a subset of peaceful, but not necessarily the same ruthless serenity he had back in the day, "the Hannibal Lecter calm," as Carter Slane liked to say. (Often adding. "…another cat who didn't curse, either").

"Whatever. Me likey." Mo was immersed now too. His dad was two under, the course was getting harder, and with no rain in sight, harder still.

Rinny and Crusty kept their distance by staying on the cart path, and well ahead of all full shots. Easier to talk non-stop that way. Mo knew that, just as he knew that the bounce in Rinny's step meant she was *major into*, which is what she called the act of being fully engaged, and was now hoping her energy could will her dad to embrace his own *major into*. Crusty told Mo the balls hitting the firm greens sounded like pop fouls landing on metal bleachers, and was convinced the scores would soar this afternoon.

When they came to the downhill 459 yard ninth hole, the group's 18th, Danny remained at two under par, and promptly rope-hooked a runner down the middle with a hooded three-wood. He hit a straight crisp shot with a five-iron that climbed into the sky, spinning, rising, and pausing before falling slightly right, and landing on the front fringe. His ball released slightly, and eventually came to rest eight feet past the front right pin.

"As good as could ever be done," said Mo. "No one." One chop.

Bob "Bob" Gregorski drove it right with Danny and hit a similar looking shot with a five-iron that carried maybe a yard further, yet he had at least 40 feet coming back for his birdie. Pig Fischer had been playing well after a rough start to the day when he went six over through four holes without actually hitting a bad shot. Pig would likely need a par to make the cut, and he put full Pig Power into a tee shot that went over 285 yards into the breeze, center cut. When he tried to muscle-up on a seven-iron, he "pulled the pig" well left of the green, into some rocks and brush about 30 yards down a dicey slope leading to a stone wall by the cliff edge. Despite it being marked as a hazard and rough terrain, Pig announced testily that he was "going after the pig." After he and Bob carted their way to the green, the Pigman grabbed his wedge and disappeared over the ridge.

Mo looked at his dad. "I'm gonna give him a hand, I got a decent look at that area yesterday…it ain't pretty there."

Danny shrugged and said to go ahead without him, certain the Pig was cooked. When Mo cleared the ridge, he saw Fischer below, his head back, shoulders heaving, with some low register noises emerging. This had to be it, at long last the Pig was "getting his pig on." He had kept his temper in check for the past two days, probably out of respect for Danny Mo and Bob "Bob," and their reputation for composure. But his two day streak had come to an end. Pig had found his ball alright, but it looked to be in a patch of high yellowish grass right behind some decrepit looking bushes. Then Pig began to curse. The cursing merged what might have been some wild boar-type snorting noises if only Mo knew what wild boar noises sounded like. Mo figured Pig was approximating how a crazy-drunk papa boar might snort-roar at misbehaving step-children boars. Maybe they'd be called step-piglets, Mo did not know.

Well down the scraggy hill, Pig, thinking he was alone, appeared to be crying during his cursing fit. Crying. Literally. His face flexed tightly against his cheek bones and he switched to a gurgle-oink of sorts that shifted to pitchy whisper-screams directed at the sky, and maybe God Himself. Mo heard some old favorites, the classics, then some fresh laid profanity mixed with the guttural hog stuff, including, but not limited to, the one that suggested he, Pig, have sex with himself. Actually, a whole lot of sex with himself. Had to be with himself, there was no one else there. Hearing it better a second time, Mo determined it to be more about how the Pig wanted to have sex with himself, and not all about where, which Mo first believed to be in the grass. When Pig finally turned and saw Mo watching him from atop a large rock, his expression went blank. "You wanna tend the flag, Mo?"

The flag wasn't even close to visible, and Mo laughed hard enough to nearly lose his balance on the rock. Next time Mo looked at Pig, Fischer was winding up, and smashing his wedge into the hay with demonic force, screaming like a chick tennis player. So much violence, and yet the ball popped up over his head, then landed three feet behind him on some flat rocky dirt. Pig wasted no time before wailing on it again. This time he skulled his ball through the decrepit bushes in front of him. It then skipped off the bluff's craggy surface before shooting forward over the ridge. A few seconds later there was laughter, and some clapping near the green.

When they made it to the green, Danny described how the ball hit the bank leading up to the green, popped straight up and trickled to within 18 inches of the cup. "Bob" Gregorski made his 40-footer for birdie, and Pig would find out much later that he made the cut on the number by tapping in his 18-incher for bogey. After all that, Danny missed his uphill eight-footer for birdie. Still, it was a solid two under par 70. Danny Mo had made the cut, and more importantly, he had butter-cut his way into contention in front of friends and family at a magnificent new course built upon land he loved in the harbor town where he grew up.

∞

Walking to the parking lot, there was a sweet peace among the three Morans and Crusty.

"Well," said Crusty, "Pardon the mixed company but all I can say is, you are Danny fu…"

"Okay Crust," Danny interrupted, "how 'bout we stick with, 'Now we go,' huh?'

"Alright," said Crusty, "Now we, in Bumphuck Harbor, go."

Rinny knuckle-bumped with Crusty. Mo was reminded of his scene with Sally. He needed a beer.

∞

Chapter 42

Meanwhile, back at the ranch, the two good friends were relaxed in the backyard shade as if nothing could be finer.

Manda was reading a book while nestled in a wooden-framed chair with a worn green canvas sling that had gotten the hang of how Manda liked to be held. Hank was curled up on the grass next to her, savoring the strokes and scratches Manda provided in an unhurried rhythm as she read. Both appeared pleased with the arrangement.

Danny was the first to join the two after his second round at The Majesty. Hank's head instantly turned toward Danny and his breathing picked up; yet, he remained at Manda's side. Not only was Hank delighting in Manda's massage, but he was also working on one of the all-natural marrow-filled beef bones she had purchased in anticipation of this week.

"You two look at peace."

Manda turned; her hearing wasn't what it used to be. "Danny, you sneak, how did it go?"

"Good enough, I guess."

"Good enough?" Crusty was right behind him and just ahead of Rinny. "Hell, I bet your boy'll be top ten by day's end, what with the wind pickin' up, and the greens baking out. Two under today? Gonna be gold."

Manda smiled wide. "Well, gold is good anywhere. Way to go, Danny Mo. You boys must be hungry, hiking those hills."

"Anyone want a beer?" Mo shouted from the balcony deck, his Rolling Rock half gone.

"Beer me," said Crusty. "Maybe it'll settle me down enough to take a nap. Too much excitement today."

A nap sounded good to Danny as well, but eating immediately was mandatory.

Manda, with a hand from Crusty and Rinny, had a top-five worldwide deli spread ready in minutes. Hank came over to Danny while Manda bustled in the kitchen and the man and his dog caught up on how the other was doing. But once Manda sat back down, Hank drifted back to the man's mom.

∞

For dinner, Manda suggested The Green Mountain Grille, a favorite of Danny's, and it turned out to be a reunion of sorts. A surprising collection of townsfolk from Danny's past turned up. By the time dinner was over, there had been toasts aplenty and pledges to come out and support Danny in the final round the next afternoon. They even moved to a private dining area in back that was more suited for the group that quickly grew to a couple dozen-strong. Danny eventually embraced the convergence as a good thing, joking about the *This Is Your Life* feel of the evening. But with the nostalgia also came the ache of missing those absent; like Curly. And Max, Danny's best buddy growing up, a guy who went on to be an Army Ranger for two tours then came home just to die of a pulmonary embolism on his boat a half mile from home on the Bay. And then there was Molly, in a category all her own. The woman whose death brought her husband a hard-earned perspective that might have impressed even her. That her death could continue to expand his introspective range sometimes slammed him to the canvas. And whether it was merely the revisionism of regret, a cruel joke or dead on, it didn't matter much anymore. He had thought her the Queen of Earthly Misery in his life, and his Irish Angel of Everything Good upon her death, and that thought, now, was like a non-fatal dagger to his heart. Danny wasn't sure what was worse - the stab, or the non-fatal part.

Still, it was a nice evening with old friends who had remained as gracious and unassuming as Danny remembered them. Deferential in conversation and clearly happy for the time with a favorite son, it was also clear that the chance to hang with Rinny and Mo was what most lit their faces. And to see your kids proffer such grace in return was, Danny and Molly had oft agreed, among the finest feelings a parent can know. The interaction was a reminder for Danny of the sincerity at the core of most folks indigenous to The Harbor. That these were people of pure intention and who cared for their own. Sure, a few of them remained a little too fixated on whoever said what about the building of The Majesty and a bit defensive over whatever Danny did or didn't do about this or that. Whatever. He knew it was just the way these mostly non-golfing folks chose to let him know they were with him.

It was understood by all that it was to be an early evening. And it the went as Danny might have hoped, even if he never would have considered planning such a thing. And despite some decent acting, there was no need to let on that his hunch had been correct. It was confirmed by Angie Mannich after one too many Merlots, that yeah, Manda Moran had arranged for the gathering at The Green Mountain Grille   They left The Grille a little after 8:30. Mo insisted on being dropped off at The Majesty; said he wanted to check the scores, get their tee time for tomorrow and see how high D Mo had actually soared on the leader board. It was a beautiful night, the course was on the way home, and Mo said he would just as soon walk back to his grandma's later. Crusty was at the wheel and executed a stealthy top-five worldwide drop-off maneuver.

Mo immediately headed to the clubhouse and purchased a couple cans of beer before returning to the big scoreboard. At 146 after 36 holes, his dad had jumped from T29 to eighth place alone. As Crusty had projected, the scores were higher for the second round in general and for those who played in the afternoon in particular. Zane Williams shot 74 and had the lead at 142, two under par. Salamone had 76 and made the cut, the highest cut ever for the Open at 158. Mo couldn't help but think of his dad's spotty putting. Danny's touch seemed fine, but nothing was going in.

It was just about as dark as it was going to get. The night was nearly perfect, with temps in the mid-60s, dry, and just enough of a breeze to move any bugs along. The players still hanging out were, like Mo, drinking. It was tough to tell by body language who had made the cut and who had simply chosen to linger at The Majesty a little longer. The patio deck still had a dozen or so people enjoying food, beverages and the view over the bay. From the clubhouse, Morgan's Forehead offered a monstrous phallic silhouette, purple-black against the remnants of reflected light off the water. From the 18th tee, the Forehead appeared quite different. Like everything in life, Morgan's appearance varied according to the angle from which it was viewed, and very few would have had the chance to see two of those views had it not been for the construction of The Majesty.

Someone approached Mo. He couldn't identify the guy at first, his face blocked of the available light coming from the clubhouse.

"Hey Mo, long time." It was Will Crinzi, a kid he played with in the Juniors.

"Willie, how you doing, Man? I was just looking at your line on the board. Tough one coming in today, huh?"

Crinzi repositioned his clubs on his shoulder. "Damn 18th green is a rock. Laid up too far back and in the rough, had to hit a seven-iron…and hit it good. The thing plowed right through that useless little bunker behind the green right into the crap. Triple. Bye-bye."

"Maybe you could use a beer?"

∞

It was a little after eleven when Mo returned to the Moran Family Manor. His cell phone clock had four aces showing. He sneaked in and was quickly in the basement without being heard. Mo cringed when he awarded himself a top-five worldwide commendation in the quiet-as-a-cat-after-six-beers-and-a-bunch-o'-shots category. Slowly, silently, he opened the patio door to let in the perfect night air. Voices. Crusty and D Mo. *Waiting up for me? What am I, a kid?* They were sitting out on the deck above him. He listened intently but could catch only snippets of what Danny was saying.

"…results…not horrible…who knows…the number. The rate's what matters…" A couple times he heard the letters PS…*PS something…A…K…?*

Crusty was a little louder. Probably a beer-related condition. Crusty liked his beer; the little guy could put 'em away like movie house Milk

Duds. "Well, Dannymo, I can tell you this, your daughter kind of wondered what was up. Thought you were going for a personal record for total pisses over 18 holes. Not that she said it like that…"

Mo heard his dad go "sshh…" and then Crusty, quieter now, continued. "That's why we walked well aheada you guys, give you some privacy."

Mo knew he was lit up, but focused now, trying to sort, straining to hear.

Danny spoke again. "Sometimes…it's just that way…" Then there was something Mo couldn't hear. Then nothing. Mo was getting tired now. Really tired. He heard his dad clear his throat. Quiet again. It was then that a drunkish Mo though he heard some words that scared him, his dad's faint voice, "…d called twice…" Or was it like the letter "t." Whispers and soft voices. Mo wasn't sure, could it be D Mo said 'Cindy?'

Then a too-loud, "Aye-yigh-yigh," from Crusty. Followed by, what seemed like "Does Carter know?"

By Crusty's reaction, Mo figured he heard right. He couldn't hear clearly anymore…garbled talk…drifting asleep…damn…he thought he'd lay down on the carpet by the patio door. *Yeah, better, much better, voices…more comfortable…silence…nothing…*

∞

Thirsty. Really thirsty. Mo rolled over and his arm smashed into the patio screen door. He figured out where he was eventually. He got up, felt the rug dents on his face, and, moving shakily, checked his phone for the time. 2:12 a.m. He checked the little basement refrigerator. A six-pack of Pabst Blue Ribbon and what looked to be some tiny bottles of prehistoric ginger ale. Mo shuddered. He went to the steps and crept up to the kitchen. His grandma kept a little lighthouse lamp on and it put out just enough light in the kitchen to get around while pulling off a snack raid in the darkness. He grabbed a 32-ounce bottle of purple Gatorade from the refrigerator and headed back down the steps.

Mo was grateful for the fourth time in two days that the steps were solidly built and carpeted and not at all creaky. Downstairs, he took in a ridiculous amount of purple fluid in one unbroken chug. He wasn't sure, but he thought he could feel his petals rise. Then he heard a noise upstairs. Very quiet, but it was something. Mo struggled to hear over his breathing after what might have been a North American record for length of chug-a-lug. He heard more sounds, muffled.

The hell... Mo still had his clothes and shoes on, the upside to passing out on nights when an intruder intrudes. He eased his way back up the steps with the patience of a groggy man with no plan; again the steps refused to squeak, solid sonsabitches. He felt his heart kick in again. He stayed behind the stairwell wall when he got to the top. Someone trying to be quiet. He heard the refrigerator door open. Mo took a quick peak. *Huh?* It was his dad poking around in the refrigerator. His back to Mo, fully dressed in black slacks and golf shirt. There were traces of powdery dirt on his slacks, the lighter kind, like infield dirt that remains after the slap-off, and his dad's hair looked pinned in and darker around the back and side hairline perimeter, symptomatic of a dried sweat situation. *Weird.*

D Mo was careful to be quick and quiet, but he had the body language of a guy not finding what he was looking for and gave up. *The purple Gatorade? Shit.* While his dad filled a glass with tap water, Mo Mo hurried back down the carpeted steps to the basement. Faster than a teen in heat he undressed to his boxers and slipped under the covers of Nana Manda's sofa sleeper. Then he listened, and waited. For what, Mo did not know. He downed some more Gatorade, spilling some on his chest and neck. *Lazy ass.* His dad did not come down. Mo's mind started working quicker. He knew there was no way his dad would not check on him, make sure he found his way home. But...he could have easily come down earlier and seen Mo face down on the carpet. Or, since he was coming in from the outside, wherever the hell he was, he could have looked in by the patio door. Mo wondered what his dad would have made of that. *Uh, yeah...I missed the pull-out bed...*

Mo was awake now. *The hell is D Mo up to? The hell was he and Crusty talking about earlier?* He was pretty certain he was awake for good.

Tomorrow. 36 holes. Check that, today, 36 holes.

∞

Chapter 43

"We're taking a cart for the first round," said Danny as they pulled into The Majesty's parking lot.

Mo was stunned. And elated.

It had been a shaky morning for him, and the thought of slogging up and down The Majesty for 10 hours over 15 miles and 36 holes didn't hold the same allure and sense of invigoration as it had when he imagined it all the day before. It wasn't that he couldn't do it. He knew he'd bounce back before they made the turn since he'd rebounded from this state many times before, but there was no escaping the current conditions. His head was partly cloudy, his stomach an uncertain squall, and his legs were dead calm (emphasis on dead). Still, his dad was a devout walker, and even at 49, the middle-aged jungle cat would concede very little to anyone physically.

Danny stared straight ahead and spoke slowly. "The fittest of the Nepalese sherpas would struggle to feather a wedge off an uneven lie to a tucked pin coming down the stretch after walking this place twice." The father looked far fresher than the son, but he hadn't said a word about anyone's condition, including his own. "Very few, whether in contention or otherwise, will walk today; we will for the final round."

"Your call, D Mo, I'm with you," said Mo. "Rain, heat, bugs and hills…we've done it all. We go cart, I'll chauffeur you to the best of my ability."

Danny looked at his son. "I'll be driving," he said.

Mo opened his mouth, but then shut it because he had no idea what he wanted to come out of it. It wasn't the time for debates. "Fine," he finally said, maybe a little too casually.

He felt like a useless doofus riding shotgun in the cart; scooting around the clubhouse area and over to the range and then down to the chipping green, so he acted like he was studying a scorecard. Kind of like when his dad would drive him to grade school on Danny's way to work and Mo would glance at a book when they passed the other subdivision kids tossing Frisbees or footballs as they waited for the school bus. He'd just go about replacing divots, raking bunkers and tending the flag for 18 holes and enjoy the ride. *Fine,* he thought. *No problems mon,* but then…ah, shit, who was he kidding. Mo was on edge. In addition, he had a case of cotton-mouth, and his stomach roiled, the beers and whiskey and purple Gatorade vying for supremacy over the absorbency of his Grandma's very game flapjacks. And, like too much of his adult life, questions were popping up like prairie dogs about too many things he wasn't all that comfortable asking about – and they weren't going to go away no matter what he put into his body or however he attempted to clear his clouded head.

Danny's two partners for the third round were just out of college and had turned pro just before The Open. A common time to turn for those with their sights set on Tour glory. They introduced themselves to Danny as Conner James and Jason Mann. James, unshaven with a white Nike hat atop close-cropped brown hair, had been the number one guy for Southern Miss, and Mann must have played at Coastal Carolina, according to the team logo on his bag. He wore black framed sunglasses with yellow lenses and seemed to have no hair anywhere on his being. Black Calloway cap.

Mo got out of the little boy side of the cart and was about to introduce himself when his dad did it for him. Mo headed toward the two guys just as Danny was shaking hands with each and introduced himself as Dan Moran. By all appearances, they had never heard of Danny Moran, nor did they seem to recognize Mo from his baseball exploits. When his dad introduced his son to Conner James and Jason Mann as "Mo-Mo, my son." Mo rolled his eyes. He would have preferred to have been just plain old Mo. "Mo-Mo my son," said quickly, sounded like a side item from a Chinese menu. Mo knew it was probably just his perception of it, that he felt uneasy for other reasons, but just hearing the words, "my son," struck him…*yeah, my son…the guy making*

out with my girlfriend or the guy passed out on the floor in his clothes...
...yeah...he's his "own damn Mo alright."

Jason Mann was up ahead by their cart, scrounging around for something in his golf bag. Mo was about to stick out his hand to Conner James, but the kid kept his distance and with a tiny smile tossed off a half-assed wave. "Yo. Is it...Mo-Mo...really?" Jason the hairless Mann then headed back to the 10th tee but simply nodded to Mo and said "Okay." Mo shrugged. *Okay?*

John G. *"Call me JG"* Schmitz smelled of a cologne that might impress certain people and his burgundy and black leather teaching saddles gleamed. Concise and friendly to a fault, he was the anti-Shelly. He wrapped up his pre-round instructions with "You guys have fun now...we got two young stallions and Danny Mo, the reincarnated thoroughbred...how 'bout that?" JG looked over at Danny, waiting for him to say something. Danny's smile wasn't much but apparently was all he had to give. He turned his back to everyone and did little half-swings with his three-wood. Mo stood at the back of the tee, watching. D Mo usually had something ready to fire back.

JG waited a beat. Then, "Best of luck to you all."

Young James and Mann each smashed drivers down the middle, towering back-to-back jacks, their balls eventually coming down over the crest of the hill and out of sight. They exchanged knowing looks... Bash Boyyzz, Brothers in the Fraternity of Power 2 Spare.

"Big balls, fellas," said Danny as he went about putting his tee into the ground.

Neither kid said anything audible in return. They paid little attention to Danny as he went through his routine, and after he turned over a hot little draw with his three-wood, also down the center, Jason Mann grunted, "Okay." Again. Mo thought it a little strange, but then neither of the bashers had exuded much warmth from the get-go. Not that it mattered; he knew his dad would not give a rip what the two "stallions" thought, said, believed in or prayed for. The kids were rolling in their cart before Danny's ball would come to rest.

Game on.

JG whispered, "Kick their ass," to Danny as he walked back to his cart.

Danny smiled wearily. "That'd be asses, JG."

Mo took his dad's three-wood and put it away before sliding into the passenger seat of the cart.

"Mo," said Danny, thumbing his son to get out of the cart. A flashing thought crossed Mo's mind…that his dad was going to make him walk. And he was right, but only over to the other side of the cart. "You drive."

Mo smiled. The combination of his growing dislike for the "stallions" along with taking over the wheel was rejuvenating. "Now we go," he said.

They found Danny's ball, which had benefited from the forward catapult from the fairway's down-slope, a good eight yards beyond the nearly side-by-side balls of the Bash Boyyzz. Mo thought the kids masked their incredulousness at being behind Old Man Mo quite well, but something was there. Mo overheard something like "sprinkler" and "kick." All three hit the green and Conner James drained a 20-footer for birdie, while Jason Mann and Danny made easy pars. Over the remainder of the front nine, Danny continued to hit the ball solidly. The wind was picking up, and getting approach shots to stop on the greens required additional calculations and trajectory management. The youngsters could hit the ball very high with their irons, which helped in holding the greens downwind, but throwing the ball way up into the air also exposed it the unpredictable spank of winds reformulated by the hills and valleys. Both Jason Mann and Connor James found themselves in some bedeviling spots early, where getting up and down had become the lesser of their worries compared to just finding their balls. Both had made a couple of birdies, but each had also made a mess of things on other holes.

Now, even Danny, who controlled his ball with high and low shots, cuts and draws, holding his flight lines with spin and finesse, missed his share of greens. But when he did, Lazarus came alive in Danny's hands and cleaned up any spillage. The game had gone from being mostly about ball striking skills, which pretty much was the key to avoiding big numbers and an early tournament flame-out, to a game of instinct and strategy, the willingness to forsake birdies for long two-putt pars and, as always in the major events, short-game confidence. Daring was usually a final round thing, and generally dumb if it wasn't.

Mo had not seen his dad in the heat of battle since caddying for him as a teenager in Danny's heyday, a time when he wasn't quite as attuned to game plans, patience and tactics. Earlier, on the sharp dogleg left 12th hole, their third, Danny had played his specially designed parachute shot with a "teed-high" three-wood, the ball coming almost straight down over a densely wooded area and short of the next batch of trouble. He made a long swing with a high, full, follow-through to achieve the hoist, the elevation required for the vertical drop. When Danny handed the club to Mo, he said, "That's as good as I've got."

"Perfect," said Mo. He had seen this swing before. It was a big action, undercut kind of shot where a lot of motion was made to achieve a softer effect. He believed it was perfect, again, for the third time in a row, but it was a blind shot, and Mo always felt better once they turned the corner of the dogleg and could see the ball in the fairway.

Conner James and Jason Mann looked at each other. They either hadn't thought of the parachute shot, or weren't completely certain of the actual over/under fit between the gangs of conifers lurking on either side of Easy Street. Both had just seen Danny knock his three-wood past their drives two holes earlier, and while they knew he used the slope to his advantage, they knew the old guy still had some pop in his bat. James was the first to go back to the cart to put his iron away and come back with a metal-wood. Then Mann followed suit. A five-wood for Southern James and a three-wood for the Coastal Carolina Mann.

They ripped high hooks further left than Danny, easily biting off even more of the dogleg. Danny had already pointed out to Mo in the practice round that he could cut off more of the dogleg on the parachute hole if he wanted, but it would leave a partial wedge from an awkward distance,' and he would never be able to attack a tight front pin on the small, crowned green. Ferguson called it "our turtleback green." The kids, however, followed the lead of the old plow horse and tried to do

him one better. Stallion James' five-wood wasn't as left as Stallion
Mann's three-wood and it never had a chance. As gorgeous as it looked
going over the trees, it was never going to settle down until it found the
far junk beyond the framing pines. No doubt he thought his five-wood
would carry roughly the same as Danny's three-wood, not knowing how
much the hall-of-famer had taken off his shot to position it in a spot that
was "as good as I've got," and what "Mo Mo, my son" called "perfect."

Lost ball. Return to tee. Three-iron. A three putt triple bogey seven
for Conner James.

Mann's ball was well left of Danny's. It had hooked forward toward
the green and finished a mere 66 yards from the center of the green and
with 57 to the pin, according to Danny's Laser Link gun that Mo liked to
use for everyone's shot. With a tight lie, a front hole location, and a steep
bunker that Loren Ferguson called "The Joker" because it was in the
shape of the smile of Batman's nemesis, protecting the front of the green,
Mann's dicey wedge was going to be long if he was smart, or in the
bunker if he got cute. Turned out he was not smart, and when he tossed
his cap into the air in dismay and fully revealed his dark-framed yellow-
eyed shades and hairless head, Mo had a hard time imagining anyone
calling him cute. Not that bald was bad, but that combined with Jason
Mann's funky glasses and look of bewilderment gave him the
appearance of a manic Mr. Potato Head.

Coming to the 18th hole, their ninth, Danny was even par. The Bash
Boyyzz, James and Mann, were five and six over respectively. Danny
had played the signature par five 18th over par for the first two rounds.
Mo told his dad that Morgan was probably not very pleased with what
he was witnessing on "his hole."

This time Danny went with his now utterly reliable three-wood. He
had thought of going with the driver, as solid contact and a helping
wind might get him past Morgan's Forehead, and maybe hit the green in
two with a tempting back hole-location. The three-iron off the tee the
day before made the lay-up a little too long for comfort.

The Bash Stallions never considered anything but drivers and
unleashed long nothing-to-lose bombs down the middle. Danny played

a perfect lay-up on his second, then hurried over to a gulch left of the fairway that separated the 18th fairway from The Forehead. There, Mo knew his dad could piss, again, in private, for the second time this nine and roughly the same spot where he had each of the first two rounds. They would have some time now. The kids would be waiting for the green to clear before trying to hit heroic, round-resuscitating second shots to the green below. Mo gave his dad some alone time before driving the cart closer to the ridge. There, he saw his dad staring up at Morgan. He continued to look upward for awhile even after having zipped. When Danny made it back to the cart, Mo noticed Danny's final round black shirt had darkened further around his chest and armpits.

"You okay, D Mo?" Mo knew it was a bit of a hike back to the level of the fairway but... "You're all sweaty."

Danny shrugged. "No breeze down there, very different from up here."

Mo left it at that. He drove the cart to the center of the fairway where they sat some 250 yards from the green far below and to their left. The view over the bay was spectacular, made all the more so with Danny Mo in all likelihood gaining on the field as the wind continued to put its sordid twist on the already difficult conditions at The Majesty. It gave them a chance to relax for a moment and take in a most glorious place.

At the bar the night before, Loren Ferguson had gone on and on telling Mo that he was extremely confident that The Majesty was going to get a US Open if he could add parking, lengthen the range, buy some inland farmland for additional corporate hospitality sites and widen two access roads, and something to do with sub-soil which was to be costly but "as good as done if it means the world would be coming to The Majesty."

Mo put his leg up on the cart just left of the steering wheel. Danny sat forward. "Rinny and Crusty, see 'em down there? To the right of the green, next to Frank Whats-his-name." Crusty had been confident he could fix a shower leak in Manda's master bath and get to The Majesty before Danny made the turn, and so Rinny stayed back as well to help with some wheelbarrow-required gardening chores that Manda had put off until the recent heat wave had passed. They would be along to walk the final 27 holes.

"I see 'em."

"Good to have the whole team."

"Wait till this afternoon…those folks from last night show up, look out."

"If they show, we'll see." Danny smiled. "Might not know what's going on…but they'll know who to pull for."

It was finally Jason the Potato Mann's turn to play and his solid three-iron bounded over the green without ever considering putting down stakes. He would soon be scouring the same heathery grass and cliff ferns behind the green where Danny had been the first day. Conner James then hit a much higher iron shot than Potato Mann, but even his high draw landed hard about mid-green and ended up in the back bunker. Both were properly dismayed and offered individual renditions from the popular post-collegiate *"can you fucking believe that"* collection of victims' rights picketing chants, nicely accessorized with some tasteful *as seen on TV* hand and head gestures designed to confirm that the Devil's lone victory over God was indeed his diabolical ability to turn the 18th green extra firm for their shots only. After those Tour de Force performances, the stallions continued their equine bond and cart camaraderie through a mutual taste in half-laugh profanity mixed with other back and forth whinnies until they got to the vicinity of their balls.

Before the lads got there, Danny nipped a wedge directly at the back left flag 136 yards away, but he carried the ball about three or four yards farther than he wanted. The ball tried to check but skipped and then rolled slowly off the back of the green, no more than 15 feet away from the hole. When Danny and Mo got to the green, Danny's ball was just past the fringe and a couple inches into some against the grain rough in what would be called an unpredictable lie.

Mo wondered about the existence of God when Mr. Potato Head found his ball sitting up sweet and lovely on a dead tuft of something yellowish brown and pitched his ball to a foot and made birdie. When Conner James blew his bunker shot a little more than 40 feet past the hole and went on to make his birdie putt, Mo no longer wondered but seriously doubted the existence of God; and when Danny, with the sweet and loving Lazarus in his hands inexplicably *double-hit* his chip from the funky, against-the-grain lie inches from the fringe, he was certain that the God he thought he knew had ceased operations and was busy outsourcing to Asia like everyone else these days – and was taking His sweet-ass time in getting the specs to Buddha at that.

Rinny gasped when the double-hit chip happened, but Danny didn't even change expressions and went ahead and made a 16-footer for bogey, the longest putt he'd made thus far in the tournament. Danny was one over for the nine, Conner James turned in four over 40, and Jason Mann was at 41, five over for the round. Driving to the first tee, Mo marveled at how his dad slouched back in the cart as if he hadn't a care in the world. Mo once double-hit his ball trying to gouge it out from under an evergreen tree in a junior tournament and was mortified; it was then he decided a double-hit in golf was like passing gas that turns out to be more substantial than just gas…on a first date. It wasn't tragic, but recovering from it took some doing.

"Man, I hit a good putt there," said Danny.

"You've hit a lot of good putts, D Mo…that one just happened to go in."

"I needed that – the need, you know - to make one. I was kind of just going along."

"I understand," said Mo. "I think."

Danny was looking straight ahead at the groups still waiting near their destination on the first tee; there would be a crossover delay. "I'm sure you do, Mo Mo, my son." he said.

Mo noticed the corner of his dad's eyes scrunching slightly. Ol' D Mo, the bastard, he knew exactly what he was doing during those first tee introductions. *Act like a kid, get treated like a kid.*

On the back, Danny Mo took command of the group for good. He played the nine in one under par - two birdies, six pars and a three putt bogey - merging gracefully with the elements, the land and the occasion.

Conner Jim and Mr. Potato Head Mann quickly plummeted from their
spate of good fortune on the ninth hole and fell apart almost completely
as the wind grew to the two-club variety. Forsaken by God and
persecuted at every turn, they gave in to their martyrdom and
floundered through weak takes on the tough-luck chuckles that identify
wannabes in denial. They fired 83 and 84 respectively, and Mo did not
care who had what. It no longer mattered. The Stallions, the Bash Boyyzz
with Power 2 Spare, were also-rans.

∞

Lunch in the clubhouse was perfect. That is to say, it was delicious
and free. Loren Ferguson had set up a semi-private area for the Moran
clan and Crusty. Rinny had called her grandmother to tell her that
Danny's even par 72 had vaulted him into third place, the lowest score
of anyone in contention due to the demanding conditions and final day
pressure. Manda was so excited she decided to join the four of them for
lunch even though she and Hank had already eaten.

Zane Williams, whose group had played longer than anyone else's
in the increasing winds, maintained his lead by posting 74, impressive
under the conditions. Not as impressive, however, as his iron to the 18th
green to set up an easy two putt birdie. Downwind, The Zaner (as he
was known to most) hit an approach so high and soft it came straight
down like an elevator and stopped 15 feet *short* of the pin on the patio-
hard green.

"That," said Danny at the time as he watched from near the first tee,
"was unbelievable."

And Danny knew that he'd get to see The Zaner up close now. As
improbable as it seemed, Danny's nostalgic, bordering on casual and
what some called "ceremonial" appearance in The Wisconsin State Open
had brought him to yet another appearance in the final group.

It had always boggled Danny Moran's unusual mind back when he
had cultivated what he defined as a passion for the work before
tournaments. Sure, he'd competed in championships for which he hadn't
"properly prepared" due to work and family commitments or obstinate
weather or niggling injuries, and actually won a few of those

tournaments without the obsessive prep work. He'd just go out and play, his expectations lessened and a freefalling "we'll-see-what-happens" mindset that sometimes led to good things and "go-figure" victories. Those wins always felt like he pulled off some kind of caper, as if he escaped with a B game and a bunch of luck. Now, it was hitting him all over again, the idea that he might have been better off without the compulsory range labor and going door-to-door in the hallways of his mind, hunting for images, swing-keys and an expanded bandwidth for better golf; the process that fertilized his range-time perfectionism and grew his expectations high enough to give life to his inner Jim Rome and his mocking voice of doubt, a voice he had to muzzle before coming up "huge." Of course, anytime he went into an event without going through his pre-tournament regimen and didn't win, Danny was convinced it was because he didn't get to do his normal preparation. Always something. Always a reason - or not. Golf.

For his three rounds at The Majesty, Danny felt he was responding to general targets that he dialed down to more specific segments, like a kid throwing snowballs at a stop sign until he was, like a lot of NFL quarterbacks, and safeties for that matter,, nailing TO with no thoughts about form. Nothing like those years spent hammering his action into a mold. Now he wondered if maybe his greatest golf achievement had been the ability to overcome his own damned work ethic to win as much as he had. How many times, hitting little checky-chips on the dormant little green in Motown, or cut-shots around the scrub oak on the range at The Ol' Barn, did he hear a more playful inner voice, his own, proclaiming himself "top-five worldwide" at hitting certain shots to random targets at guessed-at yardages with nary a thought of engineering anything. Crazy. Golf.

∞

Chapter 44

Inside the clubhouse, finishing up lunch, Mo shrugged off Crusty's prodding.

Rinny and Manda had just leveled their disgust at the man Manda called, "that evil Andy Salamone," who appeared to be fork-torturing a salad at a nearby table populated with acolytes suckling on the generous teat of B'Gandhi's very presence.

Crusty let out a grunt. "So, Sally hit you where it hurt yesterday?"

"Hardly, Crust." Mo was dismissive. "Had him on his heels so he kicks back by saying that I choked in qualifying. Right. I can mess up pretty good without blaming it on nerves. He can talk if he wants. Don't bother me."

"Your eyes were firebombs, Mo Mo," said Crusty. "Salamone had that smirk going, but I watched him close. He was a little scared, me being the only potential witness and all. He tried to hide it but for a minute he was swallowing spit like sludge from a beer can ash tray."

"That's quite colorful, Parnell," said Manda, looking at Danny. "What's this all about?"

"Nothing," said Mo. "I ran into Salamone in the men's room here, and…some small talk ensued."

"Really, Mo?" asked Danny. "You didn't say anything to me. When, yesterday?"

"Handled it. He said it was a shame I wasn't here as a player, that if I hadn't gagged away the qualifying I wouldn't have to be your, ah, 'beast of burden.'" Mo shrugged. "Just baiting me. Decided to let it go."

Danny seemed amused. "And you were there, Crusty?"

"Rinny and me were having a coffee at a table by those windows." Crusty pointed at the other side of the clubhouse. "I saw Sally head into the can and I knew Mo was still in there." Crusty shrugged. "Thought it might be interesting. I go in and they're by the sinks staring at each other," said Crusty. "Know what I mean."

"Well, what's important to remember," interjected Rinny, "is that Salamone is only, I believe, 21 shots behind you, Daddy. So watch your back."

Their plates had been taken away, but everyone was working on water refills. Danny was 25 minutes from starting the final round. He was two shots behind the newly-turned professional and former BYU All-American Zane Williams, and one behind Mike Van Sickle, a nationally ranked senior-to-be at Marquette University.

Loren Ferguson came around the corner to their semi-private table (semi-private because of some tall ferns and other potted plants that set them apart from most of the main dining area). Danny had become a big part of the Open story now, and he was grateful for the semi-privacy.

"We've rustled up some reinforcements on account of you, Danny. Some extra rangers, concession help, and the like. You should have told me." Loren was smiling.

Danny said nothing, but his expression suggested, *Get to the point, Loren*.

"Take a look," said Loren, "east windows."

Danny got up, as did Mo and Crusty. "Holy shit," said Crusty.

"Wow," said Mo. "Guess they take their Opens seriously here in the Harbor."

Manda and Rinny stood up and joined the others a couple steps into the main dining room and laughed. "They came," said Manda. "I just knew they would."

Danny looked at Loren, whose various businesses regularly employed nearly a thousand people throughout Door County; more in summer.

"Okay...I should have known," said Loren. "We worked hard to give the afternoon off to folks who wanted to come – been a scheduling nightmare - but we've got it covered." He rolled his eyes. "I think."

Rinny scanned the mass of humanity milling about by the scoreboard and the putting green. "A lot of our friends from last night at the restaurant."

"You bet," said Loren. "Quite a few took off on their own, too. Danny Mo belongs to the community."

"I'm so, so, proud," said a dewy-eyed Manda. "All these folks…after all the bitterness…"

"Do they know anything about golf?" Crusty didn't wait for an answer. "Hell, who gives a cow-pie…it's a beautiful thing."

Mo looked at his dad, who looked to be a proud man stunned, and maybe a little concerned.

"I'm gonna use the men's room and then head to the range, why don't you guys go say hello to some of the folks."

"Good idea, Danny." said Manda. "I'm going to head back home after you tee off…you know, check on Hank. I'll come back up to watch you come in on 18. However it goes today, we're all so proud of you."

"Indeed," said Loren Ferguson, nodding. "Manda, when you come back, just drive up to the clubhouse and we'll have someone park your car."

"Good," said Danny. "Mo, no need to meet me at the range. Just gonna hit a few three-woods. Keep it behaving. Meet you at the putting green."

"Got ya." Mo followed the other three as they headed toward the exit. Curious glances from the remaining clubhouse dwellers came their way, like they were a famous band or part of a dog-fighting ring or something.

Danny emerged from the restroom with purpose, but slowed quickly as if by drag-chute. The view out the south windows of the clubhouse did that to everyone, it seemed, with the purple-blue shimmer of the Green Bay as the backdrop to the 18th green and Morgan's Forehead, a giant Jenga tower of stone splitting the difference between the two. He could see the corner of the parking lot from this angle and, now, taking up that space, was a Lamers motor coach. The people disembarking had familiar faces.

The Barnstormers.

Carter, Baggie, Boots and Thad "Boo" Booher were part of a cavalcade of rubber-necking members from The Old Barn coming up the walkway to the clubhouse. Danny didn't know what to think about his growing army of supporters. *Geez, even Captain Jack.* It was a new and nostalgic feeling all at once. Many inside the clubhouse were looking at him now, not just glancing. Once again, he was *the* story. No more flying under the radar.

"Ahh...I was beginning to wonder if they were going to get here in time." Loren had just exited his office and stopped to put a hand on Danny's back. He nodded toward the bus. "What are you Danny, a star in the East?" He smiled, slapped Danny on the back and left the hall-of-famer alone to ponder whatever champions ponder in the moments before engagement.

Danny was pondering two things. The first was a minor concern, how all these people pulling for him might become a distraction. More so for his playing partners, but hell, everybody would just have to deal with it. Danny had more experience in front of galleries than most. What gnawed at him now was how all this commotion might affect something else. In the first three rounds he had stolen off to familiar little nooks and gulches along the way, semi-private spots that might not be quite as semi-private with a gallery the size to which this was growing. He had come to embrace a warm feeling from the fact that he was pissing (in some cases, exactly) where he did as a kid, when he used to go adventuring up and down the shoreline. Not only *where* he peed, but, strangely enough, *how.*

His dad had always told him he could never "go" down a hill when roaming the bluffs because you never knew who might be below you. Curly did, however, make an exception for a former friend, Conrad Philbert, the owner of a failed glass and window business in Rock Harbor. Connie, as he was known, was the former treasurer for the Rotary Club in the early '70s and reportedly emptied the club's funds into his pockets after dumping his wife and four kids and skipping town with his now-defunct company's accounts receivable clerk. Plus he once tried overcharging Curly for some shoddy work he never made good on.

"You have my permission to leak all over that guy," was Curly's metaphorical direction to the Moran boys. "He's a jerk, so piss on him."

One round at The Majesty and it all came flooding back to Danny. Some habits never leave a guy, while others lay dormant until whatever recognition factors reactivate the circle-back psychology of familiar things - and a man pissing outdoors in long-trusted places would seem to be a trigger easily pulled. Danny figured Andy Salamone was his Conrad Philbert, and that fathers and sons sometimes grew closer through the shared scorn for either's enemies. Contempt was a great unifier in many a loving family; an enemy of one meant an enemy of all. And while Danny and Molly Moran had generally steered their kids away from hating anyone, Mo Mo had come to hate Sally long before the hawk incident on the range and Danny loved him for it; just as Curly had given permission for any Moran to "piss on Connie."

But this was by far the largest gallery ever for a State Open - even bigger than when Steve Stricker took some time off from the PGA Tour to compete in 1998 and 2000. Danny would have to be covert. When he mentioned this to Mo, his son again suggested he consider using the facilities on the course. "Immaculate, nice vanilla fragrance," he had said. To Danny, it just wouldn't be the same.

With so many friends, locals and Barnstormers showing up to support his dad, Mo was relieved from having to address each individual as might be expected had it only been a dozen or so trooping along. D Mo had pointed this out to him and it was turning out to be true. There was something faceless about hundreds of people bunched together; no one set of eyes expected too much attention in return. With Crusty and Rinny shepherding them, it would be up to them to interact and/or socialize as Hospitality Reps of Team Mo.

The wind had not let up, but neither did it seem to be getting worse. The first tee was already horse-shoed with spectators 15 minutes before the final group was to go off, unheard of for a state open. Salamone's group, which included Boozer, went off the 10th hole without notice. When the introductions finally came, JG Schmitz played it straight, British Open straight. No fist pumps, commentary or neck and shoulder massages this time. Shelly was seated at the starter's table under the tent

canopy and stared straight ahead. Danny had handed Mo a piece of
paper folded into fours on which he'd written, "To Shelly," and asked
that Mo present it to the now-silent tournament official before they left
the first tee box.

Though a little younger, Mike Van Sickle seemed to have at least met
Zane Williams Jr. before, no doubt through junior events or over the
course of a couple NCAA seasons. The tall Williams was book smart,
physically gifted and, of course, scary long. Van Sickle was also big-
league long and his game featured a sense of occasion despite a putting
stroke that lived with intermittent mood swings. Danny had known
Mike's dad when he was the golf beat writer for The Milwaukee Journal
some 15 years earlier. Gary Van Sickle had gone on to write for Golf
World and was currently a senior golf writer for *Sports Illustrated*. Van
Sickle's friend (as well as Danny's), Gary D'Amato, had taken Van
Sickle's place at the state's major daily and Danny noticed the two
writers were sharing a cart, as was allowed for media types, to track the
fourth round action at The Majesty.

"Hi Fellas, I'm Zane Williams Jr., officially, but most call me The
Zaner, or when my dad is around, like today - you can just call me 'The,'
and my dad, who's going to drive our cart today, is called 'Thee.'"

Mo thought the guy had a friendly air about him, which made the
third person affectation seem almost bearable.

Zane Williams Sr., one of those heavy-set guys with chins that came
in waves and who had zero resemblance to his kid, hustled up to the tee
box. "Nice to meet you guys. Yes, I am *Thee*. It's important for Junior to
know who came first."

Mo chucked. He couldn't decide if the old man was serious or not.
His dad stepped in and introduced himself and "My son, Mo Moran."

Before he knew it, Mo found himself saying "You can call me Mo
Mo." He looked at his dad.

D Mo flashed a post-par-saving-putt look of satisfaction. Mo noticed
that *Dude's way at peace*.

Mike Van Sickle had a Marquette teammate caddying for him, a
good guy and good player named Mike McDonald. Mike the Caddie

eliminated most confusion by graciously dropping the M from his name and became Ike, as he had done for the morning round. So the final group of players and caddies was, as Mo told his dad, "*Thee* and The, Mike and Ike, and Danny Mo and Mo Mo Mo."

After a couple of tee ball bombs from Van Sickle and The Zaner, Danny didn't wait for the hometown cheers to subside, but instead played right through some ongoing hoots and started his round with a serviceable drive. Mo waved and Danny directed his big slow nod thing toward his mother as she started toward the parking lot. Before they left the first tee, Mo pulled the note to Shelly from his pocket and dutifully handed it to the old man. Shelly hesitated for a second and looked skeptically at Mo before taking the note between his thumb and forefinger as if it were a filthy sock.

Danny and Mo headed out to take on The Majesty for a final time. Rinny, Crusty and Carter led the less-than-instinctual gallery down the cart path to the left of the final threesome. As Mo walked with his dad, he glanced back at Shelly. The old man was looking at the piece of paper, confused, repeatedly flipping it over. And then he crumpled it into his fist.

"So…what was in the note to Shelly?"

"Nothing," said Danny.

"Nothing? " Mo looked at his dad.

"Absolutely nothing. "

He expected to see a smile on his dad's lips, but Danny's expression, too, gave away nothing. Mo threw his dad's clubs over his shoulder and laughed to himself. Lunch and the big crowd, including a bunch of old friends from The Old Barn, had put a little giddy-up in his step and vanquished the remnants of his early morning queasiness.

Mo had good reasons for observing his dad's behavior a little more closely of late. D Mo didn't play that "top-five worldwide" game anymore, but he was just as confounding in other ways. All harmless, Mo figured, but with Danny's concerns over his pissing freedom and, hazy as Mo was on it, that conversation he overheard between his dad and Crusty had Mo wondering if these breaks were prostate-related.

Prostate cancer was the first of the cancers Grandpa Curly had before he died. Yet the act of gaining relief seemed to be comforting, almost uplifting, for his father over their four previous rounds. His dad would mumble comments like, "going there takes me back," as well as other takes on the same theme, seemingly pleased to forsake the comforting vanilla of the swanky on-course restrooms at The Majesty. Maybe it was a part of being 49-years-old, but such a fixation, so quickly followed by the note to Shelly containing "absolutely nothing," well, it had Mo scratching his head, took him back to when his dad thought he heard the chorus of what he called the *Jesus Christ Superstar* song coming from two barking of dogs the day they buried Mo's mom. Mo wasn't sure it was what his Grandpa Curly had in mind when he would call his son, *the one and only Danny Mo*, but Grandpa sure wasn't wrong about it.

Mo decided to let further questions about the non-note drop. He knew his dad would have an answer ready that might be just as cryptic or crazy, or worse…no answer at all. Circumstances aside, this was a man who waxed sadly and loudly in a shanked eulogy for his wife about how the blue carpet of the church's alter matched his blue robe, which matched the blue of the Boise State's football field. Three years later, when Mo finally asked his dad about it, D Mo simply shrugged and suggested he ask Dummy Mo about it. "Again?" was Mo's reply, which made his dad chuckle.

Mo worked through the "absolutely nothing" note in his mind. Their last communication was Shelly flipping Danny Mo the bird. Just what could a blank note addressed to Shelly mean? "I have nothing to say to you"? Or maybe it was just D Mo's way of calling Shelly a *blankety-blank*. Or the ol' 'If you can't say something nice…' or some other Tosh.0-type riff.

The hundreds in the gallery for the final group, while quite loud in their support for Danny Mo, fell into a library-like hush whenever any of the three players were over their balls. The Zaner was a different cat, consistently referring to himself in the third person, and a monster with the driver. Mo had to admit, the guy was deserving of his bomber reputation, but Mo gave no ground on how he'd compare, how he might measure up on these holes, under these conditions, with the fairways as firm as they'd become. And until he had the chance to compete against The Zaner, he would accept no one's conclusion. When Danny reacted with mild disbelief over one of The Zaner's tee shots, Mo wasn't sure if his dad was tweaking him or The Zaner, maybe to get the kid to swing even harder later in the round. Still, Mo decided to take it a little personal, if only to feel his dad out on the subject. "You don't think I can get him, D Mo?"

"As far as that one, Mo? Is that what you're asking me? Seriously?"

"Hell yeah, I'm serious."

Danny took a deep breath and let his eyes close for a couple beats before letting the air out slowly; the look of reluctance. But he said nothing.

"Hmm..." said Mo. "Fine. But I'd take him on right now, in tennis shoes." This was Randy Ride all over again, except now it was Mo doing the lobbying instead of the salsa tycoon of West Des Moines.

"Jeez, Mo..."

Mo squinted hard at his dad, and though he appeared to be otherwise nonplussed over this, his once-prized right arm started twitching, as if its still considerable power had no place to go at the moment.

Danny raised his hand to speak.

Mo stopped walking.

Danny turned back and looked at his son. He smiled. Then he said, "No one, Mo, no one go where Mo Mo go." He did one crisp air-karate chop as he said it, then turned away and said no more.

Mo resumed walking down the seventh fairway and betrayed no emotion. But at that moment, ensconced in a bubble of love coming from so many people pulling so hard for his dad, none of it came close to how Mo felt about his dad after his proclamation of "No one!" Actually choked him up a little. Hell, maybe he was just as odd as his dad.

The Zaner proved to as explosive as advertised with three birdies and three bogies after eight holes, but Mike Van Sickle had caught him with two birdies and a bogey. Danny was hitting the ball as purely as he ever had and posted eight straight pars, two back of Van Sickle and The Zaner.

Mike and Ike debated club selection for the first time before playing to the 9th green. He eventually pulled the shot slightly, toward the left edge of the green; and the breeze, though not as strong as it was earlier, kept his ball just left enough to get a miserable break. For as little as many in the gallery knew about golf, their collective gasp at the sight of a bounding golf ball on a mad break for what looked to be a freefall to the bay from their perspective, confirmed just how bad a break it was. Van Sickle's shot was well measured for distance, but his ball took a wicked kick off the steep slope and for every unit of measurable energy that this very slope took off Pig Fisher's lucky shot the day before, it gave that much back and more to Van Sickle's ball as it bounded into the hardscrabble land where the Pigman had gotten his pig on big-time.

"Not good," said Mike, holding his finish but then dropping his club at his feet.

"No," said Ike. "Not."

"Findable?"

"It's a marked hazard," said Ike "But who knows…"

Bill Linneman, the rules official for the final group stood near a red stake and pointed to where the ball had crossed, convinced that Van Sickle would choose to drop versus going after his ball in the craggy terrain, much less try to play out of it and invite an astronomic number to his scorecard. When Pig had gone into this area he was in a desperate emotional state, fortunate to discover his ball quickly, and beyond lucky to have a swing at it. The optimism, and maybe the fitness, of youth prompted Mike and Ike to take on the terrain. Just to be sure.

"It's not good down there," said Mo, "But it was better than I thought it would be when I witnessed the Pigman's meltdown."

"He's a Warrior," said Danny, referring to Mike and the glory days of Marquette basketball. "Let's give him a hand."

"Wow."

"What?" Danny looked around and saw what Mo was looking at.

"Look at Daddy Zaner. The guy is built like a classroom globe, but he's going down to help. He could roll right through that old wall and off the cliff."

Mo sensed *Thee,* the elder Zaner, had become irritated with his son and was looking to prove a point. Boy Zaner reluctantly followed his dad, and made it apparent he felt that going on an expedition for Van Sickle's ball was a waste of time and energy. The Zaner had a championship to win.

Old Man Zaner, portly and gray-haired, showed an agility that belied his appearance. He scampered down the slope like a fat, cocksure squirrel, his gut merely a confirmation that he was more skilled at hunting for his din-din than your standard flat-bellied squirrel. *Thee* was the first after Mike and Ike to reach the rugged purgatorial surface that led to a five-foot rock wall some 12 feet short of a 100-plus-foot drop-off to the bay below. There was, however, no Titleist in sight. The thing could have ricocheted anywhere.

Mo and Danny descended a narrow dirt path that led to the ramshackle rock piles and cracked dirt and dolomite that had been partly shaped by the forces of nature and partly displaced from the construction of the course. They were the last to join the posse after first turning down an offer of help from some beer drinking Barnstormers. Senior Zaner was pretty much crab-walking the surface; his breathing was heavy and his silver hair was breaking free of whatever waxy buildup he used to keep it in captivity. Mo found *Thee's* effort inspirational. He stepped up his own efforts with little slalom actions like a skier through powder on a steep slope. He saw his dad going slowly in horizontal sweeps, regularly stopping to pull back the undergrowth, a thorough and noble technique.

Kid Zaner was looking at the bay and not much else. Every once in a while he'd move a few feet and look into the middle distance or straight down, as if in thought. Intermittently, he'd hold his golf glove with his thumb and forefinger and work it back and forth in a sweeping action as if trying to dry it in the breeze.

It wasn't much more than a minute into the search when Mo heard
Van Sickle say, "Don't bother digging into the bushes. If it isn't playable
I'll just drop where it crossed the hazard. I appreciate the help."

"Hard to believe we can't find it," said Ike, "especially with The
Zaner's superhuman effort."

Everyone stopped for a second and looked at Ike and Zane Jr. The
Zaner moved one step forward but stopped, as if the feeble bush in front
of him was preventing him from getting in Ike's face. His dad stood up,
red-faced and sweating, but said nothing. The Zaner continued to stare
at Ike, who shrugged like he could not care less. Zane the Junior
resumed drying his glove, this time with a wristier action, like a hyper-
active kid with a sparkler. He increased the speed of his glove-snapping
until it broke free of his two-finger grip and went flying a good 10 feet
and into a bush near the rock wall. He gave Ike another look, and, when
The Zaner went to pluck it from the feeble bush, he smiled at the caddie.

"Titleist Seven, Golden Eagle on it?" Zaner made a face.

"That's it," said Van Sickle. "I'll drop where it crossed."

"Now," said The Zaner, squinting at Ike, "what were you saying
there, Eisenhower?"

"Knock it off, Zane." It was his dad, chest heaving and fighting for
breath. "Let's get back to work."

After more tough luck on his drop, with the ball burrowing into the
rough, Mike Van Sickle's aggressive attempt to dig it out carried over the
green. Expressionless, he walked after it and left his next, a more delicate
pitch, short of the green. He would eventually get it to 20 feet, and three
putts later posted a quintuple bogey nine. Mo watched the kid from
Marquette go about his business, grinding over every shot. No quitting,
no apathy, nothing like Conner Jim and Mr. Potato Head Mann from the
morning. Mo felt a little bad for him, but not too bad.

Danny Mo, of course, burned the high side of the cup on his birdie
try. The Zaner, of course, buried his putt for birdie and had the lead all
alone now, three shots ahead of Danny with nine holes to play. Van
Sickle fell to six back, which tied him for third with Bob "Bob" Gregorski
and two of Wisconsin's top club professionals, Ryan Helminen and Ed

Terasa, who were playing two groups ahead of them. All three had impressive final rounds going considering the tricky winds and rock-hard greens.

Williams Jr.	-3	**Thru 9**
Moran	Even	**Thru 9**
Gregorski	+4	**Thru 11**
Helminen	+4	**Thru 11**
Terasa	+4	**Thru 11**
Van Sickle	+4	**Thru 9**

At the turn, the Morans stopped at an outdoor concession cart near the 9th green to purchase and slam a purple Gatorade. "Stuff's good, isn't it, Mo." Danny made a point of making eye contact with his son as he handed Mo the bottle.

"Rejuvenating," said Mo before quickly changing the subject. "You've lost a shot, but at least it's only two of you now."

Danny nodded and led the way toward the 10th tee. "On a course like this, major crashes can happen on any hole. Anybody's ballgame." They picked up the pace as they approached the clubhouse to avoid getting lost in a meet-and-greet mess with so many from Danny's past and other supporters looking to catch his eye and shout words of encouragement. The gallery was growing with those just getting off work and just showing up now. The difficulty of playing 36 holes at The Majesty had clogged up the pace, and getting finished before proper daylight expired was becoming a concern.

Surrounding him like the Papal Swiss Guard was a circle of stragglers with fresh beverages on the way to their posts for the first hole of the final nine. Mo couldn't escape a small sense of being on stage as he stood on the elevated 10th tee box. It was something he never even thought about when he played ball. He was a pitcher, or had been once. Pitchers pitch from a mound, the focal point of all action on the diamond. He embraced the attention, it was second nature. The spotlight was one thing, the hunger for the responsibility that came with it was everything. When it came to sports, he was wired to want, almost need, for it to be all on him. Of the many hand-me-down intangibles he shared with his dad, near the top was an aversion to any kind of competitive dependence on others. Being part of a team had its own buzz, a collective sensation unlike any other, to come through for others and other for you and everyone for all. Still, there were selfish types who could contaminate teams with their attitudes or selective effort. And then there were the over-coaching coaches; the kind that insisted on bunting early or waddling to the mound every other inning or belching out made-for-TV tirades at umpires. It reminded Mo of what his dad would say about certain executive types he'd dealt with over the years.

It was no wonder then, that the individual nature of golf had such appeal to certain types, and why his dad had started his own business, and why Mo had heard the message enough to never forget it. And why, when one of his dad's so-called corporate teammates, an old buddy named Evan Orsman, gambled away a bunch of company money, Danny shut the business down. Danny never told anyone that Orsman's indiscretions were what triggered the dissolution of MOS, and instead always gave a variation on 'enough was enough'; but Mo believed Orsman's bullshit was what did it.

∞

The wind was settling down some as it often did in Wisconsin's late afternoons and early evenings, and though the temperature probably hadn't measurably changed, it felt warmer. Using his new three-wood with surgical exactitude once again, Danny Mo placed his 10th hole tee shot within a step of perfect. A perfect tee shot after having emerged from the center of the nostalgic parade that was his walk from the ninth green to 10th tee was a critical test for him. With his past crashing into the present in a way few would understand, Danny's ability to concentrate had just been put to a test that covered a lifetime of multiple choices.

There were old friends, distant friends and miscellaneous friends; but Danny also noticed others he had forgotten… business owners and their kids who took over for them, old schoolmates, parishioners, bartenders, resort workers and park rangers, and numerous other faces he vaguely recognized from his crew-cut through bowl-cut into not-quite-mullet hair years, all filed away in places unvisited but for the odd dream or maybe triggered by something completely happenstance or silly. It was a powerful experience, as if Danny was getting a fleeting peek at his past from a different angle and with greater depth, like looking through his old View Master and glimpsing the familiar in fresh and fading light at once.

And so it was an enormously important tee shot that led to a solid six-iron to the green. Apparently, Danny must have been looking forward to pissing behind the 11th tee so much that he birdied the 10th from 20 feet with a putt he hit a tad too hard. When the ball banged the back lip, popped up and dropped in, Danny chucked, Mo Mo laughed and the crowd erupted. After The Zaner's par, Danny Mo was now two shots out of the lead.

Mo waited for his dad to finish behind the 11th tee. All three golfers had hit their tee shots already. By now, most everyone had an idea what Danny was doing and were headed down the fairway. This one was taking longer than usual, so Mo walked down and around the built-up championship tee box area to a stand of pines. His dad had his back to Mo, and was obviously relieving himself. However, as he did this, he saw that Danny was swiveling his hips in what Mo could only place as a hula dance-type of motion.

As his dad finished up, Mo stepped back and acted like he just arrived on the scene behind the 11th tee. "You okay, D Mo?"

"I am now," said Danny, smiling. "All that Gatorade, you know. You too, huh?"

"Might as well," said Mo as he watched his dad head back. "I'll catch up." He unzipped, and before beginning he noticed that his dad's "pattern" on the dirt was that of two circles, flat ovals actually, right next to each other but intersecting, like a sideways number 8, but filled in. Looked a little like a pair of sunglasses. Mo blasted away at those eyes until the pattern was one irregular blob. He couldn't work his mind around an unassailable fact. His dad had to have first cleared away the pine needles in the area of his deposit in order to make the two touching ovals, the eyes he was pissing all over. And while that explained his dad's hula dancing action, it only made him wonder all the more about his dad. In the earlier round, Mo had taken the cart to the gulch near Morgan's Forehead, left of the 18th fairway, to pick up his dad who had gone to relieve himself while The Stallions waited for the green to clear. His dad had pretty much finished, but when Mo had arrived then, too, his dad's hips were swaying. At the time, Mo didn't give it a second thought. D Mo, at heart, was a rhythmic guy.

When Mo emerged from his urination ruminations and from the pines, his dad's bag was waiting for him on the cart path. Danny and his group were nearly to their balls and the gallery was, perhaps out of respect for anyone needing to relieve themselves, moving toward the green. From this distance, Mo could tell that the gallery had grown larger still. More had joined at the turn than he had noticed at first. He picked up the bag and hustled down the fairway.

∞

Mo watched his dad do his little two-step after hoisting a gorgeous high fade from the right side of the fairway to the elevated 11th green. With the wind dying down, D Mo was no doubt going to lean on his bread-and-butter-cut shots with his long- and mid-irons (he always worked it subtly either way with the short irons), after which he habitually walked his ball toward the target with a little shuffle to the left; his "inner-Faldo," as he liked to call it. Mo had witnessed his dad's "inner-Faldo" shuffle for years. it came out when Danny's left-to-right iron shots were especially sharp; but now his little two-step was becoming more animated, and Mo wondered just where and when the strangeness would end. But strange or not, something was working.

All three players made par on 11. Danny's parachute shot with his three-wood on 12 was again perfect, making him four-for-four for the tournament. Impressive as all hell to Mo was when The Zaner hit his tee shot even higher and softer than Danny's, with a three-iron. Van Sickle smiled, then roped a cool little three-iron draw around the corner that hit hot and ran to a good place. After the disaster on the ninth, the All-American from Marquette looked like he was free to play any shot he wanted. When Mo saw Danny and The Zaner's balls side-by-side in the 12th fairway, it disturbed him that it was Danny's that was in a divot seam that someone did a half-assed job of replacing. That someone was him, and his dad knew it. After Danny played his wedge earlier that morning, Mo stopped to watch the quick playing Jason Mann, 40-some yards ahead of him, botch his L-wedge shot and then throw both his hat and a tantrum, the event from which Mo assigned the Mr. Potato Head moniker to the hairless Mann. Mo felt guilty over his sloppiness. Playing from one's morning divot was supposed to be an exaggeration on precision, the stuff of pre-television folklore.

The Zaner, somehow, spun back a full sand wedge off the back fringe to seven feet. With an impossible lie, Danny pounded down with Lazarus and drilled his ball into The Joker bunker where it half-plugged. Mo cringed. He felt alone on Idiot Island for a moment. It was his fault, and he knew it and his dad knew it. But you wouldn't have known it by Danny's reaction. Old man Moran just chucked it off. Mo wasn't sure how he felt about his dad's reaction. Danny Mo was the toughest competitor he'd ever seen, played with, or knew; and even if D Mo had the strange habit of not cursing on the course, he'd seen him get steamed over smaller incidents than this.

Danny gouged his ball from its sandy semi-grave near the lip. Lazarus's head went slamming into the lip on an abbreviated follow-through but the ball came out with no spin and wobbled, seemingly on will alone, until it was about the same distance from the hole as The Zaner's ball, but on the opposite side. After Van Sickle made his 18-footer for birdie, there was a small disagreement as to who was away, Danny or The Zaner. Van Sickle said The Zaner was away, and The Zaner said Danny was away.

Danny said "It looks like an exact tie to me."

Zaner, a little edgy, said "You're away."

Danny was squatting behind his ball. He held his putter near the clubhead and pointed the grip end straight ahead. Then he began making what appeared to be small Xs in the air, over and over, working it like it was a wand. "Whatever," he said, and stayed in his squat and closed his eyes for a few seconds while slowly reducing his X-ing action until he was motionless.

"Well, you gonna go?" The Zaner was wide-eyed, looking at Danny, perhaps unsure if he was even awake.

Mo watched his dad go through the repeating-X thing before going into statue mode. Mo again fought off the "whack-job" thought that was darting around in his brain. "Uh…D Mo…?"

"Oh," Danny smiled to himself. "Sure." He replaced his ball, picked up his lucky ball marker with the Irish slogan (the same one that he had dropped on the 72nd hole at The Hill Farm), took his stance… and slammed the putt into the back of the cup. The Zaner then matched Danny, but in aggressiveness only. Junior blew his putt five feet past the cup and missed again coming back. Irritated, he stared at Daddy Zaner for some reason, and then almost missed his bogey putt.

Danny was one back.

Tension between The Zaner and everyone else in the group thickened when he air-mailed the short par three 13th. Insta-bogey. That Van Sickle made another birdie did not help The's mood at all. Danny played an itty-bitty baby fade to the center of the green and made a stress-free par. Danny Mo had finally pulled even with Zane Williams Jr., but with the longer holes ahead, it felt more like a 2-2 count more than a ball and a strike. On the tough uphill 481 yard par four 14th, Van Sickle piled another birdie into his back nine, his third in a row. He was now two over par and only three back of Danny and The Zaner. Danny pulled his 19 degree hybrid, his beloved "Shaq-toe," left of the green from 224. He was less than 40 feet from the hole but had a funky lie on the down-slope of an igloo-like mogul. He was aggressive with his chip, a cocked-wrist vertical gouge with an open face, but caught it just thinnish enough to run it over the green. He managed the damage to one shot, however, with a sparkling vanilla bump and run chip to a foot for bogey.

Danny remained placid and was now unashamedly engaging in his new tic of manipulating whatever club he held in the same repeating crisscross motion so that he looked like an apathetic conductor for an inattentive orchestra.

When The Zaner came up an inch short on what should have been a straight uphill 13 footer for birdie, his entire appearance began to change. His shirt had been hanging out in back since the ninth, but his posture was now collapsing in tiny increments and his disposition had become more petulant than proud. Danny was now one back with four holes to go but was buoyed by The Zaner's subtle body wilt.

After they had hit their drives (and this time Danny did use his driver) on the downhill par five 15th, Mo knew what was coming. Yep, his dad had to pee again. Danny had marked his territory during the first round of the tournament and Mo had the program down now. Danny's location of choice was a seven- or eight-foot gully with a footpath that elbowed in between the 15th's tees and the fairway and led to the forested areas inland. Danny had teed off last this time, so he took a little extra time and thus nearly achieved the privacy he sought in his gully. But not entirely.

Whenever his dad needed to go, unless it was behind or near a tee-box, Mo had always walked ahead (except for the third round when he drove) with his dad's clubs. He did the same now, but made sure to drop a towel after his dad descended into the gully. When he turned back to pick up the towel, he sneaked a peek, relieved his dad was facing away. Sure enough, Danny was again doing the weird hula hip action. No visible pattern, however, to be seen against the leafy plants and long grasses on the slope. Danny's shoulders had become much more active now. Mo wondered if that was due to the fact that there was no good area to, uh…show his work. Mo felt like he was sorting out some kind of dream. Why else would he find himself breaking down the fundamentals of his dad's mid-piss dance moves? With four holes to play in the State Open and only one shot out of the lead no less. *Whack-job, whack-job, whack-job…*

When Mo and his dad caught up with their group and gallery, it was only because *they* had caught the group ahead of them. "Man, I hit that drive about as good as I can. What do you think, Mo, 310 or so? Laser the flag," said Danny, "and I'm still probably 40 behind Junior."

"At least three bills, easy. Can't feel all that unfamiliar, can it?" Mo wouldn't have any more Zaner the Bomber talk. He aimed the Laser Link at the pin once the group ahead had finished. And that group was walking to their carts like they were, indeed, finished.

Van Sickle's ball had kicked into the right rough, forcing him to lay up. Danny eventually hit his hybrid again, this time from 244 yards according to Mo's reading, and crushed it. His ball barely landed on the front, yet still bounced hard and ran slightly through the green. Even from that distance, with many in the gallery cheering Danny Mo's airborne ball, Mo could hear the unmistakable smack of the ball hitting the firm green. He flashed ahead and wondered just how impossible the 18th green would be when they got there. When they arrived at the 15th green, Danny's ball was in good shape. Easy chip. Plenty of green. No sweat.

The Zaner put his ball into what had to be much thinner air with no more than a four-iron and it disappeared in the high sky. As usual, it came down soft and left him with 25 feet for eagle. It was almost unfair. The and *Thee* knuckle-bumped.

Danny caressed the sole of Lazarus so he could feel the connection, then chipped to the length of a scorecard and made birdie. Van Sickle made par and The Zaner easily two-putted for birdie. All three players made orderly, storyless pars on the 16th and headed to the 217 yard par three 17th. Danny was one back now, and Mo knew in his heart that The Zaner had the advantage going into the final two holes. The kid was hitting his long and mid-irons so high that Mo would reflexively whip his head back to see if what he had in his hands was really the club he thought it was. And it happened again on 17. The Zaner hit still another moon-shot that, to Mo, looked to be about 15 to 18 feet to the left of the middle-right hole location. No one was surprised, nor, aside from his dad, particularly pleased. The crowd clapped with the approximate zeal they might have shown for the 9th guy to go up and receive his HVAC technician certification diploma at some tech school.

The kid did the quick, conspicuously noisy Velcro disengagement action when he took off his glove. He stuffed it in his back pocket after lifting his shirt tail, which was apparently how he wanted the fabrics of his life to be managed at the moment.

The Zaner had been a tempestuous but talented teenager turned friendly and responsible academic All-American at BYU. By his senior year he was an All-American, period, and was projected to have a bright future in professional golf according to *those in the know*. Mo had gotten the lowdown while getting drunk with Willie Crinzi the night before. Now, The Zaner elected not to go back to his cart as he had all day after hitting his tee shots. *Thee* stood on the side of the tee box near the steps that descended to the cart path, but The Zaner took a spot back and center. Chin out, he looked like a boxer getting pre-fight instructions while giving the 'yo mamma' evil-eye to his opponent in the center of the ring.

Danny played a three-iron. High cut. He held his finish for a little longer than usual. But when the ball started cutting back at the stick, he began to shuffle to the left just as many in the gallery lost all command of their decorum membranes and pure, primitive desire for a positive outcome overrode all diplomatic restraint. Loud, pleading cries ranging from, "Please God," to some drunk's, "Swallow bitch!" came echoing across the bluffs in an aural avalanche of love and support for the local boy.

Danny's ball came slamming down near the hole, and those who had already gone ahead to the green roared in a more organized manner than the begging going on back at the tee. By the sight and sound of diminishing enthusiasm, Mo knew the ball again released to the back of the green. It would end up some 45 feet away. Van Sickle's solid shot ended up just outside The Zaner's and on nearly the same line.

When they got to the green, Danny looked briefly at the lime terrain between his ball and the cup but, really, didn't appear to be focusing much on anything. "What do you think, Mo?"

"Looks like it breaks toward the cup," said Mo. It was his dad's traditional line about the meaningless truth about all putts. Mo wasn't sure how old he was when he figured out it was a kind of joke.

Danny Mo was now wandering around the green and subtly making little Xs with his putter. When Mo used his dad's 'breaks toward the cup" line, Danny smiled and gave a big, slow nod. *Some things never change* thought Mo, and he felt something indescribable come over him as his dad did this, especially when Danny held Mo's eyes for a moment longer than normal. *A premonition of some sort?*

And so it was. When Danny's putt dropped in on its last roll, the explosion from the gallery didn't even seem humanly possible, especially over the initial 15 seconds or so, and was sustained beyond that by a bunch of well-oiled Barnstormers with something of a two-note Tarzan-like yodel with beers held high. Old and young jumped up and down and hugged, and Mo saw a couple of guys just flat-out slugging each other on their shoulders repeatedly. Several state TV news stations had cameramen well positioned to capture the celebration and were panning back and forth from Danny to the crowd. Mo saw Rinny plant a kiss on Crusty's cheek, who had apparently said something funny back to her.

Mike and Ike waited it out, eventually smiling at the length and decibels of the ongoing roar. The Zaner, however, went out of his way to affect the actions of a man oblivious to the obvious. He went about some practice strokes with his putter as the high-fives and backslaps and whooping continued around him. He then went to his dad to presumably point out something about the read on his forthcoming putt, but looked to be slightly put off when his old man was busy politely clapping and nodding in the spirit of sportsmanship.

Mike Van Sickle's putt had a little too much speed and spun out. The gallery made one of those exaggerated *too bad* spectator groans, the kind born of an unmitigated bias toward a favorite son and indicative of golf's sometimes disingenuous expression of faux concern for a bastard child they care about but do not want to win. Nevertheless, the kid from Marquette received a heartfelt hand when he banged in his two-and-a-half-foot comebacker for par without marking.

Putting toward the bay and the setting sun, The Zaner left still another putt short. This time it was a 16-footer, again dead in the heart. There were whistles and *wows* and some unmistakable giggles when The

Zaner fell onto the putting surface, as if rendered motionless by his own disbelief. The giggles got to him, and he chose to play victim when he finally stood up and began to walk off the green. He stared at no one in particular with a palms-up, *What's-up-with-disrespecting-The Zaner?* gesture.

Danny Moran and Zane Williams Jr. were now tied at even par on a very difficult golf course. Van Sickle was at +3 and, according to Bill Linneman, no one else was better than +7. The Majesty had held its ground.

One hole to play.

∞

From the first time Danny Moran played The Majesty, there was never any question that the hole that struck him most was the 18th. Struck him like lightning bolts charged with currents of the past. Of all the spots on the property upon which The Majesty was built, this was the stretch of land that spoke and sang and hummed and howled to him with the echoes of long ago, through different hairstyles and evolving priorities and choices made in the name of sex and love. At the highest point along the regular bluff line, a place known as North Point, the terrain gradually descended, moving further north to a lower, smaller plateau where the 18th green now sat. And it was on this sacred land that God and C. Charles Revere had crafted what Danny Moran believed was *the* perfect golf hole.

The 18th hole at The Majesty was everything a finishing hole should be. It was a risk/reward par five, gorgeous from any angle, with the bay well below and to the left and the clubhouse in the distance at two-o'clock. And there was Morgan's Forehead, piercing the sky like a one-of-a-kind monument to nature and her forces, rising up nearly 300 feet from its shore-side to a flat, butte-like peak. On the course-side, the peak was some 145 feet above the elbow of the doglegging fairway. Danny had seen a version of this hole before, in his mind, before it was ever built. His sense of déjà vu was free and roaming on its own. As a tribute to all that karma, he had gone ahead and made two bogeys and a double on the 18th, four over par through three rounds, on this, his dream hole.

Danny stood on the 18th tee and looked around, as if alone, immersed in his own world and thus one of looser order. He'd spent so many hours awash in the shifting charms of all four seasons in these parts.

It was a place of dangerous surrounds yet the safest place he'd known, where so many truths were uncovered and where some secrets still lie. He knew how the winds blew, which paths were safest by season, where to find (and avoid) the areas of peril, and which paths offered realistic odds for reaching North Point but were a stacked deck favoring serious harm or death on a retrace down. Most of the slopes along the bay were steep, and crowded with plenty of trees, plateaus and outcroppings. They were severe but not entirely impenetrable from the waterfront. Visible to the south were cliffs with sheer walls of exposed rock with drop-offs of up to 80 feet. But there was nothing as tall or singularly prodigious as Morgan's Forehead.

Danny snapped out of his reverie when he heard Mo clear his throat as if to say, *you have the honor*. Danny looked around and re-engaged with reality. The tee was surrounded by friends and family and even strangers who had now fully embraced their local legend. The sun was low and brilliant, and the view from the 18th tee was transformed into a blinding, prismatic otherness by the fracturing effects from The Forehead's geological prominence in the west. Perhaps it was four days of streaming images and the channeling of his formative years that reawakened a feeling that The Forehead was a massive subterranean force rising up until subdued by the land itself, an unbroken stone of resistance against the harness of the Green Bay, itself the final resting place for so many shipwrecks and known to the settling French as *Porte des Morts*, or *Death's Door*, and will forever stand to preserve a community's faith in how The Harbor may budge, but never break. Danny had written a paper in high school to that effect and his teacher never looked at him quite the same. And so the cycle remained unchanged. So many thoughts now, again, firing on impulse, hearkening back to all those hours spent dreaming in the hills. Same as it ever was.

Most everyone in the gallery had a hand or two held up to shield the sun. The shadows were long and rendered a broken texture to the bentgrass fairway below, which highlighted the land's makeover more than anything else. The grass was now tighter near the surface, yet appeared to possess a depth that the longer, native grasses had a way of flattening with its swaying softness.

"Let's go with a new ball, huh Mo?" Danny turned away and looked over the bay.

"Sure," said Mo, glad that his dad had returned from wherever he'd gone. He turned and retrieved a fresh Titleist from his dad's stand-up golf bag. The wind had waned into nearly nothing; it was quiet enough for all to hear the sound of him opening the carton sleeve of new balls.

When Mo tossed a ball to his dad, D Mo immediately tossed it back. "Maybe you better mark it with something." A few from the gallery laughed for some reason.

Mo looked at his dad, confused. Danny's golf balls were all personalized with d mo, always had been. Even through his four years of so-called retirement, the local Titleist rep faithfully delivered four dozen-packs of imprinted balls to Danny Moran. In his heyday it was a dozen 12-packs.

"How do you want it marked?" Mo's throat was dry; he was more nervous than his dad.

Danny waggled his driver a couple times and wandered to the back of the tee to where Linneman was standing with his radio and cigarettes. "Surprise me, Mo." More titters from somewhere.

A moment before, and before Mo could suggest it, Danny had pulled out his driver. They knew that getting to and, more importantly, holding the green would be difficult considering the granite green 559 yards away; but they also knew that The Zaner was licking his chops, ready to bust one well past The Forehead and just short of the crossing gulch. From there, Junior would have, at most, a mid-iron shot that would rain straight down from the sky.

Mo looked at the ball and then pulled a black Sharpie™ from his back pocket, marked something on the ball and tossed it back to his dad.

Danny looked at the ball and smiled. He showed it to Bill Linneman who looked confused enough to require another puff. After Danny bent

down, Mo thought the ball was teed up a tad low for his dad's normal
tee ball.

The gallery was hushed now. Danny stood behind the ball, stepped
up to it and waggled twice as something in the bird family screeched in
the distance. Danny stepped away. Mo wasn't sure his dad even heard
the bird. To Mo, however, the sound of several hundred, hell, maybe a
thousand, people exhaling was palpable.

"Mo, get my three-wood, would ya?" Danny walked toward Mo,
holding his driver by the shaft just above the club head; he made little Xs
as he moved.

Mo handed over the three-wood, again with a puzzled expression.
He was disappointed and looked hard at his dad who delivered a subtle,
solitary nod. Mo stepped back from the tee box as if to somehow wash
his hands of the decision to go with the three-wood.

Danny Mo set up to a freshly-marked golf ball that he had no reason
to re-tee. In fact, now the ball seemed to be teed a bit high for a bullet
three-wood. Mo wondered about that. It was hard just trying to breathe
and watch. He also noticed his dad's open stance; Danny was going with
the safe cut into a fairway that sloped from right to left. Not the worst
idea, Mo thought. Get it in the fairway and the tee-shot was still no
gimmee, and it put the pressure on The Zaner. Danny could still birdie
by calling on Lazarus if he laid up to the right distance, which wasn't all
that easy, but a good three-wood would be a good start to getting that
done. Danny squinted as he took a long look down the fairway. Then Mo
noticed a graceful repositioning of his dad's body just before he took the
club back. Whatever his dad was trying to do before pulling the trigger,
however, could only be described as wrong. He swung about as hard as
he had the entire tournament and pulled his tee shot almost straight up
and into the sun. Danny Mo's shoulders sagged. A knee-high slam of his
three-wood on the tee box followed as did a heavy sigh that said it all.

The gallery was stunned. Weary from all the walking, they had hung
tough and were holding out for the justice due their boy. Danny Mo had
brought a shared elation to a community once divided by the very place
where they had now come together. They gasped, and made the gut-

wrenching sounds of calamity shared. And the thing of it, at least to Mo, was that Danny's blast into the sunlight looked downright inevitable with the way he had set up to the ball. Mo felt sick. Things were spinning, and he tried to glom onto anything that might stop it. Nothing was working.

The only discernable comment Mo heard was, "Right up Morgan's ass," and it came from a guy he'd noticed earlier. The guy's blue shirt had an oval patch with *Merle* embroidered in white. "He's dead," said Merle, shaking his head.

Mike and Ike remained expressionless. The Zaner twirled his driver a little too quickly. He stared at his dad as if he was afraid he might smile if he didn't. Daddy Zaner had already gone back for his son's three-iron, no reason to risk anything now. The Zaner took the iron and proceeded to play through a palpable fog of heavy disappointment that was now snuffing the life out of the moment. He ripped his tee shot nearly 250 laser-straight yards down the middle of the middle. Three shots back, Van Sickle killed a tee shot that may have stayed in the fairway. The spikes of splintering sunlight made it hard to see anything.

Mo was reeling. He sneaked a couple peeks at his dad who continued to stare straight ahead as they prepared to head down the fairway. Mo decided to look mostly down at his feet, because he really didn't know what to do with his face. He had found Rinny and Crusty immediately after the yank-job. They had worked to maintain straight faces with limited success. His sister was blinking back tears now, and Crusty had barely perceptible head shakes going, while his nostrils were telling in a way Mo could not articulate. Neither wanted Danny to see how crushed they were. When Mo looked down one last time, he was staggered by the fact that his dad was doing the little X thing, this time with his right index finger down near his thigh. *They're coming to take me away, ha ha…*

"We're going to have come to an agreement as to where your ball crossed the hazard, Danny." Linneman had just clicked off his radio and cruised over to Danny and Mo in a cart. "With the sun, nobody could tell for sure."

"Not a problem, Billy." Danny continued to look straight ahead. "I got a line on it.

∞

Chapter 45

Mo was looking at his feet as he walked when he was startled from his thoughts. *D Mo, my dad, my hip-shaking, bladder-draining, X-making, whack-job, nut-case, lost in space dad …my hero.*

"This way, Mo." Danny was waving Mo toward a spot that dropped about 30 feet into the ravine. It was well left of where his ball would have crossed by anyone's best guess. "Bring Lazarus and my four-iron," said Danny. "You can leave the bag."

Just ahead, Bill Linneman looked back and swung his cart around. "What's up, Danny?"

"We're going after it."

"Here?" Linneman, the chief justice of the rules of golf, took a drag on his cigarette. Crusty had heard that Linneman was a "three sport stud in high school whose feet had gone to shit." Three or four surgeries and procedures over the years and his dogs still betrayed him. Now, he avoided anything related to working out and fell into that neither fit nor fat class of comfortable American males. He took a final drag on his Winston Light and looked into the gulch that went down in three distinct stages. He looked at Mo again, who could only shrug.

"You really think you got it, Danny?"

"Know, think, hope, it's all the same," said Danny. "Gotta look in any case, right?"

"I guess," said Linneman. "I'll be coming with you then."

Mo looked over his shoulder before going into the ravine, and it was obvious the gallery hadn't a clue as to what was going on. They had been shuffling down the cart path and parts of the right rough, and now some were spilling onto the right side of the fairway. They were moving slow, as if they were coming upon an accident and in no hurry for bad news.

Mo and Danny went before Linneman, single file, down a narrow trail that was mostly just trampled grass and bent vegetation, short of where Danny had pissed earlier. They slalomed through the gaps in the taller grass, going down until there was no more down left before them. There, Danny took them on a hard right alongside a dry creek. Danny picked up the pace now that they were on a fairly level surface. Suddenly he stopped, turned, and looked toward both the fairway and in the direction of the tee, neither of which could be seen from where they were. There were, however, two officials including JG Schmitz looking at them from above.

"Danny, I'm coming down to help." JG waved as he shouted, as if a moving hand added clarity to his words.

Danny smiled, appreciative that JG offered to subject his expensive shoes to the dusty gulch. "Not necessary JG," he yelled. He looked around before turning to face Linneman. "Billy, you can head back up to the fairway if you want, Mo and I are going up."

"Probably a good idea, Danny." Linneman was visibly relieved by the prospects of escaping the big ditch. "Not that I'm advising anything. We'll work out where you can drop."

"Actually, Mo and I are going up...that way." Danny pointed to Morgan's Forehead. "My ball is up there somewhere."

Mo swallowed hard. "We are?"

Going back to his days as a middle school Mo, whenever he had asked his dad if anyone had ever been to the Forehead's peak, D Mo would say "Oh, I'm sure...and a few have died tryin'" They were at the base of the southeast slope, the side with the softest, most vegetated incline up to the top of Morgan. Still, looking at the brontosaurus back they were supposedly about to scale, and considering there was a golf tournament going on, it seemed freaking absurd.

Mo smiled. "You sure?"

Danny looked at Mo as if he didn't know him. "Absolutely." He did not smile.

"I mean, fine...it just doesn't look like a very easy thing to do, you know, without ropes." Mo was rattled. "Even if we find it...that slope...

it would have rolled back down or got caught up in some bush or a cave of bats or something.

Linneman pulled out a cigarette. "Well, uh…"

"We'll see. It's not as tough as it looks," said Danny, ignoring whatever Linneman was trying to say and took off in double time along the base of Morgan's Forehead. Mo had to hustle it up and caught his dad as they came to a small sign courtesy of the municipality of Rock Harbor:

Dangerous Area
No Climbing Allowed

Danny walked right past it. Mo looked over his shoulder, then followed.

"Uh…" Linneman lit his cigarette. "I don't know about this."

"It's a hazard; you're allowed to look for your ball in a hazard, Bill. All there is to it. I mean, you wanna call the cops?"

"Of course not. And I know the hazard rules, Danny. I just don't know…" Linneman was sorting things out, apparently not possible without another drag on his cigarette. He also knew that the sign would not deter Danny.

"We're going. You can come if you like, or not."

Linneman looked up at the peak. "I'm going back to the fairway. My feet will not get me up there. Are you guys staying on this side of the formation?"

"Of course," said Danny. "You ever see the other sides?"

Linneman took a long drag and let the smoke out in little rasp-o-laughs. This was a new one for him. He turned slowly and headed back to the trampled grass path that led to the fairway. From behind, it looked to Mo like smoke was coming from Bill's ears. More people appeared at the crest of the fairway, literally out of the blue. Waiting for someone in a blue blazer to tell them what was happening was, apparently, not happening fast enough for the gallery. Mike and Ike and a couple of Zaners were there as well. Mo saw Rinny, Crusty and Carter at the ridge further down the fairway. Rinny gave the helpless sign.

"We're going up," shouted Mo in their direction. "D Mo thinks his ball might be up there...somewhere." Rinny looked immediately at Crusty, as if seeking a translation.

"Really," said Crusty, just loud enough to hear, curious but nodding. Mo thought Crusty looked more amused than shocked.

Danny looked directly at Crusty, Rinny and Carter. "Probably be best if everyone headed back toward the green, how 'bout you guys lead the way."

Everyone was looking at Danny Mo's daughter and his two best friends. "Come on, let's go" said Crusty. "Dannymo, you sure me and Carter can't give you guys a hand?'

"We all could," said Rinny.

Danny waved them off. "We're good. We'll either find it easily or be back down quickly."

Mo gave a look of resignation and tried to recall what he saw from the 18th tee. He, like almost everyone else, except maybe Merle (and even Merle probably lost the ball at some point) had seen nothing with the sun doing its thing. He couldn't help but think the worst now. Crusty had given him all the details about what happened at The Hill Farm. How his dad had some bright idea that led to soap suds bubbling up from his clothes and some kind of lotion with rhino shit he believed was a defense against The Hill Farm's weird-ass flies. And there was always that deal with his Grandpa Curly's ashes. Mo loved his dad, but maybe this whole Open quest had finally slapped him goofy.

"Alright, Mo, we'll each take a club." Danny looked back at his son. "Just follow me, there's a trick to getting to the top. It's not a direct line. Lots of back-and-forth, like stadium ramps to the upper deck."

"Yes, sir." As Mo listened, something hopeful was breaking through his shroud of doubt. His dad was a bit unusual, always had been. The improvisational world rankings and analogies and never-before-seen dance moves at weddings, and even with the guy whizzing in circles and his air-Xing in public, there remained an irrefutable truth about so many maverick-types who were looked upon as odd. A little crazy does not mean completely crazy.

His dad had been hitting fairway after fairway with his new three-wood. But there was something about his swing on 18, something out of place. It didn't add up. Danny Mo, as tough as they come under fire, hall of fame member of the Legion of Superheroes in Wisconsin golf, suddenly jacks it into the junk when it mattered most? *That* far left? It seemed his dad made pretty solid contact, the swing was solid, if slightly... *is that even possible?* Mo trudged on, following his dad's circuitous lead up The Forehead when it dawned on him, what was out of place. His dad's swing on 18 was a lot like the one he used for his parachute tee shots on the 12th hole all four rounds – each time perfectly – only with greater force this time. *Crazy, sure. Like a freaking fox. A fox on Focus Factor even.*

Mo's legs were burning, partly from the climb, but also from his initial anxiety. Now, he could feel his energy returning. He gathered in some breath. "You hit it here on purpose, didn't you?"

"Thought about it for years." Danny anchored himself on the steep slope and then turned to look at Mo. "You think I wanted that kid hitting driver on this hole?"

∞

It was anything but a straight line to the top of Morgan's Forehead. It was not only a zigzag journey, it was also incomprehensibly up and down, and the down was necessary to achieve the up. Mo had not been sure about his dad's faculties when he said they would be scaling Morgan's Forehead, but the certainty Danny demonstrated on the ascent was something he knew not to question anymore. He did just once, a "You sure about this, D Mo?" type of question. That time, his dad just stopped and didn't even turn around to look at Mo. He just turned his head to the side before saying something that knifed into Mo.

"You know something, Mo, I brought your mother up here once. Don't know if you can believe this, but she had fewer hang-ups about the program than you. And we did it at night." His dad kept his head turned for several seconds.

His mom? At night?

At least one thing was clear, getting to the top would be next to impossible unless you knew this pinball pathway up the Forehead. Now, he believed it was actually going to happen; just a matter of time and technique. The trick included a lot of sideways, point-to-point dependence on rock outcroppings, trees, stumps, and curves of the earth that made the next angled push upward possible even if, at times, the anchor-points allowed for only one foot of solid purchase. It wasn't as dangerous as it probably looked, as there were no scary leaps or out of the ordinary physical requirements, but for sure, certain missteps and mistakes could easily have devastating results. It was ingenious in a way, and he had to give his dad props for being able to remember the route.

Mo would never forget his dad's voice when Danny called and asked him to caddie. This place was hallowed as all hell to D Mo. Mo hadn't realized how much at the time. Four rounds of playing the bounces, and getting "lucky" kicks, and secret pissing locations, what else did a guy need to know?

Mo was losing track of time. He was getting comfortable and more confident the higher they got. How long were they allowed? Five minutes to identify your ball was the rule, but five minutes from when? Mo was pretty sure it started once they get to the vicinity where his dad believed the ball to be. Mo kept glancing every which way around his feet to make sure he stepped where he was supposed to. And, on the odd chance that maybe there would be a golf ball wedged somewhere as well. They were nearly three-quarters of the way up now. He stopped for a moment, anchored on a thick rut in the rock. Grabbing onto a small tree, he turned to look out over the golf course. *Oh...my...God.*

Mo could only see the right side of the 18th green, but there were people swarming to the area and spilling up the right hillside toward the clubhouse. People, players mostly, he supposed, were leaning over railings and filling the large balcony deck and lower patio. There was a single-file line of locals and Barnstormers down the right side of the fairway as well. Newspaper types and people with cameras were all over the fairway aiming their instruments at the pair. A few had moved to the edge of the gulch, almost directly below Morgan on the fairway.

"Come on, Mo." His dad had surged ahead while he was gawking. He put on a showy little burst to catch up but his right tennis shoe spun out, which hadn't happened when his nerves kept him careful. For one second Mo felt the cold fear of losing control. He shot his right leg out instinctively and his foot hooked the thick stub of a bush root. His heart was going woodpecker on greenies.

"I meant come on, keep moving, not come on, hurry." Danny sounded winded. Mo was glad, because he was sucking wind like a Shop-Vac. His legs had transitioned to a dull ache that he knew he could push through, but it was a damn good workout. Mo didn't answer his dad; he wanted to hang on to every aerobic resource remaining. *Man... be nice if there's actually a ball up there...and what the hell was 'up there' anyway?*

Up there, at the peak of The Forehead, was beyond magnificent. Danny and Mo had crawled to the top across a stretch of cleaved, bench-like rocks. When Danny stood tall and glanced over the bay, an eruption of cheers came from below. Breathing heavily, he did not respond, not even to wave. He just stared out over the water. Mo followed and scrambled to his feet. Father and son stood together, silent but for their deep breathing as their bodies recovered. Mo drank in the incredible vista for the first time. The overall effect seemed to reinvigorate him quicker than the purple sports drink he'd slammed earlier.

When he had endeavored to describe the grandeur of The Majesty on his first tour of the course, Mo was able to confirm that there were people, places and things that defy explanation. This was like that but in panoramic overdrive. The view was dizzying, cinematic, preternatural. He wanted to see it all at once, his eyes primal, devouring everything, unable to get enough fast enough. For a moment, Mo's internal language mechanism blasted words off the walls of his brain in a manic, responsorial attempt to describe, if only to himself, his sensory experience of the summit of Morgan's Forehead. *Peak rush, eye dope, avalanching mind-blow, super psychonautical surf n' turf.* Random streams more suited for naming a trippy new jam band than helping a guy win a golf tournament. When he finally spoke aloud he was at a loss.

"Wow, just...wow," said Mo. He looked around quickly, as did Danny, hoping to see the golf ball on the windswept surface. "That's all I can say, man...is...wow." Mo looked out over the course; parts of all the inland holes were visible from where he stood. "It's just...couch and crown cool."

He felt his dad glance at him, but Mo couldn't pull his gaze from the topography. People seemed to be materializing from the hills and the size of the gallery was impressive from above. Mo looked down at them. "And I'd like to thank all the little people."

"Let's look around," said Danny, already doing so. "I hit it perfect...and it's a pretty good fit for the carry we needed, but barely. Max parachute three-wood should be good; whether it got here, or sat down once it did...who knows."

"So, how did you know the carry, D Mo?"

"I just...know, knew. Whatever."

Mo let it go. Then felt compelled to summarize in double-time, if only to get his thoughts straight. "Amazingly flat up here. More room than it looks like from below, and damn if you didn't know how it's pitches a little towards the tee box. What's with these wispy little plants coming from the cracks? I mean it, D Mo, if your aim was good we actually got a chance. We gotta find her."

"Thanks, Mo." A hint of sarcasm. Danny was already into the hunt. "Listen...as you've probably figured out, the west and north ledges go straight down, close to 300 feet. Stay away from there." Danny searched feverishly. "Wish we'd have seen it already. Not good."

Mo had recovered from the sensory rush and was enjoying his return to normal breathing. As he did, something else clicked on. Didn't make sense, but he noticed that his dad's dark slacks had some powdery dirt on them from crawling over the rocks, most of which he had slapped off with his hands. A small streak remained, however, an area he missed. The same area on his butt that Mo had noticed when his dad returned from wherever he went that made him sweat last night. *Here?*

JG, the state PGA official was yelling something up to them, possibly "Any luck?" They ignored him. They did hear, "You guys got about four minutes remaining!"

Looking back at the 18th tee, the whole madcap idea made a modicum more sense; at least more than it had from the tee. It had seemed completely ridiculous to consider such a play: nothing short, left, right or long. His dad had been up here before, of course, but how recently? D Mo had been quite confident in his selection of a four-iron.

Mo moved quickly; looking every which way, moving a bit, then stopping and looking all around him some more. Every few steps he did this, moving across the heart of the grainy surface but looking everywhere fast, like a tenderfoot testing river ice. The ideal positions on The Forehead, the middle areas void of most of the vegetation, if you could even call it vegetation, were delivering nothing. His dad was ahead, combing the areas vegetated with spotty clumps of tiny plants in large deliberate sweeps, just as he did while looking for Mike Van Sickle's ball earlier. D Mo went down on his hands and knees, crawling along with his face near the flat surface and moving toward the western face a little like Hank might. Mo struggled to deflect the heartbreak he felt coming on. *This is nuts.* The viable landing area wasn't much more than 50 or 60 yards long and no more than 40 yards wide, and it doesn't take very long for two guys to cover that. But there were still a few hundred flimsy ground plants to check out along the perimeter.

Despite his optimism of a moment ago, Mo couldn't help but weigh the merits of choosing to play the 18th straight now. His dad might have had to lay up had he done so, but Lazarus was lethal. If anyone could get a sand wedge close it was D Mo. Anything could happen - hell Danny had just made a 45-footer on 17. Playing it safe would have given him at least a fighting chance, a chance to win or go down swinging. Maybe that's what D Mo thought he was doing, taking this chance. Then again, maybe he just out-thought himself. He'd been tortured enough in this event over the years; not to mention what he'd been through in the years since his last State Open appearance.

"Mo!" Danny said it louder than needed. He was crawling slowly now, probing the intermittent plants near the ledge, but still safely enough away from danger. A cluster of maybe a half-dozen small, pale yellow butterflies were suspended in an animated weave no more than three feet above the plants. "Come down here. By me."

Mo Mo did as he was told and sprawled out next to his dad. They could hear JG yelling that they were "coming on three minutes left." And, "Any luck?" No one below would be able to see them now.

"Look. You see a ball, Laddie?" Danny's voice had taken on an Irish lilt and quavered a bit.

Mo could see the ball easily. *Laddie?* Barely detectable little laughs came from Danny, even though his expression hadn't changed.

"By the way, I like how you marked it, me boy," said Danny, still going brogue.

Mo had written the word **No** on each side of the ball, right next to the number, 1. **No 1**. *No One!*

They stood up and again took in the sights, but this time without the anxiety of whether they were going to find a golf ball. Danny walked to his ball and took a quick stance without a club. He nodded. "Those two leaves above aren't going to interfere at all. Visually maybe, but not with contact."

Father and son looked at each other. Danny's face was serene, a placid smile in place. Mo simply laughed. Everything just kept getting better, and weirder; but now Mo had no doubt that this was truly going to go down in history. If the US Open ever did come to town, the story of Danny Mo's shot to the top of The Forehead would be endlessly told, shown, shared, written about and focused upon. Everything but exaggerated - that would be impossible with the various cameras that had been aimed at them from the outset. The facts would suffice. During every round, every outing, and every tournament to be held at The Majesty, the story would be told. Golfers would tell golfers, parents would tell their children. People from the Harbor who weren't here would say they were.

Mo looked at his dad. "On this hole, under these conditions, until the end of time…No one!" He did the chop with both hands, hard, twice. "No one!"

"Don't say anything yet," said Danny, his voice hushed. "We have a couple minutes yet. Gonna take a quick leak."

"Of course," said Mo. "Been a good half hour."

Danny's eyes narrowed, "I'll be right back.".

Danny walked over to a spot near - but not too near - the farthest point of the western ledge, where he wouldn't be seen by the gallery on the fairway side below. Mo went over to Danny's ball. It was getting dark fast now but Danny's ball seemed to glow beneath the wispy leaves. It was about eight feet short of a ledge that dropped straight down to the rocky shore. Safe enough... still, the sensation of being that close to the cliff gave him the urge to squat down.

Mo looked over at his dad. Hips gyrating again. Drawing Ovals? Eyes? A modern-day Peecaso.

"You okay, D Mo?" Mo couldn't resist. He felt he could handle anything right about now.

"Sure, why not?" said Danny, looking back over his shoulder but unable to see Mo. He went back to his business, his shoulders going up and down as if he was laughing... no doubt over what his son must be thinking.

Mo shook his head and tried not to laugh. His dad kept swinging and swaying, and finished so quickly Mo wondered if he really had to go.

"Okay, I give up," said Mo. "What's up with the dancing?"

"You've noticed, huh? Wouldn't make too much of it, Mo. Just making Lazy 8s. Did 'em as a kid, not always with my, uh flow, but...a lot of times I did, out here, on the bluffs."

"I'd say Crazy 8s would be more like it." Mo was shaking his head. "The hell are Lazy 8s?"

"Actually, a Lazy 8 is a sideways 8. Some call it the infinity sign. I had a teacher in 7th grade, didn't like me much, dumped me in the class clown bucket, sent me to some school psychologist we had for a year or two; dude thought I wasn't taking things serious enough or some nonsense, said tracing the sideways 8s over and over would be a good thing for me to do when I was supposed to focus...or whatever I was or

wasn't doing. Thing is, I haven't done Lazy 8s in probably 35 years."
Danny's flat smile began to fade and his face clouded slightly. "For some
reason, I started doing it again. Of course, it could be my growing
prostate. Got some issues there."

"Your prostate?" asked Mo, unsure if his dad was just lapsing into
typical middle-aged health-related mumbo jumbo. "What issues?"

Danny looked into the distance as if the world revolved around him,
"Some bad cells, Mo. Had some tests. Should be manageable."

"The hell, D Mo, tell me you don't…" said Mo, instantly recalling
how his grandpa withered away from undetected prostate cancer. "How
bad? Why didn't you say something?" Mo, arms out, palms up.

"I just did, Mo," said Danny. "Now, anything you care to share with
me?" Danny still had a hint of a grin, but with a fresher intensity now.

Mo's thoughts went to Cindy and the heart-torching kiss that had
led to avoidance, resistance and eventually more kisses, and he thought
of her phone calls. Her confusion. The talk with his dad on the drive up
had confirmed his fears, so much so that he avoided the subject with
both Cindy and his dad. He had done his best to bury all that the past
few days.

"Probably some things you want to keep to yourself too, Mo-Mo my
son?"

"Well, ah, sure…but I'm not holding back; I mean, like you, it comes
down to timing…" Mo was rattled and jumped on the first relevant
counter that occurred to him. "Take the Salamone thing. He told me
some things you probably don't wanna know. Or maybe you do…I
don't know, this ain't the time. Now tell me you're gonna be okay,
okay?" Mo's heart was racing. Spooked, mostly by what his dad wasn't
telling him. The Salamone thing, he had to admit, was not a bad
recovery. Gave him time to think.

"I'll be fine," said Danny, dismissive. "Sally has always had some
secret he wants to leverage doesn't he…so what?"

Mo rushed through it. "Well he says that he tried to play straight
with Marty, but Marty wouldn't, said it was just a way for Marty to mess

with his head. That Marty would do anything to keep the cheating going. Plus…"

"So?" Danny interrupted, louder than normal.

"So then he said that Marty's holier-than-thou letter from the grave was bullshit, said things weren't as cut and dried as Marty made it seem."

"Not sure why we're talking about this now, but…cut and dried, Mo? These days, sheesh. Gray is the color of the day and wiggle-room is gold." Danny raised his eyebrows. "I'll be needing my four-iron, Laddie."

Mo worked to sort that out as he hurried over to get the two clubs from where he'd left them when they had mounted The Forehead. He had an impulse to bring up Bonds cheating because Sosa and McGuire did first and all that but he picked up the clubs and hustled back.

Someone must have brought JG a megaphone. "One minute, fellas. One minute left," The voice was amplified, and the megaphone crackled, but JG sounded resigned.

Mo looked at Danny. Danny shook his head. Mo then checked his watch. He went a few steps toward the east slope and waved down to JG to indicate that he understood.

Danny had more to say. "Marty never gave a rat's ass what anyone thought. Once Sally cheated on him…that was it, he didn't care." Danny looked into his son's eyes. "I almost told you on the drive up… you should know it was *me*, Mo, who wrote that letter, for him. For Marty, and, frankly, for myself, too. Marty knew someone was after him; only thing he asked of me was that if someone got him that I'd tell people that he really did know what the E stood for in the Steamin' E Burger. But it gave me the letter idea."

Mo looked at his dad in disbelief. He was concerned about Danny, but was also irritated that each of them was spilling bits of information to avoid sharing more important stuff. He didn't give a shit about the E.

"'Ephemeral' is what Marty said Kai told him." Danny started making little Xs, actually the Lazy 8s (∞) with his index finger, down low, at his side.

"But, yeah, I wrote it. Marty wasn't into that. I thought we might get Salamone to write a few checks to Overlighter's himself, maybe dupe him into trying to out-do Marty."

Mo was astounded. "You know, don't you?"

"Of course." Danny shrugged. "Sunya told me. They need the help. Marty's gone. Government support is way down and I can't help like I used to.

"Thirty seconds, fellas!" JG sounded like he was 15 feet away instead of 150 below.

Mo was looking over the horizon, weighing just how much his dad was going to admit about his health, about Cindy, about whatever. Now, however, they had a shot to play. *How the hell did we get on all this?* He handed his dad the four-iron. Lazarus remained tight in Mo's hands, held like a barbell but bowing the shaft in the middle. "Wish you'd told me about Marty."

"He needed to keep his work quiet, Mo. You weren't exactly quiet when you damned him to hell for being a cheater. Especially after a few drinks."

Mo's face flushed. He was convinced now that his dad had seen him passed out on Manda's basement carpet. Like some kid who can't get off the frat-life carousel.

Danny Mo was nodding. His eyes shone with what could have been deep love or deep concern, or both, for his son. "I wrote the letter and showed it to him long before he took the bullets. Cindy's contacts confirmed that Marty was being targeted, some kind of bounty, but that was nothing new." Danny paused. "You know Cindy, don't you, Mo?" Danny's expression was unreadable; his eyes, if not all his attention, were on his waggle. "Friend of the family, it would seem."

Mo didn't know what to say. *Come clean, play dumb, get busted? Not now.* Mo looked back up, but Danny was staring down at the green, sizing up his shot from the top of Morgan's Forehead. "I'll let them know we found our ball," he told his dad.

He walked quickly if a little unsteadily to the southeast part of The Forehead. The vertigo he'd felt earlier settled in deeper now. It was too much and not enough information at once, now, here, on top of the world of all places. He sensed that everyone below was looking at him as he moved closer to the fairway-side of Morgan. He was correct. Mo took a deep breath as he glanced down at a collection of a half dozen state PGA officials, many of whom were checking their watches.

Mo stopped and mustered up something from within. "We got it!" he yelled as he made the safe sign, the same one used in baseball. There were those in the gallery who knew what that meant and cheered. Others were puzzled and disappointed, thinking it meant "no good," like a missed field goal attempt. Mo sensed the confusion and instinctively summoned his inner Jon Bon Jovi and extended a clenched fist skyward, pumping it at least three times, and damned if he didn't slam his other fist into his hip like Superman as the crowd below erupted. The cheers thrilled Mo and he switched to the thumbs-up sign. And just like that he went from rock star to super hero to political candidate on the stump. Still, the gallery was eating everything up. And why not? Danny Mo had found his ball.

The gallery was then left to wait and watch; those by the green would be able to see more than the officials on the fairway almost directly below. Mo had lost track of most everyone while he and his dad were recovering from their climb and the hunt for the No 1 Titleist and their explorations of life, death, Lazy 8s and D Mo's prostate cells.

Mo turned back to his dad and presented him with the still-raised thumb. At the sound of the cheers, both men seemed to snap back to the magic of the moment. Mo's legs had recovered, and he hoped his dad's had too. *Bad cells? What the hell does that mean?* Mo hoped to God his dad felt as alive as he did.

"Damn," said Mo as he approached Danny, "I didn't think to bring the Laser Link gun.

"No worries, Mo Mo...been here before. And trust me, I've played plenty of imaginary shots to there." Danny pointed downward at the green. "Stock four-iron for me, pumped six for you, if you were in a mood. But there's no need to go higher." Danny held the club lightly - no crumbs - and lifted the clubhead straight up, his overlapping grip an inch from the placket of his shirt as he looked skyward.

At that moment, Mo thought his dad was the absolute high priest of the golf world. "Not sure that's possible, D Mo." Mo's face was alight. "Coming from way up here, man, it'll come straight down. You catch it clean, you could hold the parking lot."

His dad winked. Danny Mo already knew all that. Mo wondered when the idea had hit Danny. Snatching the driver right out of The Zaner's hands was like stripping the Mjolnir hammer from the hand of the Mighty Thor. And now, with solid contact, Danny would be approaching the green straight from Heaven, the only way he could possibly hold the 18th green with his second shot. Pull it off and he'd have, in all likelihood, two putts for the title.

Danny took a deep breath, face relaxed, ready to bear down. He had something powerful radiating from him, something Mo could not exactly identify. Mo knew his dad was one shot away from what had become his ultimate goal in golf. One Danny had given up on. Hell, he had retired from competitive golf. For so long, Danny Moran had believed he could compete for one of the US Am titles, or perhaps qualify for a US Open, and while he did come close, it just never worked out.

So Danny Mo kept winning everything in the state, over and over... everything but this stinkin' tournament. Snake-bitten? Perhaps. In golf, it would be more accurate to call it "Shark-bitten," considering how Greg Norman had a number of majors ripped from his grasp, to go with the ones he pissed away. So, too, was this the case with his dad's pursuit of the Open. But now, to go down in spectacular flames at The Hill Farm only to endure a tragedy infinitely worse on the same day, yeah, there was something poetic in the possibility that his dad could finally win in an even more spectacular fashion. Tally up the adventures of all the Tigers, Sharks, Bears and others of their ilk. Nothing compared to this, nor would anything ever come close.

If Danny Moran could pull off one more shot. A shot not nearly as difficult as the one D Mo had just made to set it all up.

Mo did a slow 360 and looked around. His legs may have recovered, but he could still feel the effects of having walked 18 holes before making the improbable ascent to the pinnacle of The Forehead. He thought about what his dad had said, how his mom had been here. He felt the pangs all over again, of missing her; yet knowing she had been where he now stood, this near-sacred place, made everything easier to bear. She had followed her husband on an expedition to the summit of Morgan's Forehead, an investment in faith and strength and trust in her husband by doing something crazy, out of love. Had to be out of love. The Molly Mo that Mo Mo knew and loved would sooner gut a deer than night-climb what she would surely see as a monument to death and dumb people.

But now Mo had something else welling within him, a lightness and warmth, a soft brightness that was free and comforting, like a return to a place of being, a unification of life both spiritual and corporeal even as it seemed as much a homecoming as it was a discovery for more than one heart. He'd just been through an awkward, oddly-timed exchange with his dad, touching on things they'd have to address at length later, yet he had never felt any closer to D Mo than he did right now, for many reasons but none more than the invitation from his dad to be here with him, where Danny Mo grew up. *Too?* And now, coming here, over and above, and above all else. That he felt the presence of his mom brought everything closer to divine. As Mo looked at his dad, he felt nothing but admiration and pride sweeping him away in a tide of gratitude and a profound love of family. *On Earth as it is Heaven.*

Danny was nodding as he stepped up to his ball. Mo wondered if his dad somehow know what was going on inside his son. Why not? The guy seemed to know everything else. The scene below was a collision of colors, green grass and sunlit humanity. Mo imagined that the angle of the light must have illuminated the two Morans as if they were on a one-of-a-kind stage. Tall cactus-like shadows from the folks below stretched inland, Mike and Ike among them. Mo looked for The Zaner, and when he found him further back from the hole and off the fairway, Mo fought the urge to do another fist-pump. The junior Zane, probably running low on patience, had missed the fairway with his lay-up. It would take a fluke to get within realistic birdie range from his position; he'd have to wrench his ball out of the rough, have it land just short in the clumpy greenside rough, and then bounce out with just enough release to feed onto the green. That pretty much sealed it for Mo. Hit the green, and the Open would belong to Danny Mo.

Danny addressed his ball, doing his easy pre-shot waggle now, his head and body blocking out the sun from where Mo was standing, making for a halo of sorts. Danny looked at Mo, and then as he sometimes did in casual evening rounds, those times when he was feeling at peace and carefree and free, he made a comment just before taking the club back, a la Trevino to Herman, and even Freddy and Joey in Skins Game mode. Mo had seen his dad do it many times, and then knock his shot kick-in stiff, and once, at sunset, jar an eight-iron on the fly on The Old Barn's 18th to win a skin-heavy carryover umbrella that netted him $72 that was promptly reinvested in Steamin' E Burgers at The Aftermath for everyone in the fivesome.

"It's a long story, Mo, but your mom came here with me on our wedding night." Danny Moran paused for a second or two. "And this…this is where our family began. With you."

Before Mo could process that, Danny went into his swing. His rhythm was languid and right. The click of a perfectly struck iron-shot bordered on a crack, a glorious sound, as tattered pieces of plant leaves from the follow through were yanked over the ledge and began a slow fall to the beach below. Relief flooded Mo's every pore. His dad was delivering on a feat only he, Danny Moran, could have envisioned. The ball climbed ever higher into the sky, the left half of it illuminated by the sun, which now seemed lower than where the Morans stood.

This was the shot his dad had seen in his mind, perhaps more than *three decades* ago. The ball had barely left the clubface when Danny said, "That's everything. Couch and crown everything."

There was never a doubt after the ball reached its apex that it would start cutting gently toward the flag. The ball was not only working toward the target, it was going to be *right* - the right distance, the right line and at the right angle of descent. Everything about it was just so damned… right.

Mo's eyes were stinging now. The sight of the ball in the air, the setting, the backdrop, the courage and creativity, and what would forever stand as the strongest case ever made for the value of local, or loco, knowledge. The echoes of a young father teaching his nine-year-old son about the law of the jungle was melting into Mo. *"You want to hit balls by yourself on the range, Mo? You go get your spot before you get your balls, but you need some balls to get your spot."* And when the time came, *"pounce like a jungle cat with say-so."* His dad had quoted his own dad when telling Mo this, but it was anything but a hand-me-down lesson now. Danny Mo had not only taught this to his son, he showed him how to do it, how to live it, and at this moment, Danny Mo had perfected it in a way no golfer ever would again.

D Mo held his finish. Murmurs from the gallery began to grow. The ball drifting right, carrying the bunker guarding the front left of the green, in the direction of the flag. "It's over."

At first Mo thought his dad meant he might've hit it too good, that he flew the green, but a second later the ball slammed into the green, 15 or 20 feet short and left of the hole. Amazingly, Mo swore he could hear the smacking sound the ball made, right before a blast of joy from a gallery shouting out in glee.

From their elevated vantage point, they could see the ball bobble along almost parallel to them, like a chip and run winding down. Totally focused on the ball now, Danny twisted his body, unveiling some uncharacteristic body English as if it would help get the ball closer to the hole, like Seve or Sergio. With the ball moving left-to-right and slowing, Danny's contortions gave way to his trademark little shuffle to the left, just as he had done all week and most of his competitive life. When the ball was in the air.

For some reason the scattering of the yellow butterflies in his periphery registered with Mo. Alarms went off in his head. Mo pulled his eyes away from the incredible shot and the alarms grew into sirens. Something was going horribly wrong. He saw D Mo's gaze turn kind of sleepy-eyed as he tracked his ball. His movement to the left appeared to be in slow-motion yet way too fast. A wave of dread slammed into Mo as his dad drifted toward the ledge. The man had gone to another place. Then Danny was blinking rapidly, his eyes lolling before fluttering again as if in resignation, as if he knew he was past recovery. Mo felt his legs freeze. The sound of unbridled happiness from near the green was replaced by the screams inside his head.

"That's everything," was what Danny had said seconds earlier. *What the hell is that? Everything?* His way of saying he caught his four-iron perfectly flush? Or was it just that…everything about everything? The day, the week, the last three years, his entire life, everything that came before his decision to attempt two mind-boggling golf shots and everything that happened after the first shot and before the second?

Everything.

Danny Mo returning home, to Rock Harbor, to his land, now The Majesty, to his spot, atop the sunset-side of Morgan's Forehead, "where our family began," with Molly, on their wedding night, the resulting progeny at his side now, his son his caddie his friend – Mo Mo.

Everything given, nothing left? Completing the circle of life?

Mo had neither the time nor the acuity to factor everything on the spot, but he sure as hell could feel the cumulative weight of, well, every-god-damn-thing. He wasn't sure his dad even knew where he was at the moment. Mo's mind was firing signals to move. He gurgled out a crude word just as his dad spat the same one, and the harshness of that word, so out of character, somehow broke the freeze. Mo exploded from his paralysis and pounced, certain he was too late. But like a hitter who inexplicably escapes a headhunting fastball tailing in, Mo somehow lashed his right hand out and at the small of his dad's clammy lower back and found that he was clutching Danny's leather belt before he could grasp the fact that he almost expedited his dad's plunge to the rocky shore below had he missed.

Adrenalin flooded Mo's every vessel. Part of his dad's upper body was over the ledge. Mo caught a glimpse of the view below and the momentary loss of equilibrium and surrendering panic had convinced him they were both going over. A plea for the black leather belt to hold shot through his mind before a jolt of pain shot through his shoulder. Both held up for the moment but his Adidas cross trainers were skidding on the sandy surface and as terror took over for panic, Mo pulled and lurched backward so hard they both tumbled almost sideways and crashed onto the flat of the Forehead between the spot of the historic shot and the place below where the butterflies had hovered a moment before. Mo rolled over quickly and was on his hands and knees. His heart was pounding and he struggled to breathe.

"You okay, Dad?" he said several seconds later.

Danny Mo lay flat on his back, arms and legs splayed, looking up at the sky. He wasn't breathing heavy at all. His face was blank. He didn't say anything. Mo thought maybe his dad didn't, or couldn't, hear him, that maybe the dam broke and he was completely adrift in a sea no one else could see. Worse, he feared that maybe that's where his dad wanted to be.

"Dad?" Mo was on his feet now, probably six or so feet off his dad's shoulder. Mo stayed on the balls of his feet.

Danny peered into the sky, his head cocked away from Mo. "Sorry. Seriously." Danny's voice cracked with emotion. "Pie-hole...?"

Mo stared at his dad. Yeah, he was confused, but he was pretty sure his dad wasn't talking to him. "You okay, D Mo?" Mo worked his mind hard and fast but it was like a crude broom had been taken to the elation from before and slapped it into dissipating powder.

Just that quickly, Danny Mo rolled over and sat up. He looked at his son through moist eyes, but didn't say anything right away. When he did, he led with a sheepish chuck. "Don't know if I have an answer for that, Mo." He did a quick shudder-shake of the head and got to his feet.

∞

Chapter 46

When Danny and Mo crested the side of the gulch leading to the fairway the gallery once again went gaga. John G. Schmitz and a host of other tournament officials were the first to greet the Morans. Mo was happy to see that they had retrieved Danny's clubs from where they had entered the gulch. Saved him some steps and a solid minute or more.

"Crazy, Danny," said one of the blue coats, laughing as he spoke. "Looks to be about a foot or two."

Another official opined, "The greatest shot…I mean shots…I ever…I just process what I just saw…"

The others chimed in with simple hoots or the kind of incoherent nattering that spills from minds freshly blown. A host of extended congratulatory hands were forced into backslaps when Danny blew past them, nodding politely as he did.

Mo threw the bag over his shoulder and settled into an even pace a half step behind his dad. Rinny and Crusty were practically floating across the fairway toward them, with Crusty shaking his head and Rinny smiling big.

Danny let out a long sigh.

"Runnin' out of gas, D Mo?" Mo was yawning before he finished the sentence. "Been a long day."

"Runnin' out of everything, Mo. My circuits are blown."

Mo had watched his dad closely when Danny led the way back down The Forehead. It wasn't the same route they'd taken on the way up.

"Gravity gives us a couple different options," his dad had said. "One of the options ends a little more abruptly than you might prefer." The way he said it haunted Mo, and it was all he said until they got to the fairway.

Mo shrugged. They were still a couple hundred yards away from the green. "Let's enjoy the moment."

Danny didn't seem to hear his son. "Look at Rinny, that smile, her walk, if that isn't your mother…"

"Yeah." Mo didn't know what to say.

Rinny ran the last 10 yards to her father and embraced him. "You're just so psycho, Daddy Mo," said Rinny, "I know that's not a news flash but…."

"Mmm…" said Danny, wearily. "Don't I know it, Rin."

Crusty joined the group in the middle of the fairway, but kept some distance from the three Morans. The little Sphinx could not erase his crooked grin, so he fought it off with a quip. "Not a lot of guys would play it quite that way there, Dannymo."

"Probably not," Danny agreed, walking again, smiling a little. "Alright, we'll see you guys down by the green. Manda Mo here?"

"Got here in plenty of time," said Crusty. "Rinny filled her in while you guys were dickin' around on the rock tower. She's tellin' people she used to worry about you going up there when you were younger. Now she thinks you've lost your mind."

"Mothers always know, I guess."

Finally it was just father and son striding down the center of the 18th fairway in the waning pre-dusk light. The sun and the now calmer water of the Green Bay collaborated to sparkle in the finish of one hell of day.

"Blows my mind about Mom bein' up there."

"Yours too?"

Mo thought about that. He repositioned his dad's bag on his shoulder, the irons clacking sequentially like a run of knuckle cracks. He had meant a quarter century ago or so. Did D Mo believe Molly was here, up there, now? Of course he didn't. Hell, who knew. His dad was exhausted. *The guy will soon be 50, walking, grinding, climbing, and out late the night before doing who knows what, but….*

Mo went to the well. "Remember how Mom would sing *Danny Boy?* Always knew she was in a good mood when she was singing. I could see her doing it on top of Morgan."

"Me too, Mo."

The mere mention of *Danny Boy* requires those familiar with it to rattle off the opening line of the song. Mo was not immune to the *Danny Boy* spell and actually broke into his own half-assed take. Anything to avoid getting into whatever happened near the ledge in the seconds following one historic four-iron. "Oh Danny boy...the pipes, the pipes are callin'...from glen to glen and down the mountainside..." Mo was never quite sure what came next, so he covered with "Always wished I could sing."

"You can, Mo. Just not well. But..."

"I know, but God doesn't mind." Mo chimed in with what his mom used to say about singing in church.

Father and son were walking a little slower now, angling toward the cart path bridge that led to the green 80 yards away. Zane Williams Jr. had indeed wedged his ball onto the green but it looked 40 or 50 feet away from the hole. Bill Linneman was shuffling without urgency toward Danny's ball. When Linneman got to it, he made a noticeable effort to bend over and inspect the ball and then nodded.

Danny gave a joyless chuck. "Billy's letting everyone know we really did find our ball."

Mo thought his dad was not as happy as he should be. *After so many years, after these three days, after those two shots, at this particular moment, it should be...different.* Mo cocked is head and reprised the song that was the very sound of Moran family happiness, "Oh Danny Boy..." but stopped when he saw his dad shake his head.

"It's the last line of that song that gets me, Mo."

Mo decided to say nothing, but he added the song to the list he was compiling. As soon as he could, he'd be Googling the infinity symbol, the prostate gland, and the lyrics to *Danny Boy.* See what that last line was all about.

∞

The cheers had settled down for the briefest moment then crescendoed to yet another swell. Nearly everyone joined in as the two Morans walked onto the 18th green. Mike and Ike came over to deliver quick high-fives. Mike Van Sickle shook his head, and said, "In-freaking-sane."

Mo looked around. Smiles, laughter, even some watery eyes. The joy and the sense of community would have been closer to unanimous, but for the large man in the clubhouse balcony with his back to the green. Andy Salamone was animated, talking and gesturing to some others Mo couldn't see, eclipsed by B'Gandhi's girth. Once again and forever, Mo's distaste for the man could be measured in units of hatred squared.

He pulled his dad's putter from the bag and handed it to him. Danny took it almost reluctantly, still looking at where his ball had come to rest. "If that's two feet, then I'm Andrew Bogut," he said, just loud enough for Mo to hear through the softening applause.

Mo did a little bobble-head action. His dad's ball was easily five feet away from the hole, a little above it with a slight left-to-right break. It would be delicate, but all Danny needed was two putts to win if The Zaner missed his long putt for birdie.

And Zane Williams Jr. did miss. Badly. His ball rolled at least six feet past the cup. The Zaner quickly chased after it, didn't mark, didn't line up his comebacker, didn't take a practice stroke, and then, in the peculiar way a confounding universe can turn momentarily benevolent to reward quitters for no good reason, knocked in his six-foot putt. Mike Van Sickle made his birdie putt, tipped his hat, and then melted into the surrounding mass of humanity. The spotlight was then, once again, on Danny Moran.

"Now we go," said Mo, channeling Crusty.

Danny looked at Mo and gave a tiny nod, barely perceptible to anyone but Mo, yet powerful nevertheless. This was his dad, D Mo, the one he knew, the original jungle cat; it seemed D Mo was back from wherever he had gone. Just like that.

Independent shouts of encouragement spilled onto the green from all sides and above. Mo learned long ago that for some reason, people just loved to say "Danny Mo." Some phonetic aspect of the name somehow delivered a positive vibe to the overall enunciation experience. People would come up with their own inflections, sometimes adding a colorful adverb or phrase between the Danny and the Mo. Crusty turned it into one word, "Dannymo," and after Danny walked away from the game, some Barnstormers opted for "Danny 'Here No' Mo." This all, no doubt, influenced Andy Salamone's decision to call his rival, "Dan Moran." Now, the *Danny Mos* were cascading over The Majesty with a *Johnny Comes Marching Home* fervor, and the man himself appeared to have entered yet another bubble.

Mo wondered how many different worlds his dad had visited over the course of his State Open championship. And yet he couldn't shake the feeling that what had just transpired on top of Morgan's Forehead was his dad's attempt to hit for the cycle, only to be thwarted, or maybe saved, by his only begotten son.

After a moment, the crowd quieted and a voice from above was heard. "The hell happened on that mountain, Dan? Don't think any in your congregation could see it down there, but from up here it looked like you got sacked from behind." Salamone was smiling, while a couple of his cocktail-swishing henchmen gave animated, wide-eyed looks, as if blown away by the enormity of Sally's balls.

Mo burned a stare into Salamone, who was casually leaning over the balcony railing now, but looking directly at Danny Moran. If Danny had heard the comment, he didn't show it. Whatever was going on inside his dad's head was anybody's guess, but Mo was certain that whatever it was could no longer surprise him. Salamone's comment was puzzling to the gallery, many of whom did not know much about golf, and might have wondered if "sacked from behind" was a golf expression or some low-brow sexual reference. The consensus was that Salamone was more than likely a jealous prick hungry for the attention he wasn't getting, and so Mo's blistering stare was multiplied by several hundred locals. Someone yelled, "Get security!" All of this pleased the grinning Salamone who gave a *What did I do?* shrug.

Danny didn't seem to notice anything as he circled the hole, sizing up his putt. He never once squatted to check the line from either side, but he did take his time. No need to get too crazy when two putts from five feet wins the title. The crowd hushed. Danny merely had to touch his ball and then finish it off with a one-handed tap-in. Game over. The way it should have gone down years earlier at The Hill Farm instead of Danny Mo going down.

This time Danny replaced his ball and immediately flipped his lucky Gaelic coin to Mo, who was standing off to the side on the fringe. Mo caught the coin, not really sure why his dad had sent it his way. He knew what it said, but with everyone watching, it was almost required that he inspect it. *A man's fame lasts longer than his life.* Mo put it in his pocket and watched his dad step up to the ball.

Danny took two practice strokes. Hard ones. Too firm for the distance. Still, it was vaguely familiar, but very different from what his putting routine had been for the week. Strange. Then it hit Mo. Mo recalled D Mo telling him how Grandpa Curly used to talk about competing under pressure. "Don't aim, just fire," he'd say. "Guys get crazy under the gun, they over-engineer." It was a mindset thing, a way to trust one's instincts. To let it go. On the mound it meant trust your stuff, but it held up as solid advice for almost any sport or endeavor.

And so Mo watched as his dad leaned into the lessons he learned from his own dad. Just the day before, when Mo stood with his dad in the hallway looking at a picture of Curly and Manda, D Mo mentioned how he didn't really grow up until his dad passed away. But the man never forgot what he got from his pop, the originator of the "Jungle Cat with say-so," the guy who claimed profane investments in negativity were "like freezing tainted meat," the guy who, up until the day he died, told his grandson, "You go right at 'em, Mo Mo."

Then, "the one and only Danny Mo" went right at it. He stepped to his ball with authority, no hesitation, and smacked his five-foot eagle putt into the center of the cup on the 72nd hole to win the Wisconsin State Open by two shots. At long last, the favorite son of a favorite son, with his own son at his side, in the boldest style imaginable, pouncing with say-so, went out and won that one title that came to mean more to him than anything else having to do with golf.

Danny glanced once up at the sky. When Mo arrived at his dad's side there was no hug, but there was a handshake and a moment of eye contact that Mo knew he would never forget. It gutted him when his dad quietly said, "We did it, Mo Mo. All of us."

A tangible surge of emotion came over the gallery, and gave birth to a roar that rocked The Majesty and all of Rock Harbor, across the land that no one knew better than Danny Moran. No one! The evidence was in.

∞

Chapter 47

Whether it was in response to the things he said, the things he did, or the things he imagined he did, cheers and applause had always been as therapeutic to Danny Mo as Swedish massage was to the tightly-wound. Up until three years ago, that is, when the active ingredients in the *Hip, Hip, Hoorays* no longer provided the same kind of buzz they once did.

Danny exchanged handshakes and headshakes with his playing partners and their caddies, signed his score card and made his way through the happy masses in search of his family. He shook the hands of a whole lot of people: locals, fellow players, distant relatives, golf officials, various media, and some others he at least recognized as representatives of times gone by and places traveled and traversed (if not necessarily remembering who the hell they were). He fell into a rhythm, going with a rotation of, "thank you," "thanks," and "appreciate it." Eventually, the congratulations started coming too fast and from all angles and he had to lean on the golf-speak shorthand of "Q," becoming a Q-ing, nodding, handshaking automaton.

Finally he made his way around the corner of the clubhouse to the relative safety of his trusted circle. Rinny, Mo Mo, Manda, Crusty and Carter were ready, unleashing happiness and pride with heartfelt hugs, and the priceless, biological sounds of genuine affection. Danny was smiling, but didn't have much to say. He believed one of the best things about family is that you don't have to talk all the time, the way some friends and wannabe-friends do, as if there could be no comfort without a constant flurry of words to validate the depth of a relationship. With family, sure, talking happens, lots of it in fact, but there is no immediate pressure to deliver whatever wit or wisdom makes for the perception of worthiness. In the Moran family, it was cool to simply hang out. Molly would opine that her husband needed a break from being Danny Mo from time to time, and he'd argue the implausibility of such a notion by pointing to the inability of the leopard to augment its spots. And when he did, Molly would pounce.

"Danny Mo would never be so trite," she'd say, proving her point in seven words or less.

Danny wanted only to escape The Majesty and, for however long, just hang with his family. At least for the time that was left. But he would also need some time alone to think, to reflect, to have a chance to bask in powerful memories. Most of all, to melt into the potent, interactive reverie that had become a sometimes healing, and sometimes frightening way of life for Danny Moran. Done right, Danny could think about Curly, see Curly's reaction and feel what Curly thought about everything going on. And he'd thank his father again. Most importantly, he could be with Molly. Burning memories, shared moments in another realm: the good, the bad, and the everything in-between. Everything. The presence of Curly and Molly was so near now, yet still beyond reach. At least until later, when he could properly cultivate the imagery skills that allowed him to live the lifestyle to which he had become accustomed.

Ranking himself "top-five worldwide" in the vivid daydream realm was putting it humbly. He once tried to convince Molly that his portable realities were simply his way of merging people, places and achievements with faith, hope and gratitude. That it was, in essence, a form of prayer. Molly rolled her eyes, of course, but the hint of a smile on her lips had Danny's heart swelling. Feeling needy now, he wanted the chance to lose himself in all of it as soon as possible.

But all that would have to wait. The 18th green had been transformed into a stage, with a podium and microphone, a banner dedicated to the tournament sponsor, Palermo's Pizza, a table loaded with plaques and trophies, and a gathering of navy-coated tournament officials who were issuing firm handshakes to all plaque recipients. Then, State PGA Executive director Joe Stadler took a moment to pat himself on the back for extending "a special exemption to someone special," then paused dramatically, and went into an effusive introduction that was built on the fact that it was for a man who didn't need one: "Rock Harbor's own...Danny Moran." It was embarrassing. Danny's stomach was churning. *The return of the butterflies.*

The backslaps and congratulatory commentary during his walk to the podium were like great food on a full stomach. On some disassociated level he heard the rousing nature of the lengthy ovation, and he was pretty sure he was acting the proper and humble champion.

The clubhouse was lit, as was the American flag. Some of the outside lights had been turned toward the green, creating an effect not often associated with a golf tournament. Natural light receded in the west, and electric lumens reached out to contribute, like everyone else in attendance, as well as the land itself.

Stadler handed Danny the mic, which felt surprisingly heavy. Maybe he was that tired. His hand was perspiring; he felt the wetness against the metal as he held it. Perhaps he was that nervous. His dad's ashes would've come in handy right about now. *...giving me a hand, one last time.* The quiet had become an annoying sound; he wondered just how long he'd gone without saying anything, like at the service for Molly. And so came another thought, the one which rode with him every single day for the past four years. *If you'd just shut your pie-hole...ah, Christ!* His mouth felt cakey, had that post-round parched feeling. He took a deep breath...and let it out. The sound, amplified by the microphone, echoed off the clubhouse like something from the spirit world. Embarrassing, as if he'd never done a lick of public speaking before. Him. Danny Mo. He looked out at the crowd and waited until he could come up with a cogent thought amongst the flood pooling behind the momentary famine.

Finally, he spoke. "There are so many people here I'd like to thank, and I'd really like to thank you all by name, but I cannot, of course. So please let me beg off with an old cliché, the one about 'friends too numerous to mention' but, as they say, 'you know who you are....'" Danny scanned the amphitheater of humanity that had gathered on his old turf in support of him. People who knew him as a little kid, either when he was one or they were; people with strong convictions for or against the building of The Majesty, people who'd only heard of Danny

Mo through others through local scuttlebutt, and, despite the fact that Door County boasted 10 other golf courses of varying challenge, many locals who had never set foot on a golf course in their lives. Until now.

He continued, "And, let me say that *that* is a good thing, a very good thing, that you know who you are, because that would be my wish for everyone, always…to know exactly…who you are." There were groups in the gallery who cheered, and others who looked a little confused. *Pasta speech, part deaux?*

Danny saw his mother nodding, willing him. Crusty and Rinny exchanged glances, something in the *can't-argue-with-that* family of expressions. "But…the people I find myself wanting to thank most of all…well…can't hardly say they aren't with us today, because I surely felt their presence all week." Danny reflexively gestured with his hand to cover a need to swallow hard. "But, you see, in our family, we win as a family and we lose as a family. Family multiplies the good but quick and pacifies the bad even quicker. Happens with a lot of families. *Happens* is the way to say it, too. It can happen… if you let it. Hard to teach it. Books try, words fail, and nobody really learns a lot from lectures anyway. Gotta kind of live it, or pay attention long enough. I'm talking about a long-term, slow-burn, unspectacular love with no retail value whatsoever, but with a net worth you can't believe. There's a lot to be said for the love of doing absolutely nothing much if you're with the right people. I wasn't in top form entering this championship, there was nothing much to expect, but I knew I'd be with the right people, at least." There were cheers and applause at that and Danny paused to regroup.

"I take pride in nothing much, really, menial stuff, like sorting socks and buttering toast. Or more important things like taking the time to learn a color-coded kitchen sponge program, yellow, blue, green - dishes, floor, counter, – which, I'm sorry to say, took me longer than it should have, but I got it down now." Danny Mo's eyes watered. He didn't care.

"As for losing, yeah, well, hard to apply the word 'lose' to a golf tournament for me these days. You know, you can't win 'em all, which I suppose is good. Keeps a person humble as my wife always tells me.

But, truth be told, you can learn a hell of a lot from blowing it. Believe me on that one." Danny let out a long breath, this time away from the mic, proving that very point to himself. "I had come to accept that I wasn't going to win this championship, no matter how hard I tried. And that's the thing. You see, a lot of years ago, I went to talk with a smart person on a regular basis. A counselor. Learned plenty. It's different for everyone, but one thing I learned was… to not try so hard. I didn't get it then. Now, it seems like it applies to everything. The smart person told me that if the matches get wet, then give it some time, let the matches dry. The fire and heat can return." Danny was flying too close to the flame now, close to going to a place where he might not be able to reel himself back in. He was gesturing with the mic, a slow back and forth weave (*infinity*), nervous. He tried to settle himself. "So…as a lot of you know Molly and Curly Moran, they've been gone awhile. But, before I finally shut my pie-hole…I just want you to know…they were with me all week, and always will be. I believe we won this championship because of so many things I learned from them. Some of it didn't get through to me until they were gone. Maybe *because* they were gone. But please know this: we Morans, we thank you, *WE* won today…"

The microphone slipped from his now beading right hand. It hit the 18th green with a loud bang. Danny smiled and shook his head, but didn't miss a beat. He looked to the sky and finished his sentence in a semi-embarrassing shout "…as a family!" And then - having completed a most discomfiting mission, evidenced by his choice of words, his very public act of contrition and prayer of thanks to the many and the dead - he lifted the trophy high.

There was a final ovation, not the ear-shattering sort but the kind with depth, deep sounding, thick with emotion, but mostly white noise to Danny. He felt lightheaded, doubled over for a few seconds and covered it with a shoe re-tie. After his talk he managed a few brief interviews, making sure he took care of his friend Gary D'Amato first. Thank God for Crusty, who appeared at his side soon after, and ushered him out from under the demands for his time.

Walking to the car, Danny was afraid to ask how bizarre he came across. Finally, he looked at Crusty until his friend looked back. "Well?"

Danny kept walking down the path to the parking lot. It was now dark enough to feel a bit inconspicuous. "They think I'm nuts?"

"I think," said Crusty, expressionless, "the microphone hitting the green sounded exactly like your ball did when you hit that shot from Mount Morgan."

"Gotcha," said Danny, laughing at Crusty's command of everything. "Goin' out with a bang, we did."

∞

Chapter 48

Mo had stayed behind at The Majesty after Danny left with Crusty, Manda, Rinny, all the Morans from the past and any other imaginary friends his dad may have been harboring in his head and heart. Mo said he'd wait for the memorabilia that Loren Ferguson promised to gather up for Danny. Things like the scoreboard sheet and the flags from both the 1st and the 18th holes. Danny had smiled and politely thanked Loren for the thought, but it all seemed of little interest to him. Mo, however, said he'd bring the stuff back in case his dad had a change of heart later.

Mo chugged a quick beer with a few of the Barnstormers before their bus hit the road. After that, he handled some additional questions from various writers seeking insight on Danny's strategic vision for the final hole, and what it was like looking for a golf ball where one had never before been hit (*something he knew all about, but went with "one small step for Mo-kind"*). Inside the clubhouse, people were buzzing, mostly locals and players staying over an extra night. Many of them had their own questions about Danny Mo's bizarre and ballsy use of the geological landmark now known to some "Rockers" as "Mo Fo." And most of them were hell-bent on buying Danny Mo's boy a beer.

No one mentioned what nearly happened atop The Forehead. Hell, Mo wasn't sure he was ready to even think about that. His dad had told Gary D'Amato that he simply lost his balance on the sandy surface, and that would be that, as far as anyone knew. And so Mo stuck to the facts, including how he knew nothing beforehand of his dad's decision to invent a shortcut (that took more time) on the 18th hole by hoisting a three-wood to the peak of "Mo Fo." Mo wolfed down The Majesty's signature burger called The Royal Highness, which he thought was good but no Steamin' E. With his base in place, a procession of Jagermeister shots started appearing, courtesy of some hard-living locals who saw D

Mo's victory as a sign to become one with the spirits world. And so Mo picked 'em up and put 'em down. It was the polite thing to do. He took the long way home, with a stop along the side of the road to honor his father with a liquid lazy eight that wasn't half-bad, yet it seemed to take no time at all. When he arrived at his grandmother's home, it was nearly 11 p.m. Mo was surprised to find Crusty sitting on the deck. A half dozen empty Heineken bottles lined the rail.

"Crusty-dude, did everyone go to bed already?"

"Hey Mo, yeah, everyone's gassed. They started dropping, ah, maybe 45 minutes ago."

"Didn't think it was that late." Mo sat down next to Crusty.

"Well, once we had our fill of perfectly seasoned poultry from your granny's magical crock-pot, on those soft Sheboygan hard rolls with some tater salad, you know... Your dad held out the longest, thought you might show up any minute, but the man was falling asleep in his chair. Told him I'd wait up for you."

"Wait up? The hell..." Mo, overreacting. He wasn't completely drunk, only functionally drunk. He moved on. "Anyway, there were a whole lot of people celebrating at The Majesty. Everyone wantin' to know every detail about everything. It was hard to escape."

"I know how it goes, Mo."

"If you can't celebrate this, what can you celebrate?" said Mo, a defensive edge to his voice.

"Damn straight," Crusty nodded. "Your dad figured as much, said it was either that or something about you having some girl probably wanting to hear from you soon."

No doubt. Mo had a hell of a lot to process. "Yeah, well, I didn't have my phone with me. Cell service sorta sucks here anyway." He hadn't been sure how to deal with any of that, so he drank toasts to his dad and celebrated with the Harbor folk. It was the thing to do. Things as they were, he was both curious and a little nervous about checking his voicemails, wondering if there might be a clue as to who had spoken with Cindy last.

"Your Grandma left the crock on warm for you," said Crusty. "Told me to tell you to go right at it. If not, to add some water and leave it on."

"Thanks Crust. Guess you can go to bed now, you know, now that I'm home safe."

"Guess so, Mo." Crusty stood up. "Say, let's take a quick peek at the scoreboard sheet. Like to see who shot what."

It hit Mo as Crusty was saying it. "Damn it, Crusty, I forgot it. Mr. Ferguson had it all packed up for me..."

"No biggie." Crusty shrugged. "We'll pick it up in the morning before we head home. Won't be at first light, though. Everyone was unanimous about sleeping in."

"Would've been my vote too." Mo sighed, exhausted. "Say Crusty, you know the words to *Danny Boy*?"

"Can't say I do, not all of 'em. Just the beginning." Crusty looked like he was going to say something more then thought the better of it. "Might find it in one of those music books on your granny's piani. Why?"

"Ah, it's nothing. Something my dad said." Mo regretted bringing it up.

"Okay then. Night, Mo." Crusty opened the sliding glass door that led into the kitchen. Then he turned, Marty-like. "Your dad, he couldn't say enough about having you on his bag. Said no way he gets through today without you."

"Yeah? Cool. Still can't believe it actually happened, you know, how it happened."

Mo went in after Crusty and headed to the living room, to the piano in the corner. After a little shuffling of the music books, he found *The Little Irish Songbook.* Fatigue had taken over. Mo decided to forgo the perfectly seasoned crock-pot poultry and went to the basement, songbook in hand. The sofa sleeper was freshly made, with the covers turned down. His clothes from the previous two days had been washed and folded and neatly placed next to his duffle bag. Manda's handiwork. Mo air-chucked and shook his head, *I'm not worthy*, he thought as he opened the songbook.

He found *Danny Boy* immediately. It was as if the book had been opened to that page enough times to maintain a binding memory, and went there of its own will. The song he'd heard so many times growing up took on new power when he read the lyrics, now, in the context of all that he had been through with his dad. *It's the last line that gets to me, Mo.* Mo shivered involuntarily.

Oh Danny boy, the pipes, the pipes are calling
From glen to glen, and down the mountain side
The summer's gone, and all the flowers are dying
'Tis you, 'tis you must go and I must bide.
But come ye back when summer's in the meadow
Or when the valley's hushed and white with snow
'Tis I'll be here in sunshine or in shadow
Oh Danny boy, oh Danny boy, I love you so.

And if you come, when all the flowers are dying
And I am dead, as dead I well may be
You'll come and find the place where I am lying
And kneel and say an "Ave" there for me.

And I shall hear, tho' soft you tread above me
And all my dreams will warm and sweeter be
If you'll not fail to tell me that you love me
I'll simply sleep in peace until you come to me.

I'll simply sleep in peace until you come to me.

Aww, dammit, D Mo.

Mo's thoughts turned and churned until he no longer knew what he was thinking, or if he was thinking, or if he was drifting in and out of the partial dreams of tentative sleep. Finally, near dawn, he went into a deep and dreamless sleep that lasted until he heard Crusty's voice once again.

"Well, we agreed to sleep in, Master Mo, but we didn't want you to miss lunch." Crusty was at the foot of the sofa sleeper.

Mo sat up, unsure of where he was at first. The songbook fell to the carpet. "Lunch?"

"Yeah, it's past noon, and it's almost ready."

"Ah, yeah…suppose everyone else is up."

"Ya think?"

"My dad's probably been up for half the day."

"Yeah, he's up, alright. Up and gone. Headed back already, before anyone was up."

"What?" Mo sat up straighter.

"Come on up. I made BLTs," said Crusty."And they're perfect."

∞

Chapter 49

Like a shock collar for the conscience, the writhing possum within him wasn't going to settle down, Mo supposed, until he got the message. Really got it. Was he going to take things for granted forever, or was he just stupid? Maybe the time had indeed come to take an honest look at what his mom had too frequently referred to as "root behavior," maybe to finally address his increasing dependence on dressing up bad form with a knack for *raison d'être* on demand.

But, what the hell? His dad was gone. Mo should have been around last night, like his dad had always been for him. Mo felt empty, even wronged at first, which he knew to be bad form. The *poor Mo Mo* reflex at work. Low-cost drive-thru comfort food for Bad-Shoulder-Boy's bum luck. Sad habits die hard, if at all. Then there was all that other stuff. Like his dad's health. Like Cindy. Mo hadn't been sure he could hold off getting into it. So he partied. Figured he could take it up with his old man on the drive home.

Nope.

Danny Mo was gone.

His note was so Danny Mo.

If a little dreaming is dangerous, then the cure is to dream all the time." - Proust

Mo, Rin, Mom and Crust,

Not sure if that's an exact quote. I'm more of a Dave Barry type than this Proust cat, but you know Molly, she cherished those classics and she believed that quote from the Frenchman was meant for me. Can't argue, there's freedom in them thar words. So I took it as a sign from Molly Mo when I stumbled across another gem from the Proustman, one that's equally emancipating.

"All our final decisions are made in a state of mind that is not going to last."

Don't know if that's exactly right either, but that's my recollection and it <u>feels</u> exactly right.

I've made a couple decisions I believe are exactly right too. I've decided that Hank and Manda Mo should be together, should look out for each other, and maybe grow old together if it feels right. Trust me, I've done a lot of thinking about who's right for who.

Now, I know this family shares contempt for anyone who's wronged any one of us. Molly calls it the underbelly of love. But coming through for the people who believe in us has always been and still remains more rewarding for me than proving the cynics and know-it-alls wrong. A mindset for better living and living longer and why I said "we" won the Open together. For that, I thank you and love you more than you can know. So please pass these lines from the lads on to Hank, et al.

Slan leat anois mo stor
There's no need to see me to me door
We'll meet again, I hope and pray
Now I'll be on my way

D Mo

After Mo read the note, he said nothing. Then, only, "That guy…I mean, is he going somewhere?" He was shaking his head. "I'll be on my way…" said Mo, looking at nothing. "The Saw Doctors."

"Yes," said Rinny, ""I was just telling Crusty that's the song Daddy said he wanted played at his funeral. Remember how Mom thought it was way vain sometimes, and other times perfect."

"I know, I know. But I mean, what the..." Mo pulled out his cell phone and called his dad's number. After a few seconds they heard Danny's phone vibrating on the kitchen counter next to the little lighthouse lamp. Mo clenched his jaw and stared out the kitchen window to the back yard. He didn't see anything for a spell. When things came into focus, and it was possible Crusty and Rinny were talking, maybe even to him, he saw his grandma. She had her face near Hank's as she massaged under his collar. They looked happy.

"Who's right for who?" he said in a near whisper.

∞

Chapter 50

Mo sat motionless on a backyard deck in need of a power wash and seal - his responsibility now, though his dad had thought of just about everything else. Bills paid by auto-pay, lawn service scheduled, newspaper and mail discontinued. Maybe the mail was being redirected.

Lost in thought. A wisp of an Indian summer breeze blew back a page of the Sports Illustrated magazine that was at the top of his stack, and it was the sound of that single page that snapped him back to the moment. *Sports freaking Illustrated.* The article that turned a State Open golf championship into a human interest story and the disappearance of the story's protagonist into national headlines. Gary D'Amato was being quoted in newspapers around the country and was offering commentary for local and national sports talk radio. Gary Van Sickle was all over The Golf Channel and blogging regularly on Golf.com, where he frequently and bitingly admonished gossip-mongers. Two-time US Open champion and Danny's friend from Madison, Andy North, offered his insights on ESPN, both radio and TV. Even most of the cable news networks dabbled in the story of Wisconsin's vanished champion. As the story leveled off, a friend of Danny's, a former stand up comedian and now morning radio personality who goes by the initials of KB, talked on air about the dark side he'd seen in some comedic types and how Danny Mo had "wandered off the reservation," just like a comic friend of his from Sheboygan had done, who as it turned out had inoperable cancer and was operating a street corner popcorn wagon in Oahu when he died. By his own hand. How, just like that guy, Danny had disappeared from some of their shared social circles for a period of years after his wife died. "I'm not sayin', I'm just sayin'," was how KB ended his thoughts on his friend; but the hint of veiled inference was quickly amplified by some local sports talk show types who pointed to KB as the first actual friend of Danny's to, if not suggest then at least not dismiss, the suicide scenarios that Andy Salamone had suggested as possibilities. KB's comments were like gas on brown grass and Salamone was only too happy to set the fields afire by indulging himself in new requests for interviews and comments from a reinvigorated media. The resulting speculation and half-assed information brought a second and more powerful wind to the story, and it was then that Mo Moran, like D Mo did after Molly died, went underground.

Mo Mo closed his eyes and exhaled… a long sustained release, as if his unsolicited role in what had become a national curiosity could be expunged with his breath.

The Ballad of Danny Mo
BY GARY VAN SICKLE - Senior golf writer SI/Golf.com

"That shot was a defining moment and when a defining moment comes along, you define the moment… or the moment defines you." - Roy McAvoy (Kevin Costner), "Tin Cup."

In golf, a stroke of genius is like a bolt of lightning and just as unpredictable. The conditions have to be perfect - a hurricane mix of guts and glory, desperation and determination, skill and setting where one swing of a club can transcend the game and, in a flash, become a timeless moment etched into history.

Call the roll. Gene Sarazen and Larry Mize at the Masters. Arnold Palmer at Cherry Hills. The Shot Heard 'Round the World. Tom Watson's chip at Pebble Beach. Jack Nicklaus and the 1-iron off the flagstick at Pebble, or any part of the one-man thunderstorm he unleashed on the back nine at Augusta in 1986. And, finally, take your pick of Tiger Woods' inhuman on-course highlights. Probably nothing can top his bump-and-run, bat-turn-reverse chip at Augusta's 16th for sheer ingenuity and slow-motion, lip-hanging, Nike-promoting drama.

Until last month. August 21st. The Wisconsin State Open at The Majesty, an awe-inspiring golf course that virtually overlooks the entirety of Wisconsin's Door County. A finish that had to be seen to be believed. You can be certain there has never been a shot, make that two shots, like the two played by 49-year-

old Danny Moran - aka Danny Mo - a golfing legend in the Badger State for the better part of three decades and the youngest golfer ever inducted into the Wisconsin golf Hall of Fame. There has never been a more defining moment that nonetheless defies definition.

In a nutshell, Danny Mo came to the final hole of the Wisconsin State Open with a chance to finally win the only major state title that had eluded his grasp in a spectacular amateur career. If you're reading this in Idaho or Texas, well, that probably doesn't seem to matter much. But in Wisconsin, trust me, it is a big deal. The State Open was to Danny Mo what the U.S. Open was to Snead, the PGA was to Palmer and Watson, the Masters was to Greg Norman. Moran took an unimaginable shortcut on The Majesty's dramatic doglegged par 5 18th hole up a severe mountain of rock and random vegetation - the greatest shot in the history of any Open anywhere on earth, the craziest, or both - then played the shot of his life from the bluff's edge to the green. If the course hadn't already been called The Majesty, it would've been renamed that after these two shots beyond anyone's comprehension.

After an unusually indirect and what looked to be a harrowing climb to the peak, Moran's second shot, the 4-iron from a sandy lie atop The Forehead, seemingly descended from the stratosphere before smack-thudding into the green and tracking slowly toward the cup. After descending and accepting congratulatory slaps on the back as he made his way to the green, Moran calmly rolled the 3-foot eagle putt into the heart of the cup to put an exclamation mark on an inconceivable finish to a golf tournament.

"The only way I could get there in two and still hold the green was to use The Forehead. I can hit my irons pretty high, but Zane (Williams) Jr, man, he can hit it as high as anyone I've ever seen" said Moran, who grew up less than a mile from the land that has become, despite some community splintering controversy over its construction, the most heralded new golf course in America. "I needed birdie and just as much I needed to keep Zane Jr. from making birdie (by influencing him to play the hole conservatively)."

Williams, the former All-American from BYU, hit an iron off the tee after Moran's seemingly wild 3-wood sailed into the blinding sun and apparent oblivion. Most everyone was puzzled, tournament officials included, when Moran and his son, Maurice, headed up the less severe but still treacherous south side of Morgan's Forehead. After Moran reached the peak and used nearly all of the allotted five minutes to locate his ball, Williams watched in stunned silence as Moran's 4-iron shot found its mark, crashing into the green with otherworldly force. Williams then missed his own long birdie putt that in the end would not have mattered. He finished second, two shots back. "We couldn't see anything really; we were playing right into the sun. You talk about bizarre; he had me thinking he was toast. He must've believed he really could pull it off, maybe he felt it was his only chance. He'd for sure be the only guy who'd know what's up there, but whatever…I played it safe and hit 3-iron off the tee," Williams said, shaking his head. "I guess the guy knew what he was doing all along.

"He set me up."

Full disclosure: I was there - as a dad. My son Mike was in the final group and finished third. And what Danny Moran did on the final hole of the tournament was the most cunning and resourceful and flat-out life-endangering play I've witnessed in nearly three decades of covering golf at the highest level. Just to think of it, to see the possibility, it boggles the mind. But let it be said Danny Mo finally won his elusive Open. Family, friends and history - all there to witness an individual feat that, in his victory speech, Moran claimed was a collective effort.

And it was an unusual victory speech, to say the least. Both heartwarming and heartbreaking, possessing both true joy and a sense of resignation, it was a loving tribute to the living and the dead, and about family, which included a brief lecture about the folly of lectures and advice about color-coding kitchen sponges. (Seriously.) And it was through this tournament and his speech that many from the Harbor community, most of whom do not play golf, were finally introduced - or reintroduced - to their local hero, Danny Mo. It was hello, and thank you. The question that grows daily now - was it actually a farewell speech?

According to his family, at some point in the early morning hours after a performance for the ages in the town where he grew up -- Danny Moran disappeared.

He hasn't been seen or heard from since.

"On the golf course, a man may be the dogged victim of inexorable fate, be struck down by an appalling stroke of tragedy, become the hero of unbelievable melodrama or the clown in a side-splitting comedy - any of these within a few hours, and all without having to bury a corpse or repair a tangled personality."
— *Bobby Jones.*

Danny Mo's brimming trophy case proves he knew about winning. His State Open record proves he knew plenty about failure. This isn't the place to document his golfing gaffes, several of which I covered. What mattered about them is that he never blamed anything else for his finishes. Not luck, not bad weather, not a bad lie, not demons in his head or bluebirds chirping on his backswing (one PGA Tour player I know actually tried to use that last excuse once at the U.S. Open). He took the blame himself. At The Hill Farm, Danny Mo actually lost the State Open when he fumbled his "good luck" ball marker - it hit his ball - on the 72nd hole. He consulted with a rules official and then called it on himself. After which, he returned home to discover his wife had been killed in a car accident, an accident that would have happened right about the time he was making the turn for the tournament's final nine holes, a back nine experience that included an insect plague, a ruptured disc, and a bizarre riverside rescue of a fellow competitor along The Hill Farm's 15th hole, all of which was rendered insignificant after discovery of his unspeakable loss. There were those who attributed that entire experience to fate. I asked Danny about that and he answered quickly. "I'm not big on fate as an explanation, seems to me it's is just a romantic word for 'just because, or stuff happens.'"

That, more than anything else, is what you need to know about the circumstances of his disappearance. There are questions, sure, that may be answered soon, or go unanswered indefinitely. One question that has grown in relevance, involves whether Moran actually considered walking off the peak of Morgan's Forehead, a drop of over 290 feet on the western side to the rocky shore below. It is a question that wasn't even on the radar until Andy Salamone, a lifelong competitor and rival of Danny Mo's, volunteered it.

"I don't think the people below, the people by the green, could see him up there like me and my buddies up on the clubhouse balcony could. I paid close attention. Looked to me like he was going over the ledge - like he wanted to. Now I'm getting hate mail for suggesting it as a mere possibility, people telling me he

lost his balance for a moment and to shut the hell up, well all I'm saying is…I'm
not so sure," said Salamone, perhaps the only amateur golfer who couldn't be
considered a friendly rival of Danny Mo's. "I mean, to me, it looked like the guy
was walking right off the edge when his kid grabbed him. Then the guy goes into
hiding? Really? I mean, if he's even still alive. Not to speak ill, but dead or alive,
it's a copout either way."

No one else, publicly, claims to have seen what Salamone saw. For that
matter, no one else claims to have been looking at anything other than Danny
Mo's outlandish approach shot to the last hole since the whole State Open was
riding on it. No one even considered suicide as a possibility until Salamone
brought it up, and after he did, no one at The Majesty that day believed it.
Perhaps no one wanted to believe it.

Salamone said Moran had been despondent since the death of his wife, and
that it was a major reason he had not played competitive golf in three years.
"Dan Moran has always been a bit dramatic to begin with, the type who likes
the attention, but he's been a completely different guy since his wife died, as any
of us would be. Face it, the guy's business went under, his kid's arm blew up
one step from the show. Let's just say there's been some whispers. And
something else no one has mentioned; can anyone be sure he really found his ball
other than what his buddy Bill Linneman claims? I mean, I know the guy's
supposed to be the Jesus of Rules but…they're buddies. I mean, maybe Dan
Moran was afraid of being found out?"

"All I can tell you is that Danny asked for a new ball on the 18th tee and
his son Mo marked it right in front of me," said Linneman, Director of Rules
and Competition for the WSGA. "Mo even asked how he should mark it and his
dad's exact words were 'surprise me.' Following the most incredible shot,
probably ever, I looked at the ball on the green before the Morans even got
there."

"There's no doubt he found his ball," said Chuck Garbedian, host of
Garbedian on Golf on ESPN Radio 540 in Milwaukee and himself a tournament
golfer in Wisconsin's amateur scene. He was, however, uncharacteristically at a
loss for words about his friend's disappearing act. After a long sigh, he waxed
philosophical "Who can say, a long time ago Danny told me 'I wish I could
control my life as well as my Titlist,' and, yeah, he was laughing at the time, but
now I wonder. It's no secret Danny was dealing with some challenges in his life,

and what is it they say...'the only difference between a rut and a grave are the dimensions...but...like I said, who can say."

Exactly what happened up on Morgan's Forehead, and just where he is at this moment, is a mystery. Danny Mo's son, Maurice (Mo Mo), who was caddying, says he had helped his dad find what he thought was, at first, a surprisingly errant drive - only after nearing the top of The Forehead did he suspect, and after finding the ball eventually realize, that it was an incredible - make that, insane - piece of golfing strategy. Maurice watched the ensuing 4-iron's mesmerizing flight, turned and saw his dad "lose his bearings."

There was no delicate way to ask so I put it out there bluntly: Was there any chance that his dad had some reason for disappearing...or worse? Something we don't know or can't fathom, perhaps some ongoing complication? I didn't mention the obvious, the death of his mother. Molly Moran was a special person, as are all women who put up with being married to men who are committed to golf. That Danny Mo hadn't been quite the same man since, as I too had heard from Badgerland sources. That he'd given up golf in his grief. That he'd shuttered his business. That his approaching 50th birthday was not a time to revel and lick his chops about future easy pickings in senior golf but an event to which he attached no particular significance. Some fifteen years ago told me he would be surprised if he would still be competing at 50. Were these warning signals or part of the normal grieving process? Or, normal period. Then again, what's normal when you lose your life partner? And with all due respect to the individual nature of grief, those who've suffered such losses say that "time heals, but not necessarily time alone."

Mo weighed the question and, at first, simply said that he didn't know anything, offering only "No one..." and a shrug. After another moment of thought he added "My dad has his reasons...and I know this is going to sound weird, but, he left a note and...let's just say, looking back now...our family found that note reassuring. And that's about all our family will have to say about that."

The Milwaukee Journal-Sentinel's golf beat writer, Gary D'Amato, took over covering Danny Mo's exploits when I left Milwaukee. "Did he find his ball? Of course," said D'Amato. "Is he okay? I believe he is, but only time will tell. Is he a different kind of guy? Sure. Refreshing might be a better word."

I can attest to that. It was over a decade ago, we were sitting around BS-ing an hour after Danny had bladed a bunker shot off the roof of the pro shop at Milwaukee Country Club on the 18th hole to cost himself a spot in local US Open qualifying. I'd attempted to qualify myself and missed as well – that year – but Danny, he'd tossed back a few beers very rapidly and we got to talking, rehashing the old days, when he confessed something to me. He claimed that he never really gets nervous in tournaments but that when he get's a little hard on himself on the range, like when he's preparing for a big tournament or even during the first few holes of a big tournament, he'll hear a voice in his head, mocking him, doubting him, calling him out…and that it's in the voice and clipped delivery of Jim Rome. "You know, repetitious takes, cutting through the crap " Danny had said, "like some gifted autistic dude calling it as he sees it. Over and over again." I wasn't sure if he was serious, but I do know that Danny Mo is nobody's clone.

I phoned Steve Stricker, the PGA Tour star who was at home on a travel break in Madison and someone who'd played with Moran many times, to ask what he thought about all the talk surrounding Danny Moran's disappearance. I asked him, cautiously, if he believed Danny Moran was still alive.

"I do," Stricker said without hesitation. "Absolutely. Nobody knows what a guy is going through in his life, and I don't know all the facts, but the guy was always as solid as they come. Cracked us all up…a lot. It's a little strange, a bit mysterious, but…Danny Mo deserves the benefit of the doubt." Stricker paused then before adding. "I've played The Majesty. What Danny did, you'd have to be crazy. Even if you knew what was at the top of that rock tower. It's unbelievable."

It has been nearly six weeks now since Danny Mo disappeared. There is an anonymously posted photo - courtesy of the double-edged sword of technology in a wi-fi, Facebook, Smartphone world – that showed a man who could be Danny Moran, a baseball hat partially concealing a much shorter haircut, greeting a woman at the George Bush Intercontinental Airport in Houston. I asked Maurice about this and another camera phone photo posted on Facebook taken in Ireland at a Saw Doctors' concert, Danny Moran's favorite band. The photo shows someone in the background who some claim could be Danny Mo as well. "Not even his mom and my sister can tell if it's him in those photos, but I wouldn't be surprised if it is. He's always wanted to see Ireland," said Mo. "We've got a distant cousin, at least my dad claims he's a cousin, a guy by the name of Leo Moran, plays guitar and is one of the leaders of The Saw Doctors…God knows he loves those guys. Sees them every time they come to the states, chats them up a little. I've been listening to a song of theirs a lot lately called 'I'll Be On My Way.' In fact, my sister and my grandma and lot of us are leaning on this song of late."

There hasn't been a song written yet, as far as I know, The Ballad of Danny Mo. Maybe, because unlike 'Ode to Billie Joe' and that character's dive off the Tallahatchie Bridge, this tale doesn't have an ending. There are no answers. Just a burgeoning legend that grows more enigmatic every day.

All we know for sure is that Danny Moran is gone.

I enlisted the help of a local free climber in Rock Harbor to be my Sherpa and take me up The Forehead. (After securing authorization for this piece: it is otherwise a $5,000 fine for curiosity seekers since the State Open.) The way to the top requires a bizarre up, down, crossover route; one Moran obviously had burned into his brain over the years when that very area was more or less his backyard. At the peak, one look around and…well, there is no way to explain the majesty of it. Taking it in, even through my labored breathing, I wondered how many times Danny Mo had been there, done that, and the stories he might be able share about The Forehead. We found the approximate area where Danny Mo had ripped his incredible 4-iron. I was stunned by the altitude - looking down at the 18th green and the clubhouse beyond, I felt like I was on top of the world. Over my shoulder was a delirium-inducing view of the bay. I could not fathom that anyone could've imagined hitting a tee shot to such a location. Looking back at the tee, it made me think that Danny Mo's final tee shot – with a slightly oversized, custom-made three-wood - was even more amazing than his shot to the green.

I remembered something Manuel de la Torre said about Danny Mo's swing. De la Torre is the 80-something Hall of Fame golf instructor and legendary pro at Milwaukee Country Club, a man who knows as much about the golf swing as anyone alive. The secret to Danny Mo's success, I quoted de la Torre years earlier, was that "he always had perfect balance."

I inched as near to the cliff's edge as I dared. Gray and white clouds posed above the Green Bay of Lake Michigan, which stretches across the horizon. It could be an ocean, for all you know from here, and Japan or Africa could be on the other side, not Marinette. There is indeed majesty to this place, and will forever be the site of one incredible story. Especially since The USGA is reportedly set on bringing its Open to what's officially known as The Majesty at Harrow Bluffs.

I wondered if the loss of one's partner, compounded by the unfortunate turns that life can take, could affect a man's balance. It is certainly possible. I stepped well back from the edge and looked across the water. An ore freighter in the distance seemed to be barely moving, a statue among blinking whitecaps. A punctuating gust of wind came off the water and it made me shudder.

∞

Mo sat back in his chase and, again, drifted off to a dreamland that, again, confirmed the fact that he was always going to be a lot like his dad. He recalled their drive up to Rock Harbor, the conversation, how they danced in and out of topics fathers and sons almost never have to face. And he kept going back to the moment his dad turned up the music in the car. "…tryin' to get the balance right, the health, the drugs, the lovin' and the beer."

He replayed the flurry of revelations atop Morgan's Forehead, and how long his dad had kept secrets both complicated and fascinating while never letting on that he owned them.

Until the time was right.

Timing.

Everything.

He understood early on that his dad's note from the morning after his victory in Rock Harbor revealed more than what the note actually said, and how Hank, now a totally spoiled granddog, had helped him out with that. And he understood there was more than one reason why D Mo disappeared. Houston. Ireland. He thought he recognized the woman in the airport photo and had it at least tacitly confirmed by the nature of Carter Slane's silent reaction. A little scary, but it made sense. Maybe more than a little scary. That the concert photo in Ireland had been taken over a month later than the one Houston was of some comfort to Mo. Some.

He could see, too, that his dad was a lot like his own dad, Grandpa Curly. And fiercely proud of it. *Nothing wrong with that.*

And he realized that it was now his turn, that there were secrets that Mo Mo Moran was going to have to keep. And he would prove to his dad that he could and would honor such a covenant, so with every lapsing day and a generous God, the more he too would be able to one day share with the man who showed him how it's done.

Like no one.

∞

Epilogue

The man tried to look casual.

As with most pre-tournament efforts at effortlessness, the hop in the man's step was contradiction in action. The crammed cobalt blue golf bag over his left shoulder looked to weigh him down as much as a plastic quiver of toy arrows. With his free arm sweeping in front of him, he had the look of a speed skater willing himself to relax down the homestretch. He offered friendly, but rote, greetings to others milling around as he made his way to the range, but he was laser-locked on the open spot that would soon be his. Flat, with perfectly manicured bent grass, and more importantly, it was as far as he could be from the large golfer with the long silver hair and still be on the range.

It was Thursday morning and the State Golf Association's Match Play Championship was down to the final four competitors. It was the first tournament to be held at The Majesty since the man's father had won the State Open there in historic fashion about 20 months earlier by playing a shot to-and-from a tower of rock that guards the corner of the dogleg on the par five 18th hole. Incredible shots and an amazing local story to be sure, but when the man, Danny Moran, vanished the next morning, the whole affair became a national news story rife with mystery and runaway speculation. Back then, The Majesty was fast becoming a destination course, with golfers coming from nearly every state. When word spread about the legend of Danny Mo, the demand for tee times and media access intensified and came from all over the world. The course, of course, was part of the story.

Mo Moran was the surprise of this match play tournament. But his opponent, Andy Salamone, had been the hottest amateur golfer in the state for the past year and a half. Fresh off becoming the oldest amateur from Wisconsin to qualify for the US Open, Salamone was using the

WSGA Match Play championship at The Majesty as a tune-up for the following week at Bethpage Black in Farmingdale, New York.

"Can't think of a better way to prepare for a US Open course than winning on a US Open course the week before," was the quote that made the papers and rankled more than a few competitors. Now, the two were set to clash in a semi-final match that could easily render the final anti-climactic.

Before the event, there were plenty of stories in both the print and broadcast media about the return to The Majesty, including recaps of Danny Mo's unthinkable final hole strategy. Mentions of his disappearance, however, had been muted and respectful.

An attorney now for the Foley and Lardner Law Firm in Milwaukee, Corrine "Rinny" Moran had managed to get the day off so she could caddie for her brother. Rinny had told Mo she would quit her job before she'd have her brother square off against Andy Salamone at The Majesty without her. She had worked late into Wednesday night and then left Milwaukee at 4 a.m. Thursday morning and drove straight to the course. Now, she did some stretches at the far end of the range, effectively protecting the spot she knew her brother preferred.

Mo gave his sister a hug. "Early one, huh Sis?" he said. "Thanks for getting my spot."

"No. Thank *you*… for winning both matches yesterday so we could have today," she said. "How's Grandma?"

"Good," he said. "She and Hank look after each other. She's coming up later." Mo smiled. "She said she and some friends were going to load up on Celebrex and walk the back nine."

Rinny's eyes sparkled, reflecting the cloudless sky. "Cindy?"

"Unbelievable," said Mo. "Keeping me out of trouble."

"You'll always find trouble. Like today."

"I suppose." Mo shrugged and smiled. "Fewer things to blame now." Mo changed the subject. "Gonna have to be better than good today. The Great White Hairdude is playing great." Mo felt his own nerves jangle as he talked. He covered it with his stretching ritual.

Rinny sniffed. "He's always played better when Daddy's not around."

"You know, Rin, just walking around here, for some reason…" Mo took a deep breath. "Seems like he *is* around."

Brother and sister gazed over the landscape of The Majesty, eventually settling on the soothing panorama of the bay. Morgan in the foreground had always been a magnet. Door County's preeminent landmark had become a must-see point of reference for all who visited the course and Rock Harbor these days. But neither Moran would look up. It wasn't a moment for glimpsing the peak of The Forehead. It was time to peak. Period.

There had not been more than a handful of spectators for any one match thus far in the Match Play Championship. Now there were at least 100 lining the area near the first tee before the Morans even arrived. Rinny walked at a casual pace to keep Mo from rushing. She was smiling, the picture of confidence. Mo was squinting and silent. Salamone stood near the first tee casually tossing a ball in the air and catching it between yawns. He left for the clubhouse before Mo and Rinny got near him. Salamone's henchmen bathed in the aura and various exhausts of the big man. His crew consisted of Jumbo Larson from The Old Barn, another guy who looked familiar to Mo, and two well-tanned, bling-draped, cologne-soaked 50-something smokers in flashy golf shirts.

Rinny stopped short as she and Mo approached the first tee. She didn't have to point at the stained-black hole sign. Being the first hole there was large silver number 1 and small silver script at the bottom that read, **The Majesty**. Next to the **1** was a thickly chalked **NO**. No One.

Mo looked at Rinny. "You think…?" Mo was blinking fast. "Hell…was it commissioned? There aren't 10 people who'd know the 'no one' thing, and three of 'em are dead."

A second later, Salamone emerged from the clubhouse with an unlit cigar jutting from his mouth and made his grand entrance to the first tee box. He looked lovingly at the cigar in his hand. "Cohiba," he said softly as he turned toward his four-minion gallery. They smiled and nodded.

Salamone threw the expensive cigar to the ground like it was a lesser man's cigarette before producing a burp that sounded like a lion interrupted from a nap. A few in the gallery laughed. It looked to Mo as if the familiar looking guy might have tried to breath in some of the vapors.

Doug Fry of the Wisconsin State Golf Association would referee their match. Salamone had appealed to Executive Director Emeritus, Gene Haas, that Bill Linneman, the Director of Rules and Competition for the WSGA, was too close to the Moran family to be involved with their match. Haas quickly went over the rules and conditions for the match. The players had been informed at the beginning of the tournament that most of Morgan's Forehead was now out of bounds.

Salamone had the honor, but before the man he used to call The Hair Dude could place his tee in the ground, Mo walked up to him.

"Big Andy," he said as if he was darn near a friend. "You and me, we got plenty to disagree about. Especially the stuff about my dad. You guys had a hell of a rivalry."

"I suppose we did. Good competitor. Bet he woulda loved to qualify for a US Open." Salamone looked confused.

"Yeah, right," said Mo. "I know you guys battled since before I was born. But, listen to me. That stuff was between you two. I want you to know that." Mo's smile was pasted on. He looked straight into Salamone's eyes. "Okay?" Some in the gallery were straining to hear. Everyone was watching.

Salamone raised his eyebrows. "Ooo-kay."

"Alright then," said Mo, sharply. "That shit is between you and my dad. Not me or my sister. Got it?"

Salamone went with a *this-is-too-weird* look with his eyes.

"I mean, my dad couldn't stand you. And my sister and I, Salamone," Mo smiled wide, "We think a lot less of you than my dad ever did." Mo burned his jungle cat glare right through the heavy man. Salamone tried to give it right back. Their eyes locked, Mo cocked his head almost imperceptibly, the sight of his scars unavoidable now. The tissue torn by the talons from a red tail hawk some 20 years ago didn't tan, and the healed marks stood out like little question marks made with fine chalk. Mo smiled all friendly-like and said, "Just so we're clear." Then he walked away, the gallery none-the-wiser.

Salamone's eyes narrowed. He was flushed, but kept up the smirk of a man sizing up a crazy man. "Whatever you say!" he said, loud enough for everyone to hear.

"We're good then," said Mo, just as loud. Then Mo turned and walked right back to Salamone, who looked like he wasn't sure what Mo might do. Mo beamed. Then, quietly, he said, "You can concede putts, or the match. Otherwise, shut the hell up. You hear me? Do *not* talk to my sister or me."

Salamone had already turned and made wide eyes as he walked away with a slightly weak-kneed affectation, letting everyone watching know he was dealing with a nut-job. He was, however, flustered enough to step on his precious Cohiba, breaking it in two, and crushing most of it. His face went maroon and his nostrils flared. "Motherfff…" he said before mouthing the rest.

Mo had imagined for years how he might deal with Salamone when there came a time where neither could avoid the other. Not anymore.

Whatever psychological coup Mo might have felt he'd pulled off when Sally hooked his tee-shot into some thorny trash left of the first fairway was quashed when, nervous as he'd ever felt in any sport, he barely three-putted to win the first hole of their match. His second putt was two feet short and the third barely lipped in. Felt like dropping an easy pop-up and forcing the lead runner out at second.

Salamone then birdied the next three holes to take a two up lead. Mo felt less pressure once he was down a couple holes. He'd taken some blows, but focused on the fact he was hitting the ball solidly. This was a new level for him. He was three down at the turn despite playing the front in a respectable one over par. Neither player spoke to the other. Not a single putt was conceded. The gallery was, but for Sally's four fast-tiring valets, pulling for Mo Mo Moran.

Manda was waiting by the 10th tee with a few of her friends, and they had apparently agreed that nylon warm-up suits and matching

terrycloth visors would be the uniform *du jour*. The breeze seemed to
pick up and disappear at random. Mo felt this was a good thing.

Rinny pointed out how Salamone's look of satisfaction was "too
pleased, too soon." As usual, she was correct. Salamone gave away the
10th with a showy, Neapolitan flop-shot that should have been a basic
chocolate chip and run. Mo birdied the 12th by hoisting a hybrid over
the corner of the woods, nearly identical to his dad's 'Made for The
Majesty' three-wood shot. A sand wedge to six unconceded inches, and
Mo was only one down when he buried the half-footer in the heart.

The wind was acting funny. A "televangelist breeze," his dad would
have called it, blowing hard and soft at different times and proving
costly to those participating. The dramatic changes wreaked havoc on
Salamone's product-heavy hair, which sometimes billowed like
storefront awnings and it seemed to be messing with his head.
Throughout the back nine, Mo went about smashing low bullets off the
tee that the wind couldn't touch. His ball-speed was astonishing, but by
keeping it low, he was able to carry his ball fairly close to the down-
slopes where his dad had been landing his three-wood on so many of the
holes. Loren Ferguson had added over 350 yards to the course in
accordance with USGA directives for The US Open some years down the
road. There would be more "suggestions," but the effect of the added
yardage and Mo's calculated bullet-ball carries put him an average of 50
yards past most of his opponents, the still big-hitting Salamone included.

But Andy Salamone could golf his ball. Wisconsin's Amateur Player
of the Year for two years running was undaunted by youthful power or
anything else, and seemed only to be getting better as he got older.
Salamone's four tag-along soup-tasters, however, were wearing down. If
they had been confident they could walk The Majesty, they certainly
underestimated the work involved. Before taking over chauffeur duties
on the cart, Jumbo Larson had turned darn near purple, and his ever-
slowing waddle suggested acute chafing. The familiar looking guy
turned out to be Salamone's brother-in-law, who, Rinny pointed out, had
been recently released from jail after his third OWI. The deeply tanned
Bling Twins were winded, raspy-voiced and sweaty, yet seemed wholly
incapable of remaining silent for longer 15 seconds. They lagged behind

and talked the entire way unless they were shouting praise to their beloved B'Gandhi. It was now a three-minion man march with the Bookend Buddhas hanging out of the laboring electric cart. Manda and friends whispered amongst each other throughout and seemed to mosey more than hike. Like Rinny, the older ladies wore smiles that validated the fact that Mo was loved no matter what happened in the match.

Both players went two over par over the next four holes: 13, 14, 15 and 16. But it was on the par five 16th where Mo's superior length and a good club selection guess led to a two-putt birdie that squared the match.

The greens at The Majesty were firm but not quite as hard as they had been for the State Open, thanks to some of Loren's investments in soil management consultants and some latest, greatest irrigation improvements. Rinny aimed the Laser Link measurement gun at the par three 17th hole's flagstick and reported the yardage to Mo, who nodded. He knew exactly what the yardage would be – 217 yards. The wind was relaxing now, stretching only occasionally. He committed to the relaxation, and his high five-iron came straight down, and still rolled out some 25 feet past the middle right pin. Mo knew after four holes or so that the pin positions on this final day of the State Match Play Championship were either identical, or very close, to the positions on that final day of the Open two years prior.

Mo watched Salamone step up to his ball. The man had a disconcerting amount of confidence about him. Sally had to have been comfortable with the yardage because his hybrid went as high or higher than Mo's five-iron, and smash-landed into the front fringe before trickling in the direction of the flag. Salamone and his four fans barked as his ball was in the air, and then as it rolled slowly toward the hole. Sally hissed "Just go down, Honey!" His ball did not go down, but did come to rest three feet from the cup. The only applause came from Sally's homeys, their hoots in defiance of the unspoken dis from the locals. "Ahhh, listen to the silence of the lambs," said one of the Bling Brothers, laughing.

Evaluating his putt, Mo found himself echoing his "looks like it breaks toward the cup," comment before ol' D Mo buried the 45-foot bomb that had set off an eruption he'd never imagined possible in a state golf tournament. At this moment, an outside observer might have perceived a stony indifference among the gallery surrounding the green, but it was more the pregnant hush of silent prayers going out to a God who simply had to allow Mo Moran to make this putt. They sure as hell knew Andy Salamone wasn't going to miss his three-footer. The man hadn't missed a meaningful putt all day. And whatever else anyone thought of Andy Salamone, his putting skills were unquestioned.

With the past converging with the present, Mo discovered he was smiling and making tiny Xs, little Lazy 8s, as he lined up his putt. Maybe he only thought he was. Rinny was behind him, also sizing up the line. "Something tells me this one's out of your hands, Mo. It's going in if you get it there, isn't it?"

"I know the line, Rin, that's for sure." He stood up and one of his knees made a popping noise. There was no pain.

"Then just roll it in," said Rinny.

He didn't just make it; he stuffed it in like a famished man would a meatball. Though there were fewer in the gallery, the overall gaga per capita was just as great as when Danny Mo made his 45-footer on the same hole in the final round of the State Open two years ago. But this was match play, and match play was different. More personal. These cheers had an attitude, more haymaker thrill than touchdown bliss. More visceral than even that, closer to the bloodlust rush of a sword plunged into a bull made weary at last. Yeah, this was different alright. In match play, especially against Andy Salamone, damage to the opponent was as important as the welfare of the hero.

There were a couple of cameras from the local affiliates to capture it all. A smiling Manda was hugging herself and nodding to those saluting her, while one of her friends, Rita, proved she could whistle like a rancher, and then performed a quick muscleman pose with both arms flexed like Clay Matthews after a sack. The woman was into it. Salamone immediately put his ball down on the green and picked up his mark before Mo could pluck his ball from the cup. Sally quickly walked to the other side of the cup as the cheering continued. He milked the drama, knowing full well his putt would once again bring on enough silence to warm his cockles and keep the cackles coming from his supporting lounge-lizards.

Mo retrieved his golf ball and tossed it to the young son of a cheering man in a blue shirt – Merle, according to his oval patch. Mo then walked back to the hole and matter-of-factly slapped Salamone's ball away from the hole with his putter, toward no one in particular, conceding the short uphill putt. Salamone reacted with a sawed-off chuckle before offering a "whatever" type shrug. No golfer ever minds having a putt conceded, but Sally seemed a little let down, as if burying the putt before the faithful followers of Mo was some kind of pre-kill ritual to enjoy before charging into the final hole of this semi-final match.

Rinny gave Mo a narrow-eyed look, not liking the charity. Mo just winked and walked toward the 18th tee. Rinny called his name. He turned in time to catch the ball she had tossed to him. He looked at it. Then brother and sister looked at each other for a moment.

The 18th at The Majesty had remained exactly as it was three years ago, 559 yards, a dogleg left around Morgan's Forehead. The green, as it was from the beginning, was still firmer than the other 17. It was now partially surrounded by people, with others filing toward it, many no doubt taking an early lunch to catch the end of the morning match.

Mo may have had the serene, calculating appearance of a stoic warrior, but he was jacked and jumpy inside his skin. His instincts were telling him to adapt. This was the goddamn Hair Dude, with his big goddamn mouth, and those goddamn tits bobbing with a life of their own. There was too much history still too fresh for forgiveness. Too much bullshit unbalanced by any semblance of anything worthwhile in the man besides a remarkably complete golf game. Mo had long claimed there was really only one person he could honestly say he hated. Andy Salamone. Now, the revulsion in Mo hardened him like cast iron. He'd certainly been in tougher situations than being tied after 17 holes at the semi-finals of the State Match Play Championship, but never had anything seemed this important. He needed to adjust.

Mo laughed inwardly. He recalled his dad once telling him how Grandpa Curly hated a local guy named Connie, how he'd say, "piss on Connie." Now he wondered if that was actually his grandpa's way to rid himself of hate. Maybe it wasn't all that different from Pig Fischer getting his "pig on," how Pig sometimes "had to lose it, just to find it." His dad admitted to having hated some people over the years, claimed to know firsthand how counterproductive it was. He'd say that if you want to play good golf you had to find a way get rid of the venom. Mo remembered how his dad laughed when an 11 year-old Mo Mo immediately replied that, "you have to bite someone to get the venom out."

Maybe it was the back-to-back birdies that turned out to be his so-called bite. Mo felt the rancor level dropping, and something else taking its place. Something beyond the easy-open package of satisfaction that comes standard with every birdie. It was more a convergence of energy and clarity. The déjà vu on the 17th green had come in powerful waves, and he was rolling with the challenge like some surfer god. A sense came over him that everything was happening for a reason. He embraced a feeling of near mirth, the thought of how far he'd come, how cynical he used to be, and the whole notion of becoming his "own damn Mo." It was almost humorous, but it was, really, about love. He would have had no argument with anyone crowning him King Cornelius in the Kingdom of Corniness, but the truth was he felt flushed with love, even charged with it.

Yep, love. And freedom, to go after big things, like this today, things considered to be big by very few. It was his dad who'd shown him how big they could be, and it was in the showing that Mo had come to understand. This is was what he loved, doing exactly this. He had new dreams now to replace the broken ones. He recalled his dad's note the morning he disappeared. How he got more out of coming through for those who believed in him than shoving it up the ass of the naysayers. Or something like that.

In any case, his folks had covered all the bases. His dad, the crazy-like-a-fox whack-job, wherever he was, along with his mom, probably the only woman smart enough to love his dad in the way that drove him to become Top-Five Worldwide in so many categories that just happened to please her. Mo learned balance, to draw the best from the systematic rhythms of his mom and the galvanizing spontaneity of his dad. He learned that the truth ain't always what's accepted as truth. And with Cindy's unrushed and invaluable support, he was able to overcome his growing dependence on alcohol. Something that may have had him headed toward, as his mother used to say, "total anarchy," by bowing to the pressures of what his dad called "Lemminghood." Finally, and in the Moran family this was big, he learned how to compete like a jungle cat with say-so, and to love the hunt as much as or more than the prize.

It was as if every ounce of power in his heart had been converted to clubhead speed, speed colliding squarely with a golf ball, a golf ball marked with a *No* before the number *1*. The same ball from two years ago, a version of the Titleist Pro V series that was no longer manufactured. The new Pro V1Xs were advertised as going six to eight yards longer. Six to eight yards Mo hardly needed. Mo let out the anger and tension and breathed in the willingness to believe. Maybe it wasn't rhino dung, or the cremated remains of Grandpa Curly, or a lucky coin. No, it wasn't any *one* of those things. It was *all* of those things, of that spirit, a faith-based initiative for finding a way, and failing that, to go right at 'em as long as the battle was just.

The swing was without exertion, yet the unmistakable sound of whatever adds up to "that's everything" came through. The ball hung in the air about as long as it took Bill Linneman to finish half a cigarette. From the tee, the white speck looked to have nearly reached the rough that crossed the fairway almost 370 yards away. The Moran fans who weren't cheering could only laugh.

"Uh, that'll work," said Rinny, quietly.

Mo barely reacted but for the hint of a squint that only Rinny could read.

Salamone, to his credit, smashed one down the fairway as well. His ball, however, would be in a distant hamlet from downtown Mo-Mo town.

Mo heard a whistle from Salamone or possibly one of the four table-fillers some 70 yards back in the fairway. Sally wanted to play his lay-up shot. Mo, standing by his ball, was apparently in his way. Mo's Titleist had, prior to this tee shot, been hit by his dad only twice and putted once. His ball sat in the first cut of the rough leading to the crossing ravine. Mo smiled. Five more yards, and it would have been in the hazard and unplayable. As it was, the ball was sitting up, making it an easier lie from which to hit a high shot. Rinny led Mo to the left side of the fairway and waited for Sally to play. Brother and sister were now slightly past The Forehead but close enough to feel its presence. They both took a moment to look up. Salamone laid-up perfectly. Neither Rinny nor Mo said anything about anything.

Mo waited for the green to clear. For the moment the wind was gone. Rinny aimed the Laser Link measuring gun. It read 188 yards.

Mo thought for a moment and, as he often did, said "Audit, please." Rinny smiled and retrieved the gun from the case clipped to Mo's golf bag. As she pulled it out, she must have accidentally pulled the trigger because it beeped when it connected with a small reflector device that is either attached to or embedded in each flagstick. Rinny made a funny face as at the gun displayed 57 yards. She and Mo followed the aim of the gun with their gaze… to the top of Morgan's Forehead. They looked at each other. Mo took the gun and aimed it upward again and fanned it slowly until it beeped again. Fifty-five yards. Mo started laughing as he put it together. "Our father, wherever he is, hallowed be thy name…"

"What?" said Rinny.

Mo shook his head. "Dad put a reflector up there, at the peak. I get it now. How he knew, or knew for sure. Must've attached it to a branch of one of those little trees clustered together by the south ledge. I'll bet that's it. He knew exactly how far he had to carry his ball." Then he looked at the ball he was about to hit and pointed *"That* ball."

"Oh…my…God." Rinny laughed, her eyes tearing up. "That's so…Daddy."

"He went up the night before the final two rounds," said Mo. "Remember, I told you how Dad had returned to Grandma's in the middle of the night, sweating, and his clothes were all dusty?"

"I remember," said Rinny, shaking her head. They looked at each other, entranced. Then the jungle cat in her took command. "Okay…what do you think? Six? Smooth." said Rinny. "Pin's up, if it trickles off the back you're okay."

Mo nodded but begged to differ. "I'm pumped. Seven." Mo chucked one more time, still amazed about his dad's premeditated spontaneity.

"Make it a solid seven." Rinny looked inland at the trees to see the effects of any wind.

Mo took the seven and wasted little time. The hole location was the same as it had been two years ago. Mo could feel what his dad must have felt from the peak; he just knew it was the right club.

And it would have been if Mo hadn't pulled it slightly going for some extra altitude, or maybe from the excitement he felt. He flushed the shot and it hung in the sky forever, but the tall draw drew a little *too* much. It hit the slope precisely pin-high and kicked left into the bunker. Five feet right and he would have had, *maybe,* 15 feet for eagle, if not less.

"Let's go get it up and down," said Rinny pulling the bag over her shoulders.

Mo could feel it. It was getting to him. He waggled his sand wedge as he wiggled into his stance in the bunker. Rinny's last words, "You are Mo Mo Moran," went beyond comforting. Salamone had played a near-perfect wedge to about eight feet, and was left with a straight uphill putt. More than likely Mo would need to get up and down to stay in the match.

Danny Mo, with his beloved Lazarus, was far better out of the sand than Mo could ever hope to be. Mo could hardly swallow. The lie was fair and on the edge of a shadow made by the bunker's revetment wall lip. The gallery was still, the quiet complete. Mo's legs felt heavy. He nearly forgot that there wasn't a penalty for breathing. Salamone stood in his view with the expression of a guy a little too fascinated watching a flustered puppy in a busy intersection.

Mo took a deep, dramatic breath. He knew it was too obvious so he countered with his look of spreading relish, the one reserved for certain competitive challenges, on the field and off. Mo's experience in various sports and a handful of fights came to bear. The internal alarms triggered a rescuing calm at the moment he took the club away. He splashed the sand and the ball came out clean. It was a good shot, but it wasn't great. It was on line, but too far. The ball, *that ball*, his dad's ball, clanged into the flagstick and dropped straight down. Not into the cup, but inches from it, spinning crazily in place.

The crowd went stark raving glad. If Salamone was saying a prayer, he didn't get past, "Jesus Christ!" Shaking his head, his expression suggested he may have thrown up a little. He swatted Mo's ball away from the hole and back into the bunker from whence it came, conceding the birdie. Disapproving groans came from around the green as the ball nearly hit Rinny who was already in the bunker and raking it smooth. Rinny was glowing as she scooped it up cleanly. Mo felt tremendous relief. His body was electric. Salamone now needed to make his putt to stay alive. 'Stay alive' had popped into his mind before grasping the level of hyperbole in such a phrase. Mom. Grandpa Curly. Marty. Soldiers.

Salamone took more time stalking this putt than he had on any of the previous 17 holes. Perhaps waiting until everyone settled down after Mo's bunker shot. Salamone's body bounced with every step. He kept shaking his head. It wasn't clear if he was still begrudging what he had to see as a lucky break, or whether he was unsure of his line on the eight-footer he needed to halve the hole. Mo stood off to the front left part of the green. Rinny joined him, and the two Morans stood motionless as everything again became eerily quiet. Apparently, even the wind had stopped to watch. Rinny put her head down as if unable to watch, but only for a second. Slowly she allowed her head back up, and turned a look of cold evil at Salamone, as if she knew some spirit-slaughtering but unteachable technique known only to courtroom carnivores.

After delaying, Salamone stepped up to his putt a little too quickly. Mo thought that was a good sign. Rinny's stare continued to slice and dice when Mo felt something stirring within him, something extraordinary. Salamone was a statue over his ball. The something Mo felt was getting stronger. Powerful. Unnerving. He gathered himself by looking into the middle distance, over the land that led to the inland holes, the land his father had roamed growing up, land he had been so excited to revisit once it became The Majesty. The feeling in Mo was weird and wonderful at once and on the verge of overwhelming. He saw something, but wasn't sure what. Mo watched as it came into focus.

Over the horizon, high above the land and then circling south before coming in lower, then lower still, tracing the fairway, was a fast moving creature of astonishing grace. Mo had come to know this bird of prey quite well; he had studied it since his intimate encounter with one almost two decades earlier. The bird came even lower, and angled as if about to drop further.

Salamone's back was to the bird, and as the he took back his putter, the red tail hawk silently sailed some 20 feet above him at a moment just before impact. Salamone appeared to flinch from the sudden flash of the passing shadow, and pulled his putt an inch too much. And... missed. He had no idea what had happened. When the Hair Dude looked around there was nothing to see.

At that moment, Rinny's look softened as the putt missed. A moment later, she had the look of one who'd seen a ghost. She followed Mo's eyes, and together they watched the hawk circle over the bay, and dip its near wing before ascending quickly into the sky. Rinny let out a quiet gasp as the bird rose to the peak of Morgan's Forehead and disappeared.

∞

Walking off the 18th green at The Majesty, there was one thing left for Mo to do. He asked to speak with Bill Linneman outside the scorer's tent. He had a single question for the WSGA's Director of Rules and Competition, which Linneman answered in the affirmative. Mo laughed to himself, thought about his dad and, of all people, Marty Archibald.

Then Mo Mo Moran announced that he was conceding the match to Andy Salamone. Rules breach. He had violated the One Ball Rule when he switched to the ball his dad had hit to and from The Forehead. He knew all along that the same brand and model of golf ball had to be used for a 'stipulated round' in any tournament worth anything. He'd once heard his dad joking at The Aftermath that the rule was like a marital vow.

"Ah, Jeez, Mo," Linneman closed his eyes for a couple beats before putting out his cigarette in an empty can of Diet Coke. "You can't, technically, concede."

Mo didn't care. "Call it whatever you want," he said before turning to walk away from any further debate. He headed toward Rinny and Crusty who were purposefully discussing something, but quieted when Mo arrived. He explained the DQ, and the reaction from the two was strange.

"Got it," said Crusty, nodding, "I'll let the ladies know." He quickly went ahead to explain the developments to Manda and her group, who were positioned around the corner of the clubhouse, the same area where Danny had gathered with family after winning the Open. For a moment, clouds shielded the sun and it made the peak of Morgan's Forehead easier to see. Walking side-by-side now with Rinny, Mo slowed and stared upward at The Forehead, until the sun reappeared, forcing him to look away.

Mo glanced at Rinny and continued walking. "You know, when Mom died, I still had conversations with her. For awhile anyway, but I knew she was gone. With Dad, it felt like he was here today." Mo was blinking away the sun's effect on his eyes just as he and Rinny joined Crusty and Manda. "It was weird. Coming down the stretch, especially heading to the tee at 18, it was like I could feel him with me."

Everyone looked at Mo, kind of funny-like, and then at Manda who had just snapped shut her cell phone. She was also blinking back the effects of whatever burned within her. Rinny muffled a sniffle, and Crusty was suddenly looking straight down. The Matriarchal Mo finally spoke. "You're like your Grandpa Curly, Mo Mo. He could always sense whenever I or the kids were nearby, and your dad claimed the same thing with your mom, even after her reunion with the angels, but…"

Mo fought to grasp where his grandma was going, even as images of his dad mumbling to Molly Mo atop Morgan's Forehead came flashing back.

"There was indeed reason to feel your father's presence, he indeed saw his two kids in action today, especially the back nine. He took up his position quite early." Manda's tiny nods grew in size and emphasis. "He knows the sightlines and vantage points along this harbor like, well…"

"No one," said Rinny, beaming as she delivered a karate chop to give her brother time to process things.

Mo was smiling. "He got his spot, huh?"

Manda looked at her wrist like she was checking the time though she wasn't wearing a watch. "I'll bet he's back at the house and catching up with Hank right now."

∞

About the Author

 John Haines has won over a dozen state and local golf championships and has represented Wisconsin in four USGA Amateur Championships. He is a sales rep and packaging consultant for The Sheboygan Paper Box Co and lives with his family in Mequon, WI. DANNY MO is his first novel

9 780983 324973